DANGEROUS DESIRE

Swinging her around, Lucien moved her back against the rock wall and used the length of his body to hold her there. "You always push," he ground out. "What is it you hope to gain, Alessandra? Think you I will throw up my hands and allow you to return to Algiers?"

That was precisely what she had hoped would happen. "I do not understand why you don't!" she retorted.

"Don't you?" He pressed himself against her, every swell and hollow of his body finding a place to rest in her supple curves.

Her breath caught as the desire of weeks past rekindled.

Desperate to shatter the response building in her, Alessandra turned her head. "No," she said, her voice a weak whisper.

"Yes," Lucien rasped.

She did not want this, Alessandra told herself as she evaded his mouth. He had made himself her enemy, had he not?

She tried to latch on to the anger she'd felt, but Lucien's mouth was playing music over her heated skin.

"This is why I cannot allow you to return," he said, lifting his head. "I still want you, Alessandra."

PAGAN BRIDE

Bantam Books by Tamara Leigh

WARRIOR BRIDE

VIRGIN BRIDE

PAGAN BRIDE

PAGAN BRIDE

Tamara Leigh

BANTAM
NEW YORK • TORONTO • LONDON
SYDNEY • AUCKLAND

PAGAN BRIDE

A Bantam Book/March 1995

ISBN 0-553-56535-4

Published simultaneously in the United States and Canada

Bantam Books are published by Bantam Books, a division of Bantam
Doubleday Dell Publishing Group, Inc. Its trademark, consisting of the words
"Bantam Books" and the portrayal of a rooster, is Registered in U.S. Patent
and Trademark Office and in other countries. Marca Registrada. Bantam
Books, 1540 Broadway, New York, New York 10036.

PRINTED IN THE UNITED STATES OF AMERICA

RAD   0 9 8 7 6 5 4 3 2 1

To my sister, Lisa Marie—

You always knew, always believed, and never gave up the faith. Lizanne and Ranulf, Graeye and Gilbert, Alessandra and Lucien, and the others yet to come thank you, but more, I thank you.

PAGAN
BRIDE

CHAPTER I

Algiers, 1454

Not even the chains of his bondage could make him look the slave. Wearing only loose-fitting hose, the waistband riding low upon his tapered hips, the bronze-headed giant was dragged to the platform to stand before the astonished crowd. The three men holding him scowled as he thrust his muscular body against them, his loud, wrathful curses understood only by those who knew his language.

An Englishman, Sabine silently rejoiced, and an enraged one at that. She had never expected to encounter such a fine specimen. Though he could not be a nobleman, for surely he would have been ransomed if he were, he carried himself as one.

She gripped the arm of the chief eunuch, who had accompanied her to the auction. "That one, Khalid," she said.

His eyes widened. "Mistress, he is not a eunuch."

That was true. The auctioneer had not prefaced the summons to bid with such information. But it did not matter. This was the one she had been waiting for these past two months, and she was not about to let him slip through her desperate fingers.

"It matters not," she said sharply. "I will have him."

His brow furrowed, Khalid leaned down from his great

height. "Only a eunuch is allowed within the walls of a harem," he reminded her.

"None need know," she argued, growing anxious as the bidding began.

Khalid shook his head. "Nay, this man is fit only for the stone quarries. There will be others suited for your purpose." Which only he, her confidant for the past ten years, knew of.

"Time is running out for me," she said, her voice catching. "Do not deny me this, Khalid. It may be my last chance."

The corners of his mouth tightened. "He is a poor choice, mistress. Have you not seen the stripes upon his back? A man is not beat so viciously unless he deserves it."

Of course she had seen the scars he bore, the recently acquired ones still livid and swollen. Regardless, she was determined to have him, for she had seen none worthier to carry out her plan.

"Do you not feel his anger—his hate?" Khalid pressed. "I tell you, he is a dangerous man."

"Only a fool would be devoid of such emotions," Sabine retorted, "and a fool is not what I seek. Nay, his anger will serve me well."

Khalid was still not convinced. "Pray, choose another, mistress."

"I have chosen."

As the bidding turned fierce among those who sought to acquire the strong Englishman for their mines and quarries, Khalid found himself in the midst of an internal struggle. He wanted to help his mistress, but knew it could mean his life. What if this man proved obstinate, which seemed likely, and revealed himself to the master? What if he ran rampant through the harem and seduced the women?

"Do you not bid, I will," Sabine threatened.

Khalid's frown deepened. "He will cost much."

In response, she wrenched the gold bracelet from her wrist, thrust it into his hand, then began to work a ring from her finger. "I do not care what he costs," she said.

Khalid stayed her desperate movements with a hand to her shoulder, then grudgingly stepped forward.

Watching through the veil that hid her face, Sabine anxiously smoothed her fingers over the black cloak she wore. Draped from the crown of her head, the garment fell straight to the ground, concealing the colorful finery beneath. It was the same for all respectable women who went out in public in this place so far removed from Europe.

As the bidding continued, with Khalid adding his deep voice to the shouts, the slave still fought his captors. Heavy perspiration glistened on his chest and arms, and darkened the hose encasing his legs. From what well did he draw his strength? Sabine wondered. What sustained his spirit in the face of such adversity?

Suddenly the man broke an arm free and slung his chains into the faces of two of the guards. Yelping their pain, the men flew backward, leaving only one to deal with the slave's violent fury.

As the crowd rumbled with alarm, those nearest the platform—save Khalid—hastened back as the slave fell upon the remaining guard.

For the first time Sabine questioned whether she could handle this Englishman. Had she been too hasty in her decision to purchase him? After all, she was no longer the young woman she had been twenty years ago. Far from it. Had she three more years left in her, which she did not, she would see the age of forty.

Leaping to the platform, Khalid lunged for the slave and dragged him from atop the bloodied guard. The two others, having finally regained their feet, hurried to assist him.

Still the slave continued to thrash, and not until Khalid brought his knee sharply up between his thighs was the fight wrested from him.

Pained, the Englishman threw his head back, his eyes tightly closed and teeth clenched. No sound, however, issued from his lips. A moment later he slumped against his captors.

A cheer rose from the crowd, their fear deserting them as they looked to the formidable black eunuch.

Khalid turned and searched out his mistress, his brow creased with doubt.

Knowing he sought confirmation of her decision to purchase the slave, and that he was more strongly opposed than before, Sabine hesitated. However, in the end she nodded.

His displeasure evident, Khalid looked to the auctioneer. "I will pay no more," he said, letting his last offer stand. "Is there another who would challenge me?"

The beady-eyed auctioneer looked out across the throng, but none came forward. With a shrug and a toothy smile, he accepted the eunuch's bid.

Smiling behind her veil, Sabine watched as the slave was dragged from the platform.

"It is done," Khalid growled when he rejoined her. "I pray you do not come to regret it as much as I."

She placed a hand on his arm. "I thank you, my friend. Your loyalty will not go unrewarded."

This, Khalid knew well, for his mistress had always been most generous. He only prayed Allah would protect him that he might enjoy the harvest soon to be his.

Feigning a boredom she could not possibly feel with all the excitement and fear twisting her insides into knots, Sabine levered herself up from the pillows. Though angry eyes bored into her as she rearranged her slender form amid the profusion of color, she refused to acknowledge the man until she was once again settled comfortably.

Wrapping her composure around herself, she lifted her gaze and focused on the slave's manacled ankles before beginning a leisurely, upward perusal. By the time she reached his face, his indignation was evident in every contour of his muscled flesh, in the tension that linked captor with captive, and in eyes filled with rage.

Sabine's falsely bright smile wavered. Aye, this was no mere emotion to be smote with a pretty smile and a flutter of lashes, she conceded. Here was one who, given the opportunity, could—and would—kill his captors. She steeled herself for flight should he attempt to defy his chains and the guards holding him.

But the Englishman did not spring forward. Instead, he swayed where he stood.

What was wrong with him? Sabine wondered. He acted as if . . .

Drawing a sharp breath, she turned her gaze upon Khalid. Though his face remained impassive, one look at his dark, sparkling eyes confirmed her suspicion. He had drugged the man in such a way that, though the mind remained alert, the body could not act upon its urgings.

Relieved, Sabine motioned the guards to withdraw.

The two men slipped into the darkened corners of the tent where they could watch. And watch was all they could do, for they knew nothing of the English language—though Khalid did.

She lowered her feet to the carpet covering the earthen floor and straightened. Then, thrusting her shoulders back, she walked forward.

"I am Sabine." She spoke in English, though she knew her words were strangely accented, since she'd spoken mostly Arabic for almost twenty years. "By what name are you called, Englishman?"

Though his eyes narrowed, he did not answer.

Placing herself directly before him, she raised herself onto her toes and peered into the hard countenance that was divided into two distinct halves. Whereas the right was unblemished, the left was scarred by a blade that had perfectly traced the high cheekbone there. Where had he acquired such an injury?

Her gaze shifted to eyes the color of amethysts. Incredible, she thought. Where had she seen that color before? Her mind tugged at the vague memory, but it slipped away.

Next, she looked at the bronze hair that fell in waves to his shoulders. Though dirty and unkempt, it was every bit as virile as the man. On impulse, she lifted a hand to it, the miniature bells linked around her wrist tinkling in the silence.

Pity, she thought. This man might very well give his life to achieve the goal she was about to set him. Abruptly, she interrupted her wayward thoughts. Nay, he would succeed—if for no other reason than to preserve the manhood he no doubt prized.

A smile twitching at her lips, Sabine set herself back on her heels. His face was not quite handsome, she concluded—certainly not worthy of such a magnificent body—but not unattractive either.

The sudden rattling of chains brought her back to the present. Shocked, she stumbled away from the man who had shoved his great body against her.

"Arab whore!" he spat at her.

In an instant Khalid and the guards were beside him. The guards held him by the arms while Khalid struck him in the face with the back of his hand.

The man did not even flinch.

No real danger, Sabine tried to convince herself as she fought to calm the heavy beating of her heart. Still, not until the guards began dragging the slave toward the tent opening could she bring herself to speak.

"Leave him," she commanded in Arabic.

Immediately, Khalid took up a vehement protest, but was quieted by a stern shake of her head.

"He can do me no harm," she reminded him.

Nostrils flared, the eunuch studied her determined expression before ordering the guards forward. "There." He motioned to a stool. "Then be gone."

The guards forced the man down on it, then reluctantly withdrew from the tent.

"They will talk of his defiance," Khalid warned. "If you intend to continue on this perilous course, mistress, then it is best you do so in privacy."

True, Sabine thought. An emasculated man lost much of his high spirit and unruliness and, deprived of the desire for sexual consummation, became gentler. Not surprisingly, the Englishman displayed none of these qualities. The question was, could he feign them?

Nodding her agreement, Sabine went to stand before the slave, though she did not get as near as before. "You have nothing to fear from me—" she began.

"Fear?" The word rumbled up from his deep chest. " 'Tis I who should be feared. Lovely as your heathen neck is, 'twould pleasure me greatly to crush it between my hands."

Sabine was momentarily flustered by the culture of his voice. How could a commoner have acquired such eloquent speech? Shrugging off the peculiarity, she pulled loose the pins holding her hair veil.

"You have much to learn, Englishman," she said as her glorious fall of red tresses was revealed, hair that could not possibly be of Arabic origin, and that no amount of henna could ever reproduce so vibrantly.

For a fleeting moment she glimpsed his confusion, then it was swept away.

Frustrated, she went down on her knees beside him. "I am every bit as English as you," she said. "And just as you, I, too, was a slave when I came here."

"And what is it you call yourself now?" he ground out, his gaze insulting as it swept over her Arabic costume.

Refusing to be ashamed of the lifestyle that had been forced upon her nearly twenty years past, Sabine angled her chin higher. "I am the wife of a wealthy Arab merchant," she said with all the pride warranted from having obtained such a station. She could have easily met with the same fate as so many others—becoming a concubine, or worse, a prostitute.

"A renegade," the Englishman tossed back. "A whore who has thrown off her religion and taken that of the infidel that she might know greater comfort."

Sabine considered him a moment, then lifted a chain from the neck of her caftan and held the crucifix suspended from it close to his face. "Is it still your wish to throttle me?" she asked as he stared at the piece.

A frown settling between his brows, he shifted his gaze back to hers. "What is it you want?"

"I have a proposal—one I believe you will find more than acceptable."

He waited for her to continue.

" 'Tis your freedom you seek," she said, "and if you do my bidding, you shall have it." At last she had his interest, and his anger eased perceptibly.

Still, he remained defiant. "Whether or not I do your *bidding*, I shall have my freedom," he retorted.

Recalling what Khalid had apprised her of a short time before, Sabine smiled. "If that is so, then why have you not escaped in all the time since you were taken? It has been over a year, and yet you still do not have your freedom."

His eyes darkened. "It was not for lack of trying. 'Tis no simple matter when you are chained to the oar of a galley day and night."

Pushing herself to her feet, Sabine walked to his back and lightly drew her finger down a scar that ran from shoulder to hip. He tensed beneath her touch.

"Still, you rebelled," she mused. "I like that." She sauntered back around to face him. "A pity there was none to ransom you. Had you a title, you would not have been made to suffer so."

"I do have a title," he snapped.

Though Sabine should not have been surprised, considering his speech, mannerisms, and carriage, she was. She looked to Khalid, who confirmed the truth of it with a nod.

If only she had listened better at the auction, she thought, or at least given Khalid time to tell her all of it before bringing this man to her. Still, it did not change things, she concluded. Indeed, a nobleman might better serve her purpose than a commoner.

"Why were you not ransomed?" she asked.

He left her question unanswered.

She shrugged and turned to Khalid, who handed her a sheaf of documents. Angling the papers to better read them, she found near the top what she sought. And for a long moment, she saw nothing save the name that jumped out at her—De Gautier.

Dear God, could it be? She forced her gaze farther down the document, only to have her fear confirmed. Her breath momentarily lost, she clenched the crisp documents, crumpling their edges.

What terrible fate had brought this man to her? she wondered. In all of England, there was none who would have been a poorer choice for her to entrust her most precious possession to. A De Gautier—it was unthinkable.

The coughing spell came on suddenly, as it did of late. Clutching at her heaving bosom, Sabine accepted the comfort of Khalid's arms as he lifted her against his chest.

Wordlessly, he carried her to the bed of pillows and lowered her onto it. He pressed a square of linen into her hand, his concerned face hovering above hers as she held the cloth to her mouth and coughed into it the blood from her burning lungs.

When the spell finally passed, Sabine was left more weakened than she'd ever felt, her body frail and slack.

"I will send him away," Khalid said.

She lifted a staying hand. "Nay, I am not yet finished with him." Ignoring Khalid's scowl, she turned her gaze upon De Gautier.

Aye, now she knew why her memory had stirred at the sight of those eyes. He had been but a child, perhaps all of eight years old, when she had first come face-to-face with Lucien de Gautier. Then she had been Lady Catherine, the young bride of Lord James Bayard, and the boy had been her husband's captive.

Though a good man, James had not been averse to using the De Gautier heir to obtain what he and his ancestors had so long desired. For generations, the Bayards and the De Gautiers had quarreled over a strip of land—Dewmoor Pass—that lay between their two properties. Although even kings had attempted to settle the dispute, peace had always been short-lived, for neither family was willing to relinquish hold of any portion of it. As a result, much blood had been shed, and hate amassed, during those years.

Had the De Gautier boy not proven so clever, James may well have finally secured the land for the Bayards. As the negotiations had dragged on, Lucien had quietly bided his time. Though he'd made no attempt to mask his anger, such a young child had not been thought to present any threat to the Bayards. Thus, he had been allowed to wander freely about the castle and, late one night, had finally gained his freedom through the skillful use of a dagger he had stolen. But that was nearly twenty years ago—a lifetime, Sabine told herself as she focused on the boy who had long since become a man. Were the families still feuding? She pushed the preposterous question aside. Not even England's war with France, which looked to be finally over, had lasted as long as the Bayards' and De Gautiers' war.

Even as Sabine thought to abandon her impossible plan of smuggling her daughter out of Algiers, an idea found its way into her fatigued mind. Since Lucien de Gautier did not recognize her, she might still be able to make use of him—provided she did not tell him of her true identity. Hence, he must be led to believe her daughter, Alessandra, was born of her Arab husband.

Pushing herself into a sitting position, she met his unwavering stare. "Shall we bargain?" she asked.

His eyes narrowed to suspicious slits. "First I would know what it was that upset you so greatly." He nodded to the documents that lay upon the carpet.

Delaying, Sabine draped a silk robe around her shoulders. "Naught upset me," she said. "I am simply not well."

"You lie."

Angered by his keen perception, she tossed her head back. "I am not well," she repeated, "which is the reason you are here."

Clearly, he did not believe her, but he let the issue drop. "Then speak."

"I offer you freedom."

He considered her a long moment before responding. "And what must I do for this freedom?"

Beneath the cover of her robe, Sabine clenched her hands. "Take my daughter with you when you go."

"To England?"

"Aye. I have family there."

"And that is all you would ask of me?"

"Ah, but 'tis not so simple as it sounds. My husband will not allow it, and neither will Alessandra, my daughter, go willingly."

"Then why send her away?"

Sabine was silent, pained at what she must reveal in order to gain this man's cooperation. "As I have said, I am not well. Soon Alessandra is to wed one of the Islamic faith, and when I am gone, there will be none to protect her."

"Then it is her safety that concerns you?"

"Aye, but neither do I want her to have the life I have had. Were she suited to it, it would not bother me so, but she is not."

"The life of a—"

"Life in a harem," she interrupted before he could call her that filthy name again.

A corner of Lucien's mouth lifted in what could be called neither a smile nor a sneer. "And if she will not come willingly?"

"You will come into the harem," Sabine said as if it were the simplest thing in the world. "There you will gain her trust, and if I still cannot convince her to leave, you will take her from there. All will be arranged that might see you safely from this land."

Lucien's gaze moved past Sabine to where Khalid stood. "Even I know," he said dryly, "that unless a man is no longer a man, he is not allowed in that place of women."

Sabine glanced from Lucien to Khalid, acutely aware of the silent battle raging between them. Obviously, Lucien de Gautier would not soon forget the humiliation he had suffered at Khalid's hands. Nor would Khalid overlook the insult just paid him.

"Aye," she said, "only members of the household and eunuchs are allowed within the harem. Thus, you must become a eunuch that you might enter."

"Become a eunuch?" Lucien repeated with great disbelief. "If you are suggesting I become like him"—he indicated Khalid with a thrust of his jaw—"then I decline your *generous* offer, madame. When I return home, I will return as a man."

"In pretense only would you become a eunuch," she clarified. "None but myself and Khalid would know."

"And I am to trust him?"

"He is loyal to me and will say nothing of our secret."

"And if I refuse?"

She locked eyes with him. "If you refuse, Lucien de Gautier, then you are of no use to me, and a true eunuch is what you will become."

Surprisingly, he laughed. "Again, you mistake me for a fool," he said. "Think you I do not know castration is forbidden in Islam?"

What he said was true. The emasculating procedure was allowed only outside the Muslim nations in spite of the demand for eunuchs within it. "Laws can be broken,"

Sabine tossed back. "And as I do not accept the faith of Islam, it would not weigh too heavily upon my conscience to break that particular law."

Khalid stepped forward. "I will do it myself," he said in English. As Lucien turned his wrathful stare on him Khalid raised his hands, palms heavenward. "Surely Allah will forgive one minor transgression."

A muscle in Lucien's jaw spasmed, but he did not vent his anger. He simply stared at the eunuch.

"Do not allow your pride to cloud your good judgment," Sabine said. "I have given you hope where ere you had none."

Lucien looked back at her. "Then it seems I must accept your proposal."

Relieved, she sank into the pillows. "Fine. For a sennight you will remain in the city with Khalid. It is he who will instruct you in the ways of a eunuch, and he you will answer to. After that, you will be brought to the home of Abd al-Jabbar—my husband—and enter the harem."

She turned to Khalid. "No doubt he has been long without a woman," she said, speaking in her adopted language. "Each night you are to bring him prostitutes that he might slake his thirst upon them."

"And if that is not enough?"

She smiled. "However many it takes. Just do not bring him into the women's quarters still wanting."

"It will be done, mistress."

Sabine turned her attention back to Lucien. "I have instructed Khalid—"

"I heard," he interrupted.

So he had learned their language, she thought. Although it would make it less difficult for him in the harem, it unsettled her. "Be sure you get your fill," she said, "for 'twill be all you will have until you return to England."

"Perhaps." His mocking smile showed fine white teeth that had somehow survived the ravages of life at sea.

Sabine swallowed hard on her mounting anxiety. "Do not fail me, Lucien de Gautier," she warned. "You are very much a man, and I would not want to have to change that."

His smile widened. "I will be cautious."

CHAPTER 2

The music grew louder, its vigorous beat coursing through every vein in every limb that moved to it. Tightly, it wound itself around the slender woman who swayed at the center of the large room. It pulled her head back and closed her eyes against the light. It drew her arms up from her sides and spread them wide to embrace the sensual rhythm she had given herself over to. It shook her shoulders, rotated and jerked her hips, and caused her fingers to snap.

The female dancers who had been hired to entertain the women of Abd al-Jabbar's harem drifted away, going to stand along the walls and watch this strange one who had joined in the dance.

She was different from the other women, her hair a flame amid the ashes. Skin that should have been pale was tanned and faintly touched with freckles. Though fine-boned and slim, her body curved where it ought to, her breasts full and firm. And those pale green eyes—they were full of daring and laughter when she turned them upon her captive audience.

All watched as the tempo quickened and the solitary dancer swept across the floor, sparkling laughter spilling from her throat as the music pulled her deeper into its spell.

Unmindful of the pins holding her veil in place, the young woman snatched the translucent material from her waist-length hair and drew it taut between her hands.

Then, raising her arms above her head, she pivoted on the balls of her bare feet. Faster and faster she turned, until she whirled in the wake of the diaphanous material clothing her limbs.

More laughter parted her lips, followed by a shriek of delight as the music reached its zenith. She was lost in it—completely given over to its control.

"Alessandra!" A reproving voice split the air.

The music fell away, and a din of women's voices rose to take its place.

Wrenched from the trancelike state she had slipped into, Alessandra staggered around to face her mother's displeasure. However, the room continued to revolve as if she were still dancing. She sank to her knees and sat back on her heels, the dizziness making it impossible for her to focus on the woman who stood at the far end of the room.

Standing between Sabine and Khalid, Lucien knew he was in trouble. He had known the moment Sabine had called out to the wild dancer, naming her the one. Inwardly, he groaned and cursed his man's flesh. One look at the young woman as she whirled across the floor was all it had taken to decide him. Thinking her a dancer— though with her mother's hair falling down her back, he should have known otherwise—he had determined to have her as soon as possible. Then the accursed woman at his side had shattered the possibility. Or had she?

As her dizziness subsided Alessandra blew a cooling stream of air up her face, then, reluctantly, she looked at her mother. Sabine stood just inside the doors, her face bright, her hands cradling her hips. Grimacing, Alessandra rose to her feet and walked forward. Behind her, the musicians and dancers resumed their entertainment, though Alessandra was sure their audience was far more interested in the pending encounter between mother and daughter.

Alessandra was halfway across the floor when something odd and disturbing drew her eyes to the right. Immediately, her steps faltered, and she halted.

There, alongside Khalid, stood a man of equal girth and height—as much a giant as the chief eunuch. Though fair of skin, he was clothed the same as Khalid, his head covered with a turban, a caftan falling from his shoulders, and over that, a dark robe.

Most notable were his eyes, their beauty undiminished by the brown-blue smudge ringing the right eye. Who had blackened it? she wondered.

Her answer was found in the man who stood beside him. One look at Khalid and the strange bend of his nose conjured visions of the two giants locked in mortal combat. However, it seemed neither had come out on top. A truce, then? Alessandra mused.

A peculiar feeling came over her. Frowning, she looked back at the new man and found his gaze taking a leisurely jaunt over her. At every place it lit upon her, from her flushed face to the rise and fall of her breasts, down to the toes she curled into the carpet , she felt burned.

Why did he stare at her? Did he mock her? Or was it just her imagination? Imagination, she told herself after a quick search through her memory. This must be the eunuch her mother had purchased a sennight past. Aye, none other would dare be so forward.

"Come, Alessandra," Sabine said. "I would have an explanation for this unseemly behavior."

Drawing a shaky breath, Alessandra went to her mother and pressed a kiss to her pale cheek. "Forgive me," she said, truly repentant. "I could not help myself."

Sabine's face softened. "You must learn to control these impulses, child," she said, brushing Alessandra's tousled hair off her face. "When Jabbar hears of it, he will likely forbid you entertainment again."

And he would hear of it, Alessandra thought, for Leila, the first of his three wives, would tell him. Shrugging off the inevitable, she smiled impishly. "It will have been worth it."

Sabine sighed. "Just do not complain to me when you are left to your boredom again. I will hear none of it."

"Would I do such a thing?" Alessandra's eyes grew wide and innocent.

"Yes, you would."

Alessandra laughed. "And you would still come to my aid."

Rolling her eyes, Sabine took her daughter's hand and pulled her around to face the new eunuch.

Up close, Alessandra was even more disconcerted by the man. There was none of a eunuch's serenity in that scarred face. Indeed, his expression was hard, as if engraved by anger. Yet something peculiar lurked in the depths of his eyes—amusement, perhaps?

"Why do you stare?" she bluntly asked.

"He is from England," Sabine hastened to explain. "The new eunuch has much to learn before he assumes his place in this household."

Apprehension replaced by astonishment, Alessandra stepped nearer the man. "England? Why did you not tell me, Mother?"

"I thought to surprise you."

"Surprise me?" She looked over her shoulder at Sabine. "That you have."

Her mother smiled. "I thought, perhaps, he could help you with your English, and in return, you would teach him our language."

Alessandra grimaced. She preferred the language she had spoken all her life and was not keen on being tutored in English. Though she could converse well enough in her mother's native language, it was difficult upon her tongue. Not only did it lack the richness and superb delicacy of Arabic, there was none of Arabic's singsong intonation to soften it.

"Aye, I could teach him our language," she agreed, having no intention of wasting time learning more of the English her mother would have her know intimately. She turned back to the man.

Again, his penetrating gaze unsettled her as it drifted from her face to her neck. But he did not stop there.

Never before had Alessandra felt uncomfortable in the clothes she wore within the women's quarters, but now she did. No man, not even her betrothed, Rashid, had ever looked at her in such a way.

Wondering what it was that tugged the corners of the eunuch's lips upward, she glanced down her front. Heat rose in her cheeks as she saw what the garments could not hide—the generous swell of her breasts and the flare of her hips distinctly visible through the fine material.

Her first thought was to cover herself, but she promptly squelched it. She had never felt ashamed of her body, and she would not begin now.

With a toss of her head, she asked in her accented English, "What is your name?"

"He has taken the name of Seif," Sabine said.

"Seif ..." Alessandra repeated. "And his Christian name?"

"It is of no consequence." Sabine's voice rose sharply. "In this household, his name is Seif."

Surprised by her mother's vehemence, Alessandra turned back to her. "Something is wrong?" she asked.

Sabine shook her head. "I am simply tired."

As she should be, Alessandra thought with a knowing smile, considering Jabbar had spent the past three nights with her. Though he had two other wives and a dozen concubines, there was none Jabbar loved or desired more than her mother. It was for this reason Leila disliked Sabine so intensely—and Alessandra.

"Come and sit down," Alessandra prompted, urging her mother toward the others with a hand beneath her elbow.

Sabine drew back. "I am going to rest now," she said. "Perhaps you could introduce Seif."

Alessandra looked to the group of women. They were showing little interest in the splendid performance of the dancers. Their eyes were all upon the new eunuch.

Knowing exactly what they were contemplating, Alessandra scowled. They were like vultures—the lot of them—hungry for what Jabbar gave them too little of. Even Leila, who usually hid her emotions well, was clearly fascinated.

"Very well," Alessandra said. "Come, Seif."

He started to follow, but Sabine caught hold of his arm. "One more thing, Lucien—Seif," she whispered. "None is to know of my illness, including my daughter. Do you understand?"

He stared at her a long moment, then dipped his head. "They will not hear of it from me, mistress."

Wishing she could find greater confidence in his words, Sabine dropped her hand. "Remember our bargain," she reminded him.

"How could I forget?"

With growing unease, she watched him cross the room to where Alessandra stood. Though one would have to be blind not to notice her daughter's unusual beauty, never before had Alessandra seemed so sensual or provocative—nor so ready to know the knowledge of man and woman.

It was something Lucien had also noticed, of that Sabine was certain. Though he had striven to keep his face impassive while he'd watched Alessandra's seductive dance, Sabine had seen the light of desire flash in his eyes, seen the flaring of his nostrils and the spasming of the muscles of his jaw.

Was it possible he had not quenched his desire these past nights? she wondered. Khalid had informed her of Lucien's great appetite and the many women it had taken to tire him each evening, but he had assured her the man was ready to come among the women. But was he?

Her misgivings mounting one upon the other, she twisted her cold hands together. Even if her plan succeeded, would Alessandra reach England intact? Or would this giant of a man forever spoil her? And what if he discovered who Alessandra was? What then would be his vengeance?

Oh, foolish plan of hers, she silently lamented. She ought to abandon it this moment. However, on reflection, the alternative was far worse. Concern over whether Alessandra reached England with her virtue intact was far preferable to knowing the sort of life Rashid would give her; and once on English soil, she could escape Lucien de Gautier if need be. It was a chance Sabine had to take.

"The Englishman will be watched," Khalid said, as if reading her thoughts.

Sabine tilted her head back and stared at him, grimacing at the sight of that splendid nose knocked askew by the Englishman. Though Khalid had told her they had come to an understanding of sorts, and that there would be no more trouble between them, she was less than certain herself.

"I trust you will keep me apprised of any further problems," she said.

Ever solemn, Khalid nodded. With one last glance at her daughter and the man standing beside her, Sabine left the room.

Alessandra determinedly ignored the new eunuch in an attempt to block her acute awareness of him. She focused on the dancers instead, admiring their colorful garments, and the trinkets they wore about their wrists, waists, and ankles that flashed color and sound as they moved. She envied their freedom, and wished herself as unfettered as they.

Again, the music and dance poured into her, threatening to draw her back to the floor. Making a conscious effort to still her restless movements, she crossed her arms over her chest and squeezed her thighs together, but her body did not obey for long. Finding the rhythm, it opened and began to sway.

Finally, reasoning that she was already found out and that her punishment would be no greater if she compounded her crime, Alessandra tossed off the stifling inhibitions and stepped forward. She did not get far before being pulled back.

Startled, she looked down to where she was held, her pulse leaping as her gaze fixed upon the long, tanned fingers encircling her wrist. Jerking her head back, she met Seif's eyes. There was laughter there, though not of the humorous sort. It was mocking.

"Release me," she demanded in English as she attempted to pull her hand free. She was unsuccessful, though it was not because he held her tightly. Indeed, his touch was almost like a caress.

Her breath catching as some strange sensation inched its way up her spine, Alessandra tugged again. "Do you not let go," she warned, "I will call the other eunuchs and have you removed."

His eyebrows arched high. "The dance has been forbidden you," he said.

Though Khalid could get away with handling her so,

Alessandra was not about to allow the new eunuch such liberties. "I do as I please," she retorted, uncaring that her raised voice was drawing attention to them, especially since the others could not understand the words they spoke. "Now release me!"

He drew his thumb across the pulse point in her wrist. "I am waiting for this to calm," he said.

Quite the opposite, her pulse leaped higher. Gasping, Alessandra wrenched her hand free and jumped back from him. "You are too bold for a eunuch," she whispered fiercely. "Perhaps a whip across your back would put you in your place."

Immediately, his face shuttered, all derision wiped clean. "Forgive me, mistress," he said, crossing his arms over his broad chest. "As your mother has stated, I have much to learn."

Had it been a genuine apology, Alessandra might have made allowances for him, but she knew it was not. He was simply trying to appease her.

Still, that did not explain why her anger was so great. Her anger, she reluctantly acknowledged, had more to do with the sensations he had roused with only the touch of his eyes and his fingers—sensations she had never experienced and that frightened her more than she cared to admit. They were far too much like the music she could not resist.

Abruptly, the musicians and dancers ended their performance. The air still vibrating with their energy, they were rewarded by loud, boisterous applause.

Feeling a sudden need to speak with her mother, Alessandra seized the opportunity to slip away unnoticed. She had taken barely two steps when Seif stepped in her path, blocking her escape.

"You are not going to introduce me?" he asked, one eyebrow raised higher than the other.

"Introduce yourself," she snapped, then stepped around him. Fortunately, he did not follow, for she would not have known how to deal with him then. Ignoring Khalid's questioning gaze, she hurried from the hall, all the while imagining that deep, masculine laughter followed her.

• • •

"Insufferable!" Alessandra exclaimed, throwing her hands into the air.

Propping herself on an elbow, Sabine watched her daughter pace back and forth, her hair a splash of color against the softly painted walls. "Aye, he is that," she agreed.

"Then why would you purchase him?"

"You are spoiled, Alessandra," Sabine chided. "It takes time for a man who has recently become a eunuch to accept his fate. The Englishman will come around."

Alessandra shook her head. "I do not think so. He is not like the others."

"Ah, but given time, he will be."

Alessandra rubbed her hands over her arms. "I do not like it when he touches me," she said absently, remembering the heat of his eyes and the feel of his warm hand upon her.

Angry color sweeping across her pale face, Sabine sat straight up. Had it already started, then? she wondered. And if so, how long before her daughter surrendered to Lucien's seduction? Though steps could be taken to ensure Alessandra's virtue while she remained in Algiers, once she was in Lucien's hands, Sabine had only his word that he would leave Alessandra untouched. But his word was not enough, especially considering Alessandra's newly heightened awareness of those things far removed from a child's world.

Silently, Sabine cursed the illness that was eating at her tortured body. If not for it, she could have continued to control Alessandra's exposure to the harem women and their boastful, vulgar tongues. Now, however, Alessandra knew by word what she had long been shielded from, and her insatiable curiosity demanded knowledge from experience.

"He touched you?" Sabine asked, unable to keep the angry tremor from her voice.

Realizing the mistake she had made, Alessandra attempted to shrug off the incident. "It was nothing really. He grabbed my wrist, that is all."

"Why would he do that?"

Alessandra ceased her pacing and met her mother's wide-eyed stare. "He . . . did not like what I was doing."

"Which was?"

"Dancing," she mumbled.

"What did you say?"

Alessandra breathed a long sigh. "I was dancing," she said in a rush. "I know I should not have, but it seemed that if I was to be punished for doing it once, then—"

"Alessandra, will you never learn?" Exasperated, Sabine lay back upon her divan. "And you think you are suited to life in a harem." She shook her head. "You would be better off in England."

Hoping to avoid the argument that was fast approaching, Alessandra walked over to the divan and perched herself on its edge. "Let us speak of the marketplace," she prompted. "You have not told me what else you purchased besides that dreadful eunuch."

"Nay, we will speak of England," Sabine insisted. "There is so much I have not yet told you."

Alessandra's shoulders slumped. "I know enough," she said, cupping her chin in her palm. "I am the firstborn child of Lady Catherine—you, Mother—and Lord James Bayard of Corburry. My father is wealthy and noble, a good man. Though you did not know it, you were pregnant with me when you were stolen from your home and sold into slavery—"

"Enough," Sabine interrupted. "I would tell you of Agnes."

"Agnes?"

"Aye, the cousin I came to live with when my parents died. I was only ten years of age."

Alessandra's interest was piqued, for she had not heard of this Agnes before. She leaned nearer. "Were you great friends?"

A bitter laugh escaped Sabine's lips. "Quite the opposite. We were rivals from the beginning."

"In what way?"

"Every way. Agnes was a year older than I, and quite lovely. Her parents doted on her and gave her everything."

"And you?"

Sabine shrugged. "They were good to me. I was not neglected. Though my clothes were those Agnes grew out of, my playthings those she threw aside, I was content."

Alessandra felt a sharp pang of sorrow for the lost little girl her mother must have been. "Did you and Agnes quarrel much?"

"All the time. In fact, we fought like boys—rolling on the ground, kicking and pulling each other's hair. . . ."

It was difficult to believe her gentle mother had ever engaged in such sport, but Alessandra found it amusing to envision. "And who won?"

"Agnes—every time. You see, she was larger than me."

Alessandra was disappointed. "You never bettered her? Not even once?"

Sabine's face lit. "Aye, though not in wrestling."

"Do tell."

Her smile grew wider. "Agnes very much wanted James Bayard for her own. She courted him day and night, flirted outrageously with him, even asked him to marry her."

"And?"

Her mother laughed. "Though I had not encouraged him in any way, James chose me instead."

It seemed a fitting enough revenge, Alessandra thought. "He loved you?"

"Very much. It mattered not that I brought such a paltry dowry, he wanted only me."

"And you—you loved him as well."

The triumphant smile faded from Sabine's face. She shook her head. "Nay, I cannot lie to you, Alessandra," she said, lifting a hand to caress her daughter's cheek. "Never did I love your father, though I did have great affection for him."

A look of hurt crossed Alessandra's face. "But you love Jabbar. I have heard you say so."

"Aye, though it was not so in the beginning. I hated the infidel who bought me and sought to make me his concubine. But Jabbar was patient with my strange Christian ways, and so very handsome, my tongue cleaved to the roof of my mouth each time I looked at him. Not until after you were born did he lay a finger to me." She sighed.

"Though I did not wish it, I fell in love with him—and he with me."

"And so you became his wife."

She nodded. "One of three."

"And you have been happy with him, have you not?"

Sabine shook her head. "Not always. It is difficult sharing the man you love with so many others, which is the reason I do not want this match between you and Rashid. It is not Christian—nor is it English."

"But I am not English—"

" 'Tis the only blood that runs through your veins, daughter," Sabine snapped. She'd pointed this out several times before. "Though you have been raised among Muslims, you are wholly English and serve no other god but that of the Christians. This is not the life I wish for you, nor the life you could live."

"You do not know that!"

"Do I not? Then who is the child who cannot stand to be too long indoors, who waxes impatient when there is naught to do but sit around the fountain and eat sweets, who longs to dance and go unveiled before all, who plays foolish pranks and grows indignant when Rashid takes a concubine to bed?" Who, Sabine did not say aloud, had grown restless to know of men what the other women of the harem had long known. All the more reason to send her to England.

Alessandra surged to her feet, the bells around her ankles sounding harsh in the tense room. "I will listen to no more!"

Urgency lending her speed, Sabine caught hold of her daughter's arm. "You are too strong-willed, and to become one of several wives would not long satisfy you. I know you, Alessandra, better than you know yourself. This is not the life for one such as you."

Alessandra looked into her mother's desperate face. "You would send me away, then? To England and people I do not know? People like that eunuch you have brought into our home? Why, he has not a smile with which to smite the devil from his eye!"

Fearful that Alessandra might stumble upon the true purpose of Lucien de Gautier, Sabine softened her approach. "You know 'tis my greatest desire that you return to your father," she said, moisture gathering on her lashes.

"And what of you? If you plan to send me to him, why would you not come also?"

As if pained, Sabine closed her eyes. "There is naught for me in England. I could never leave Jabbar. My place is here, with him. This is my life now—"

"As it is mine!"

Sabine opened her eyes. "Nay, Alessandra, it will never be yours. You are your father's daughter. So like him. You are not like those simpering, conniving creatures Rashid will wed and take to his bed, rivals who will make you consider each morsel you place in your mouth for fear it could be your last."

Sabine was remembering Leila's ill-fated attempt to poison her shortly after she had come to live in Jabbar's harem. Though the woman had already born him his first son—Rashid—earning for herself the esteemed position of mother of the heir, she had become intensely jealous as Jabbar showed his preference for Sabine over any other. Threatened, Leila had tried to murder her rival.

Sabine had shielded Alessandra from such things all her life, but the danger was ever present, and it was time she learned of it. "Leila is as opposed to you wedding Rashid as I," she said. "She would think nothing of poisoning your food to be rid of you. Do you not see it is your life I fear for?"

Alessandra considered her mother's words. Well she knew Leila's animosity, but she did not believe the woman capable of murder. "I think you exaggerate, Mother. And even were that true, Rashid would not allow her to do me harm."

Exasperated, Sabine shook her head. "A fortnight before you were born, Leila poisoned my food. Fortunately, I was so nauseated with pregnancy I ate very little of it. Though it was not enough to kill me, I was sick unto death for days thereafter. Nay, Alessandra, there is nothing Rashid could do to prevent Leila from doing the same to you. I was fortunate, but you may not be."

Suddenly chilled, Alessandra wrapped her arms

around herself. " 'Tis why Khalid oversees the preparation of everything we eat, isn't it? Why I am forbidden to take anything from Leila . . ."

Sabine stroked her arm. "Aye. Now you understand why I do not want this life for you."

"But if Jabbar loved you so much, why wasn't Leila punished for what she did?"

"She was punished. Jabbar took Rashid from her and sent her back to her family. And he would not have allowed her to return had her son not needed her so much. You see, Rashid became so distraught that he refused to eat, day and night he cried, his small body growing ever weaker, until . . ." Sabine sighed. "Loving him as he did, Jabbar could not bring himself to send his son away. He had to bring Leila back."

"Yet you would send me away."

"England is your home. You will be safer there."

Though she now knew a fear she had never known before, Alessandra still could not accept the thought of leaving. "I will not go, Mother. I will not leave you, nor those I have grown up with."

"You will go."

She shook her head. "Nay, there is naught you can do to change my mind."

"Then I will not change your mind."

Suspicious, Alessandra narrowed her eyes, studying her mother's face. "Jabbar will not send me away, and he will not allow you to, either."

"I ask no man's permission to do with my daughter what I desire. I bore you, and only I will decide what is to be your fate."

The cool words shook Alessandra. This was a completely different woman from the one who had gently raised her. This woman was unyielding.

"Because I love you so much," Sabine went on, her voice softening, " 'tis why you cannot stay."

Alessandra gripped her mother's hand. "And because I love you so much, Mother, I will resist any attempt to send me away. You are all I know. I want naught to do with those in England who would look upon me as an oddity. I may not be Arab, but neither am I English. This is where I belong and where I will stay."

Sabine's shoulders slumped. "Then you will fight me."

"Aye, though I do not wish to."

A sad smile upon her lovely face, Sabine placed her hands on her daughter's shoulders. "I cannot win this argument, hmm?"

"Nay."

A deep sigh. "I so dislike losing, you know."

Praying the matter was finally settled, Alessandra kissed her mother's cheek. "You are not losing," she said. "We both gain."

Sabine made no response to that. "There is something else we must speak of," she said. "The new eunuch—Seif—I do not want you telling him of your English background."

Alessandra frowned. "He is a eunuch. There is not much chance of us carrying on such a conversation."

"Nevertheless, you are not to tell him who your father is, nor speak of your father's lands."

Puzzled by this strange command, Alessandra folded her arms across her chest. "You have never before forbidden me to speak of such things. Why do you now?"

Sabine shook her head. "It does not matter. Just do not speak of it."

"You are hiding something, Mother. What is it?" Always, she and her mother had been close, no secrets between them. Why now, and why with this Englishman?

Sabine twined her fingers together and stared at them. "Is it not enough that I ask this of you?"

Alessandra laid her hand over her mother's. "It is difficult for me to accept that you would put secrets between us," she said softly. "And you know how deep my curiosity."

Sabine closed her eyes briefly, then nodded. "Very well. I will tell you, but ask me no more."

"Agreed."

"Though I did not know it when I purchased him, the eunuch's English name is Lucien de Gautier."

Alessandra tried to remember where she had heard the

name before; it was one her mother had mentioned in the past.

"He is of the same family whose land adjoins that of the Bayards," Sabine helped her. "The same family who has been feuding with your father's for so many years."

Now she remembered, though the details were vague. "Continue," Alessandra prompted.

"For many years theirs was a blood feud," Sabine said with obvious distaste. "Before I was taken from England, it had lessened to petty skirmishes, but still they hated one another. It was frightening."

"Was it the De Gautiers who sold you into slavery?"

Sabine shrugged. "I do not know, though I have always considered it a strong possibility."

"And as Seif is a relation," Alessandra filled in, "then you fear he might do us harm should he discover our true identity."

"It is possible, especially now that he has recently become a eunuch. I think, in time, he will settle down, but one should never knowingly cross swords with the devil."

Alessandra smiled at the comparison. "I understand," she said, "and will say nothing of my lineage."

"Do not forget," Sabine cautioned. "You know not how important it is."

CHAPTER 3

Rising before the other women of the harem, Alessandra dressed and made her way to the roof terrace she frequented each morning. From there she could observe the comings and goings of the boats on the Mediterranean, and watch the sun rise above the city of Algiers.

Though it was not always convenient, Abd al-Jabbar, an intensely private man, had chosen to build his sprawling home inland, away from the city. If one traveled by donkey, it could take as much as half a day to reach Algiers's bustling marketplace, though by swift horse, the trip would be less than two hours.

Plagued as always by a restlessness she had never understood—though Sabine said it was her father in her—Alessandra had been disappointed not to be allowed to accompany her mother into the city the last few times she had gone. In her search for a new eunuch, Sabine had been adamant that Alessandra remain behind. They had even argued over it.

Soon, however, Alessandra would have to be allowed to go, for she needed cloth for her wedding attire. Although she and Rashid were not to be wed for several months yet, it would take much time to complete the intricate embroidery that would adorn her costume.

She wrinkled her nose in anticipation of the endless hours of boredom that would then be hers. Though competent with a needle, she found taking one in hand to always be a chore. But, as with nearly everything her mother insisted she master, it was a skill of gentle Englishwomen.

With the coming of dawn, Alessandra went down upon her knees and clasped her hands before her. She had only just begun her prayers when she was interrupted.

"To which god do you pray?" a scornful voice asked. "The accursed Muhammad's, or that of the Christians?"

Her heart jolting, she jumped to her feet and spun around to face the new eunuch. "What are you doing here?" she demanded.

He straightened from the wall and stepped toward her. "I followed you," he said.

Then he had been watching her all this time? The thought unnerved her. "Why?" she asked, resentful that the nearer he came, the farther back she had to tilt her head.

Stopping less than an arm's reach away from her, he narrowed his gaze and stared out across the land to where the city lay. "I thought, perhaps, we might begin our lessons," he said. "It seems I must know more of your language if I am ever to converse with the women."

"It is not among your duties to *converse* with the women," Alessandra retorted. Her irritation deepened as she imagined how the wives and concubines must have vied for his attention after she had deserted him two days earlier. Since then, she had seen little of him, for Khalid had commanded all of his time.

"I would not think it my duty, either," he agreed, "but they seem to be of a different mind."

That did not surprise Alessandra, though it vexed her beyond reason. Pulling her cloak more tightly about her, she thrust her chin high. "Until you have learned your place, eunuch, I have no intention of teaching you anything. You are far too ill-mannered and rude."

He looked down at her. "All because I prevented you from making a spectacle of yourself?"

She knew he referred to her dancing. "I did no such thing!" she huffed. At least she would not admit to having done so.

"Didn't you?"

Rankled, she turned her back on him. "Once again, you

overstep your bounds, Seif." She lowered her eyelids against the brilliance of the ascending sun. "Leave me now."

She listened for his departure, but he did not move, the heat from his body warming her back as the sun did her front. Thinking she could wait him out, that he would eventually grow bored and wander off, she feigned ignorance of his continued presence. However, her body paid no heed to the pretense, as acutely aware of his proximity as if it were his hands caressing her rather than his heat.

Frantically, she wondered why this man—a eunuch—could have such an effect upon her. And what, exactly, was the effect? It certainly felt like nothing she had ever before experienced. Was this, perhaps, what the women chattered about and called desire?

Impossible. The man was not even handsome—at least not in the way Rashid was.

"You have not answered my question." His warm breath swept across her ear.

A tremor of pleasure shot through Alessandra, radiating to the farthest reaches of her limbs. "What—what question was that?" she asked, keeping her back to him for fear of what might show on her face.

"Whether or not you are a pagan. Are you, Sabine's daughter?"

The sun was not up a full ten minutes, yet she felt as if she could abandon her cloak for all the warmth that suffused her body.

"I do not have to answer that," she said flippantly.

Without warning, he settled his hands on her shoulders and turned her to face him. Before she realized his intent, his fingers glided down her throat and found the chain about her neck. Pulling it free of her caftan, he cradled the crucifix in his large palm.

"Christian," he pronounced, letting it catch the light. Smiling slightly, he met her startled gaze. "Though you are still a bit of a pagan, aren't you, Alessandra?"

Again, she knew, he was remembering her dancing. Snatching the crucifix from him, Alessandra jumped away. "How dare you!" she stormed. Without thinking, she rubbed a hand over her throat, where his fingers had seemed to scorch her skin.

His eyes laughed at her. "Would you like me to put it back?"

He knew, she realized. Knew exactly the effect he was having on her. She cursed herself for behaving exactly as those women in Jabbar's harem who had been long without his attentions. And she had not even known such attentions that she should be missing them!

Hitching up her cloak, Alessandra darted past him and hurried to the stairs. Thinking her escape assured, she lunged forward, only to come up against a firm chest and to be wrapped in arms that had only held her so near when she'd been a child.

"Rashid!" she exclaimed, leaning back to look into his startled face.

"You are in a hurry," he said, setting her away from him. "I had hoped to have a few minutes with you before leaving for the city. Father and I will be gone a sennight."

Nervous, Alessandra looked over her shoulder to where Seif stood. His arms crossed over his chest, his legs spread wide, he stared back . . . and laughed at her. She could feel it as distinctly as if the sound filled the air. It was the recklessness her mother had tried so hard to wrest from her that was responsible for what she did next.

Alessandra threw her arms around Rashid's neck and, as he staggered back, pressed her body against him and her mouth to his. It was her first kiss, but what should have been saved for her wedding night was nothing like what she had hoped it would be. She waited for something to happen, to experience a greater thrill than the eunuch's touch had aroused, but there was only emptiness.

"Alessandra!" Rashid exclaimed as he forced her back. "This is highly improper. What is wrong with you?"

Shame washing over her, she stared at the ground. "I am sorry. I don't know what . . ."

What *was* wrong with her? she wondered. Why had she felt nothing? Why had Rashid not responded? Had it been the same for him, that he'd felt nothing, or was it propriety that held him back? She loved him, didn't she? Felt the same for him that her mother did for Jabbar?

Perhaps not. They had grown up side by side and, in spite of Leila's attempts to keep them apart, had been as close as any brother and sister. Was that all there was between them? Had it not blossomed into something greater?

"Is this the new eunuch?" Rashid asked, stepping away from her.

Reluctantly, Alessandra followed him back across the terrace. "Aye, he is the one Mother recently purchased."

Rashid looked back at her, a frown gathering his dark eyebrows together. "What is he doing here with you?"

Panicked by what he might suspect, Alessandra grasped at the only excuse she could think of. "Mother asked me to teach him our language. It seems the best time to do it, since his duties are many once the household awakens."

"Hmm," Rashid grunted. Hands clasped behind his back, he went to stand before Seif.

Silence, drawn out and terribly uncomfortable, ensued as the two men examined each other.

Standing to the side, her bottom lip caught between her teeth, Alessandra silently implored the eunuch not to be so bold, to lower his eyes in deference to the master's son. But he did not, his gaze as sharp and unwavering as ever.

Fortunately, Rashid was even-tempered, his ire not easily aroused. In contrast, Jabbar would likely have ordered the eunuch bastinadoed for such a lack of respect.

"He has more to learn than our language," Rashid finally said. "I think his time would be better spent with Khalid, don't you?"

"I . . . yes," Alessandra agreed.

Rashid stepped nearer Seif. "I am Rashid, firstborn of Abd al-Jabbar," he said in Arabic. "And you are?"

"He does not yet—" Alessandra began.

"Seif," the eunuch answered.

Smiling faintly, Rashid looked to Alessandra. "He learns fast."

Forcing a smile to her lips, she raised her gaze to the

eunuch's. "Yes, he does." That he had corroborated her
story didn't even occur to her. All she could think was
that he understood far more than she had been led to believe. How she wished she could wipe the smug expression from his face.

Without further word, Rashid turned on his heel and
strode away.

Having no desire to be alone with the eunuch again,
Alessandra followed. "You wished to speak with me,"
she reminded Rashid.

"I had thought there might be some bauble you would
like me to bring you from the city," he said as he descended the stairs.

Unable to resist the urge, Alessandra looked back at the
lone figure silhouetted against the new sky. Though he
had turned to stare at the city, she knew he still laughed
at her.

Long after Alessandra and Rashid had gone, Lucien remained atop the roof and surveyed the home of Abd al-
Jabbar. It was immense, spread out over nearly as much
land as the whole of the De Gautier castle in England.
Like the castle, it was fortified with walls patrolled by
guards, but there the resemblance ended.

The main house itself, a large, flat-topped structure
built of ponderous blocks of stone, was only two stories
high. Therein was housed the hall, the kitchens, and the
meeting rooms for the men. Three single-storied buildings jutted out from it, one being the harem and apartments of the women, the second the bathhouse, and the
third the men's apartments.

In between the harem and bathhouse lay a spacious
garden with a marble-tiled fishpond at its center. Farther
out were the eunuchs' quarters, the servants' quarters,
the stables, and storehouses. Though not as imposing as
most castles in England, the mansion was far more opu-
lent, with its tiled floors, arcades formed by marble pil-
lars, and numerous fountains. Luxury, not security, had
been the primary consideration in its construction.

Lucien grimaced. Had he not given his word to Sabine,

it would have been only a small challenge to escape this place, but now he must wait on the impetuous Alessandra.

Teeth clenched, he wondered at the dangerous game he was playing with her. He had not intended to engage in such sport. But then, not once had it entered his mind that she would be anything but a blushing young girl, and certainly he had not expected her to be so lovely. Except for her warm skin tone, it was impossible to tell that any blood other than English coursed through her veins. She had all the looks and beauty of her mother—and more.

It had been a long time since he'd felt such intense desire for a woman. Years, in fact. And that he would feel it for this one, a woman whose Arab descent condemned her in his eyes, astounded him. He did not want to feel such emotion for his enemy. He did not want to feel the jealousy he had a short time ago.

Involuntarily, his thoughts turned to the man Alessandra was to wed—the arrogant Rashid. Lucien had learned of the pending marriage from Khalid, but only from the young man's boasting that morning had he discovered that, like Alessandra, Rashid was an offspring of Jabbar. The two were half siblings, then.

Did the Islamic faith permit such close marriages? Though he had learned much of the Arab people and their culture in the past year, this was one area he had little knowledge of. Surely this was Sabine's real reason for wanting her daughter taken to England. Having remained a Christian, she could not possibly approve of such a union.

And there would not be one, Lucien told himself, suddenly determined to fulfill his end of the bargain. As planned, he would deliver Alessandra to England and see her safely into the hands of her mother's relatives.

Odd, he thought, but he was no longer concerned about their escape. It would be dangerous, but the temptation he would be faced with once the fiery young woman was completely in his care would be even more perilous. It would be a long journey back to England.

"Damn!" he cursed. Though he had thought himself well sated with the numerous prostitutes Khalid had supplied him, he felt as if it still had been well over a year since he had last lain with a woman. If he was not careful, he would, indeed, find himself a true eunuch.

CHAPTER 4

"Alessandra," a young voice called out. "Come join us."

Idly pushing herself back and forth on the swing, Alessandra turned to look at the spectacle emerging from the trees. Her interest was piqued as she saw the daughters of the wives and concubines entering the garden, a donkey between them. They were all younger than she by at least four years, the older ones having long since been married off.

With childish glee, Alessandra slipped off the swing. However, the feel of Seif's eyes upon her halted her before she had taken more than a step. Shaking her head, she reseated herself.

"You can be the gentleman first," said Nada, an exotic, sable-headed girl.

She was tempted, but Alessandra remained resolute, telling herself it would be enough to watch the others enjoy themselves. It was not, though.

Longingly, she watched as Nada was made ready for her ride. Dressed as a man, her brows thickened with kohl, a mustache painted above her upper lip, and a carved melon perched upon her head, she was helped onto the donkey. She sat facing backward, and the animal's tail was handed to her. One kick, and away she went.

Squealing her delight, the girl held tight and tried to maintain her balance as the donkey trotted through the garden. As was most often the case, the melon was the

first to go, cracking and spilling its seeds onto the stone
path. Startled, the animal leaped forward, and a moment
later Nada slipped sideways and fell into a flower bed.

Rushing forward, the women and children laughed
loudly as the girl struggled upright. It was an entertainment they never tired of.

If only Seif would go indoors, Alessandra thought.
There was none better at the game than she; almost every
time she made the full circuit of the garden, melon and
all. Fearful that she might give in to the impulsiveness
that too often landed her in trouble, she gripped the
ropes of the swing tighter.

A moment later Leila's husky laughter drew Alessandra's attention away from the game. Peering over her
shoulder, she saw that the woman stood very near Seif.
Her hand resting on his forearm, she smiled up at him.

Though the eunuch did not seem to be encouraging
her, something stirred inside Alessandra. She could not
name the emotion, but knew she did not like what she
saw.

How soon before the still-beautiful Leila made him
hers? she wondered. With the exception of Khalid, all the
eunuchs had succumbed to her wiles at one time or another.

Leila laughed again and stepped nearer Seif, her eyes
boldly caressing him. Seif ignored her, though, looking
past her, and his gaze met Alessandra's. Though his face
reflected little emotion, his eyes sparkled with something
she did not understand.

Berating herself for having been caught staring,
Alessandra turned her attention back to the game. However, she enjoyed it less than before, a gnawing need to
look at Seif again making it difficult to concentrate.

With each successive rider, the donkey grew less and
less accommodating, its irritation manifested in its increased speed, quivering hindquarters, and temperamental braying. Thus, it was not surprising when it kicked its
hind legs and threw its rider. The girl sailed through the
air and landed in a thicket of spiny bushes near Alessandra. Immediately she began to wail.

Launching herself from the swing, Alessandra hurried to disentangle the girl from the greedy thorns. "It was foolish of you to ride him," she said.

"And you would not have?" the girl retorted.

Brushing the thorns from the other's clothes, Alessandra shrugged. "I am better experienced than you," she said as the several girls and women gathered around them.

"Then let us see if you can ride the beast," Leila slyly suggested. "Or do you grow too old for such games?"

A challenge . . . Alessandra looked over her shoulder at her mother's adversary, the woman who was soon to be her mother-in-law.

Her small dog clasped beneath one arm, her mouth curved in a taunting smile, Leila raised her brows in silent question.

Wavering, Alessandra looked to where Seif stood near the fishpond. It was not dancing, after all, she rationalized. She'd never been forbidden to take part in the garden games, and quite often the older women participated as well. What harm could there be in it, and why should she care what the new eunuch thought of her?

She turned back to the girl who had last ridden the donkey. "Give me the man's clothes."

A buzz of excitement rose from the dark-browed, mustached girls as Alessandra gave herself over to the preparation. Throughout, she kept her gaze averted from Seif, though it did not diminish her awareness of the silent laughter he directed at her.

She would not fail, she assured herself. She would keep the melon atop her head and traverse the entire garden without mishap. She would make that insufferable man swallow his laughter.

Transformed into the "gentleman," she was seated upon the animal and clenched its tail in one hand. Knowing it would be a difficult ride, for the donkey was decidedly agitated, Alessandra tightened her legs about him and steeled herself for the coming jolt.

"Away!" Nada shouted as she landed her hand to the animal's rump.

Though Alessandra did not lose her seat, the melon began to slip sideways, forcing her to angle her head to keep it from falling.

The donkey followed the pathway at a brisk pace, jostling its stubborn, unwelcome rider, but to no avail. As it approached the first curve of the path, it increased its speed and, when that did not unseat Alessandra, leaned hard into it.

Still she held on. Her thighs were strong, and she had only to concentrate on the melon balanced upon her head. This she did with utmost concentration, blurring her eyes so nothing would distract her.

Though she could not see the fishpond from her backward-facing position, she knew she was nearing it, and the end of her ride. However, in her silent rejoicing, she nearly lost the melon. Righting it, she breathed a sigh of relief and anxiously awaited her first glimpse of the water.

There it was. Triumphant, Alessandra threw both hands into the air and let the melon fall away.

Nearly all within the garden applauded her accomplishment, and the din masked the yipping of the small dog that darted between the donkey's legs.

With an angry bray, the animal reacted violently, bucking with such force, Alessandra was thrown from its back.

It all happened too quickly for her to comprehend. One moment she was filled with exultation, and the next, engulfed by pain and cold.

Struggling up from the water of the fishpond, she managed to make it to her knees before the sharp ache in her head forced her onto all fours. Her outstretched arms bracing her, she stared disbelievingly at the pink-tinged water.

Blood, she realized, and it was hers.

She had only a moment to settle her faltering gaze upon the wet hair falling over her face and the crimson streaming down its length, before strong arms plucked her from the water. Khalid, she thought as oblivion beckoned to her and deadened the babble of female voices. Only one did she clearly discern—Leila's.

"I do not know how it happened," the woman exclaimed, her voice pitched high above the rest. "Somehow he got away from me."

Who had gotten away from her? Alessandra wondered, squeezing her eyes against the fierce pounding in her head. "Ah, Khalid, am I going to die?" she whispered.

But it was not Khalid who answered her. "Nay, little one," Seif said in English. "All will be well."

Odd, but she sensed no more of his horrid, voiceless laughter, and his arms were so comforting. Dropping her head against his chest, she nuzzled into his warmth and drifted off.

She felt so terribly cold. Turning onto her side, Alessandra drew her knees to her chest and wrapped her arms around them, but the effort produced nothing save a dull throb in her head.

Moaning, she threw out a hand and groped for something to pull over her, but found only pillows. A whimper rose from her throat as she hugged her arms more tightly about her shivering limbs.

Suddenly an orange light forced its way through her closed lids. "Mother?" she murmured.

Warm hands moved over her legs, lifting them and pulling at something wrapped around them.

It would have been easy to drift back to sleep, but her curiosity would not allow her to. Squinting against the harsh light, she looked at the large figure standing at the foot of her divan.

Who was it? she wondered. She forced her eyes to focus on the man and realized it was Seif who tended her.

Why was he there? Once night fell, even eunuchs were forbidden the harem—except Khalid. She was about to ask when she remembered that she had awakened before, and each time Seif had been there beside her mother. Was it her imagination, or had Sabine said he was to watch over her?

Scowling, Seif pulled the cover free from its entanglement with her feet and shook it out.

"Where is my mother?" Alessandra asked.

For a brief moment his piercing gaze met hers, but he said nothing until he had dropped the cover over her and tucked it around her huddled form. "Likely she is sleeping," he said, straightening to his overwhelming height.

"And why are you here?" Alessandra blurted, disturbed by the warmth his impersonal hands had left upon her.

He folded his arms over his chest. "Your mother and Khalid ordered me to sleep outside your apartment until Jabbar returns. They are concerned for your welfare."

The accident. It came back to Alessandra, explaining the pain in her head and the loss of the hours since. She fingered the bandage wound around her head.

"You saw ..." She faltered as the memories assailed her. She felt again the cold water and saw it stained with blood, remembered the arms that had lifted her and held her close, heard the words Leila had spoken. . . .

"How did it happen?" she asked.

"Leila's dog. He frightened the donkey."

The warmth that had begun to suffuse Alessandra's limbs receded as her mother's disclosure of days earlier, and the taunting words Leila had used to entice her into mounting the donkey, melded. Had it been an accident, or had Leila purposely set out to do her harm as Sabine had warned?

She had to ask. "Think you it was an accident, Seif?" she said between teeth that had begun to chatter.

He hesitated. Then, pulling his robe from his shoulders, he draped it over her. "Your mother does not believe so," he said.

Of course not. Alessandra grabbed his arm before he could withdraw. "What do you think?"

He stared into her eyes. "It may have been accidental," he murmured, "or deliberate."

"You do not know which?" Her voice rose in the still room.

Lifting her hand from his arm, he turned it palm up and stared at her smooth ivory skin. "As your betrothed pointed out," he said, his thumb feathering across her wrist, "I have much more to learn than your language."

Rendered breathless by this small intimacy that warmed her as no amount of covering could, Alessandra stared wide-eyed at him. It didn't matter any longer whether Leila had attempted to do her harm. All that mattered was that she not lose this incredible warmth.

Seif urged her arm back beneath the covers, and fearful he meant to leave, Alessandra said the first thing that came to mind. "Is it late?"

"Actually, 'tis quite early. In little more than two hours it will be day again." He turned and said over his shoulder, "Sleep now and I will summon your mother at first light."

"Do not go," Alessandra pleaded, pushing herself into a sitting position that worsened the pain.

Lifting the lamp he had brought with him, Seif looked back at her. "My place is outside your door, mistress."

"Can you not stay until dawn? I am so cold and . . ." Unable to believe the shameless words she was about to speak, she lowered her eyes. "And I need your warmth."

Lucien stared at the long lashes that feathered shadows beneath her eyes, then shifted his gaze to the soft bow of her lips. Lord, but he was tempted. Just one taste of those innocent lips—

Nay, he shook off the forbidden. Alessandra was vulnerable now, and would no doubt regret asking him to stay. "It would be improper," he said. "Also, I would not want to feel Khalid's whip across my back."

Alessandra had never known a greater humiliation. Wishing she could erase these last minutes, she slid down beneath the cover and buried her face in the pillows. "Leave, then," she said, her voice muffled.

He did not leave, though, and the silence grew expectant as the minutes passed. Finally, curiosity eating at her, Alessandra lifted her head. Seif was standing alongside the divan, his eyebrows drawn together.

"What is it?" she whispered as a fluttering in her belly warned her of things better left unknown.

His face smoothed, and a faint smile lifted the corners of his mouth. Then, without a word, he extinguished the lamp. The room in total darkness, he urged her across the divan and made himself a place on it.

Confused, Alessandra clutched at the cover. "But I thought—"

"Shh. 'Twill be our secret, hmm?" Sitting with his back

to the wall, he pulled her into the curve of his body and pressed her head to his chest.

Awareness tugged at Alessandra as she breathed in his scent, a scent unlike any she had ever known. No perfumes masked the smell of him, the strangely pleasant odor. In fact, the only thing she could liken him to was Rashid's prize stallion.

She had loved the smell of that high-strung, temperamental animal, had buried her face in its neck and inhaled it when Rashid had not been looking. Though forbidden, she had longed to ride it, to have it surging beneath her, to feel its labored breathing against the insides of her thighs as it carried her far away. But no matter how she had begged, Rashid had denied her, even refusing to take her up before him. So masculine and strong the stallion had been, just like this man who was no longer a man.

"If you relax," Seif said, stroking a hand down her back, "sleep will come more easily."

With a nervous laugh, Alessandra settled herself more comfortably and drew a leg up over his.

He shifted slightly. "Better?" he asked.

"Umm, yes," she murmured, her arm sliding around his waist. "Do you know what I was thinking, Seif?"

"Nay, I do not."

"I was thinking how like a horse you are," she murmured. "A great stallion that runs with the wind."

"Is that so?"

Was it humor she detected in his voice? She couldn't be certain. "Aye. Rashid has such a stallion," she continued. "Its name is Altair, which means flying eagle."

"And does he fly like an eagle?"

"He looks to, but I have never been allowed to ride him."

"Though you would like to."

She sighed. "Very much. However, Rashid says Altair will not tolerate a woman on his back."

"That is true of some stallions."

"I do not see why," Alessandra said. "I can sit a horse the same as Rashid." She did not tell him that her experience was limited to donkeys, that she had only been on horses with Rashid at her back and controlling the reins.

"You think so?"

"Of course." Settling deeper against him, Alessandra unthinkingly slid a hand inside his caftan and put her palm to the mat of hair on his chest.

Seif shifted again, as if uncomfortable. "And you liken me to this stallion?" he asked.

"I know it sounds strange, but yes, you are much like Altair."

He bent his head and put his mouth to her hair. "Are you thinking you would like to ride me, then?" he asked softly.

Alessandra was about to protest the ridiculous question when a vision of doing just that rose up before her and swept her with sudden heat. It had seemed the most natural thing to compare Seif to Altair, though now she saw the folly of it. She had spoken the same as some of the harem women, though unintentionally, drawing parallels between man and beast.

"I . . ." She fumbled with denial, shame warming her. "I didn't mean . . ."

Lifting her hand from his chest, Seif laid it against her side. "I know what you meant," he said, his voice serious. "Now sleep, Alessandra. Morning comes soon."

She wanted to explain, but suddenly felt too weary. "I thank you for staying. It is kind of you."

Was that the reason he had stayed? Lucien wondered in the silence that followed. Kindness, or the desire to know the feel of her?

Long after she had fallen back to sleep, he asked himself time and again what he was getting into. After all, this was not part of the bargain he had struck with Sabine. Indeed, he was risking emasculation if he was discovered abed with her daughter, no matter how innocent it might be. And it truly was no longer innocent, considering their conversation, or the paths his mind kept wandering down.

He sighed. A wise man would not have placed himself in such a precarious situation. He considered slipping away now that she was asleep, but could not bring himself to. Too much, he liked the feel and scent of her, but that was not all. He admired her spirit, which was refreshing in light of the women he had associated with in the past.

There had been so many, he reflected, unable to link names with the blurred faces he beckoned from his memory. Even those he had been betrothed to—two of them—were now as indistinct as the others.

Absently stroking Alessandra's hair, he wondered at his failing memory.

CHAPTER 5

Since Sabine refused to believe her daughter's fall had been anything but the result of a deliberate attempt to harm her, Alessandra found herself in Seif's company thereafter.

He followed her everywhere, forgoing only those places he was not allowed. It would not have been so bad had she not shamed herself so terribly, pleading with him to stay with her three nights past, or if she had not likened him to a stallion she would like to ride. But she had. Perhaps worse, she still felt the terrible sense of loss she'd had when she'd wakened alone after those few hours spent in his arms.

Fortunately, he had not mentioned the incident, and the days had passed with relative ease. Now, feeling healed after the rest her mother had insisted upon, Alessandra decided it was past time she had the bath she so desperately desired. She waited until it was the time of day when most of the women congregated in the bathhouse, then left her room.

She walked past Seif, who immediately stepped away from the wall, his shadow falling over her as he followed.

Not until the sulfurous vapor greeted her as she neared the bathhouse did it occur to Alessandra that he might follow her within. Though she had never felt uncomfortable in the presence of eunuchs, the thought of disrobing in front of this one disturbed her greatly.

At the door, she paused and turned to him. "You may wait here," she said. "I will not be long."

"The baths are not forbidden me." His eyes sparkled. "I tended them my first day here."

Then he knew exactly why she did not wish his accompaniment. "You will wait here," she repeated, then turned from him.

Seif's hand fell to the door, preventing her from opening it. "If you go, so do I."

Gritting her teeth, Alessandra looked at his hand, then faced him again. "No harm can be done me in the baths."

"Unless it is forbidden me, I am to go wherever you go," he reminded her. "That includes the baths. Am I any different from the other eunuchs?"

She wanted to scream that yes, he was different, but she had yet to understand what it was that set him so far apart from the others. After all, it was only a feeling she had about him—one that appalled and confused her.

Stubborn to the end, she decided she would have her bath, even if it meant he would be in attendance. "Very well," she said. "You may accompany me."

She was pleased by the surprise that flashed across his face. Clearly, he had thought she would decline the bath altogether.

He pulled the door open, and she walked inside.

In the antechamber a servant girl greeted her. "Ah, mistress," she exclaimed. "You are better now?"

Alessandra nodded. "I but require a bath to wash these past days away."

The girl turned to a table laden with various items, from which she removed a thick bathrobe, a towel, and high-stilted wooden clogs.

"You may go ahead," Alessandra said to Seif, not wishing to disrobe before him.

"I will wait for you."

She would have protested, but he considerately turned and went to stand before the table. Not knowing how much time he would give her before turning back around, she threw off her clothes and thrust her arms into the robe the girl held for her. Then, slipping her feet into the clogs that would spare her the heat of the marble floor, she took the proffered towel and hurried forward.

"You are prompt," Seif said.

Now closer to his height, though she still had to angle her head to meet his gaze, Alessandra raised her brows. "You expected otherwise?"

Reaching for the door, he shook his head. "Not really."

The bathhouse was spacious, a large pool at its center, marble sinks spaced along the walls for bathing.

As Alessandra had known they would be, most of the women were there, their curious gazes turning to her and Seif as the two of them crossed the floor. While some were being bathed at the sinks by servant girls, others languished beside the pool, eating sweetmeats and engaging in idle talk, their naked bodies shamelessly exposed. Only two—one of them being Nada—had actually ventured into the pool, whose warm water caused a haze to cloak the entire bathhouse.

Alessandra was thankful Leila was absent. As first wife she had her own private bathing chamber, but it was not unusual to find her gossiping in the bathhouse.

"You should have worn pattens as well," Alessandra whispered to Seif.

"Pattens? What—"

"Clogs." She nodded to hers.

He grimaced. "I fear I do not have the grace, nor the tolerance, to balance upon such peculiar footwear."

"The other eunuchs do."

Peering through the haze, Seif picked out the two other men in the bathhouse. "So they do," was his only comment.

"Alessandra!" Nada cried, her body streaming wet as she emerged from the pool. Grabbing a towel, she blotted herself dry as she hastened forward. "You are well?" she asked, embracing Alessandra briefly.

Alessandra stole a glance at Seif to discover his reaction to the naked girl. His face was an impassive mask. She looked back at Nada. "I am healed," she said.

"Allah is merciful," Nada said, then turned and ran back to the pool.

God is merciful, Alessandra silently amended, knowing better than to speak it aloud.

The servant girl who stood ready to bathe her beckoned her forward.

"This I do alone," Alessandra said, stepping away from Seif. "You will wait here."

Though his feet did not follow, his eyes did. She knew it as surely as she knew she would soon be as naked as the others. Hoping the haze would dull his vision, she kept her back to him as the servant removed the robe that the heat had plastered to her skin.

Though it was only her backside any but the servant girl could see, embarrassment suffused her as she was urged down upon the stool before the sink.

If only he would look elsewhere, she thought, her discomfort growing as her hair was gathered and piled atop her head. Perhaps he was, and it was only her imagination telling her otherwise.

On impulse, she looked over her shoulder to where she had left him, but he was no longer there.

Where? she wondered, sweeping her gaze left and right. She was just beginning to relax, crediting her imagination with the discomfort she had felt, when her eyes locked with his.

Her breath caught, heat pooling in her face as she realized the vantage he had gained in moving to the opposite side of the pool. He no longer had a view of merely her naked back, but her profile.

Alessandra wanted to look away from that consuming gaze, to break the contact that stretched between them like a taut, unraveling rope, but was unable to.

Slowly, a different kind of heat wended its way through her, one that tightened her nipples, warmed her belly, and settled in the forbidden region of her body. It was as if she were melting.

If his eyes could do this to her, what would his hands do if ever she allowed them to touch her as boldly? This had to be what the wives and concubines spoke of when their conversation turned to lovemaking.

But he was a eunuch! Though her rational reminder banished the sensations claiming her body, she still could not bring herself to look away. Then an outlandish thought crept in. Or *was* he a eunuch?

Was it mere coincidence her mother had purchased an Englishman to replace the eunuch who had fallen into disfavor? Eunuchs were not so scarce that she would have had to settle for one so rebellious. And then for her to force his company upon her . . .

The appearance of a concubine at Seif's side finally broke their eye contact.

Instantly, a strange exhaustion claimed Alessandra, and she slumped forward.

"You are ill?" the servant girl asked, pausing in her vigorous soaping of Alessandra's legs.

Alessandra straightened. "I am fine," she said, shifting on the stool so Seif would see only her back again. "Perhaps a bit tired."

The girl resumed her duties. "The waters of the pool will refresh you," she said, slipping the clogs off so she could clean Alessandra's feet. "And when you are sated, I will henna your hands and feet for you. Then you will feel yourself again."

If only she *could* feel herself again, Alessandra lamented. She did not like this inner turmoil she'd been suffering since Seif's arrival. It bothered her that she could have such sinful feelings for the eunuch when she had never felt anything similar for Rashid. Never had he made her feel the woman's emotions that Seif did.

The ablutions at an end, her skin scrubbed clean, kneaded, rubbed, and rinsed of soap, her hair washed and hanging wet down her back, Alessandra rose from the stool. "My robe," she said, nodding to where it lay.

The girl handed it and the towel to her, showing surprise when Alessandra donned the garment. "You are leaving?" she asked. "What of the pool—and the henna I have promised you?"

"I am not leaving. I have simply grown cold." Alessandra hated to lie, and it was not a very good lie considering the perspiration dotting her brow, but she could not admit her reluctance to go naked before Seif. It was better to let the girl think she was still suffering from her head injury.

Refusing to look in Seif's direction, Alessandra walked to the group of women clustered at the pool's edge and sat beside them. Lifting the hem of her robe, she submerged her feet in the water.

Immediately, Hayfa, second wife to Jabbar, scooted near her. "You will faint if you keep that on," she said, flicking the sleeve of the robe.

Perhaps, Alessandra thought, but at least she would be clothed. "When I am warm again, I will remove it," she said, eyeing the woman whose once slender body had grown heavy with overindulgence.

Conspiratorially, Hayfa leaned near her. "Tell me of this new eunuch," she said, the tip of her tongue touching her upper lip. "What type is he?"

Alessandra knew full well what the woman referred to, but could not prevent her cheeks from burning bright with embarrassment. "I can tell you nothing," she snapped.

"Hmmph," a concubine who had been listening grunted. "Is it not you he has spent these last days with?"

The woman made it sound as if she and Seif had become lovers! Though Alessandra knew she should not allow herself to be drawn into such conversation, she felt a great need to defend her innocence.

"He follows me everywhere I go and sleeps outside my apartment," she said, "and that is all."

Clearly, neither woman believed her, and Alessandra's palms itched to slap their smirks away.

"If it is true our innocent Alessandra knows nothing of his anatomy, perhaps she should ask him," Hayfa suggested, her gaze flicking to where Seif stood.

"Ask him yourself," Alessandra retorted.

"I think she is frightened of him," Hayfa said. "See how she covers herself in his presence. Perhaps he has warmed her cold English blood, and she knows not what to do."

It was too close to the truth. Although she knew she should ignore the thinly veiled challenge, Alessandra jumped to her feet. "I will show you I am not frightened of him," she said, then turned and walked toward Seif.

Legs spread wide, his hands clasped behind his back,

he watched her approach through narrowed eyes, making each of Alessandra's steps more difficult than the last.

Coming to stand before him, her heart pounding wildly, she forced a mask of indifference to her face. "Hayfa ..." She nodded to the woman. "She wishes to know ... what type of eunuch you are."

Puzzlement wrinkled his brow. "What do you mean?"

Alessandra groaned inwardly. Oh, why did he have to be so difficult? Surely he knew to what she referred. She could not return without the information she had been sent for, so she fisted her hands upon her hips and thrust her chin forward.

"Some eunuchs simply have their seed taken," she said, angry at the betraying tremble of her voice. "Thus, they can still give pleasure to a woman without spoiling her with a child the master would refuse as his. Others, like Khalid, have both seed and ... device removed."

His brows lowered over his incredible eyes. "How do you know such things?"

Alessandra wished the ground would open up and swallow her whole. However, she was determined not to lose face, especially now that she had come this far. "Yusuf"—she indicated a eunuch on the other side of the pool—"is only without seed, so he gives Hayfa much pleasure. She boasts of this constantly."

"Has he given you pleasure as well?"

Alessandra's knees nearly buckled. How dare he! That he would even suggest ...

It was the same as Hayfa and the concubine had alluded to. That a girl could reach the age of eight and ten and still be a virgin was virtually unheard-of in a land where girls were often wed by their thirteenth birthday. Alessandra would have been, too, had her mother not interceded time and again. She was an untouched woman among women who had long known a man's touch, and she was pitied her lack of experience. Not even her marriage to Rashid would ever erase that.

Though the denial had been ready upon Alessandra's lips, it never made it past them. Instead, she found herself speaking another lie. "I am no virgin," she retorted.

For long, interminable moments, he simply stared at her, as if attempting to discover whether she spoke true.

"And I am no Yusuf," he finally said. "You may tell Hayfa and her friends that I am the same as Khalid."

Truly? Alessandra thought. Not so long ago she had entertained thoughts that he might not even be a eunuch, and now to be told he was one in every sense of the word . . .

"I—I do not believe you," she said.

He shrugged. "As you have no virginal senses left to offend, mistress, perhaps you would like me to show you."

Alessandra's eyes grew large, her mouth dropping open. Then, forgetting the soothing waters of the pool and the promised henna treatment, she whirled around and made as speedy a retreat from the bathhouse as she could manage.

Long after she had enclosed herself in her apartment, she still felt his laughter, and heard that of the concubines that had followed her from that place.

As Lucien left the bathhouse Sabine slipped back into the shadows, where she had hidden when she'd glimpsed Alessandra's earlier flight from that place. Hand to her breast, she searched Lucien's profile as he swept past her, certain he had the answers to the questions spinning in her mind.

What had been the cause for Alessandra's haste? she wondered again. Why the flush upon her skin that could not be attributed solely to heat? Why her trembling lips and the sparkle of tears in her eyes? Why the unintelligible mutterings she had spoken to the walls?

All manner of imaginings ran through Sabine's mind, each tied to Lucien de Gautier, and none without foundation. He had been in the bathhouse as Alessandra had bathed, and had undoubtedly seen what was denied Englishmen until they had wed the lady.

So what, exactly, had happened between them? Certainly nothing untoward with so many other women there, but something . . .

The coughing came again, though Sabine held it in until Lucien was well out of sight. When she released it, wheezing and great gasping breaths threatened to prostrate her. She lifted the skirt of her caftan, pressed it to her mouth to muffle the terrible sounds, and lurched toward her apartment.

If only she could reach it without calling attention to herself, then she could lie down and perhaps clear her mind enough to know what to do. If only—

Khalid's concerned face appeared before her, and the next moment she felt his arms lift her up against him.

"Hush, mistress," he soothed, pressing her face to his chest. "Give over to me."

Nodding, she clenched fistfuls of his robe and coughed into his chest, mollified by the knowledge that, as always, Khalid would take care of everything.

"Enter," Alessandra called when she heard the knock on her door. Without turning from the latticed window, she motioned her visitor forward. "Come see."

It was a mistake, for immediately her attention was drawn from the playful romp of two gazelles in the garden to an unsettling awareness of the man who came to stand beside her. Try as she might to recapture her enthusiasm for the scene, it paled.

"What is it?" Seif asked, his arm brushing hers.

Alessandra pulled her arms nearer her body. "Look closer, you will see."

"Ah, gazelles," he murmured.

She nodded. "A mother and her baby. It is the first I have seen of the little one since it was birthed."

"I have come to apologize," he said, abruptly changing the subject.

She felt his gaze upon her, but did not look his way. She did not want him to see her surprise. "For?"

"I should not have been so forward with you in the bathhouse."

"That is true."

"Then you accept my apology?"

She shrugged. "Mother says allowances must be made for you, so I have done so."

"Allowances?" he repeated. "Such as?"

Wishing she had simply accepted his apology, Alessandra chewed her lower lip a moment before answering. "You are English. Thus, you do not know our ways."

"And how are your ways different from the English?"

She reflected on his question before shrugging it off. "I don't really know. They just are."

He chuckled, a sound made new by the unexpectedness of it coming from him. "The differences are great, mistress. For instance . . ." His hand covered hers where it held the lattice, and he gently pried her fingers loose.

Surprised that he would touch her again, and so soon after apologizing for being forward with her, Alessandra tried to pull her hand free, but he held tight.

Lucien himself was surprised that he was so drawn to touch her, for he'd had no intention of taking such liberties again. He'd only come to apologize, but now found himself wanting to stay—wanting very badly to stay.

"It would not be untoward for a man to kiss a woman's hand in England," he continued. Making a concentrated effort to ignore the warning voices clamoring in his head, he carried her hand to his mouth. He pressed his lips to the inside of her wrist and reveled in the tremor that raced up her arm.

"Do . . . not," she protested.

He smiled. "Here, though, a man could lose his head over such a small thing." Or his manhood. Though that last thought impinged upon his desires, he thrust it aside.

She stared at her hand still clasped in his. "Which is what will happen if you are caught," she whispered.

"You think so?" Having no intention of being discovered, he shook his head. "Tell me, what other allowances have you made, Alessandra?"

Though she could have loosed her hand, something would not allow her to. Perhaps it was her name on his lips—spoken so softly, and yet with such meaning underlying it. She looked back at him.

"What? Oh!" She moistened her lips. "Unlike the other eunuchs, your manhood was taken from you much later in life, which causes restlessness. You know what it is like to—" Embarrassed, she snapped her teeth closed. What had possessed her to speak so freely of such things?

"To?" he prompted, pulling her closer. "To make love to a woman as a whole man?" The pupils of his eyes dilated until only a narrow ring of violet remained. "Yes, I remember what it is like. Should I show you what I can still do? I vow you will not be disappointed."

She pulled her gaze from his, only to have it light upon his fascinating mouth. "Let—let me go," she whispered.

He waited until she'd lifted her gaze to his again, then released her. "Go if that is what you desire," he said.

Though there was nothing holding her to him, Alessandra could not grasp the presence of mind to move away.

"Come to me, Alessandra," he beckoned. "Let me taste you."

She did not want to, fought it for what seemed an eternity, but found her hands lifting of their own accord. Drawn into his spell, she placed her palms on his chest, then, slowly, inched them up to the back of his neck.

"Tell no one," she said, and pulled his head down.

It was like nothing she had ever felt. The meeting of their mouths sparked a hunger she had never known, though many had spoken of it. "More, Seif," she moaned.

"I am Lucien," he said harshly, drawing her forward until there was no space between them.

He wanted to feel all of her, to know every curve and swell beneath her shapeless caftan. He wanted to know her fire, the impetuous workings of her mind. He wanted to wipe away this past year that had embittered and hardened him more than all the previous years spent battling the Bayards. There was something about Alessandra that had been missing in all the women he had ever known. He wanted to capture it—even if only for a moment.

Her hips pressed just below his, Alessandra felt something warm and hard lengthen against her belly. She barely registered the strange sensation before Lucien's tongue slipped between her teeth and stroked hers.

The shock of it nearly freed her of the dangerous game she played, but she held to him. This kiss was nothing like what the women talked of. Seif—or was it Lucien?—

had not lied when he'd said she would not be disappointed.

He ringed her lips with his tongue, then abruptly put her at arm's length. "How is it your mouth is untried, and yet you no longer possess your virginity?" he asked.

As if awakening from a dream, Alessandra put a hand to her lips and looked questioningly at surroundings that seemed only vaguely familiar. Frowning, she shifted her gaze to Seif, staring at him for a long moment before she shook herself free of his spell.

Dear God, she had kissed him! Gone willingly into his arms without thought of the consequences—or Rashid.

Mortified, she quickly stepped away and went to stand before her dressing table. "You should not have done that," she said, though she knew it had not been only his doing.

He moved behind her, but did not touch her again. "It was merely a demonstration of the differences between our cultures."

Alessandra picked up her comb and began to draw it through her hair. "That is all it was? A lesson, then?"

"And desire for that which is forbidden me," he admitted. "I can still feel such emotion."

He had made that painfully obvious. "You desire me?"

"I would not have touched you otherwise."

Laying the comb down, Alessandra turned to face him. "I am promised to Rashid," she said firmly, though she felt far from resolute. "There can be no more of this between us. Do you understand?"

A faint smile curved his mouth. "It is you who controls it, mistress. I am but a slave."

Why was there no comfort in that? Disturbed by his proximity, Alessandra slipped past him and went to stand in the center of her apartment. "Then I've nothing to worry about," she concluded.

"Nothing," he agreed, reclining against the edge of the dressing table.

"You ... wanted something else?" she asked.

His gaze swept her from head to toe, but all he said was, "I thought, perhaps, we might begin my lessons."

Alessandra nearly laughed. "You seem to have already

acquired a fair grasp of our language. It would not be time well spent teaching you what you already know."

He retrieved her comb. "I know not what this is called."

She hurried forward and took it from him. "A *misht*," she answered, returning it to the tabletop.

"And this color." He flicked the skirt of her yellow caftan.

"*Asfar*. I—"

"What is the name of that which lines your eyes?"

Self-consciously, Alessandra ran a fingertip beneath her lower lid. "It is called *mirwad*."

Nodding, he looked for something else to inquire about.

Alessandra threw her hands into the air. "If you are determined to remain, why don't you tell me of England instead."

"You would like further demonstrations of the differences between our two countries? If that is what you desire, I will oblige, but it is likely we will end up where we left off."

Her cheeks warming, Alessandra turned and busied herself with the pillows strewn about her divan. "That is not what I meant," she said over her shoulder. "Tell me . . ." She searched for a topic. "Tell me how it is you became a slave."

A long, uncomfortable silence followed that she tried to ignore. However, there was nothing left to arrange on her divan, so she seated herself on it and looked at him.

His face had darkened, creating a sharp contrast against the white of his turban. His body had become rigid, where it had previously been relaxed. Gone was the light in his eyes and the smile on his mouth. And there was none of his silent laughter.

"Have I asked something I should not have?" she said tentatively.

He did not answer. Instead, he walked to the door and left.

Had he ever really been there? Alessandra wondered after several minutes had passed. She touched her mouth, felt its swollen flesh, then put the tip of her tongue to her upper lip and tasted him.

Aye, he had been there. Even the lower reaches of her body, still warm and aware, knew it.

Though she tried to put it from her mind, once again her thoughts turned to the stallion she had compared him to. Willful, virile, dangerous . . .

Lucien held his rage until he had gained the privacy of the garden. Then he erupted, his curses shouted to the sky, his fists slamming into the unforgiving bark of a tree.

Finally, throat hoarse, knuckles scraped raw and hurting, he leaned back against the tree and stared blindly at the pitiful walls that stood between him and freedom.

Since coming to Jabbar's home, he had not allowed himself to dwell on the injustices that had been done him during his captivity. Alessandra's innocent question, though, had strained the barriers he had erected, had evoked images that would have been better left buried.

"Damn the woman. Damn all women!" he cursed beneath his breath. They were faithless—the lot of them. The two he had been betrothed to, even Alessandra . . .

She was betrothed to Rashid, yet allowed another man to touch her. Despite her protests, had he wanted to, Lucien was certain he could have had her. But he *had* wanted to, so what had stopped him?

He shook his head. Though he would never trust a woman with his heart, his present anger was not against them. Acknowledging that, he directed his enmity back at the living nightmare of slavery.

CHAPTER 6

At the end of a sennight, Jabbar and Rashid returned bearing gifts of silk, jewelry, and gilded slippers.

Amid the excited buzz of women showing off their new treasures, there was music and dancing in the hall. Trays laden with pastries and sweetmeats were brought by servant girls, though they were largely ignored by the women who were too elated and preoccupied to indulge.

All were dressed for the occasion of the master's visit, each hoping to catch his eye so that she would be the one with whom he spent the night. As usual, there was little modesty about any of them. Their light, colorful trousers and vests allowed glimpses of curved breasts and buttocks, slim thighs and small ankles. Their hands, feet, and hair were hennaed, their faces heavily made up.

At the far end of the hall sat Jabbar, surveying all with a faint smile. On his left sat Rashid, on his right, Sabine. Unlike the others, she was dressed in a caftan. Though the garment was elaborate, its silver and gold threads catching the light, it revealed little of her figure, attesting to the fact that she remained Jabbar's favorite. He did not need tantalizing glimpses of her body to desire her above all others. Undoubtedly, it was her he would spend the night with.

Though Alessandra always enjoyed occasions such as this, her pleasure this afternoon was overshadowed by the present Rashid had brought her.

Removed from the others, she fingered the cloth that

was to be fashioned into her wedding gown. Though it was beyond lovely, and would complement her hair and complexion perfectly, she could not help but be disappointed that she had not been allowed to choose the material herself.

It was such a small thing, she knew, but it had meant a great deal to her. Above all, the trip into the city had meant a break from the monotony of the harem. It had meant wonderful hot hours in the marketplace haggling with the vendors and seeing the sights she had not laid eyes upon for two years now. It had meant freedom of a kind she'd had so little of, and of which she dreamed constantly.

Perhaps her mother was right, she grudgingly conceded. Perhaps this was not the life for her. But would England be any different? Would she—

"You do not like the cloth?"

Alessandra jumped at Seif's voice. Eyes wide, she looked up to where he loomed over her. Since he had walked out on her several days past, the air between them had been strained. For the first time she felt an easing of that tension.

"What?" she asked.

Hands behind his back, he nodded to the fabric.

"Oh, yes," she said with false enthusiasm, her mouth hurting from the effort to force it into a smile. "It is beautiful."

"For your wedding?"

"How did you know?"

He shrugged, though his eyes did not mirror disinterest. They were intense, their depths pulling at her. "A guess," he said.

"Oh." Turning her gaze from his, she pretended interest in the group of women to her right.

"If it is not the cloth that makes you so unhappy," Seif said, "then what is it?"

"Do I look unhappy?"

"Very. Not even the music and dance interests you."

What he said was true. At the very least, her feet should have caught the rhythm by now. Instead, she had hardly noticed it.

She looked back at him. "Sometimes I feel as if . . ." She

searched for the English words that would best express her emotions. "As if I cannot get a full breath. Like there is a great weight upon my chest."

His eyebrows drew together. "You are ill?"

"I do not speak of an ailment," she said quickly. His words, though, made her think of her mother, and she wondered why Sabine had not yet shaken the burden from her chest that made her cough so much. "Nay, this comes from my head, making me restless and impatient for freedom. Surely you have experienced it yourself."

He smiled. "You are saying, then, that you feel enslaved as I do."

"Enslaved," she repeated, considering the word before shaking her head. "That is too harsh. It would be unfair to name it that."

"What else would you call it?"

She sighed. "I do not know. Perhaps it has no name."

Glimpsing Sabine's approach, Seif turned and stepped back to his place against the wall.

"Alessandra." Sabine gracefully lowered herself to the divan where her daughter sat. "Are you not going to show me what Rashid brought you?"

Alessandra looked into her mother's drawn face and saw that she was pale. Dark circles beneath her eyes told of the sleepless nights she must have been suffering of late.

This was the first time Alessandra had seen her in two days. In all that time, Sabine had not emerged from her apartment, nor allowed any but Khalid within. Alessandra had not worried overly much about it, for she had grown accustomed to her mother's peculiar habit of locking herself away for days on end. She had been doing it for nearly two years now, offering only the excuse of needing time alone with God. Though it always unsettled Alessandra and made her feel abandoned, she, like Jabbar, simply waited it out.

Now, however, seeing how tired, even aged, her mother looked, she was not so sure she should have. "Mother, you do not look well." She pressed a hand over Sabine's.

"No?" Grimacing, Sabine drew her fingers through her hair. "Better?"

"You know that is not what I meant," Alessandra said. "You look ill."

Sabine brushed aside her daughter's concern. "It is always difficult for me when Jabbar goes away. Worse when Leila takes advantage of the situation and tries to do you harm."

Perhaps that was some of it, but not all. "What of the cough? You still—"

"I have yet to speak to Jabbar about what that woman did, but when I have him alone tonight, you can be assured I will."

"You still have that cough," Alessandra pressed on. "Has the physician nothing to rid you of it?"

Sighing, Sabine looked across the hall. "He says there is nothing to worry about. 'Tis a cough, naught else."

Alessandra was not convinced. "Perhaps we should summon another. After all, the man is quite old."

"Alessandra, you weary me with all this needless concern," Sabine reprimanded. "Do let us speak of other things."

From the determined set of her mother's face, Alessandra knew she would get no further. "What is it you wish to speak of?" she asked, settling into the abundance of pillows.

"Khalid tells me you and the new eunuch are getting along better now." Her mother smiled a smile that did not reach her eyes.

Something was wrong with her mother, terribly wrong. Alessandra was convinced of it. Likely, Khalid was the only one who knew, but would he tell her if asked? Fool, she told herself. He would never betray Sabine's confidence, not even to her daughter.

"Alessandra, did you not hear me?"

With a start, she met her mother's gaze. "Oh, yes," she said, "Seif and I are getting along fine."

"I am pleased. He has guarded you well these past days."

"There is something about him," Alessandra mused,

leaving off her ponderings over her mother's health. "Most curious."

Sabine stiffened. "And what is that?"

Alessandra stole a glance at Seif and saw his attention was upon Jabbar and Rashid. "I do not know, but I intend to discover what it is."

"Methinks it may be he is simply different from the other eunuchs," Sabine said. "He is, after all, an Englishman, his culture far different from that of the others."

"Yes," Alessandra agreed. "He is an Englishman, and therein lies the answer if ever I can unearth it."

"The cloth," Sabine said in a deliberate change of subject, "is it for your wedding g—"

"It is me Jabbar desires." Leila's loud boast interrupted Sabine. Both she and Alessandra looked up to see the other woman staring at them. "I had but to press my body to his to know it. There, against my belly, he hardened and grew long. I vow, this night he will come to me and no other."

The women she had surrounded herself with tittered and tossed sly glances in Sabine's direction.

Such taunting was not unusual from Leila, and all had grown accustomed to it, especially since her boasts usually proved empty. As always, though, Alessandra was angered by Leila's posturing. Although her mother smiled, Alessandra knew Sabine was saddened by having to share Jabbar with these women. Alessandra prayed she would be as gracious once Rashid began taking other wives and filling his harem with concubines.

Suddenly a thought struck her, a distinct memory of her intimacy with Seif several days past. Frowning, she heard again Leila's words, relived the wondrous kiss she had shared with the eunuch, and felt again the insistent press of his man's flesh against her belly.

Flushed and warmed by her vivid remembrance, she shook her head. Impossible! If Seif was the same as Khalid, then she should not have felt that part of him.

He had lied to her, then. But why? Was he only half a eunuch, and had told her otherwise simply to discourage her and the others from making demands on him? Or was he not a eunuch at all?

She turned and looked at him, and this time found him waiting for her gaze. It was as if he knew exactly what she was thinking. Dragging her eyes from his, she looked down at his hips, hidden beneath the voluminous caftan and robes.

If he was not a eunuch, then why would Khalid allow—

Alessandra halted her questioning thoughts. It was a waste of time to ponder the reasons until she knew for certain whether this Seif was, indeed, a eunuch. But how?

CHAPTER 7

It took two more days for Alessandra to gather the courage to do what she had set herself to. Clothed in colors that blended with the night, she climbed out her window and lowered herself into the fragrant bushes of the garden.

The moon was high and full, clearly illuminating the path she must parallel to gain the eunuchs' quarters. She did not hasten, though, for there were guards about who might catch sight of her.

It seemed hours before she had traversed the garden, but it was, in fact, only minutes. Easing open the gate, she winced as it creaked on its hinges. In case she might need to make a speedy retreat, she left it ajar and stole toward the low-lying building that housed the eunuchs.

A tremor of excitement rippled through her as she neared the building. It had been a long time since she'd undertaken such an adventure, and she would not have had the opportunity had Jabbar not dismissed Sabine's accusations against Leila. After speaking with all those who had been present in the garden that day, he had pardoned the woman of any wrongdoing. Thus, Seif had been excused from the duty of guarding Alessandra's apartment, and he now slept in the eunuchs' quarters with the others.

Thankful she was slender, Alessandra squeezed behind the bushes that lined the back of the building and slowly picked her way along the wall. At each window, she peered within in an attempt to discern which of the eunuchs slept there. The moonlight that streamed into each room aided her.

Beginning to wonder if Seif had been given quarters elsewhere, she nearly clapped her hands in delight when she peeked into the last room. There he lay on a pallet against the far wall. Though he faced away from her, she knew it was he from the width and length of his body. It could be no other.

Briefly, she considered the first obstacle. Seif was clothed—or partially so. As children, she and Rashid had sneaked into Khalid's quarters once during the night and found him naked, his gleaming backside like twin moons. Alessandra had hoped to find Seif the same way, but it was not to be.

He'd thrown off his covering sometime during the night, and was wearing only a pair of full trousers that allowed a glimpse of firm upper buttocks. Above that, tapered hips flared into a wide expanse of bare back and shoulders that strained beneath the swell of muscle.

She had known he would be like this—known from the strength of his arms that beneath his robes he was hard and thick.

Shameless sensations coiled up from the nether regions of her body, turning her breath shallow and constricting her throat. Though she tried to focus on the real purpose of her reckless venture, it was difficult. Already her mind was afire with imaginings of her hands gliding over Seif's flesh as she slid the trousers down past his hips to discover his state of masculinity.

Could she do it without awakening him? she wondered. And if he awakened, what then?

What then, indeed! She chastised herself back to the present. She must not forget whom she was betrothed to. She did this only to satisfy her insatiable curiosity—naught else.

Naught else? another part of her derided. What of the restlessness that had grown to nearly uncontrollable proportions since Seif's arrival? She had felt some of it before he'd come, but had always been able to stifle it. Now, however, with his glances that looked into her soul, his touch that fired her entire body, the kiss . . .

Naught else but curiosity, Alessandra repeated silently, trying to convince herself of the untruth. Chanting it to herself, she raised her gaze to Seif's hair. What color was it? she mused. It looked neither yellow nor brown, but somewhere in between. Having only ever seen red and dark hair, she longed to see it better, to—

She frowned, realizing something was wrong with his back. She looked on either side of the window for the lattice coverings that threw their shadows upon his back, but there were none. Then how was it his back was crisscrossed with dark lines? The moment the question formulated itself, she knew the answer—a whip had done that.

As if her own back burned with the harsh punishment that had been meted out to him, she felt the pain of such torture. Though she had doubted it before, she knew with dread certainty that Seif would find his escape from this place, even if it meant his death.

She turned to retrace her steps back to her apartment, but pulled herself up short. No, she thought, she had come to discover this man's secret, and she would not leave until satisfied.

She placed her hands on the windowsill and, as quietly as possible, hoisted herself onto the ledge. Crouching there, she waited a long moment to see if she had disturbed Seif's sleep, but he did not move, nor did his breathing change. Twisting around, she lowered her bare feet to the floor, then crept forward. Still no indication that she had awakened him.

At his feet, she crouched low and stared at the shadow of his face. He continued to sleep, unaware of his late-night visitor.

Eyeing the narrow space between his pallet and the wall, she wondered if there was some way to roll him over without awakening him. Her gaze wandered to his feet. Perhaps if she lightly stroked the sole—

She drew a sharp breath, then peered closer. Was it possible? Unable to check the impulse, she traced the vertical groove that ran the length of his right foot, then did the same with the horizontal groove. Sinking back onto her heels, she stared in disbelief at the crucifix burned into the bottom of his foot. Why? Was this some strange English custom she had never heard of? Her mother bore no such mark. It seemed sacrilegious.

Alessandra's breath was knocked from her as a great body suddenly surged upward and fell upon her. Rough hands fastened around her upper arms, wrenched her forward, and shoved her down upon the mattress. Then an oppressive weight fell on her, giving her no room to breathe.

"You could wake a sleeping baby," Seif ground out, his eyes glittering above her.

"Get . . . off," Alessandra wheezed, thinking any moment she might lose consciousness if she did not fill her lungs.

He made her suffer a moment longer, then raised himself enough to give her breath. Eagerly, she gulped the precious air.

"What are you doing here?" he demanded, his voice low so he would not awaken those in nearby rooms.

As she could conjure no believable excuse for intruding upon him, she decided on the truth. "I came to discover whether you are the eunuch you claim to be," she said, shifting beneath him in hopes he would move off her.

Instead, he clamped his thighs tighter about her legs and lowered his chest so it brushed the peaks of her breasts. "And you thought to do this without awakening me?"

"I would have succeeded had I not been so foolish as to touch your foot," she retorted, trying to ignore the stirring in her taut nipples.

"I was awake long before then," he informed her. "Before you entered my room."

"I do not believe you."

He shook his head, his hair falling forward to brush her cheek. "It would have been wiser for you to climb the wall than go through the gate."

Alessandra was struck speechless. Was it possible one could sleep so lightly as to have heard that small sound? And if he had heard it, why hadn't the guards?

"Did you know it was me?" she asked.

"Only when you came to my window. It was then I caught your scent."

"My scent?"

"Attar of the orange blossom," he said. "The others prefer roses or jasmine."

"Oh." Why did it make her feel vulnerable that he would know such a thing? After all, it was not as if she doused herself in the sweet perfume.

With a sudden yearning for the familiarity and safety of her apartment, she pressed her hands to his chest and attempted to push him away. Her efforts gained her nothing but a taunting smile.

"Please, Seif," she pleaded, "get off me."

Dipping his head, he lightly touched his lips to her ear. "Is the flame too hot?" he murmured.

"What?" she gasped, squirming as his caress kindled a hunger she had only experienced with him.

His tongue flicked the lobe of her ear. "Has no one ever warned you about playing with fire, Alessandra?"

Try as she might to douse her burgeoning desire, it leaped to life when his mouth trailed over her neck. "I—I wish to return to my apartment," she panted.

He swept the hollow of her throat with his tongue, then lifted his head. "You came here to learn something," he said, his voice strained. "Now I am going to teach you what kind of man I am."

The feel of him hardening against her stole the last of her weak protests. Curling her fingers into the crisp hairs covering his chest, she moaned, "Yes, teach me."

Though what Lucien really had meant was to teach her a much-needed lesson, he suddenly wanted more. Promising himself he would let it go only a bit further, he lowered his head, took possession of her lips, and, with no thought of taking her slowly through their lovemaking, plundered their tenderness.

Alessandra groaned her pleasure when his tongue thrust between her lips and stroked the sensitive inner flesh there. Wanting more, she opened her mouth and touched her tongue to his. Immediately, his entwined with hers, engaging in a frenzied dance that made her heart race and her body sing.

He was moving against her, she realized a moment later, his hard staff lengthening as he stroked it over the soft place between her quivering thighs.

As if it knew well the secret she had yet to discover, Alessandra's body responded of its own accord, her hips thrusting upward in an attempt to match his urgent movements.

Lucien groaned into her mouth, then relinquished her lips to fasten upon the soft place where her neck and shoulder met. Only a bit more, he reminded himself, then he would stop.

"Yes," she breathed. Gliding her hands down his sides, she slipped them beneath the waist of his trousers and cupped his rigid buttocks.

As if he could penetrate the barrier of their clothing, he thrust harder against her. Stop now, he told himself, else it will be too late.

"How many men have you had, Alessandra?" he rasped as his hands worked free the fastening of her vest and began to tug her chemise up.

It took Alessandra a few moments to decipher the un-expected words. "Only one," she lied, though it was not quite a lie, for he was about to make her a woman.

Muttering something she could not understand, he pushed the chemise high and revealed her breasts to the moonlight.

"I knew they would fit my hand," he said as he cupped each in turn. The rhythm of his hips never faltering, he stared at the rigid peaks before finally lowering his head and taking one in his mouth.

Alessandra gasped as the sensation shot through her and uncoiled itself in the cradle of her woman's place. Though she closed her mouth against the cry, it escaped and burst upon the room.

"Shh," Lucien hissed, his hand closing over her mouth, his body tensing. Lifting his head, he listened for sounds from the other rooms. It seemed to Alessandra a terribly long time before he finally eased.

Removing his hand, he looked down at her.

"I am sorry," she whispered. "I could not help myself."

She thought his face softened, but couldn't be sure with the shadow of his hair upon it.

"Control, Alessandra," he said. "If you hold those feelings in until the end, you will see that it increases the pleasure tenfold. Can you do that?"

"I do not know."

He sighed. "Then we must go slower."

"You are not going to stop?"

He hesitated. "Do you wish me to?"

Alessandra knew she should bring an end to their love-making, but her body still hummed and ached for the promised consummation. "I have not yet learned what I came for," she whispered.

He put the palm of his hand on her belly and glided it downward. "Then open to me."

"Open?" she breathed, not understanding.

He pushed a knee between her legs and gently urged them apart. "Yes, that's it," he said. Looming over her, he deftly loosened her trousers, then began to draw the thin material down.

Quivering, Alessandra placed her hands on his shoulders and lifted her hips to assist him. A moment later she was exposed to the moonlight and eyes that burned her as they gazed upon her pale flesh.

"Beautiful," he murmured. Though he did not touch her, he dipped his head and blew softly upon the mat of hair between her thighs.

Alessandra gasped as he fanned the flames of the fire he had set, her nails digging into his shoulders as she raised her hips higher.

He lifted his head and looked at her. "Are you sure?" he asked, his voice strangled.

"Please."

Shifting his weight, he pulled the trousers past her thighs and calves, momentarily delayed by the fastenings at her ankles.

"Wh-what now?" Alessandra asked as he tossed the garment behind him. Wasn't there something she ought to be doing? Touching him, caressing him, stroking him as she had overheard the harem women speak of? Vividly, she recalled Hayfa's description of the position she had taken with Yusuf, and how she had made him cry with ecstasy. Could she do that with Seif?

His gaze swept over her, then he lowered himself, his hands sliding up her legs as he came to her.

At the first touch of his mouth upon that most private of places, Alessandra jerked against him, her cry muffled by the fist she pressed to her lips.

"Hold to it," he said before his tongue touched her and began an exploration similar to that he had undertaken upon her mouth.

Hold to it? How? Alessandra wondered as her body reacted to his expert lovemaking. She did not think she could. Something far too immense and taut was growing within her—something that possessed the power to set her body into motion. Completely out of her control, it found the rhythm he coaxed it to.

Teeth clenched, eyes tightly closed, she reached out and found his head. Pushing her fingers through his hair, she pressed her hand to the back of his head and urged him deeper. He complied, his mouth hot and magical upon her.

Never had Alessandra felt such incredible sensations. She was soaring higher and higher, the air she breathed oppressive as she gained elevation. It did not matter, though, for there was something more essential to her being than drawing a full breath. She could fill her lungs later. First she had to reach that elusive pinnacle. . . .

He must have known of her ascent by the change in her breathing, for he stopped and lifted his head. "Not yet, Alessandra," he said hoarsely, beginning to work himself free of his trousers.

She wanted to scream her frustration, quick tears brimming as the ache deep within her found none of the promised release. Remembering the danger around them, she bit hard on her lower lip to keep the sound from surfacing.

Though he quickly shed the garment, Seif did not come to her immediately. Instead, he lowered his mouth to her once more. And there was something else. . .

His fingers parted her, then slid inside her tightness

and found her moisture. She felt some discomfort, but it soothed and became pleasure as he began to stroke her.

"Ah, Seif," she whispered.

He stilled. "Lucien!" he demanded.

Confused, she raised her head and met his glittering gaze across her body.

"Never call me that heathen name when I am touching you like this," he growled. "My name is Lucien."

It did not matter. All that mattered was the melding of their bodies—that she become one with him. "Lucien," she groaned, tossing her head back. "Lucien!"

Satisfied, Lucien leveraged his body up and settled into the cradle of her thighs, his manhood erect as he thrust his fingers deeper to widen her for his penetration.

Eagerly, he pressed himself to her opening, but before he could enter and forever damage the thin barrier of flesh his fingers had discovered, realization washed over him.

She was untouched—a virgin!

For long moments he agonized between the needs of his flesh and his sense of honor, trying to ignore the seeking body beneath his. His desire for her was so great, it would have been more than simple to sample what she had already given to another, but he was strangely loath to be the first to spoil her.

He cursed himself for that weakness, for he had never before allowed his honor to govern him where lovemaking was concerned. Providing he desired a woman, he had always taken what she offered. Somehow, he grudgingly acknowledged, he cared too much for Alessandra to steal her virtue.

"You lied," he said bitterly.

It took a moment for his words to penetrate Alessandra's sensual haze, but when they did, the harsh reality forced her up onto her elbows. "Lied?" she repeated, her gaze drawn to that part of him that was to have slaked her hunger. It was in shadow, but here was the visual proof that he was not the full eunuch he had claimed to be.

"I will not be the one to take your virginity," he ground out.

He knew. "Why?" she whispered, desperate to feel again what his hands and mouth had given her.

Though Lucien told himself honor was the foremost reason he stayed himself from taking her, he also remembered Sabine's threat to emasculate him if he violated her daughter. "The price is too high," he said.

"Price?" She shook her head. "None need know but you and I."

"Do you not think Rashid will know when he lies with you on your wedding night? He is no fool. And what if—" He broke off. He had nearly pointed out that her belly might grow large with his child. She would know he was not a eunuch had he spoken those words.

Alessandra wanted to weep. She could not remember ever wanting anything as badly as she wanted this man. Not even the possibility of losing Rashid would have deterred her were the matter in her hands. Indeed, her betrothed seemed more like a brother with each day that had passed since the coming of Lucien.

Lying back, she threw an arm across her eyes. "I am sorry," she choked. " 'Tis my shame that I am no better than the others who would use you for the same purpose."

His anger at having been deceived receding, Lucien felt her need more deeply than his own. After all, he had promised her something she had never known, given her a taste of it, then cruelly snatched it away.

"Nay." He sighed, unaware that his fingers stroked her inner thigh. "You are not like the others, Alessandra. Were you, I would not have touched you."

Her shudder of reawakening stilled his hand, and he admonished himself for rousing her again. Lord, but he had never known such a responsive woman.

"Don't stop," she pleaded.

Lucien engaged in an inner struggle that tore at his every fiber. Then, against his better judgment, he slid down her body and began caressing her with his mouth again.

Since he'd delayed for so long, Alessandra's response was more intense than before, her body demanding and frenzied as she reached for the completion he had so far denied her. When it came, it was thunderous, racking her entire frame and raising a shout of satisfaction that would have been their undoing had Lucien not anticipated it. His hand to her mouth, he endured the sharp teeth she sank into his palm.

When the shudders passed and her mind and body settled back to the mattress, Alessandra experienced a calm of a kind she had never known before. Satiated, she lay unmoving as she sorted through all the sensations she had just experienced. They had left no part of her untouched, not even her innermost core that had been denied Lucien's manhood. Though it was only her imagination, she felt as if he had filled her completely.

"Better?" His voice broke into her dreamy consciousness.

Opening her eyes, she saw that he had moved away and was donning his trousers. "Mmm, yes," she breathed, wishing he would come back and lie beside her.

Moving lightly for such a large man, he retrieved her trousers. "You should leave now," he said, dropping to his haunches and holding the garment out to her.

Alessandra fingered the material. "I do not want to."

"Nevertheless, you will," he said, thrusting the trousers into her hand. "It is not safe here."

Dismissing his urgency, she turned onto her side to face him. "You worry too much." She traced the scar upon his cheek. "It is yet many hours till dawn."

As if her touched pained him, he jerked his head back and rose quickly to his feet. "Too many hours," he said. "Now dress yourself."

Hurt by his rejection and his eagerness to be rid of her, Alessandra lost her smile. "I had thought perhaps we could talk for a while," she murmured as she sat up. She wanted to know more of him, to know of the scars upon his back and face, and the cross burned into his foot.

Head bowed, she tried to make sense of the disarray of her chemise and vest amid a sudden blur of tears, but could not pull herself together.

When Lucien dropped down beside her and impatiently took over the simple task, she could not have been more grateful. "Thank you," she managed, her voice choked with tears she vowed she would not shed.

"Alessandra," he groaned, forcing her chin up to stare into her eyes, "you are far too naive. Can you not understand my suffering?"

"Your suffering?"

He sighed. "What you felt, I also felt. I satisfied your desire, but mine has yet to be quenched. If I allowed you to stay, I might do something we would both regret. Now do you understand why you must leave?"

Once again, Alessandra felt a fool. Though talk of lovemaking was everyday conversation, it seemed there was much she had yet to learn about men.

"Is there not a way to satisfy you as you've done me?" she asked, wanting to give to him what he had given to her—to hear his cries of ecstasy as Hayfa had heard Yusuf's.

"Nay," he said shortly, scooping up her trousers and helping her to her feet. "There is naught you can do for me."

Using him for balance, Alessandra donned the garment in thoughtful silence. It did not make sense that he could pleasure her body without violating her, yet she could not do the same for him. Hadn't she overhead the women speaking of such things? If only she had listened closer, rather than shying away.

Tucking her chemise into her trousers, she turned to face him. "I thank you," she said, thinking she had never seen him look more handsome. Perhaps it was only the kindness of the moonlight, but not even the scar detracted from his masculine beauty. Boldly, she stepped between his feet, slid her arms around his neck, and lifted her mouth.

"Did you get what you came for?" he asked, ignoring her invitation.

Immediately, her reason for coming to his room returned to her. She shrugged. "I know only for certain that you are not the same as Khalid. Hence, you are either the same as Yusuf, or not a eunuch at all."

"And of what use would I be in a harem if I was not a eunuch?"

She lowered her gaze to his muscular chest. "I thought you might tell me. I can see no reason for my mother purchasing you in the first place unless she had other plans for you."

"Such as?"

To voice aloud her suspicion was a difficult thing to do, but Alessandra forced herself to. "Did you know she wishes me to go to England? That she does not want this marriage between Rashid and me?"

"I am but a slave," Lucien said. "Why would she discuss such things with me?"

Alessandra tilted her head back and stared hard at him. "Why do you answer my question with another question? Do you do it to avoid speaking the truth?"

She was to receive no answer from him, for in the next instant the door was thrown open and a light thrust inside the room.

Gasping, Alessandra swung around to face the accusing stares of the two who stepped within.

"What do you here, Alessandra?" her mother demanded, her face bright with anger.

"I . . ." Alessandra faltered. Swallowing hard, she looked back at Lucien, but found him expressionless, as if removed from the entire situation. Desperate, she looked to Khalid for help, but his usually placid face was set with fury.

"I warned you, Lucien," Sabine said, pushing her daughter aside and confronting him. "Now you will suffer the consequences."

Consequences? Alessandra thought. For something she was responsible for? Gaining her wits, she placed a beseeching hand on her mother's arm. "He has done nothing," she said. "He—I came to speak with him, that is all."

Her mother turned to her, more angry than Alessandra had ever seen her. "In the middle of the night?"

"I could not sleep."

Clearly, she was not believed. "If you came only to speak, why were you in his arms?" Sabine pressed.

It was true. She'd had her arms around his neck. How to explain that? "I was thanking him." It sounded weak to Alessandra's ears, but she could think of no other excuse. "That is all."

God is merciful, Alessandra thought as uncertainty flashed across her mother's face. "Whatever you may think happened, Mother, the blame is mine alone. Is it not his room I am in?"

Sabine looked from her daughter's imploring face to Lucien, then back again. "Are you still virtuous, Alessandra?"

It was so blunt and disconcerting a question that Alessandra started. *Was* she still virtuous after what had passed between her and Lucien? she wondered. Though he had made her a woman in one sense, he had refused to fully initiate her into the rites of womanhood. He had left her a virgin.

Recovering, she silently thanked him for his strength of mind, for otherwise, it would be a lie she spoke. "You think I would shame you by giving this eunuch what is to be my husband's?"

Her mother stared at her. "Answer me."

Alessandra lifted her chin high. "You can be assured Rashid will find me untouched on our wedding night."

"I would know now," a brazen, smug voice said from behind Khalid.

Leila . . .

They all turned to stare at the woman who had draped herself against the door frame, her expression triumphant. Worse, beyond her stood Rashid, his face tormented as he looked past the others to Alessandra.

Alessandra had never known such regret. It had not occurred to her that her actions might hurt her friend, the man she was to wed. What must he think of her?

Pushing away from the door frame, Leila sauntered past a stunned Khalid and placed herself before Alessandra. "On the morrow we will send for the physician," she stated, her gaze unmerciful. "And you had best be chaste, for not even your mother can prevent the punishment required of a whore."

Sabine shoved Leila away from her daughter. "There is no need for a physician," she spat. "My daughter speaks true."

Leila was too certain of herself to become ruffled. Smiling broadly, she brushed the sleeve of her robe where

Sabine had touched her. "We will soon know for certain." She turned her attention to Lucien.

"And what punishment is there for this eunuch, Khalid?" she asked, her eyes glowing appreciatively as they swept over Lucien's exposed torso and the bronze-colored hair falling to his shoulders.

Remembering his duty, Khalid stepped forward and gripped Lucien's upper arm. "He will be placed in confinement until it is known whether he has done any wrong."

"Hmm," Leila murmured as she drew a sharp fingernail down Lucien's chest. "Has he not done wrong by being alone with Alessandra?"

"Fifty strokes of the bastinado," Rashid ordered as he walked toward Lucien.

Alessandra swung around to face her betrothed. "Nay," she cried, "he has done nothing wrong." In her distress, she barely registered the eunuchs gathering at the door. They'd obviously awakened and had come from their rooms to discover the cause for the commotion.

Leila turned to Alessandra. "My son, heir of Jabbar, has spoken," she said. "So be it."

Alessandra's first thought was to plead with Rashid, but she realized it would be useless the moment she saw his face. Flushed with bright color, lips twisted with anger, it was a face she did not recognize. No longer was it handsome and familiar. Indeed, it was frightening.

"Mother," she implored, tears flooding her eyes.

Sabine shook her head. There was naught she could do.

"Come," Khalid said, urging Lucien from the room.

Alessandra swung back around to face Lucien. For one agonizing moment her gaze met his, her breath catching as she recognized the raging anger in the depths of those amethyst eyes. Something dangerous and feral exuded from him, warning of the clash to come the moment before he thrust Khalid from him.

In spite of his incredible strength, which could have taken on several at once, the odds were against him from the start. One word from Khalid and the other eunuchs surged into the room and fell upon him. He fought them, inflicting brutal blows, but it was only a short time before he was overpowered by the sheer strength of numbers. Bloodied and beaten, he was dragged to his feet.

At the sight of him, Alessandra turned and accepted the comfort of her mother's arms. Lowering her face to the smaller woman's shoulder, she let loose the sobs of anguish that had been building inside her.

"Now, Englishman, you will learn some respect!" She heard Rashid shout as if from a distance. A moment later the sound of flesh striking flesh fell upon the room like a thunderclap. Then again . . . and again.

Would it never stop? Alessandra bit hard on her lip, drawing blood, but could not bring herself to watch Lucien's suffering. She had done this to him. Could he ever forgive her?

At long last, silence.

"One hundred strokes of the bastinado," Rashid ordered.

"Two hundred would be better," Leila suggested.

Alessandra swung around to face the man she did not know. "Pray, Rashid, do not do this injustice," she begged, keeping her eyes averted from Lucien, who had been forced to his knees, and whose only support was those who held him.

Rashid stared at her a long time, his eyes searching for something she prayed he would not find. Then a scornful smile turned his mouth. "One hundred strokes," he repeated.

"Why do you cry for him?" Sabine asked hours later as the sun shed its first light over the land.

Her eyes tender and swollen, Alessandra pressed nearer her mother. "It is my fault," she whispered.

Smiling ruefully, Sabine lifted a bright tress of her daughter's hair and watched as it curled around her fingers. "That is not the only reason you cry," she murmured.

Alessandra wiped the back of her hand across her eyes, then lifted her head from her mother's lap and peered at her. "I do not understand why it hurts so much," she said. "It just does."

Sabine urged her back down, stroking a hand over her

head. "Could it be you feel something for this man that you do not for Rashid?"

After a moment's hesitation, Alessandra nodded. "It is true I have feelings for him, but I do not know what they are."

Sabine closed her eyes. "Does your heart beat most painfully when he is near?"

Alessandra nodded again. "It is difficult to breathe sometimes."

"Does he come upon your thoughts often and disrupt whatever it is you are doing?"

"Even when he is not within sight."

"What is it like when he touches you, lays a hand on your arm?"

Almost, Alessandra could feel the caresses of the night before. "I want more," she answered honestly, a shudder going through her.

Sabine sighed. "Could it be love?"

Alessandra stiffened. "I do not know. Do you think it possible?"

"Only you can be certain, Alessandra, but remember this. Regardless of what happens, Lucien de Gautier is the enemy of your father. He is not to be trusted. And he is a eunuch."

Alessandra considered her mother's warning, then asked, "Do you think he is in pain?"

Sabine pressed her lips together. Only if Rashid had stayed to ensure that his punishment was given as ordered would Khalid have carried it out to its full extent. Otherwise, Khalid would lessen the severity to be sure the Englishman was able to complete the bargain he had struck with her.

"Try not to think about it," she said.

CHAPTER 8

Had Alessandra not been so preoccupied with Lucien's fate, it would have been a humiliation she would have felt straight through her soul. Instead, the impersonal hands examining her went almost unnoticed.

"She is intact," the physician announced.

Her mother's sigh of relief startled Alessandra back to the present. Pulling a cover over her exposed limbs, she looked at Sabine, her expression reflecting hurt. "You did not believe me."

Quickly, Sabine crossed to her side and put an arm around her. "Forgive me," she said. "I have been foolish."

Alessandra chastised herself for the guilt she had laid upon her mother's already burdened shoulders. It was true that had Lucien taken what she'd so shamelessly offered, she still would have denied it. She would have lied to save him from punishment—lied to her mother.

"There is nothing to forgive," she said, a tremulous smile finding its way to her lips.

"I will inform your husband the wedding may go forward," the old physician said as he walked to the door.

A moment later Sabine was alone with her daughter once more. "Come," she said, "let us dress you."

In silence, Alessandra allowed her mother to attend to her needs, her every thought centered on the man who had been made to suffer for her reckless abandon the night before.

How had he fared? she wondered as she conjured a

ten-year-old memory of the cruel punishment she had once witnessed. Though her mother had forbidden her to go anywhere near the stables while the manservant was put to the bastinado, curiosity had made her rebel—and been responsible for the nightmares that had plagued her sleep for months thereafter.

Seeing it all again, Alessandra shuddered. The helpless man's feet had been locked between two pieces of wood, then raised high so that only his neck and shoulders rested on the ground. Using a short stick, a guard had then delivered violent blows to the soles of the servant's feet. He had thrashed about on the ground, his screams of pain so loud that, though Alessandra had tried to block the sound, she'd been unable to. Blessedly, the man had lost consciousness halfway through the thirty strokes of his sentence, but still the punishment had been carried out to its completion.

Lucien was larger, by far stronger and younger than that servant had been, but could he bear more than three times the punishment? Would he be forever disabled?

Alessandra wanted to weep, but had no more tears left.

Outfitted in a long caftan, trousers, and slippers, she yielded to the pressure of her mother's hands and sank down upon the stool before her dressing table. Staring sightlessly at her reflection in the mirror, she shifted her thoughts to how she might learn of Lucien's well-being. Dare she seek him out and risk being discovered yet again?

"What are you thinking?" Sabine asked as she brushed the snarls from her daughter's hair.

Alessandra met her gaze in the mirror. "Lucien."

Sabine sighed. "You should not call him that. Here he is Seif."

Strange, Alessandra mused, but since last night, she had thought of him only as Lucien. Though these last weeks she had called him by his Arab name, it no longer seemed to fit. Had it ever?

Sectioning Alessandra's hair, Sabine began to plait it.

"Where is he?" Alessandra asked.

Without looking up from her task, her mother shrugged. "Likely returned to the eunuchs' quarters."

"I wish to see him," Alessandra said with resolve.

Sabine's jaw clenched, but still she did not look up. "And see him punished again, daughter?"

Alessandra lowered her eyes as guilt washed over her anew. Her mother was right. Such foolishness would only bring more harm to him. "I must know," she whispered.

Sabine reached around and lifted her daughter's chin so their eyes met in the mirror. "Do not worry," she said. "Khalid will bring news soon."

As if on cue, there came a light tap on the door.

"Enter," Sabine called, unable to disguise her eagerness.

It was Khalid, but the message he carried allowed no time for questions. "Mistress," he said, "the master requests your presence in the hall."

It boded no good, Sabine sensed. Had the matter of Alessandra's chastity not been settled? What else was there to discuss? "And Alessandra?" she asked.

"She is to accompany you."

Nodding, Sabine quickly finished the braid and secured it with a ribbon. "Come, Alessandra," she said. "Jabbar awaits."

An uneasy silence hung over the three of them as they made their way to the hall, a silence so intense, Alessandra thought she might scream. Fists clenched, lips pressed tightly together, she followed her mother into the great room.

With a flick of the wrist, Jabbar beckoned them forward.

Though there were servants about, Rashid and his mother were the only other occupants of the hall. Unmoving, the two stood on opposite sides of Jabbar.

Alessandra looked first to Rashid, surprised when he offered a reassuring smile. Some of her tension eased as she saw that here was the boy she had grown up with— the one with whom she had shared so much laughter and adventure. The vengeful man of the night before appeared to be no more. Still, she did not think she would ever forget what he had become.

Anticipating Leila's anger, she should not have been startled by what she saw in that lovely face turned hideous by hatred, but she was. In the instant their eyes met, Alessandra knew her mother's fear of Jabbar's first wife had not been unfounded. It had been no accident that the woman's little dog had escaped and frightened the donkey. It had been intentional. She looked away from Leila's murderous gaze as she and her mother came to stand before Jabbar.

It seemed they stood there a long time, but finally he spoke. "Alessandra, come forward."

Obediently, she went down on her knees before him.

He stroked her head, his eyes appreciative of the flame-colored hair that had years ago attracted him to her mother. "Though you are of another man's seed," he said, "you have been like a daughter to me."

Alessandra smiled, her affection for this man shadowed only by her worry for Lucien.

"It is because of this I have long overlooked your unbecoming conduct," he continued, "and why I have given Rashid permission to wed you against my better judgment. I do not doubt you will make him a difficult wife, but he has chosen you, and I will not stand in his way. However, it is time you accept the customs of our people and shed those of your mother's."

"I do not understand," Alessandra said. "I wear the costume of the Arab people. I—"

"I speak of your conduct, Alessandra. No more will you venture out-of-doors without escort, nor uncover yourself to darken your skin. You will observe the mealtimes and remain seated when there is music and dancing. Never again will you leave your apartment in the middle of the night. You will show respect for men and keep your tongue inside your mouth unless a question is asked of you. You will join the others for prayers—"

"She is a Christian!" Sabine interrupted.

Jabbar considered that a moment, then nodded. "So she is." He turned to Rashid. "Would you have her convert?"

Rashid shook his head. "Though our children will be raised in the faith of Islam, this I would not ask of her."

Jabbar looked back at Alessandra. "Do you understand what will be required of you henceforth?"

She felt caged, trapped. Enslaved. For a brief, wistful

moment she fantasized running from this place and mounting a swift horse that would grant her the freedom her heart ached for, but she pushed that fantasy aside. Difficult as it would be to assume the role Jabbar demanded of her, this was where she belonged. Though her mother wished it otherwise, it was all she had ever known, and she would not abandon it.

"I understand," she said, lowering her eyes to stare at the colorful tiles beneath her knees.

Jabbar must have sensed her inner turmoil, for he dropped his hand to her shoulder and gave her a reassuring squeeze. "I am pleased," he said.

Thinking the interview at an end, Alessandra started to rise, but he urged her back down. "I give you five days in which to prepare yourself," he said. "Then you and Rashid will be wed."

"Five days!" Sabine exclaimed, taking the two steps that placed her directly before her husband. "Jabbar, it is too soon!"

Tolerant as always with the Englishwoman he had taken to wife, Jabbar merely shook his head. "That is what you have been telling me for the past four years, wife. Did not the events of last night convince you Alessandra has been too long without benefit of a marriage bed?"

"But nothing happened that she need be ashamed of. The physician—"

"Yes, she is untouched, but for how much longer? She grows restless to know what you have so long denied her. I say it is past time she wed."

Sabine grasped for an argument, anything to prevent her plans from being rendered useless. "The wedding dress," she said, swallowing hard on the cough that rose from her pained chest. "It will take many weeks to complete."

"Alessandra is nearly your size," he said. "Only minor alterations need be made to the dress you wore when we were wed."

"But she should have her own. And what of the celebration? There is no time to—"

Jabbar stood, bringing the discussion to an end. "Five days," he said, then left the hall.

CHAPTER 9

After a day spent at the bathhouse, where she was bathed, groomed, and pampered to distraction, the last thing Alessandra wanted was to attend the women's celebration known as "henna night." On this, the eve of her wedding, she longed for the comfort of her mother's company and nothing else, but that would be frowned upon. Hence, she had no choice but to submit to the women who came for her in the late afternoon.

Sabine at her side, she was led into the hall with great ceremony. Even those women who typically shunned her greeted her warmly. Leila was the only one who distanced herself.

Within the vast room there was music, dancing, and trays laden with every food imaginable. There were bowls filled with flowers, the heavy scent of frankincense and myrrh, and a table heaped with gifts for the bride. As nearly all the women wore the brightly colored garments that showed their bodies to best advantage, the room was a wondrous rainbow of shifting colors. Most noticeable, though, was the hum of excitement and gaiety.

Though Alessandra had not cast off the anxiety that had burdened her the past four days, she smiled as she was led to her place of honor at the center of the hall. No sooner was she seated than the younger women surged forward, carrying pots of henna, cosmetics, hair oils, and aromatics for the body. Giggling and chattering, they surrounded Alessandra and began the ceremonial decoration of her person.

With a wooden stick, henna was carefully applied to her palms, the insteps of her feet, and her face, the latter being the most painstaking and time-consuming of the entire procedure. While the intricate, lacy patterns were traced on her face Alessandra sat as still as possible. However, as it was quite ticklish, the women had to reprimand her several times for twitching her nose and mouth.

While the henna dried, body oils were touched to her skin and her hair tended to. Grimacing and grunting with discomfort as her red tresses were tightly fashioned into nine plaits, Alessandra glanced about the hall. Her mother, she noticed, was conversing with Khalid.

Were it not for the fact that the eunuch's usually expressionless face was creased with distress, it would not have seemed unusual. Alessandra, though, sensed something was definitely wrong.

Her heart lurched. Had something happened to Lucien? she wondered. Following their meeting with Jabbar four days earlier, Khalid had reassured both her and her mother that Lucien was well and would not be long in healing. Rashid had not, in fact, stayed to witness that the entire sentence was carried out. Thus, Lucien had only had to suffer twenty strokes of the bastinado. However, Khalid had also told them of Rashid's plan to sell the Englishman the next time he went into the city.

Though Alessandra had longed to go to Lucien and beg his forgiveness, she had stayed the foolish urge and tried to be content with the infrequent news Khalid brought. She could not risk any more harm being done him.

"There." Nada broke into Alessandra's thoughts. She thrust a hand mirror before her. "What do you think?"

There were two plaits on either side of Alessandra's hennaed face, six thinner ones falling from her crown, and one at the nape of her neck. "Lovely," she murmured, and turned her thoughts back to Lucien.

Disappointed by her lack of enthusiasm, Nada rolled her eyes and began to peel the dried henna from

Alessandra's face. Once the residue of paste was wiped away, all that remained of the ceremonial preparations was the application of cosmetics.

To a restless Alessandra, it seemed a waste of time—they would have to be reapplied on the morrow—but she knew it was useless to protest. This was the women's night, and they would be satisfied with nothing less than everything.

Hence, it was with great relief that she finally rose from the stool in all her prewedding splendor. The women exclaimed over her, touched her hair, admired the orange henna stains, and breathed deeply of the fragrant scents wafting from her.

Alessandra yielded to them grudgingly. There would be time aplenty to discover the cause for Khalid's distress once the women had had their fill, she told herself. Soon they would drift away and immerse themselves in the revelry of the long night to follow.

It took longer than she'd hoped, but finally she was free to seek her mother's company.

"You look lovely, daughter," Sabine said, patting the cushion beside her.

Alessandra sank down upon the divan. "Has something happened to Lucien?" she asked.

Sabine glanced around to be certain there were none who might overhear their conversation. "Why do you ask?"

Alessandra heaved an impatient sigh. Her mother was being evasive again. "I saw you speaking with Khalid. He seemed upset."

"Oh, that." Sabine's attempt at a smile fell flat. "It was nothing. All has been taken care of."

"And Lucien?"

"You can be assured it had naught to do with him," she said, her gaze fixed elsewhere.

Curious, Alessandra followed her mother's line of sight and saw that she watched Leila.

"A dangerous woman," Sabine remarked, "and an even more dangerous mother-in-law."

Alessandra could no longer argue that. "I will be cautious," she said.

Assuring herself that Khalid's full attention was on the woman, Sabine turned back to her daughter. "There is no need," she said.

Alessandra frowned. "I do not understand. Have you not told me—"

"Yes, yes." Sabine waved an impatient hand. "She is a viper and will stop at nothing to harm either of us."

"Then . . . why should I not be cautious?"

Sabine leaned near and spoke in her ear. "Because after tonight you will be gone from this place."

Alessandra's eyes widened. "Nay, I will not. I have told you—"

"Do not speak so loud!" her mother harshly reprimanded. "And try to smile."

One glance around the hall told Alessandra her outburst had not gone unnoticed. Forcing a smile, she stared straight ahead and pretended an interest in the dancers. "I am not going," she whispered a short time later. "I will not leave you."

Sabine reached for Alessandra's hand and squeezed it. "You cannot stay," she said in a low voice. "The danger is ever present."

"As it was for you," Alessandra pointed out, glancing at her mother, then back to the dancing. "If you can survive, so can I."

"I have been fortunate thus far, but someday my luck will come to an end."

Alessandra shook her head. "Nay, you are too wise, Mother. Methinks you may even live forever."

Sabine closed her eyes. Should she have told Alessandra of her illness? Would her knowing make any difference?

Sabine thought hard on it, but in the end came to the same conclusion she had so many times before. It would only make her daughter that much more determined to remain at her side. By the time the sickness finally took her, it would be too late to get Alessandra to England. She would be wed to Rashid then, his child growing in her belly.

Had Khalid not caught her eye and given her the signal they had agreed upon, Sabine would have continued with the argument. Instead, she gave Alessandra a push. "Go," she said. "I wish to see you dance one last time before you are wed."

Alessandra was astonished. Dance? Her mother was granting her permission to indulge in what was forbidden her? And what of their argument? "But—"

Sabine shooed her away. "Enjoy yourself, for when you are wed, Rashid will not allow it."

Slowly, Alessandra rose to her feet. "You are sure?"

Sabine stood as well. "Go, Alessandra, quickly, before I change my mind."

To lose herself and all the worries of these past days in the furor of the dance was too much to resist. As if her feet had sprouted wings, Alessandra rushed to join the dancers.

"It is done," Khalid told Sabine as they watched Alessandra take up the dance.

"You saw her?"

He nodded. "It was hidden inside her vest."

He spoke of Leila and the lethal drug he had discovered missing from his closet of medicines less than an hour earlier.

"And what did she put it on?"

"Dates. Those on the platter the girl brings you." With a lift of his chin, Khalid indicated the servant girl threading her way toward them.

"I will take them to Jabbar and show him Leila's deceit," he continued.

"No," Sabine said, her voice resolute. "That will not stop the wedding. And even if Leila is removed, in time another will take her place."

Suspicion gathering his brows, Khalid looked down at her. "What do you propose, mistress?"

"Let the girl bring me the food," she said. "Leila will have one small triumph this night."

"Mistress, you do not intend—"

"I am dying, Khalid," she snapped. "Whether it be today or months from now, the end is the same."

"And what of Alessandra?"

It grieved Sabine deeply that her daughter might see her in the throes of death, but there seemed no other way.

"It will convince her to leave, that the dangers are real. Once I am gone, she will see there is nothing left for her here."

Khalid nearly laughed. Was it possible he knew her daughter better than she? "Nothing except that which she has always known," he reminded her.

He was right, of course, but Sabine had to believe in this. "She will go with Lucien," she spoke confidently.

In spite of her misgivings over being able to trust Lucien with Alessandra, Sabine had come to realize their mutual attraction might be the bond that held them together until they reached England. She only prayed Alessandra would not reveal her relationship to the Bayards before then.

Unaware that she bore death upon her arms, the girl set the platter of beautifully prepared food on the table beside Sabine. "For you and your daughter, mistress," she said, then scurried away.

Sabine eyed the half-dozen gleaming dates before choosing a sweetmeat instead. "Does Leila watch?" she asked as she carried it to her mouth.

A muscle in Khalid's jaw clenched. "Yes, mistress."

"Good."

Sabine took her time chewing the sweetmeat, then chose the plumpest date. "I have prepared a bag for Alessandra's journey," she said. "You will find it beneath my dressing table."

"I beg you, mistress," Khalid said hoarsely, his eyes imploring. "Do not do this."

"You have been a good friend, Khalid," she continued as if he had not spoken at all. "As promised, all except that which I have given Alessandra and the Englishman will be yours."

"The Englishman is more than capable of forcing her to go with him," Khalid said, reminding her of their original plan.

Thoughtful, Sabine rolled the fruit between thumb and forefinger. "She holds her breath, doesn't she?"

Nostrils flaring, his fists clenched at his sides, Khalid glanced to where Leila reclined. "She does."

"I wonder how long she can go without air before

fainting," Sabine said as she lifted the poisoned fruit to her lips. Holding it there, she hesitated, waiting for Khalid to turn his coal-black gaze upon her. When he did, she smiled.

"Do not mourn me, old friend," she said, "for at last I am to be free of the pain."

Something warm and unspoken passed between them.

As she looked back at her lovely, vivacious daughter, an inner peace came over Sabine, and she took her first bite of the poisoned fruit. She had won.

Unhurriedly, she ate the remainder of the date, and then four others. "A pity she did not put it on something else," she said as she licked the sticky juice from her fingers. "I've never been very fond of dates."

Lowering herself to the divan that was to be her death-bed, she made herself comfortable among the pillows, then folded her hands over her stomach. "But then, they were intended for Alessandra, weren't they?" It was well known that her daughter had a passion for the little fruits.

Khalid poured a goblet of honeyed lemon juice and passed it to her.

Wondering when she would feel the beginnings of death, Sabine sipped the cool liquid, then reached for another sweetmeat. "This," she said, nudging the last date, "you must take to Jabbar."

A gleam of satisfaction entered Khalid's eyes. "He will feed it to Leila himself."

True, Sabine thought, he probably would—which was good. Even if Lucien de Gautier failed her, an unthinkable event, at least Leila would never be given another chance to harm Alessandra.

"Will it be long, Khalid?" she asked after several minutes had passed and she still felt nothing untoward.

"Though it is deadly," he said, "it is slow to act."

She should have known Leila would not choose something that would deprive her of the pleasure of a slow death. "It is painful, then?"

He nodded. "But if you do not fight it, the pain will be less."

There was not much comfort in that, but at least she

knew what was to come. Looking past the dancers, Sabine picked out Leila's flushed countenance. Poor woman, she thought. She knows not whether to celebrate or lament. I have truly foiled her plans.

Sabine's wry smile faded as she caught sight of an exhausted Alessandra making her way back across the hall.

"Wonderful!" Alessandra exclaimed as she approached, her face glowing with excitement. "I do not think I shall ever forget this night."

For an entirely different reason, Sabine hoped not.

Plopping down beside her mother, Alessandra poured herself a drink and quickly downed it.

"Why do you waste your time with me when you could be dancing?" Sabine asked, running her hand up and down her daughter's arm. As she did so it occurred to her that this was the last time they would touch. Her eyes filling with tears, she looked away.

Alessandra laughed. "Even I must rest sometime, Mother." Leaning sideways, she planted a quick, affectionate kiss upon Sabine's smooth brow. Then she reached for the last date.

Having anticipated such a possibility, Khalid got it first, all but snatching it from her fingers.

"Khalid!" Alessandra exclaimed. Never before had she seen the chief eunuch take food in front of the harem women.

He smiled, though the smile did not reach his eyes or soften the grooves alongside his mouth.

"You are acting most strange," Alessandra said.

He shrugged. "I am but hungry."

She eyed the fruit. "Then why do you not eat it?"

"Later."

More and more curious. Frowning, Alessandra stood. "If you are not going to eat it now, then give it to me," she said, holding out her hand.

Crossing his arms over his chest, he shook his head.

Was it a game he played? she wondered. Impossible, the man was far too solemn. She looked down at her mother, and in the next moment was beside her.

"What is wrong?" she demanded, entirely forgetting about the date as she gazed into Sabine's contorted face.

"I—" Sabine attempted to speak, but nothing more came out. Lurching against the pillows, she threw her head back and wheezed noisily to draw breath.

Immediately, Khalid was there, pushing Alessandra aside.

"What is wrong with her?" Alessandra cried, her pitched voice alerting the others.

He did not answer. Instead, he pulled Sabine into his arms and spoke low in her ear so none but she could hear. "Do not fight it," he reminded her, a single tear rolling down his face and falling to her hair. "A small breath is all you need."

Sabine convulsed against him, but managed to drag air into her lungs. "Hurts," she rasped.

"Mother!" Alessandra called as she forced a place for herself beside Khalid, tears and kohl streaking a dark path down her face. "What is happening?"

Drawing short, jerky breaths, Sabine opened her eyes and stared at her daughter. "Poison," she said, her hand trembling violently as she tried to raise it to Alessandra's face. "I . . . warned . . ."

Alessandra caught her mother's hand and pressed it to her heart. "What do you mean?" She shook her head. "Poison?"

Sabine's gaze flickered over the myriad faces that had come to surround her, then a gleam entered her eyes. "Leila," she said, staring at the woman a moment before her body convulsed again.

A cold shroud descended upon Alessandra. Her mouth trembling, she turned and looked into eyes that radiated evil delight. It was true, then. . .

As her mother continued to agonize Alessandra rose to her feet. Though her heart bled with pain and sorrow, she had only one thought as she stepped forward.

As if they knew her intent, the other women moved back, clearing a path for her.

It seemed she walked a long way, but finally she stood before Leila. "You did this," she said.

Leila shrugged. "I know not what you speak of."

Alessandra stared at the woman, her hands curling into fists as she experienced an anger so great, she did not recognize herself. A moment later she lunged forward, fingers hooked and a terrible scream of rage parting her lips.

The two fell as one, Leila taking the brunt of the fall to the hard tiles.

"Murderer!" Alessandra shrieked, drawing blood as she raked her nails down the older woman's face and neck.

Leila retaliated with a slap that snapped her opponent's head back, then caught hold of Alessandra's braids and jerked hard on them.

Feeling no pain, Alessandra bunched her fists and drove them into Leila's sides, again and again. She did not hear the woman's cries of pain, nor feel the desperate hands that tried to pull her away. She knew only a need to avenge her mother.

It seemed she had hardly begun when rough hands seized her and dragged her off Leila.

"What are you doing?" Rashid demanded, giving her a hard shake.

"Release me!" she spat, her teeth bared as she watched Leila's awkward attempts to stand. Straining and thrusting her body forward, Alessandra tried to break free of Rashid's hold, but he tightened his arms around her.

"You will cease this moment!" he ordered.

Fury vibrating through her, Alessandra looked over her shoulder at him. "You are not my master," she hissed.

Shock widened his eyes and swept the confused outrage from them. "Alessandra, what—"

A great, mournful cry wrenched the air, causing all within the hall to fall silent.

Turning, Alessandra and Rashid watched as Jabbar pushed Khalid aside and fell to his knees beside the divan. "No!" he shouted over and over as he gathered Sabine's limp form to him.

Alessandra pulled free of Rashid's hold and took a hesitant step forward. "Mother?" she called. Then, on legs that felt as if they might collapse beneath her, she stumbled forward and lowered herself beside Jabbar.

The man whom none had ever seen shed a single tear was sobbing, his face buried in Sabine's thick hair.

Unable to believe her mother was gone from her,

Alessandra pressed a hand to Sabine's back and waited to feel the heartbeat that had to be there. There was no movement, only a terrible calm.

"Nay," she choked. She lifted Sabine's wrist and pressed her fingers to where there should have been a strong pulse. Again, there was nothing to evidence life.

Nothing . . .

Her chin dropping to her chest, her arms falling like deadweights to her sides, Alessandra sank back on her heels. Unless this was some terrible dream that she would shortly awaken from, her mother, Lady Catherine Bayard of Corburry, was dead.

Though Alessandra's misery demanded an outlet, the tears and sobs of grief remained locked within her. "No," she whispered as she stared at the blur of tiles. "No."

It was a long time before anyone came near Alessandra. When Sabine had been carried away at last and nearly all sent from the hall, it was Rashid who came to her. Murmuring soft words, he stroked her hair and tried to draw her to her feet.

Alessandra tipped her head back and stared at the dark-headed man. For a moment she was comforted by the familiar face, but that comfort was soon replaced with fear.

Here was the son of the woman who had murdered her mother. He had Leila's heavy-lidded eyes, her mouth, and the same high forehead. He was of the evil woman's blood—blood that had run so thick and hot with jealousy, only murder could cool it.

"Come," Rashid said, his eyes kind. "I will see you to your apartment."

She wrenched her arm from his grasp. "Do not touch me!" she screamed, and began to crawl away.

"Alessandra, it is me . . . Rashid."

She recoiled when he caught hold of her shoulder. "Leave me be," she cried. Covering her head with her hands, she curled herself into a tight ball.

He knelt beside her and tried to pull her into his arms, but she continued to resist, wildly lashing out at him. He was persistent, earning for himself numerous slaps and scratches, but in the end he yielded to another.

Alessandra did not realize Rashid had moved away until Khalid's voice warmed her ear. "Mistress," he said, "if you put your arms around my neck, I will carry you to your bed."

She peered up at him, confusion wrinkling her brow as she searched his dark, lined face. He looked so much older, she thought. Everywhere there were deep grooves she could not remember having seen before, and his eyes . . . Sorrow had stolen all light from their dark depths.

"My . . . mother," she said.

He nodded. "She is at rest, little one. No more harm can be done her."

"Truly?"

"Is that not what your god promises?"

She thought on it a moment, found solace in it, then sat up and put her arms around his neck.

"Yes," she said. "He does." Settling her head against his shoulder, she surrendered to the exhaustion weighting her lids and was asleep before they reached her apartment.

CHAPTER 10

Surfacing from a sleep she did not wish to be awakened from, Alessandra heard her name being called and felt warm fingers slide up and down her arm. Groaning, she rolled onto her stomach and buried her face in a pillow.

"Alessandra!" Though it was no louder than before, the voice was more insistent.

Shaking her head, she tried to shrug off the hand that fell to her shoulder, but it was like a vise.

"Go away," she muttered, desperately trying to recapture the oblivion she had been pulled from. However, in the next instant, she was turned and lifted to her knees.

Forced to abandon her sleep, she raised her head and stared at the shadowed figure who supported her. Though it was too dark to make out his features, she realized almost instantly who it was that had come to her in the dark of night.

"Lucien!" she gasped, coming fully awake. "What . . . ?"

"Quiet!"

Remembering what had happened the last time they had been caught together, Alessandra lowered her voice. "I was worried about you," she whispered. "Are you in much pain?"

"No more than I am accustomed to," he answered, his voice gruff and impatient.

She winced. "Can you ever forgive me?"

At his hesitation, feelings of uncertainty and distress

welled within her. But then he lowered his head and pressed a fleeting kiss to her lips. "Now—"

"Ah, Lucien." She sighed, leaning into him and sliding her arms around his neck. "I do so like the feel of you." Her mother had guessed right. She did have feelings for this man—feelings she had never experienced with Rashid. Smiling, she touched her mouth to the exposed skin above the neck of his caftan.

"Alessandra—"

"I had the most terrible dream," she murmured as blurred images filtered into her consciousness. She saw a woman gasping for breath and the evil eyes of another. She saw— She shook it off. Disturbing as it was, it had only been a nightmare.

An uncomfortable silence ensued, then Lucien unlinked her hands from his neck. "Tell me of it later," he said. "We must hurry."

"Hurry?" Tilting her head back, she tried to make out his features, but caught only the glitter of his eyes. "I don't understand."

Gripping her waist, he lifted her from the divan and set her feet to the floor. "We are leaving here, tonight." He turned to the latticed windows through which he had entered her apartment. "Come, there is no time to waste."

Leave? Confused and suddenly suspicious, Alessandra took an uncertain step backward. Did he intend to spirit her away that he might make love to her, or . . .

Of a sudden, her earlier suspicions came back to her. Her mother's determination to see her taken to England. The long search for a new eunuch. The purchase of the Englishman who was by no means suited to harem life. His false claim to being a full eunuch.

Alessandra closed her eyes. Was this her mother's doing? It had to be, which meant Lucien was not a eunuch in any sense. He was a man who had been paid well to play the part, and whose only purpose was to steal her away to England. Then what of their lovemaking? Had it meant nothing to him? Had it been simply a means of gaining her trust?

She felt dirty—used—a pawn. "Ah, nay," she lamented, praying it was not so, but knowing it was.

Immediately, Lucien was beside her. Without a word, he took her arm and began pulling her toward the window.

A blossoming anger freed Alessandra. "I have been tricked," she accused as she jumped back from his grasping hands.

"God's teeth!" Cursing, Lucien reached for her again.

Alessandra evaded him and slipped into deeper shadows on the far side of the room. "It is my mother's bidding you do, isn't it?" she said.

He walked toward her voice. "I will explain later."

"There is no later." She fumbled for something—anything—with which to strike him should he come too near. Her hand closed over the brush on her dressing table. "Do you come any nearer, I will scream. I swear it."

He kept coming. "And be responsible for my death?"

His death . . . Alessandra momentarily waged a battle between preservation and conscience. She could not allow him to take her from here, but neither could she sentence him to certain death.

"Go, Lucien," she pleaded. "Take your freedom, but leave me be."

"Not without you. You are leaving this night, even if it is over my shoulder."

Like a sword, she held the brush before her. "Then that is how you must take me," she warned, praying he would think better of it.

Accepting that this was, indeed, what he must do, Lucien closed the gap between them in two long strides and caught her arm before she could dodge him again.

"Let me go!" she demanded, straining against his bruising hold.

"If it must be by force, so be it," he said, pulling her nearer.

Alessandra twisted around and raised her hand above her head. A moment later she brought the ivory handle of the brush down upon his skull.

Grunting his discomfort and muttering curses, Lucien wrested the brush from her and tossed it to the floor.

"I will not go with you," she declared as she struggled against him. "I will not leave my mother!"

Like steel hands, his arms tightened around her, crushing her breasts to his chest and leaving too little room for breathing.

"Alessandra." His voice was hesitant, regretful. "It was no dream you had. Your mother is dead."

It took a moment for the words to sink in, but when they did, she grew still.

"Don't you see?" he went on. "There is no longer any reason for you to remain here."

Denying the vivid memories that rushed at her, Alessandra shook her head. "Nay, you lie, Lucien de Gautier. It was only a dream I had."

His sigh rent the air. "Leila," he said. "She poisoned your mother. Do you not remember attacking her?"

Too well she remembered it once he spoke the words. Though she tried to thrust it from her mind, she saw it all again. It seemed so real—hardly like a dream at all.

"How would I know your dream if that is all it was?" he asked.

He could not. "My mother is dead?" Alessandra asked in a small, grieved voice.

"Yes."

Fighting the anguish, not wanting to cry for fear it would make it that much more real, she went rigid in his arms. "Leila," she mumbled, turning away from the wrenching sorrow in favor of the less painful emotion of hate. "I will see her dead."

"Her punishment will be just," Lucien assured her. "Now we must leave."

Alessandra shook her head. "Nay. Not until I have seen with my own eyes that she suffers the same fate as my mother."

Having no more patience to draw from, Lucien swung her into his arms and began walking toward the open window. Alessandra immediately commenced anew with her struggles, punching, kicking, and bucking all the way.

Lucien had never done such a thing before, certainly did not like the thought of it, but she left him no choice. Dropping her to her feet, he held her with one hand and raised the other. "One day you will thank me for this," he said, then reluctantly landed his fist to her jaw.

Not knowing what hit her, Alessandra staggered and fell into his waiting arms.

Unable to sleep for fear of the terrible punishment that awaited her on the morrow, Leila gripped the lattice of the window and stared out at the dark night.

She was no fool, accepting that these were her last hours. Although she was the mother of Jabbar's heir, which had saved her from banishment once, nothing could save her now. There had been a chance Jabbar would have simply sent her away again had it been the daughter, not the mother, who had died, but his love for Sabine was too great. Even without the evidence Khalid had produced—the poisoned date—the end would have been the same.

Leila drew a hand down her face, wincing at the stinging scrapes Alessandra's nails had raked into her skin. Worse, all the blows the bitch had driven into her sides made it painful and difficult to breathe.

A hatred which Leila had not believed could ever grow any stronger, swelled in her breast. If only it had been Alessandra's young body that had shuddered and gasped for breath. Then, even had her sentence been death, all would have been worth it. But Rashid would still wed her.

Though Leila had tried these last years to convince him otherwise, he was determined to have the flame-headed bitch for his wife. His perverse desire was the same as his father's.

Her head beginning to throb, she pressed fingers to her temples and reflected on the victory that had nearly been hers four nights past. Hoping to discover what pleasure the English eunuch might be capable of giving her, though he had callously rejected her every attempt to seduce him, she had decided it was time to seek him out.

She had gone via the garden, as she always did when she desired a tryst with one of the eunuchs. However, as she had slipped through the gate, an unexpected sight had greeted her—Alessandra climbing in through the window of the English eunuch's room. At first Leila had been outraged, intensely jealous that another was enjoying what she had been denied, but sanity had prevailed.

Realizing that here was the way to ensure Rashid never married the English whore, she had given the two sufficient time to compromise themselves, then gone for her son. Unfortunately, Sabine and Khalid had gotten there ahead of them.

Still, Leila had been secure in the belief that the physician would give testimony to Alessandra's loss of chastity, and she'd nearly gone mad when the old man had said otherwise. And then Jabbar had commanded that the wedding go forward without further delay. . . .

It would have been so easy had Alessandra lost her virginity to the English eunuch. That, Rashid could not have forgiven, for he was the same as most Arab men. The purity of his bride was all-important. So much that, had it been any but Sabine's daughter, her merely being alone with another man at night, even a eunuch, would have been sufficient cause to reject her. But Rashid had been adamant, leaving Leila with no choice but to use poison to achieve her end.

A sound that should not have been there, slight as it was, had Leila searching the garden. She was beginning to think it had been her imagination when she caught sight of a movement. She peered closer. Though there was not much moonlight, she picked out the shadowy figure of an immense man.

A guard, she thought, then realized that none were so large. Could it be Khalid . . . or the Englishman? As the man slipped through the trees a sliver of moonlight fell upon something in his arms before being enveloped once again by shadow.

Red hair. Unmistakable.

Leila had thought she would never smile again. But here was the Englishman, and it could be none other than Alessandra with him. Where would they consummate their desire? His quarters . . . the stables . . . perhaps right there in the garden?

She began to tremble at the thought that she had been given one last chance to expose the lovers and free her son from wedding the whore. In gratitude, she sank to her knees. Merciful Allah had chosen to smile upon her in her last hours. Perhaps He might even deliver her from Jabbar's sentence of death.

Though Leila burned to raise the alarm, she quelled the impulse, telling herself she must be patient. This time she wanted no question as to what had transpired between the two. Whether or not Alessandra remained a virgin, her behavior could not possibly be overlooked a second time.

"At last I have won," she whispered into the dark, tears of joy streaming down her cheeks. "Won."

CHAPTER II

As promised, the horses had been waiting beyond the walls. Though Lucien and Alessandra had only to go as far as Algiers, where a ship waited to take them up the coast, through the Strait of Gibraltar, and on to England, the ever-loyal Khalid had left nothing to chance. Both animals were well equipped with provisions should the plan go awry. And Lucien had the unsettling feeling it would . . . or already had.

Although he would have preferred that Alessandra remain unconscious throughout the entire ride, they were less than halfway into it when she began to rouse. Pushing his mount harder, the second horse trailing behind by a length of rope, he held tight to Alessandra in readiness for the fight she would no doubt give him.

For an instant he entertained the idea of knocking her senseless a second time, but abandoned it. It had bothered him to have to do it in the first place, and since there was no immediate danger, he would not do it again unless forced to.

The moment Alessandra opened her eyes, she knew who held her before him, and his purpose. Worse, she knew agonizing pain as the terrible events that had led her to this came rushing back.

Lucien had not lied. It was no dream that had taken her mother from her. It was a vicious woman who was responsible for that—the woman who was to have been her mother-in-law.

The determination to seek vengeance lent Alessandra enough strength to fight back the torrent of grief threatening to break open her emotions. Later, she promised herself. Later she would indulge in the tears banking behind her eyes, the sobs straining her throat. Now she must focus all her efforts on escaping the deceitful man who had made himself her unwanted savior.

Swallowing hard, she pushed aside the fold of robe that had been drawn over her face and looked up at the figure silhouetted against the night sky.

How far had he taken her from her home and the revenge that was her due? she wondered. And what was the miscreant's destination? Algiers?

Defiantly, she slapped her hands to Lucien's broad chest and tried to push away from him, uncaring that such foolishness might result in a fall from the horse. However, Lucien was not of a mind to indulge her useless struggles. His arm simply tightened around her waist until it was difficult to breathe.

Grudgingly, Alessandra stilled. Shortly thereafter, Lucien eased his hold, allowing her the breath to vent her rage.

She began cursing in Arabic, raising her voice to be heard over the air rushing past them and the pounding of hooves. Whether he reacted to her obscenities was impossible to tell in the darkness. Still, that did not prevent her from hurling insult upon insult, until her voice became hoarse and her throat raw.

Forced to silence, she noticed the discomfort of the ride for the first time. Cradled as she was against Lucien, her rear end wedged between his hard thighs and her legs dangling over one side, she had no defense against the horse's jarring movements. In contrast, Lucien was able to move with them.

Alessandra's resentment grew, her mind crowding with all the venomous words she intended to scream at him given the first opportunity. He would rue the day he had made a pact with her mother.

On the final approach to the city, Lucien slowed the horses to a trot and proceeded with caution. Alessandra decided to voice her indignation again.

"How dare you take me from my home!" she spat. "You are nothing but a—"

"Quiet!" His arm tightened around her once more.

She strained against his punishing grip. "I will not be quiet. If it will gain me freedom, I will gladly waken the entire city."

He reined the horse in, then grasped her shoulders and pulled her around. "Would you prefer I strike you again?" he asked, his warm breath stirring her hair.

Alessandra opened her mouth to issue a challenge, but snapped it closed at the remembered pain that had preceded her fall into unconsciousness a short time ago. Consideringly, she shifted her sore jaw from side to side.

Aye, he would do it, she acknowledged, and likely without any remorse. And then what advantage would she have? Though it was not easy to reason herself out of causing a commotion, logic told her it was best to wait.

"You are the lowliest cur," she muttered.

A rush of scornful air escaped his nostrils. "You do not even know the half of it. Now behave." In silence, he guided the horses behind the covering of trees not far from a row of buildings that marked the farthest reaches of the city.

"We will leave the horses here," he said. Steadying Alessandra, he dismounted first, then lifted her down.

Though it was still too dark to see well, Alessandra felt his regard and knew he was questioning whether she could be trusted to stay put. She had no intention of doing so.

As if he knew her mind, he growled, "I have given you fair warning." He turned his attention to the packs strapped to the horse. He was selective, removing only what would be needed for the sea journey. The provisions for a land journey were left untouched.

Leaving her side, he strode to the second horse. "You will need to change," he said over his shoulder.

Throwing off the robe that would only prove a hindrance, Alessandra spun around and began running toward the buildings. The ground was soft beneath her feet, slowing her, but neither would it prove a benefit to the man who would soon be after her. Although certain she could escape him, for the soles of his feet could not have fully recovered from the punishment of the bastinado, she vigorously pumped her arms and legs.

She thought she heard him behind her, but attributed it to her imagination. His only chance was if he remounted the horse and came after her, and that would be too great a risk for the amount of noise it would make.

Thus, she was shocked when Lucien's body collided with hers. Her legs knocked from beneath her, Alessandra instinctively threw her arms out a moment before she slammed to the ground.

The breath emptied from her lungs in a painful rush, the dirt tearing into her palms and grazing her face. Though the abrasions stung, her only thought was to draw a breath. Desperately, she gulped air, but could get none past her constricted throat.

"Little fool!" Lucien's angry voice resounded in her ear. Raising himself from her, he flipped her over and dragged her onto her knees between his thighs.

Her head thrown back, Alessandra's throat finally opened, allowing a full breath.

"Fool," he muttered again, his fingers biting into her shoulders.

The pressure in her chest easing, she stared at his shadowed face. "Fool?" she gasped. "Because I refuse to allow you . . ." She took another breath. ". . . to take me to a place . . . I do not wish to go?"

As if he thought it might make her see sense, he gave her a brisk shake. "I made a bargain with your mother, and I intend to keep it. Fight me all the way if you must, but you are going to England."

"I will not!"

He breathed a harsh sigh. "Why are you so frightened of change, Alessandra? Believe me, 'tis for the better."

"It is not change I fear," she said, lying to herself and him. "I seek retribution. Leila will not go unpunished for what she has done."

"Aye, and Khalid will make certain she is punished like for like. Why can you not leave it at that?"

Alessandra was grateful he could not see her jaw tremble, nor her eyes flood with tears she continued to deny herself. "I will not rest until I have seen with my own eyes that evil woman draw her last breath."

"And then what? Will you wed Rashid and spend the rest of your days in this godforsaken place? What of the children you will raise under the constant threat of intrigues such as that which killed your mother?"

Alessandra forced the grief down once again. " 'Tis none of your concern, Englishman." She ground the words out from between her teeth. "If you want to escape, then go, but leave me. I have no intention of ever setting foot on English soil."

Lucien pulled her to him. His thighs hard against hers, an unyielding arm curved around her waist, he grasped her chin and raised it.

"Release me!" she commanded. "I loathe your touch."

"You are a liar, Alessandra," he said softly, his fingers tightening when she tried to jerk her head back. "You desire me as much as I do you."

"Desire?" she repeated, secretly pained that he had given her feelings such a lascivious name. "Is that all you feel? The lust of your flesh?"

His thumb brushed her lower lip. "What would you prefer I call it? Love?"

Alessandra closed her eyes and savored his touch. Aye, love . . . It was as her mother had guessed. Love, not desire, was the powerful emotion she had come to feel for this deceitful man. Certainly she also desired him, but that was such a small part of her feelings.

"Nay, I would not believe you if you called it that," she tossed back.

He was silent, as if he was considering a matter of great import, then he shrugged. "Then I won't," he said. "Desire it is—the same as you."

"You conceited—"

"Have you so soon forgotten this?" he asked, then his mouth was on hers. Brutal, yet passionate, it demanded a response. As his tongue attempted to urge her teeth apart, he swept his hands over those places only he had ever known.

Alessandra struggled against him, vainly trying to feel

nothing for this man who had deceived her so completely. She would not give in to him. Could not.

Though she tried to remain indifferent to his seduction, her body thought otherwise. She detested the fluttering in her stomach and the pricking sensation in her breasts that should not have been there—loathed the warmth flooding her being.

Closing her eyes tightly, she battled the unwanted feelings he roused by forcing her thoughts back in time. Unwittingly, she came upon the memory of the first day he had come into the harem. As if she had been but an observer, she saw and heard again the conversation with her mother regarding the new eunuch. Allowances were to be made for him. . . . He was an enemy of the Bayards. . . .

Lucien lifted his head. "Deny it you may," he said, his voice thick and husky, "but Rashid will never make you feel what you do in my arms."

She could just make out the sparkle in his eyes. "I doubt you even desire me, Lucien," she said. "It was all an act to gain my trust and entice me to England with you."

He touched her face, his thumb tracing her swollen lips. "I do not think there is anything I would not have done to gain my freedom," he said, "but desire is not something one can force. Either it is there, or it is not."

"You expect me to believe you?"

"Aye, Alessandra, I do. The thought of my flesh swelling inside you near drives me mad with wanting. Eagerly I would breach that which guards your virtue and bury myself in your depths." He caught her hand and pressed it to his rigid length. "Just the remembrance of the sweet, womanly scent and taste of you makes me so hard, it is painful. 'Tis a long time since I have felt anything for a woman."

Though his words stirred her deeply, Alessandra could not forgo the only opportunity she might have to convince him to leave her behind. Disregarding her mother's warning, she wrested her hand free and said, "Then it must surely pain you to feel anything but hate for a Bayard."

He tensed. "A Bayard? What game are you playing now, Alessandra?"

She moistened her lips. "No game. I am simply telling you what my mother feared to reveal. Before she was stolen from her home and sold into slavery, Sabine, as you knew her, was Lady Catherine Bayard of Corburry—wife of Lord James Bayard. I am their daughter."

Lucien struggled with the unexpected revelation. Dear God, he had risked all to help a Bayard when he could have been well on his way to England before now? Suddenly it all made sense—Sabine's reaction to his papers, her secretiveness, Alessandra's lack of resemblance to Jabbar. . . .

"We are enemies, you and I," Alessandra continued. "And as such, it would not be unseemly for the bargain you struck with my mother to go unfulfilled. Thus, I release you from the obligation."

All but shoving her from him, he rose to his feet, molten anger pouring into his veins. "A stinking Bayard!" he shouted to the heavens. "I should have guessed. How could I have been so blind?"

Why the sinking feeling? Alessandra wondered. Was this not what she wanted? After all, his contempt was the key to gaining her freedom.

Lucien shoved a hand through his tangled hair as he conjured a vague memory of the lovely, redheaded woman James Bayard had taken to wife. He had seen her only the one time he had been at Corburry as a youth. Unfortunately, he had paid little heed to her, for he had been too intent on plotting his escape. And escape he had. Then, a month later, Bayard's wife had disappeared.

"Though I was still a boy," he said, "well I remember when Lady Catherine disappeared. Aye, how could I forget, for it was the De Gautiers who were accused of having taken her." He looked down at her. "Do you know our people nearly starved the following winter?"

Alessandra shook her head. "How could I know anything of what transpired after my mother's abduction?"

Bitter laughter erupted from his throat, then died. "Indeed. Hence, I will tell you what happened."

"I do not wish to—"

"James Bayard set fire to half our harvest," he harshly interrupted. "And he would have burned all had the other half not already been gathered in. Then, as if that was not enough, throughout winter he led raids against our villages. He took what little the people had and left them more hungry than before."

There had to be a reason her father would do such a thing, Alessandra reasoned. Her mother had said he was a good man. "Was it not your family who abducted my mother?" she asked.

Again, he laughed. "Though we would have been more than justified in doing what we were wrongly accused of, my family had naught to do with her disappearance."

Curiously, Alessandra believed him. Someone else had been responsible then. Standing, she tentatively touched Lucien's chest. "Then it is just as well I will not be accompanying you," she said. "God speed your journey, Lucien de Gautier."

As she pulled back he grabbed her wrist. "*Our* journey," he corrected her.

Alessandra was stunned. He still intended to force her to England? "But I am a Bayard," she protested. "Why would you wish to help me?"

"I assure you, help no longer has anything to do with it," he said, his tone cold. "Your mother was wise to hide your identity from me. And you are a fool to have divulged it." Taking advantage of her confusion, he began to pull her back to where the horses waited.

"What do you intend?" she asked, suddenly fearful of this man who had become a stranger in the space of mere minutes, and who had usurped her anger and indignation with his own ominous emotions. Aye, here was the angry man she had first glimpsed upon his arrival in the harem. Gone was the one who had touched her so deeply with his caring when she had been injured, then with his hands when she had ventured into his quarters.

Lucien retrieved the pack he had tossed aside when she had run from him. "Here," he said, thrusting dark garments to her chest. "Put these on."

Alessandra did not need the light of day to know he held the traditional costume Arab women wore when they went about in public—a heavy caftan, a cloak, and a concealing veil.

She had to make him see sense. "Lucien, please," she said, gripping his arm. "Do not—"

He thrust her hand aside. "I will gag, bind, and carry you over my shoulder if need be. Now either you put these on, or I will do it for you."

She hesitated, then reluctantly took the garments. "You know not what you do," she murmured.

He released her. "There you are wrong." Stepping away, he retrieved a length of cloth and began to fashion a turban about his head.

How was she to escape him? Alessandra wondered as she pulled on the caftan. Not until its warmth settled over her did she realize how chilled she'd become in the night air. Grateful, she positioned the veil, then draped the cloak from the crown of her head.

Lucien wasted no time. The packs secured beneath his robes, he took Alessandra's arm and steered her in the direction of the buildings she had been running toward.

"Not a word," he said as they neared. "Do you understand, Alessandra?"

"Lucien, can't you see how foolish—"

Halting abruptly, he pulled her around and lowered his face near hers. "I have no more patience for you. All I have asked for is a yes or a no. Which is it?"

Her whole world having turned upside down in a matter of hours, anger, grief, and now fear tearing up her insides, Alessandra wanted very much to cry. But she would not. "Yes, I understand," she said in a choked voice.

Sensing her anguish, he hesitated, but in the next moment was guiding her forward again.

The steep, narrow streets they negotiated in silence were nearly deserted. Fortunately, when they chanced to cross another's path, they were afforded no more than a cursory glance.

Alessandra had never seen Algiers at night. For a few minutes she arose from her misery and allowed the silhouetted city to impact upon her senses. It was almost beautiful, she thought. Unlike during the day when it was a dirty, teeming, yet exciting place just begging to be explored, it now radiated magic beneath the stars.

Shortly, she was forced back to her present circumstances by the robust smell of the sea and the clamor of a lit harbor that merely napped while the city slept. Here there were people about—mostly drunken seamen in search of another drink or a woman's thighs to make their bed upon. They were loud and coarse, staggering and spouting vulgarities as they went.

Slipping in and out of the shadows, Lucien pulled Alessandra after him. "Where is she?" he muttered, his eyes searching the calm waters of the harbor.

She? Though Alessandra wanted to ask the question, she kept her mouth closed. Was it a ship he spoke of? A short time later she had her answer.

"There," he said. "The *Sea Scourge*."

Alessandra followed his line of sight to the ship that rocked in the harbor. Unlike the others anchored nearby, it was not very wide of beam or long of reach, but it appeared solid.

" 'Tis the one that will take you to England?" she whispered.

"Do not exclude yourself, Alessandra." His voice rumbled with displeasure. "Be assured you will accompany me."

She had not meant to provoke him. It was simply that she had not yet accepted that she would, indeed, be leaving Algiers. Nay, even now she could not abandon hope of escaping him.

Thinking it best to change the subject, she looked up at him. "How are we to . . ." Her voice trailed off. A harbor light revealed Lucien's features, and she saw for the first time the damage Rashid had inflicted upon his face. Though it had healed these past days, the remains of bruises and lacerations were evident.

Never had she imagined the extent of Rashid's anger. "Dear God, Lucien," she breathed, reaching up to touch him.

He jerked his head back. "Do not."

Her guilt deepening, Alessandra was grateful for the veil that hid her own face. She lowered her hand. "It is my fault," she mumbled, her throat and eyes burning with tears.

"Think you I expect any less from a Bayard?"

Though his words cut, she could not blame him for his bitterness. After all, it was his due.

He gripped her arm. "Come. There is to be a boat waiting to take us out to the ship."

If they were seen, as was likely, what would be thought of a proper Arab woman and a eunuch wandering about the harbor in the last hours of night? Alessandra wondered as she was pulled into the street. An oddity for certain.

An old seaman, a bottle of spirits dangling from his fingers, turned his attention upon them. Staggering to a halt, he thrust his chin forward and stared at them through puffy lids.

Ignoring the man, Alessandra and Lucien were nearly across the street when the vibration of pounding hooves pulled them up short of their destination.

"What is it?" Alessandra asked.

"Damnation!" Spinning her around, Lucien dragged her back into the alley, deeper this time, and pressed himself and her against the wall of one of the two buildings.

"Lucien—"

"Do not speak another word, or I will be forced to strike you again."

Biting her lip, Alessandra waited to discover who the horsemen were that descended upon the harbor with such fury. Was it possible she had been discovered missing and Jabbar had sent men in search of her? Although it seemed implausible her absence would be noted before daylight, there was a remote chance.

Shouted orders and the clatter of horses preceded the riders.

Peering around Lucien, Alessandra saw the first of them. Though the man's profile was difficult to discern for that brief moment it was visible to her, it was the familiarity of the horse that identified him.

"Rashid," she gasped.

Even as the thought to call out to him surfaced, she found herself being propelled farther down the alley. Not until they reached the opposite end did Lucien turn her to face him.

"One of two things will happen if you alert them," he said. "Either you will be returned to Rashid and I will be put to death, or you will simply make it more difficult for me."

He spoke true, Alessandra thought. For the offense he had committed, there was no other course but death. And only a slow, torturous one would satisfy the Rashid who had sentenced him to a hundred strokes of the bastinado.

A thought struck her. Perhaps this was all that was needed to convince Lucien to leave her behind. "Think you I care what happens to you?" she bluffed.

Lucien clenched his teeth. Lord knew, he did not have time to engage in a verbal sparring match with her. Provided he was coherent, the old seaman would not be long in pointing out the direction they had taken. Still, he needed Alessandra's cooperation.

He tipped her chin up. "Unlike your father, you do have a conscience, Alessandra Bayard. You will not make yourself responsible for my death. And though we are now enemies, you cannot deny what you feel when I touch you."

She thrust his hand away. "Speak for yourself," she snapped. "You do not know my mind."

Slipping a hand inside her cloak, he curved it around her breast. " 'Tis not necessary," he said, feeling her involuntary shiver of response, "for I already know your body. And that is enough."

Before she could protest, he removed his hand and, after glancing both ways, hurried her across the street and down another alley. Fortunately, it was a large city, and there were many darkened corners in which to conceal themselves as they traversed it.

All the while, Lucien prayed the horses had not been discovered. It was their only hope of escape. Even then, it would not be easy. A land journey would be dangerous, taking a considerable amount of time compared with travel by ship. Worse, he would have to deal with Alessandra's rebellion and determination to remain in Algiers.

Damn! Though it explained much, he almost wished she had not told him of her loathsome sire. Until that moment, he had been more than willing to take her to England. Now it was a struggle not to leave her behind to her fate.

What was preventing him from doing just that? he wondered as they continued their escape. The answer came to him immediately. Though he hated to admit it, it was more than attraction he felt for the impetuous desert flame. What had sustained him throughout the punishment Rashid had ordered was the thought of one day having Alessandra to himself. And he still intended to, though now it could very well serve the additional purpose of gaining vengeance on the Bayards.

How sweet the revenge to return her spoiled to her father, he thought. And if a child resulted from their union, the old man's torment would be that much greater. Though part of him found satisfaction in such musings, another part was reluctant to consider them.

Lucien's wandering thoughts were nearly his undoing. Just in time he caught sight of the horse loping down the street they were about to cross. Pulling back into the shadows, he snatched Alessandra against his side and pressed her face to his chest.

He was surprised when she melted into him, her labored breathing evidence of her exhaustion. He had pushed her hard, he realized. It was a wonder she hadn't collapsed.

"Leave me, Lucien," she whispered as the rider drew near. "I will only slow you. Then you will have gained nothing."

"If you truly wish to remain in Algiers," he said in her ear, "then here is your chance. Go ahead, Alessandra, call to him."

Alessandra drew back and looked into his shadowed face. It was a dare, and she very nearly rose to it. However, it would mean jeopardizing his life, and she could not do that. Nay, if she was to escape him, she must do so in such a way that would see no harm done him. Regardless of his deception, she could not bear the thought of him dying.

She buried her face against his chest and waited for the rider to pass. But he did not.

The man halted his horse at the mouth of the alley where they hid and leaned forward to peer its length. "Who is there?" he demanded in Arabic.

Loosening his hold on Alessandra, Lucien reached inside his robes and retrieved the dagger he had concealed there.

The man dismounted, drew his sword, and after a brief hesitation, stepped into the pit of darkness.

There would be bloodshed, Alessandra knew, fear trembling through her. As soon as the man's eyes adjusted to the dark, he would see them pressed against the wall.

Lucien was not about to let that happen. Pushing Alessandra away, he leaped forward and fell upon the man.

Her fist pressed to her mouth, Alessandra watched the two shadows become one. She heard their grunts and curses, and the sound of bone striking bone, but could not tell who had the advantage.

Dear God, do not see Lucien harmed, she prayed. Though she wished no ill upon Rashid's man, she knew that one would be sacrificed. "Let it not be Lucien," she mumbled.

Both men went crashing to the ground. The struggle continued, but shortly thereafter, one rose victorious.

Alessandra held her breath. It had to be Lucien, for the man walking toward her looked to be of his proportions.

"Lucien," she breathed, taking a tentative step forward. "Is it you?"

"Aye." He took her arm. "I hope you are not disappointed."

Disappointed? Dear God, she was relieved. She barely suppressed the impulse to throw her arms around him. As they were enemies now, it would be unseemly.

"Is he dead?" she asked as he guided her around the silent form that lay in the alley.

"I may be a De Gautier," Lucien muttered, "but I am not so cruel as to leave a man suffering." Gripping her waist, he lifted her onto the dead man's horse, then swung up behind her.

Although he knew it a risk to go by horse, for they were more vulnerable to being caught in the open, time was of the essence. Once Rashid's men were spread over the city, their chance of reaching the horses was greatly reduced.

As the alleys were too narrow and cluttered for the large animal, Lucien was forced to negotiate the streets, which offered little cover. He was tempted to set the horse to full speed, but he proceeded with caution, using the side streets for cover when other riders approached.

After what seemed like an eternity to Alessandra, they were free of the city and, it seemed, any hope of her escaping Lucien de Gautier.

CHAPTER 12

All through that day and into the night, Alessandra and Lucien rode, pausing only to refresh the horses and share the food Khalid had packed for them.

Throughout, hardly a word passed between them. Alessandra was too preoccupied with her grief and plans for revenge upon Leila once she escaped Lucien, and he was too angry with himself and her.

Not until the sun rose on the second day did they stop for rest, Lucien having determined it would be best if they henceforth traveled by night to elude those who were probably still searching for them. Though they had followed the caravan routes heading west, he now turned the horses north to the sanctuary offered by the rocky Mediterranean coast. It was there, in one of the many caves, they bedded down to await the coming of night.

"I'm cold," Alessandra said, finally admitting one of the two reasons her body could not find the sleep it so longed for. Though the terrible memories of her mother's death were more weighty than the chill pervading her every limb, she still could find no voice for her anguish.

Lucien sighed. He had hoped it would not come to this—at least not yet. The thought of getting too near Alessandra unsettled him. It had been torturous enough sharing his mount with her during the long ride, but he had not trusted her alone on the other horse. When they rode again at twilight, though, she would ride alongside him rather than in his lap.

"Are you awake, Lucien?" she asked, raising herself from the damp floor of the cave.

"Aye."

Carrying her blanket, she crossed the short distance to him and knelt beside him. "I'm cold," she repeated.

Though it was midmorning, the cave had not warmed, nor was it likely to for some time, considering its west-facing location on the rocky shores.

Lucien looked up at her, but there was not enough light to distinguish her features. "What do you want?" he asked.

Alessandra did not immediately answer, resentful of his deliberate obtuseness. "You are going to make me beg, hmm?"

"A Bayard beg? Never."

Already she was weary of being compared with a family she had never known. "Can you not forget for one moment who my father is?" she snapped. "You make me responsible for things I have had no hand in."

Levering himself onto an elbow, he reached up and pressed his fingers alongside the pulse in her throat. " 'Tis the same blood," he said.

She thrust his hand away and started to rise, but he caught hold of her and tugged her back down. "You have not yet told me what it is you want," he reminded her.

She had wanted to lie beside him, to garner some of his heat, but would not admit it now. "I want nothing from you," she declared. "If you are going to hate me for being a Bayard, then I will hate you for being a De Gautier."

"As it has always been thus between our families, it seems fair."

She strained away from him. "Let me go!"

Yanking her forward, he unbalanced her and sprawled her across his chest. "Would you like me to warm you, Lady Alessandra?" he asked as he tugged his blanket from beneath her and swept it over them both.

Alessandra's pride urged her to fight him. However, the moment his vast heat seeped through her clothing, she was lost. Stilling, she lay atop him and savored the warmth he had forced upon her, surprised his arms had lost none of their previous appeal. Ah, if only things could be different.

Realizing she was not going to resist as he'd expected, Lucien wondered at his disappointment. Odd, but he had no desire for her yielding.

Why? He knew the answer the moment he asked the question. It was far easier to remember who had sired Alessandra when she acted like a Bayard. He must be cautious lest he find himself once more ensnared by her charms.

Easing her against his side, he pillowed her head on his shoulder. "Sleep now," he said. "We have a long ride ahead of us this night."

Huddled against him, Alessandra closed her eyes and tried to find rest for her fatigued mind and body. However, it was not to be. She was too aware of the tension in Lucien's body and his own wakefulness.

"Why must we be enemies, Lucien?" she asked. "There is no ill between us."

He heaved an exasperated sigh. "There you are wrong. You and your mother deceived me." Though his anger was less evident than before, it was still present.

"I did not do so knowingly. I knew nothing of the plans my mother had laid. And do not forget that you also deceived me in pretending to be a eunuch."

"Thus we have deceived each other, which is exactly what our families have been doing for the past one hundred and twenty-five years."

"It must end sometime."

"Perhaps, but not in my lifetime."

"Why?"

His hand strayed from her waist to the undercurve of her buttocks, something Alessandra was more than aware of.

When next he spoke, he sounded weary. "Alessandra, there is so much you do not know, nor understand."

"Then tell me of it."

"You will know soon enough."

"Was my family responsible for your enslavement?" she pressed. As the Bayards had thought the De Gautiers responsible for her mother's disappearance, perhaps they had retaliated in kind.

Bitter laughter answered her. "Nay, that is one burden that cannot be put upon them. 'Twas my own doing."

"Tell me."

Minutes passed, and when it seemed he had no intention of enlightening her further, he obliged. "What know you of the war between England and France?"'

Alessandra reflected on that. Though it was a subject much removed from everyday life in the Maghrib—the coastal portion of North Africa that included Algiers—her mother had kept herself apprised of the long-standing conflict and spoken of it occasionally.

The backs of Alessandra's eyes pricked as a vision of her mother rose before her. Swallowing hard, she forced her thoughts to the war instead.

It had come about when the English had laid claim to the French throne during the last century. Though it had not been a continuous war, for the most part, England had been victorious throughout. Only recently had it met its downfall. Now, it seemed, France would remain a separate country under the rule of a French king, and England would have to content itself with its island kingdom.

"It is a war that looks to have finally been lost by the English," she said with a shrug.

"Aye. A foolish war that should have ended more than a hundred years earlier."

"You fought in it?"

He was silent a long moment. "Aye, that I did."

"Why?"

"Pride, arrogance. Against my better judgment, I crossed the channel to fight for a king who does not even know his own feeble mind."

"You speak of Henry the Sixth?"

He nodded. "The same."

"What happened?"

"What happened was Lord John Talbot, the Earl of Shrewsbury."

Not understanding, Alessandra shook her head.

"The old man was impetuous—reckless. At Castillon, I

and another tried to convince him against the frontal attack he insisted upon, at least until our infantry arrived, but he refused to listen."

The strategies of war meant little to Alessandra. Though she was well learned in many subjects, owing to her mother's carefully devised studies, war was not one that had ever been covered in any detail. "Why would the earl not listen?" she asked.

He barked caustic laughter. "If the English have a failing, it is that of stubbornness. It prevents them from knowing when the game is well and truly lost."

"And it was lost at Castillon?"

"Nay, it was lost long before then."

"Then what happened at Castillon?"

"Talbot died, along with nearly all those that fought for him. They were blown apart by the French artillery. Like rain, their life's blood sprayed upon the battlefield."

Alessandra was disturbed by his description, her vivid imagination painting the scene for her. She moved nearer him in an attempt to chase away the prickly bumps that had risen along her arms. "How did you survive?" she asked.

Again, silence. "I fell with the others," he finally said, "but was more fortunate. Mine was not a mortal wound, and I rose again to take up my sword against the French."

"Did you kill anyone?"

"Aye, one of them being the eldest son of a duke. 'Tis the reason I was sold into slavery after I was captured."

"You were not ransomed?"

"Not by the French. The duke vowed I was to suffer a fate worse than death, and it nearly was. Only after I had been sold into Muslim hands and served several months on a galley did the captain attempt to ransom me. Then . . ."

"Then?"

He shook his head. "You wanted to know how I became a slave. That is all there is to it."

"That cannot be all," Alessandra said. "Why did your family not pay the ransom to bring you home?"

It was a question Lucien wanted to know the answer to

himself. When the ransom demand had been sent, his freedom had been assured—or so he had thought. The long, agonizing months of waiting, however, had finally brought news that the payment of monies had been denied. It had made as little sense then as it did now.

Why would his father, with whom he had always been close, refuse to pay a ransom he could easily afford? True, he had been against his eldest son going to France to defend the English claim to the throne, but that had been the extent of their disagreement. What had transpired at Falstaff these past two years to change that?

"Lucien?" Alessandra touched his cheek.

Hardening his jaw against the pleasant sensations her fingertips aroused, he pulled back to the present. "I do not know why the ransom was refused, but I intend to find out."

She slid her hand back to his chest. "Perhaps they had not enough money to pay it."

"My family does not want for anything," he snapped, angry he felt any emotion other than revulsion for a Bayard. "Indeed, the De Gautiers are every bit as prosperous as the Bayards."

"Then something must have happened."

Why was she defending his family? Lucien wondered, resentful that she was again not acting like those he had been raised to hate. He turned his head away. "Go to sleep, Alessandra."

Though she could not remember having felt greater fatigue, Alessandra did not want to sleep, for it was in that place of dreams that the memory of her mother's death lurked. Thinking to delay a bit longer, she turned to questions Lucien had yet to answer. "What of the cross burned into your foot, and the scar upon your face?"

He drew a breath of patience. "Alessandra, we have not many hours ere we must ride again."

She drew her knee up his thigh and shifted more of her weight onto him. "I would but know," she beseeched as she slid her hand up and around his neck.

Pulling her hand away, Lucien pressed her more firmly to his side. "Do not, Alessandra," he growled. "You know I still desire you."

Not even the sudden shame that suffused her could prevent her from challenging him. "Do you?"

Knowing it was a dangerous game she was trying to draw him into, Lucien abandoned the subject and turned, instead, to her earlier question.

"The scar on my face is the symbol of the Islamic faith—the crescent." Though he thought he spoke matter-of-factly, his voice was tinged with a bitterness still raw and hurting. "It and a hundred lashes was the reward for my second attempt to escape the galley where I was enslaved."

Alessandra could not suppress the shudder that shot through her. "Then it was intentional," she said, her imagination conjuring this time a disturbing vision of the torture Lucien had been made to suffer.

"As intentional as Rashid's sentence," he growled.

Alessandra did not want to be reminded of that night. "And the cross?" she prompted.

As if he were reliving the actual event, his body tensed, his muscles bunching rock hard. "That was for my third attempt."

"But why the cross? And why the sole of your foot?"

"Can you not guess?"

Alessandra did not want to. She shook her head.

False laughter burst from Lucien's chest, then abruptly died. "I was branded that I might forever trample the symbol of my faith."

Now she understood. "And forever display your enemy's," she murmured.

"Aye." Lucien saw again the cutter's dagger, his smile, the glitter of his cruel black eyes the moment before the blade had painstakingly traced the crescent. He saw the red, glowing poker and felt the searing pain as it had been applied to the bottom of his foot. The scarred flesh of his back crawled as he recalled the numerous times his defiance had earned him the whip. In that brief moment he lived again the rage that had fired his being and kept him barely sane throughout his ordeal.

Still, he had never cried out—never begged for mercy as others had. Though his stubbornness had angered his captors, earning him greater punishment, he had refused to yield anything to the infidels.

"I am sorry," Alessandra said softly, "that my people—"

"Your people! Accept it, Alessandra. The Muslims are no more your people than they are mine."

"That's not true," she argued. "I was raised among them. Though I do not share their god, I have shared all else. It is their ways I have embraced since I was a child."

"And soon you will know the ways of the Bayards," Lucien reminded her. "Regretfully, they *are* your people."

What of his earlier threats? Alessandra wondered. "Then you do intend to return me to my father?"

It was several minutes before Lucien answered. "Perhaps not straightaway," he said, "but yes, you will eventually come to know the man who fathered you."

Alessandra experienced only a moment of fear before she thrust it aside. Clearly, Lucien was undecided as to whether he would use her against her father. He was not the heartless brute he wanted her to believe him to be. "Then you have made no plans?"

He shook his head. "Nay, but we've a long journey ahead of us. Be assured I will devise something ere we reach England."

His nonchalance piqued Alessandra's anger. "*If* we reach England," she retorted.

"It is my destination," he said. "And so it is yours."

She wanted to argue that, but she knew she would only waste her breath. Biting back the words, she closed her eyes and resigned herself to the beckoning arms of the rest she needed.

What was he going to do with her? Lucien asked himself when, at long last, she slept. By sire only was she a Bayard. Did that make her innocent of their wrongdoings? If so, what of his plan to take her virtue and gain revenge upon her family? Try as he might to recapture the hate he had felt when she'd first disclosed her identity, he found he could not.

At an impasse, he turned his head and breathed in the wonderful scent of her. In spite of the long ride's accumulation of dust and perspiration, he found her no less appealing than she had been the night of her visit to his quarters.

The sudden, involuntary stirring of his loins disturbed him. Fighting it, he turned his head the other way and tried to forget the deliciously feminine body curled against his.

There was far too much at stake to allow his emotions to dictate his actions, he sternly reminded himself. Perhaps later, when they were safely bound for England, but not now.

Wide-eyed, Alessandra stared at the reins Lucien had pressed into her hand. "Is it much different from riding a donkey?" she asked.

Lucien stilled. A donkey? Surely she jested. Slowly, he turned from the setting sun to face her. "What?"

"A donkey," she repeated, smoothing her hand over the stallion's thickly corded neck. "You see, I've only ridden donkeys by myself, never a horse."

With a loud groan, Lucien clapped a hand to his forehead. Considering Alessandra's unruly disposition, he had assumed she would know how to handle such an animal. Too, she had claimed to be able to sit a horse the same as Rashid . . .

Telling himself he must be patient, he walked over to where she stood beside the stallion. "There are similarities in that if one can ride a horse, likely one can also ride a donkey," he said.

She averted her gaze. "But that is not the circumstance."

"Aye." Taking the reins from her, he turned her to face him, but the words he had been about to speak bottled in his throat.

As Alessandra had not donned the cloak and veil, he saw for the first time the intricate designs that had been stained upon her skin for her marriage. Mostly, though, he saw the sorrow in her eyes. He had known it would be there, had felt it each time they touched, but had not expected such a rush of compassion for her plight.

"When are you going to cry?" he asked.

She looked down.

Crooking a finger beneath her chin, he brought her gaze back to his. "Hmm?" he prompted.

"I have no need for tears," she said pridefully, her eyes glazing with their unshed evidence. "There can be no benefit in such displays of weakness."

As if she were a child, Lucien smoothed the hair off her brow. "Your mother is dead, Alessandra," he said softly. " 'Twould not be unseemly for you to grieve."

Sniffling back the tears, she stepped away from him, coming up against the stallion. "You think I have not?" she asked. "I loved her."

He nodded. "Yet you will not allow yourself to weep as other women. Why?"

She nervously threaded her fingers through the horse's tangled mane. "Until you came, I knew little of tears," she finally said. "In Jabbar's household, it seems there was only happiness."

Lucien knew he should keep his distance, but something drew him closer. "Crying is not something you need practice, Alessandra." He laid a comforting hand upon her shoulder. "You just do it."

Ducking beneath his arm, she put distance between them, then turned back around to face him. "Perhaps I don't wish to!"

He shook his head. "Nay, you'd rather allow yourself to be eaten with plans for revenge against Leila than give your mother her due."

She stiffened. "You think to give me advice, Lucien de Gautier, when your whole life has been filled with naught but devising ways to obtain vengeance against the Bayards?" she shouted. "Do not waste your breath, for I will hear no more of it."

He could not argue that, he realized. She was right. He was not in the position to give advice when he was still inclined to use her against her father. However, her cooperation was necessary to ensure that they reach England safely. And if she knew the truth about her mother's death, perhaps she might give up her foolish idea of returning to Algiers.

"I had hoped not to have to tell you this," he said, "but

it is time you knew your mother was an accomplice to her own death."

An accomplice? Alessandra's anger lessened as she floundered over his meaning. "What speak you of?" she demanded.

"Sabine knew of the poison—that it was meant for you and not her."

Preposterous! "You lie," she gasped. "My mother would do nothing of the sort. She was a good Christian."

"Nay, I do not lie, Alessandra. Sabine knowingly ate the dates to prove to you how dangerous the harem was. It was her greatest desire that you leave Algiers."

Then it was the dates that had delivered the fatal poison. "Khalid ..." Alessandra whispered, remembering the eunuch's refusal to hand over the last date. "He knew." Which meant he and Leila must have planned her mother's death together. It did not seem possible. Yet was there any other explanation?

"Aye, Khalid knew," Lucien confirmed. "He saw Leila poison the dates, but when he warned Sabine of their poison, she ate them anyway."

Alessandra shook her head. "My mother would not have gone to such an extreme. She was still young and—"

"She was dying, Alessandra."

She stared wide-eyed at him. It was impossible what he said. Her mother had been youthful and vibrant. True, she'd had a bad cough for some time, but otherwise had been healthy.

"No, again you lie," she vehemently denied. "Is it the same with all your countrymen?"

Returning to his horse, Lucien threw open a pack and rummaged within. Shortly, he found a sealed letter. "Here," he said, thrusting it into her hand. "This should explain a few things. Then, perhaps, you will put aside these foolish ideas of yours."

Alessandra looked dumbly at the letter, then turned it over to see her name scrawled across the back—her mother's handwriting. "Where did you get this?" she demanded.

"Khalid. Although I was instructed not to present it to

you until we reached England, under the circumstances it hardly seems to matter."

Breaking the seal, Alessandra unfolded the letter and stared at the Arabic words. Clearly, her mother hadn't trusted Lucien not to read it; though she had never quite mastered the written language of her adopted country, in this instance, she had chosen it over English.

Turning away from Lucien, Alessandra walked to an outcropping of rock that had been weathered smooth by the sea's spray, and lowered herself to its hard surface. Her hands quaking, she began to read.

"My dearest Alessandra," the letter began:

I pray one day you will forgive me for this deception. Unfortunately, you have left me with no other choice. As I have said time and again, you do not belong in Algiers. Your place is with your father in England. It is there you will find the world you should have been born into, and which you so long for. Perhaps you will understand better when you know the secret I have kept for more than two years now. I am dying. Each day that passes makes this cough worse and its pain more intense. The physician says it will be over with soon. Eagerly, I await the blessed day. As it is imperative that Lucien not know your true identity, I have given him instructions to deliver you into the care of my aunt and uncle, Harold and Bethilde Crennan of Glasbrook. They will take you to your father. Pray, do not vex the Englishman overly much. Farewell, daughter, and always remember I love you above all else.

Alessandra read the letter through twice more. However, except for her tears blurring them, the words remained the same. She felt her face crumple and a sob catch in her throat the moment before a hand descended to her shoulder.

Her mind protested the comfort of Lucien's arms. Though she wanted to turn to him and give herself over to the terrible grief, he was her father's enemy—and had made himself hers. In his arms lay a dependency that, in her present circumstances, she could ill afford.

Her mind grew firm with resolve, but in the end, her aching heart proved the stronger of the two. Letting go her emotions, she turned into the arms she knew she should run from and buried her face against Lucien's chest. Desperate, she grasped fistfuls of his cloak and clung to him as the pent-up tears and sobs began to spill.

Warring with his sensibilities, Lucien hesitated, but then put his arms around her and drew her closer. Though it meant a delay in their journey, he let her cry until his garments were wet through to his flesh, her sobs had subsided into miserable hiccups, and the day sky had turned to twilight. Only then did he draw back and gaze into her flushed face and swollen eyes.

" 'Tis past time we were on our way," he said, then lightly swept a thumb over her lower lashes to remove the moisture. "There is much ground to cover this night."

Ground that would take Alessandra farther from the revenge she so desperately longed to have against Leila. It mattered not that her mother would have died from her illness anyway. All that mattered were the remaining precious days Alessandra might have spent with Sabine—days that had been stolen from her by the evil woman who had brought about the inevitable so much sooner.

And now Lucien de Gautier was also acting the thief by denying her the satisfaction of ensuring Leila's punishment. Was there not some way to convince him to leave her behind? She saw compassion in his eyes where earlier there had been anger and loathing, but was that enough? Nay, it was not, she concluded. Whatever Lucien's plans, they were set.

Bitterness welled within her. For too long she had been sheltered from the harsh realities of the world, and now that they had descended upon her ingenuous shoulders, it was time to rise above them and prove she was not the child her mother had so often called her. She was a full-grown woman, and would no more behave like a girl.

Thrusting her arms against Lucien's chest, she freed

herself and scrambled to her feet. "Do not touch me," she said. "Neither do I want, nor need, anything from you."

At first, Lucien was too taken aback to hide his surprise. However, seeing the challenging set of her jaw, the flash of her moist eyes, he allowed his face to harden and his hands to clench into fists. A thousand times a fool was he. He knew better than to let a cursed Bayard touch his emotions. What in God's name had compelled him to offer comfort? Damn this weakness! Damn these unwanted feelings! Damn her!

Lucien straightened. "Fine," he said, then turned on his heel and began the trek back to the horses. "Do not be long, for we ride shortly."

"You ride, not I, Lucien de Gautier. Even if I must walk, I will return to Algiers." The moment the words passed her lips, she knew her threat was empty, and that she had no other choice but to go with him. Silently, she cursed herself for the childish boast.

Lucien halted. Had not the letter convinced her there was naught left for her in that place? What vengeance did Alessandra think to gain upon Leila? If she would only be honest with herself, she would see that the woman had actually done Sabine a favor. Gone was the torturous, racking pain he had witnessed many times. At last, she was at peace.

He took a deep, sustaining breath. "I am in no mood to be tested, Alessandra," he said without turning to look at her. "Do you not come of your own will, upon my soul I swear you will learn the extent of my loathing for your family."

There followed a long stretch of quiet broken only by the slapping surf, then he heard the scrape of her shoes over the rocks.

"If you succeed in forcing me to England," she said when she reached his side, "I will eagerly join with my father against you."

He gazed down at the determined face that had been wiped clean of nearly all its child's unknowing innocence. Though he should have been relieved that the Alessandra he had come to care about was gone, he could

not deny the pain of her passing. It seemed she was fully
Bayard now.

"I cannot imagine it being any other way," he retorted.
"But do not forget that you must first escape me."

She stared at him a long moment, then nodded. "But
escape I will."

CHAPTER 13

And escape Alessandra attempted more than a dozen times over the next ten days of their journey.

Though it soon became apparent she was gifted with natural horsemanship, fortunately for Lucien, her mount was far less worthy than his. Thus, the chases she forced him to were mere diversions—diversions that frustrated him and sorely tested the strength of his patience.

Hours of tense silence marked their journey, the eruption of angry words their only communication. Their situation was made worse by gnawing hunger as the provisions Khalid had supplied dwindled and fresh water became increasingly difficult to find. Had Lucien been alone, he would have had no trouble supplementing the food supplies with wild game, or stealing into the merchant camps erected around fresh water, but he could not trust Alessandra to stay put.

Days earlier, he had tried taking her with him in pursuit of game, but she had only seen it as an opportunity to provoke him by scaring the quarry away. In fact, though it would have been far easier for Lucien if the two of them slept apart as he'd intended, each time they bedded down, he had to hold her to his side in order to get any sleep. And though each night took them farther from Algiers, with every mile they covered, Alessandra grew more determined to escape him.

Shaking himself back to the present, Lucien looked at the pitiful leavings of the provisions. Two more days, he estimated. Two more days before they reached Tangier and a ship that might carry them to England.

His stomach rumbled, kindling his surface-deep anger. Thinking of the nourishing meat he could hunt, he looked over his shoulder to where Alessandra had positioned herself near the cave opening. Completely oblivious to him, she was dragging her fingers through her matted hair, her movements jerky yet determined.

There was a solution to this dilemma, he reminded himself. He had considered it several times these past days, but had been loath to carry it out. Now, with the certainty that the next day would find them without any food, he realized he had no choice.

His mind made up, he retrieved a coil of rope and determinedly advanced on Alessandra. Doubtless, she heard his approach, but she stubbornly refused to turn around. So much the better, Lucien mused.

Lowering himself beside her, he grasped her wrists in one hand and, the element of surprise on his side, began binding her.

Alessandra's head shot back, her startled gaze meeting his. "What are you doing?" she exclaimed.

He lifted a brow, but offered no explanation as he deftly secured the rope.

Alessandra began to struggle. "Stop!" she shrieked, her voice echoing in the cave.

Finished with her hands, Lucien forced her onto her back and ran the rope down between her legs. Then, thrusting aside her cloak and caftan, he reached for her flailing legs. It was no easy task, but amid her high-pitched screams of rage, he brought her ankles together and hurriedly bound them.

Not until he reached to tear a piece of material from his cloak did Lucien realize Alessandra was cursing him in her native tongue. She spoke rapidly, but he followed much of what she said, picking out the expletives he had become familiar with during his time on the galley.

"What a brazen tongue you have," he scolded.

"Brazen?" she stormed, propelling her body sideways. "I—"

With no thought of proceeding gently, Lucien made

quick work of securing the gag in her mouth, then sat back on his heels to face her voiceless indignation.

"I regret having to do this," he said, "but you leave me no other choice." He rose to his feet. "Sleep now. When I return, we will have a real meal."

Although sleep was something Alessandra was badly in need of, she had no other thought but freeing herself and using Lucien's absence to escape him. With much effort, she put aside her anger and listened for the sounds of his leaving. When she was certain he was gone, she resumed her struggles—kicking, thrashing, twisting this way and that, and rolling around on the hard ground. In the end, she only succeeded in dislodging the gag, sustaining multiple scrapes, and tiring herself needlessly. Much to her detriment, it appeared Lucien was no longer underestimating her.

For what seemed an eternity, she lay in a tangled mass upon the ground and entertained visions of the retaliation she would work against him. He would pay for this humiliation, she vowed. The question was how.

Rested, Alessandra lifted her bound wrists and, in the dim light, focused on the rope. For all her efforts, it looked like the knot had not loosened. In fact, from the tingling in her hands, it seemed to have grown tighter.

After clenching and unclenching her hands to restore circulation to them, she lifted them to her mouth and began gnawing at the fibrous rope. It seemed an animallike thing to do, but she didn't care. She wanted to be free, and she would do whatever it took to gain freedom.

She was too immersed in the seemingly impossible task to realize when she was no longer alone. Her eyes closed as she continued to work her way through the rope, her jaw and teeth aching, she did not see the shadow that fell over her. Only when hands grabbed her shoulders and yanked her into a sitting position did she come to awareness.

"Good God, Alessandra!" Lucien exclaimed as he stared at the damage she had done to the rope. She had chewed almost halfway through it.

Her hopes of escape dashed, Alessandra thrust her face near his. "Bastard!" she hissed. "How dare you—"

He clapped a hand to her mouth. "Keep your anger to yourself," he commanded her, "else I will see fit to leave you bound."

And he would, Alessandra knew. Curse him for the power he wielded over her. Curse him for being the one born a man. . . .

This last thought struck Alessandra as odd. Never before had she desired to be anything other than what she was. She had always enjoyed being a female. Now, however, there seemed no advantage to it.

"Well?" Lucien asked. "Which is it to be?"

Grinding her teeth, she nodded her acquiescence.

Obviously not trusting her, he slowly lifted his hand from her mouth. She uttered no sound. At her continued silence, he began to remove the rope.

Once freed, Alessandra scurried away from him and took up her place before the cave opening. "Knave," she muttered just over her breath so that he might hear. "Cur . . . blackguard . . . beast."

She had taken the chance he would ignore her insults as he had so many times before, but a moment later discovered otherwise.

Swinging her around, Lucien shoved her back against the rock wall and used the length of his body to hold her there. "Always you push," he ground out. "What is it you hope to gain, Alessandra? Do you think I will throw up my hands and allow you to return to Algiers?"

That was precisely what she had hoped would happen. "I do not understand why you don't!" she retorted.

"Don't you?" He pressed himself against her, every swell and hollow of his body finding a place to rest in her supple curves.

It was what happened against Alessandra's belly that stole the heated rejoinder from her lips, that swept her back to the one night of love he had given her. On that night turned tragic, Lucien had denied her his man's flesh. Would he do so again if she allowed herself to feel anew the feelings he aroused in her?

That thought alone, and the threat it presented, set her into motion. Raising her arms, she pummeled his chest with her fists. "Let me go!" she shouted.

He stopped her assault, capturing her wrists and pinning them on either side of her before turning his attention to the flailing legs that threatened to unman him. Forcing his way between them so that she straddled his thighs, he waited for her to give up the fight.

She did so reluctantly, and only after several minutes of useless thrashing against his hard, unmovable length. Expelling a ragged breath, she tilted her head back and met his eyes.

Her breath caught. It was not so much what she saw in that shadowed face, but what she felt.

For the longest time, neither moved as the desire of weeks past was rekindled. Though each had tried to deny it, to place obstacles in its path, it was more alive than ever.

Slowly, Lucien lowered his mouth until it hovered above hers. He waited, giving her the chance to turn away. When she didn't, he lightly brushed his lips over hers.

Her breath shuddering from her, Alessandra slid her mouth from his and turned her head to the side. It had felt too good—too dangerously good—to allow it to go any further.

However, Lucien was not of the same mind. He followed and teased the corner of her mouth with his tongue.

Desperate to dispel the response building in her, Alessandra turned her head again. "No," she said, her voice a weak whisper.

"Yes," he countered, his own voice strong and deep.

She did not want this, Alessandra told herself as she once again evaded his mouth. He had made himself her enemy, had he not? And only a short time ago, he had tied her up as if she were an animal!

She tried to latch onto the anger she'd felt as she'd struggled to free herself from the ropes, but Lucien's mouth was playing music over her heated skin as it traveled from her lips to her ear, then to the sensitive place between neck and shoulder.

"This is why I cannot allow you to return," he said, lifting his head. "I still want you, Alessandra."

Uncertain hope fluttered through her. Then he would release her once she had lain with him? "If that is true, why don't you just force yourself on me and have done with it?" she asked. "Is that not what a De Gautier would do?"

She felt him stiffen, but he didn't move away as she'd thought he might.

"I would not think I would have to force you," he said softly. "Do you?"

Delicious, unbidden memories of days long past flooded Alessandra, but she threw them off in favor of something she had considered more than once these past days. "If—if I give myself to you, will you release me?"

He did not seem at all surprised by her proposal. Thoughtfully, he feathered a finger down her throat. "Am I to believe you place such small value on your virtue?" he asked. "Or is it possible you do, in fact, desire me and wish to continue where we left off the night you came into my room?"

Insufferable! From the heat that rose in her face, Alessandra knew she blushed furious red. For the first time she was grateful for the shadowy interior of the cave. "I have told you, I do not desire you!"

There was no mistaking Lucien's humor when he let loose a burst of laughter. "Ah, then 'tis that you do not value your virtue."

Of course she valued it, but if it was the price she must pay for freedom, then perhaps it was not such a bad pact she might make with this devil. "There are some things more important," she retorted.

"Revenge?" Suddenly serious, he lifted her chin. "In England, a woman's virtue is everything, Alessandra. Do you not have it, then it is unlikely you will ever capture a worthy husband."

"And what makes you think I want a husband?"

He shrugged. "It is what your father will want."

Aye, her father ... Would the man even acknowledge her as his? she wondered. Though her mother had said he was good and kind of heart, what of those things Lucien had revealed about him? If Lucien spoke true.

Determinedly, she made her offer a second time. "You

have not answered my question. Will my virginity buy freedom?"

"Nay, it will not."

"But you said you wanted me. That—"

"Aye, and I meant it. I do want you, Alessandra, which is why I have tolerated your antics thus far. But I must also consider your value once we reach England."

Her heart wrenched. How cold and calculating this man was—how deep his hate for the Bayards. Catching him unawares, she ducked beneath his arm and quickly distanced herself. "You are despicable!" she declared. "An animal."

Surprisingly, he did not pursue her. "I am what my captors made me."

"Nay, the blame is not theirs," she said, "but the De Gautiers'. 'Tis they who made you."

He seemed to consider this. Then, again to her surprise, he conceded. "You are probably right, but enough of this. There is meat to be fired and sleep to be had ere night falls."

That he had yielded to her shocked Alessandra and left her grappling for further argument. There was none to be had. Indisputably, Lucien de Gautier was still in control, and too soon they would be in Tangier.

CHAPTER 14

Dangerous as it might be for a woman alone in a city so far from Algiers, it was a chance Alessandra could not pass up. As she and Lucien were swallowed up by the horde of people frequenting Tangier's marketplace, she waited impatiently for the right moment.

Why he had brought her so far west was a question that would never be answered if she succeeded in losing herself among the crowd. She had asked, but each time her query had been met with a silencing glare. All she knew for certain was that he was looking for something . . . or someone.

Holding tight to the reins of her horse as she led him forward, Alessandra slowed her steps and fell back into the thickening crowd.

Soon, she told herself, smiling behind her veil as she realized how easy it was going to be to lose herself among the hundreds of women clothed identically as she. Nearly all wore the cloak and veil of Muslim tradition. Soon . . .

Unfortunately, Lucien also slowed, so much that Alessandra was forced to draw even with him once again.

"Stay close," he growled in the language of his enemies.

Gnashing her teeth over the lost opportunity, Alessandra stole a glance at him.

Earlier that morning, on the outskirts of the city, he had arranged the excessive material of his headcloth to cover the lower half of his face. Garbed as he was, and with only a strip of tanned skin visible, he melded easily with those around him. However, his brilliant eyes still revealed that he was not the Arab he portrayed, and for that reason he kept them downcast.

A major port bordering on the Atlantic and the Mediterranean, Tangier was a place of many faces where trade between countries was rampant. Thus, a disguise would have been unnecessary if not for the possibility that Rashid might still be in pursuit.

Was he? Alessandra wondered. Or had he given up and taken another for his bride? Long gone were the intricate henna markings she would have worn to her marriage bed, and the mass of braids had come unraveled days earlier. Also in the past was her wide-eyed innocence and the mother who had so opposed her wedding Rashid. She was no man's bride now.

But she could well become one man's mistress, she harshly reminded herself, glaring at the angry giant who strode alongside her. With that thought, she again turned her attention to escape. The opportunity presented itself minutes later when Lucien paused before a vendor's stall that was strewn with textiles and woolens of every imaginable color.

Keeping one eye on Alessandra, he spoke in a low voice to the little man who'd rushed forward to present his wares and extol their quality. The vendor was to be disappointed, for it soon became obvious that Lucien was interested in something other than material.

Pressed against her horse by the bustling people eager to make a place for themselves in the cramped street, Alessandra prayed for Lucien to look away for just one second. He obliged her less than a minute later.

Barely an arm's reach from him, she ducked and scrambled beneath her horse. Her heart pounding furiously, she threw herself into the mass of people and was immediately swallowed whole. One black-clad woman among many, she pushed her way through the suffocating press of bodies.

Behind she heard Lucien call her name, his voice an angry bellow above the excited buzz. How near he was, she didn't know. All that mattered was that she find her way out of the market and out of his reach.

She knew a deep regret as she hastened past the stalls, merchants, and patrons. If she succeeded, she would never again know Lucien's touch, the wonderful, masculine scent of him, or the sensations he roused in her. He would be lost to her forever—a man for whom, in spite of these past days that had been rife with discord, she still harbored intense feelings.

Had the gap between them not widened so terribly when she'd told him she was a Bayard, she might have forgotten about her revenge against Leila, and even set aside her fears of what awaited her in England. It was too late, though. Lucien hated her, and she had every reason to hate him—if only she could.

Her vision blurred by unexpected tears, she slipped into the narrow space between two buildings and hid herself in the shadows there. Leaning back against a wall, her breathing ragged, she stared at the patch of daylight whence she had come.

She was just beginning to relax when Lucien's unmistakable figure blocked the light.

Dear God! How was it possible he had followed her? Holding her breath, she tensed for flight lest he come any closer.

He did. "Alessandra," he called as he stepped into the passageway, his wide shoulders brushing the walls on either side.

Alessandra whirled and ran to the light at the other end. For once, she had the advantage of size, easily negotiating the tight space that hindered Lucien.

Unfortunately, it was too dark to see the barrel she collided with. Scrambling to her feet, her veil torn away, her cloak askew, and the taste of dirt on her lips, she lunged forward into the light.

The street she emerged upon was not nearly as busy as that of the marketplace. Even had it been, its advantage would have been limited, for her red hair had come uncovered. No longer was she one of hundreds.

Men stopped and stared as she ran past, women scurried away as if death had come into their presence, and Lucien thrust them all aside in his quest to recapture her.

Alessandra ran with all her might, her arms and legs pumping vigorously. Stealing a glance over her shoulder, she saw Lucien still close behind, as determined to catch her as she was to escape him. Desperate, she turned right, left, then left again in an attempt to lose him among the buildings. Still he came, as if guided by scent alone.

Why didn't he just let her go? Didn't he realize the danger he was putting himself in by pursuing her?

She made another sharp turn, sprinted between two crudely constructed buildings, then turned again. In spite of the deepening stench, she didn't realize she had entered the roughest part of the city. Likewise, she did not notice the poverty or the coarseness of the people she passed—or the lascivious stares that followed her.

Ahead, a half-open doorway beckoned, offering refuge from a man who could not be far behind. Alessandra didn't hesitate. She leaped through the opening and quickly pushed the door closed. Her back to it, she faced an empty room as she listened for the sound of Lucien's passing. It was a short time in coming, preceded only by the curses he hurled before him.

Then she waited. Would he retrace his steps once he realized she had slipped away? Likely, but by then she would be long gone, she reassured herself.

"Farewell, Lucien de Gautier," she whispered, tears stinging her eyes.

The room she found herself in appeared to be a storehouse. All around were shelves lined with encrusted bottles. Open barrels wafted alcohol fumes upon the air. Sacks strewn about the floor spilled grain that large, fat rats were leisurely feeding upon.

She grimaced. Only from a great distance had she ever seen the vile creatures. As if they were scratching their way over her bare limbs, her skin began to crawl and grow cold.

Shaking off her vivid imaginings, she looked across the room, where light showed beneath another door. Beyond it came the muted sounds of merrymaking.

She couldn't stay long, she knew. She must find the authority who could help her return to Algiers. Blessedly, she was not without coin. That much she had planned for by raiding the pouch containing untold sums while Lucien had gone to relieve himself one afternoon. But would it be enough? She only prayed the name of Abd al-Jabbar was as well-known in this westernmost country as it was throughout the central Maghrib.

First, though, she must restore order to her clothing. As she straightened her cloak Alessandra envisioned the bath she would have once she had secured her passage to Algiers. Unfortunately, fresh water had been far too precious these past weeks to allow such luxury, and the accumulation of dirt and grime upon her skin made her wrinkle her nose in distaste.

Having lost her veil, she reached for the excess material of the hood of her cloak to cover her face—but too late. Her hand stopped in midair as the door before her was suddenly thrown open, emitting a rush of light that made her squint.

Her first thought was that Lucien had discovered her hiding place. However, her fearful eyes told her otherwise. The man before her was nowhere near the size of Lucien. Not that he was small, by any means. It was just that if he was put alongside Lucien, he would certainly lose the height he enjoyed over the average man.

The man was obviously surprised to see her, but then he stepped forward. "Thief!" he bellowed.

Abruptly coming to her senses, and spurred on by a new kind of fear, Alessandra swung around and reached for the door behind her. She managed to open it only a few inches before it was thrust closed again and she was hurled across the room.

Landing in a heap among the scattered grain, the terrible rats protesting shrilly over her intrusion, Alessandra knew she was in grave trouble. Though she could prove she'd stolen nothing, the man thought her a thief . . . and thieves were not kindly looked upon in the Muslim world.

The hand that she might well lose was grabbed at the wrist and wrenched so forcibly, she was propelled upright. "Stop!" she cried in Arabic. "I have stolen nothing."

Her fluency in his own language gave the man pause, his brow furrowing as he looked from the disarray of her red hair to her eyes, her nose, and lastly her mouth. She hoped he'd release her, but in the next instant he was dragging her from the storeroom and out into a lit room packed with tables and chairs. The handful of men seated there looked up from their drinks and stared at the unexpected spectacle that was being dragged into their midst.

Kicking and scratching all the way, angry words tumbling from her lips, Alessandra paid no heed to any of them until the man holding her grabbed her hair and forced her head back.

A tavern, she realized. It was a tavern she had unwittingly come upon. Dread poured into her as she looked frantically around the room in hopes of discovering one sympathetic face among the leers. She found none, and her fear quickened. These were not men, but animals, the very same her mother had more than once warned her of.

"Master, a thief!" her captor cried.

A heavy man, darker than most Arabs and most certainly of mixed race, rose from a nearby table. "A prostitute," he branded her, his pitch-black eyes raking over her. "Perhaps she can pay for what she has taken."

Alessandra did not immediately comprehend his meaning, but when he pushed her cloak aside and cruelly grabbed her breast, she had no doubt as to his proposal. "No!" she shrieked, slapping his hand away and struggling anew.

His arm swung up and his open palm smacked her face.

Her fear increasing tenfold, Alessandra cried out and lifted her hand to her stinging cheek. However, the man who had first discovered her caught hold of her arm and pinned it behind her back with the other.

"My father is Abd al-Jabbar, a wealthy Algerian merchant," she said rapidly, desperately. "I was stolen from him a fortnight past. He will reward you richly for my safe return."

Silence fell as the men digested her absurd claim, then the room burst with raucous laughter that breathed the foul scent of alcohol upon her.

Of course they would not believe her, for she had none of the looks she had just laid claim to, Alessandra realized. And not only was she obviously of European descent, she was more bedraggled than the sorry souls she found herself faced with.

"A whore and a liar," the dark man said as he reached for her again. "Come, let us see what you have to offer."

"I have coin," she said, knowing it only a matter of time before it was discovered and taken from her anyway. "I will pay—"

Her words changed to a cry as her caftan was torn from neck to waist.

Heavenly Father, deliver Lucien unto me! she silently pleaded as her flesh was exposed to eager eyes. What had she done? How foolish she had been to believe it possible to escape without mishap—to go out into a man's world and remain unscathed.

A blend of fear, anger, and despair filled her as hands roamed her body—fear for what they meant to do to her, anger that there was naught she could do to prevent it, and despair over what she had lost in fleeing Lucien. Though she had tried to hate him for his deception, she saw now how futile that had been. Lucien had been her last hold on life, the only thing worthwhile in a world slipping through her fingers.

The other men joined the first, violating her with their pinching, grasping fingers, speaking vile, boastful words that turned her stomach, nauseating and terrifying her.

Withdraw, she urged herself. Remove yourself in mind, if not body. However, her mind stayed exactly where her body was. In fact, so caught up in the heinous act was she, she didn't notice when the pouch containing her precious coins was discovered and taken from her.

"Lucien," she gasped, tears streaming down her face. "Lucien." Though he was no more, another man rose from a table in the back of the room. He was followed by two others.

"Enough." The man spoke in the lingua franca recognized by Arab-speaking people. His heavy accent evidenced that he was of French descent.

Surprised, Alessandra's assailants drew back, allowing

her a view of the handsome, dark-headed man who
strode confidently forward. In European dress, he and his
men stood out among the many draped in the shapeless
robes of Muslim tradition. Hope surged through her.
Would he help her?

He stopped several feet away, spread his legs, and
propped his hands on his hips. His gaze swept Alessandra, an appreciative gleam entering his eyes when
they lit upon her exposed breasts. "For what price this
woman?" he asked.

Alessandra cringed, wanting more than anything to
cover herself.

The tavern owner waved the others back from her.
"Ah, Monsieur LeBrec, you would pay to have her first?"
he asked.

The man laughed. "Nay, I will pay to have her to myself. I share with no man."

Though his words were of little comfort to Alessandra,
some hope blossomed. Compared with the others who
clearly intended to rape her, this man seemed respectable.
Perhaps she could convince him that what she spoke was
true.

The dark man thought a moment, then grinned. "You
are a selfish man," he said. "And when you are finished
with her?"

"You know my business, Asim."

His grin widening, Asim nodded. "Indeed," he murmured, then named an exorbitant price.

The man called LeBrec shook his head. "Too much," he
said. "Look at her. She is no prize. And smell ..." He
sniffed the air. "It will take much purging before she is of
any use to me." He offered a quarter of Asim's asking
price.

Asim pulled Alessandra forward and thrust her before
LeBrec. "Look, friend, she is of fine frame and slender of
limb." He swept an expressive hand downward. "She
will bring you much pleasure."

LeBrec's gaze flicked over her. "She smells even worse
than I first thought," he said dryly. Still, there was a twin-
kle in his eye.

Humiliation replacing fear, Alessandra's immediate response was to spout wrathful, indignant words, but she checked it. She could not afford to anger the Frenchman. He looked to be her only hope.

Asim leaned forward and breathed in Alessandra's scent. Then, with a shrug, he lowered his price. LeBrec argued it, and shortly an agreement was reached at less than half the original figure.

Asim eagerly took the money, pushed Alessandra forward, and trotted off to count his wealth. The other men also dispersed, albeit reluctantly.

Reaching forward, LeBrec pulled Alessandra's cloak closed to conceal her nakedness. "You need not fear me," he said when she turned distrustful eyes upon him. "You are safe now."

She stared hard at him, trying to see beyond his wonderful smile. "*Merci, monsieur,*" she said in a voice that trembled with relief. It seemed the Frenchman was not an animal, but would he aid in her return to Algiers? And if so, at what price?

"So you know my language, eh?" he asked.

Nodding, Alessandra met his dark gaze. "And English." Sabine had neglected no area of her daughter's education, endowing her with the fluency of three languages and the fundamentals of several others.

LeBrec grasped her elbow and guided her to the tavern's main entrance, his two companions following in silence. "Yet you speak Arabic as if it were your native language," he mused.

Alessandra halted and turned to face him. "But it is. I am not a liar, monsieur. I was born and raised in Algiers. My father is Abd al-Jabbar."

LeBrec smiled wider, the corners of his eyes crinkling. "And what is your name, *chérie*?"

"Alessandra."

His eyebrows rose. "Well, Alessandra, when all this grime is removed from your fair skin"—he drew a thumb down her cheek and came away with a smudge of dirt—"we will know for certain, won't we?"

She would have to tell him all of it, Alessandra realized. She only hoped the price of his assistance would not be lying with him.

"Come." He urged her forward. "I will take you to my home, where you can have a long bath. Then we will talk."

A bath. The dirt was no longer Alessandra's main concern, but the cleansing away of the feel of those hands that had nearly violated her. Optimistic though wary, she placed herself in LeBrec's hands.

CHAPTER 15

Pity, Jacques LeBrec thought as he stood over Alessandra's sleeping form. Leaning forward, he lifted a lock of her lustrous red hair and rubbed it between thumb and forefinger.

He was truly taken with the beautiful, impetuous woman who had emerged from the mire of filth to grace his table only hours before. She was refreshing, her manners impeccable and testimony to the incredible story she had told him, and of which he now had written proof.

Straightening, he glanced at the letter he'd found among her scant belongings. It was from her mother, and its poignancy had gripped him with intense emotion when he'd read it minutes ago. Carefully, he refolded it and tucked it inside his overtunic.

As he looked again at Alessandra his loins stirred at the remembrance of the shapely figure he had glimpsed beneath the layers of diaphanous material she had been clothed in, and that was now hidden beneath the blanket she'd pulled over herself. Hopeful, he smoothed a hand over his crotch, but was disappointed in the weakness of his response.

Having long ago accepted his impotence, he was not at all surprised. Still, he continued to harbor hope of one day finding a woman capable of bringing him to life. Though Alessandra did not appear to be the one, she had moved him more than any other. Sighing, he turned away.

It was just as well, he consoled himself. Otherwise, he might not be able to part with her, which he must do—and soon.

It was unusual for him to become emotionally attached to one of his investments, but this woman was an exception. Had he the time to send a messenger to Algiers to discover the reward for her return, he would keep the promise she had extracted from him to return her to Abd al-Jabbar. Unfortunately, he had a debt coming due shortly and his coffers were in dire need of replenishing.

At the door he paused and looked over his shoulder. In sleep, Alessandra was even more exquisite than awake. The light sprinkling of freckles enhanced, rather than detracted from, her beauty. Her long sweep of lashes, pert nose, and lovely, bowed mouth were an artist's dream. And her spirit, which transcended slumber, was irresistible. It was no wonder this Lucien she pretended to hate was so determined to take her to England with him. No doubt he knew how to pleasure a woman . . . and himself.

The bitterness that Jacques had long ago come to terms with crept back in. It tore at his insides and hardened him against unwanted feelings that were determined to interfere with what he must do.

No matter, he tried to convince himself. If Alessandra could not satisfy the elusive passion of his body, then she would satisfy the one passion he could easily indulge—gambling.

"There is an auction today," Jacques said as he lifted Alessandra down from the carriage that had delivered them to the marketplace.

Assuring herself her veil was in place, Alessandra tilted her head back and looked up at the man who had generously made himself her guardian three days past. During that time he had proven himself a gentleman through and through—unlike Lucien, she reminded herself when a deep pang of longing assailed her.

"Auction?" she queried.

A hand to her back, Jacques guided her forward. "*Oui*, a slave auction."

"I have never seen one," she murmured, her thoughts going again to Lucien. It was at such an auction that her mother had purchased him.

"Ah, but today you will, *chérie*," Jacques said as he led her to a stall brimming with cosmetics. "This I promise."

Alessandra did not think it was something she would enjoy attending, but held her tongue for fear of offending this man who had been so kind to her. If not for him, a terrible fate would have befallen her. Now she had only to wait for Jabbar to come. As Jacques had sent a messenger two days earlier, it was only a matter of time before vindication, and all that was familiar to her, was restored.

Telling herself this was what she wanted, Alessandra turned her attention to the vendor who was pressing pots of kohl and rouge on her.

She shook her head. However, in the next instant, Jacques tossed a coin at the man, scooped up the cosmetics, and handed them to her.

Murmuring her thanks, she placed them in the pouch beneath her cloak.

Next, Jacques led her to a small stall where trinkets blinked in the bright sunlight.

"This would look lovely with your hair," he said, dangling an intricate silver necklace before her.

She touched it. "It is beautiful."

"Then you must have it." It was questionable whether she would be allowed to keep it, Jacques knew, but the fine piece of jewelry would be his apology to her, in advance. His brows knit. Lord, how he hated doing this thing, but he must.

Alessandra shook her head. "I have no coin," she reminded him.

He smiled. "It would please me to buy it for you."

Although she had agreed to allow him to purchase caftans for her—the reason for this outing—Alessandra was uncomfortable with his offer. The garments were a necessity, a matter of comfort and modesty that the silken trousers, chemise, and vest he had loaned her did not permit. And though she'd been given no choice with the cosmetics, they and the necklace were luxuries. Nay, he had already shown her more kindness than she would ever be able to repay.

"I cannot," she said.

Jacques's disappointment was exaggerated, but nonetheless real. "Come, Alessandra, consider it a gift—repayment for your companionship these past days."

"It is you who should be thanked. If not—"

"I insist, *chérie*."

She shook her head. "It is generous of you, but I must decline."

Blast the wench! Jacques silently cursed. Why couldn't she be like the other grasping creatures that had surrounded him all his life. She should be demanding matching earrings, a bracelet, a belt of shimmering coins. . . . It was as if she knew what awaited her and was using his guilt to divert him from the course he had set himself and her. It was the same as his mother had always done, the devil rest her soul.

Charged with simmering anger, Jacques fought to keep the edge from his voice. "You will wear it for me tonight," he said, reaching for his purse.

Failing to notice the emotion darkening his eyes, Alessandra stood firm. "Thank you, Jacques, but—"

"Think you I expect repayment in flesh?" he barked, his outburst sending the merchant back a couple of steps.

Alessandra blinked in surprise. She had not meant to upset him. As this was a side to him she had not seen before, it unsettled her. "I did not mean to sound ungrateful," she apologized.

His face hard, a muscle in his jaw spasming, he turned away. However, when he turned back again, the drawn lines had softened. "Humor me, hmm?" he said, holding the necklace out to her.

Alessandra hesitated, then nodded. What harm was there in accepting? Had he not made it clear he only wished to be her friend? "Very well," she agreed, "but I will repay you as soon as I am able."

Displeasure over her stipulation flitted across his handsome face, but just as quickly dissolved. "This I know," he murmured.

It took only minutes for Jacques to bargain the merchant down to the price he was willing to pay, then he was pushing aside Alessandra's cloak to secure the necklace about her throat.

Reminding herself he was European and therefore unfamiliar with the strict decorum of the Muslims, she swallowed her discomfort at being revealed before strangers and stood still while he fastened the clasp.

"I knew it would suit you," he said, a stiff smile thinning his lips.

Grateful for the veil that at least hid her face, Alessandra pulled her cloak closed over the filmy garments. "*Merci*, Jacques."

He searched her eyes a long moment, then shrugged and turned her around. "You are a strange one, Alessandra," he said as he led her between the stalls.

"How is that?"

By the time he finally answered, Alessandra had nearly forgotten what she had asked. "You are different from the other women I have known," he said.

"And have there been many?" The moment the words passed her lips, she would have given anything to take them back. They were far too bold and personal. Heat swept her face.

Jacques, however, seemed unaffected by her query. "Ah, yes." He sighed. "Though few were virgins like you, *chérie*."

Alessandra stumbled to a halt. "H-how do you know that?" she stammered. It was certainly not anything they had discussed. In fact, considering the tale she had told him, she would not have been surprised if he had assumed otherwise.

Taking her arm, Jacques urged her forward again. "I know the face of innocence," he said as he turned off the main street and steered her down a much narrower one. "Though yours is no longer in full bloom, the final barrier has yet to be breached."

Embarrassed and intensely uncomfortable that he would speak of such things, Alessandra was at a loss as to how to respond. Strange, but this Jacques deviated considerably from the one she had come to know in the comfort of his home. What had brought about the change?

"It surprises me," he continued, "that this Lucien you speak of did not steal your virtue in all the time you were together. Or that you did not surrender it to him."

Alessandra would have stopped again, but his lengthy stride would not permit it. "You cannot possibly know that," she said, making no effort to hide her indignation.

He turned down another street, at the end of which lay a large, decrepit building. "But I do. It is, after all, my business."

Warning bells rang in Alessandra's head. Something was wrong. Very wrong. "Your business?" she repeated, remembering he had said something similar to the tavern owner. "I don't understand."

He avoided her gaze, his own fixed straight ahead. "All will be explained momentarily."

She looked to the building that lay before them and, for the first time, realized the marketplace had been left far behind. What of the caftans Jacques had promised her? Were they not the purpose of their outing?

Determined to have an answer, she dug her heels in and pulled her arm free of his grasp. "Where are you taking me?" she demanded.

He turned toward her. "You will see."

She took a step back. "No, I will know. You are behaving most strangely, Jacques, and I will go no farther until you have told me the reason."

"I've a surprise for you," he said. "Would you ruin it by asking that I reveal it?"

Alessandra stood firm. "Yes."

His mouth twisted consideringly, then he lifted his palms heavenward. "Ah, *chérie*, must you make this so difficult for me?"

"I am sorry, but I must know."

He shook his head, then suddenly grabbed her, his arms lifting her high against his chest.

"Put me down!" she shrieked, her arms and legs flailing.

He stumbled, but did not go down. Though Lucien would certainly dwarf him, Jacques was no weakling, his stout, broad-shouldered frame surprisingly muscular beneath the gentleman's clothes he wore.

Without a doubt, Alessandra had lost the battle before it had even begun. But knowing that and accepting it were two different things. She fought him all the way, and not until she was dropped into a chair did her blows fall upon thin air. Well past modesty, she swept her veil off and threw back her cloak.

"How dare you!" she seethed, her peripheral vision revealing to her the stark and filthy room she'd been deposited in.

The admiration, gratitude, and trust Jacques had reveled in was gone from her face, replaced by suspicion and accusation. Unfortunately, much as he would like to be the champion he had pretended to be these last days, circumstances necessitated otherwise. Circumstances that bluntly reminded him of who he was—Jacques LeBrec, slave trader and gambler unextraordinaire.

He heaved a weary sigh. "I am sorry, *chérie*," he said, sliding the back of his hand down her smooth cheek. "It is with great regret that I do this." Eyes remorseful, he brushed his thumb across her lips.

With sudden understanding and a wrenching sense of betrayal, Alessandra thrust his hand aside. She was being thrown to the wolves. Jacques had never intended to help her. All along he'd had other plans for her. Certain as she was, she needed to hear the words from him.

Steeling herself, she stood. "What is it you do, Jacques?"

Unable to hold her accusing gaze, he looked past her. "Understand, *chérie*, it is business—strictly business."

The business of knowing whether or not a woman was virgin or tainted. The business of women. Slavery? "And what is your business?" she asked, a trembling in her belly spreading outward.

He was silent a long time, then he looked back at her. "Slaving, Alessandra."

She closed her eyes, her mind searching for a way out of this new dilemma. Could she escape Jacques? And if so, what new dangers awaited her? Her mind reeled back to the rape he had rescued her from, taunting her with the knowledge that his reason for doing so had been purely self-serving. Was there no safety for a woman alone in this world? she wondered desperately.

Self-pity hastened the tears from her eyes. Now everything was lost to her—her mother, her home, Lucien. . . .

Lucien. How she yearned to see his face again. To feel those angry arms around her, his warm breath in her ear, the promise of his mouth on hers. To know that even in hate, there beat a heart full of grudging compassion.

In his absence, his loathing no longer seemed such a terrible thing. It was an obstacle, naught else. And the revenge she had sworn on Leila . . . Amazingly, it had grown distant, almost trivial. Sabine was gone, and though her memory was without end, the mourning would someday come to a close.

Alessandra suppressed the sob that rose to her throat. Foolish child, she scolded herself. Would she never grow up?

Jacques brought her back to the present by thrusting a crisply folded kerchief in her face. "Wipe your tears, *chérie*."

She stared at the linen, then defiantly scrubbed her forearm across her eyes. "Why, Jacques?" she asked.

One corner of his mouth lifted in an apologetic smile. On Lucien it would have looked scornful, but on this man it was charming in spite of the true character he had revealed.

"You will bring a good sum," he said. "A virgin with hair of fire who speaks the language of the Arabs." He reached to touch her silken strands, but grasped only air.

The chair upended by her hasty retreat, Alessandra was forced to step over it to put more distance between herself and Jacques. "You are despicable," she hissed. "A man who is not a man, but a weasel!"

Did she know how true she spoke? Jacques wondered, cut to the quick by words that echoed his own beliefs. His hands clenched into fists, his anger coming to a boil. However, he did not turn it on her. He owed her that much.

"I could have sold you into prostitution," he said.

Her short burst of laughter was filled with scorn and

disgust. "And I suppose I should be grateful you mean to only sell me into slavery?"

He did not immediately answer, but when he spoke, it was as if to a child. "There will be many vying to bring you into their harem, Alessandra. I would think you would prefer the prospect of one lover to many."

"I prefer none," she retorted. None but Lucien ...

His brow furrowing, Jacques dragged a hand down his face, cupped his chin, and stared at the toes of his polished boots.

There might never be another chance, Alessandra realized as her gaze pounced upon the open pathway to the door. What lay beyond, she had no notion, for she had been too preoccupied with fighting Jacques to notice her surroundings when he'd carried her into the building.

Freedom, she assured herself. Freedom was what lay beyond. Spurred on by its beacon, she flew toward the door. Over the thrumming of her heart, she heard Jacques call to her and the sound of his heels on the wooden floor, but nothing could deter her from her course.

Nothing except the burly woman who suddenly appeared in the doorway and caught her by the shoulders.

Alessandra's momentum carried her forward, slamming her face into the well-endowed chest that was the woman's only claim to being of that gender.

Gasping, Alessandra tried to extricate herself from the brutal hold. The grip on her merely tightened until she nearly cried out.

"You would have lost her, Jacques dear," the woman boomed, the French words crude and uncultured upon her tongue. She extended her arms to better see Alessandra.

"Not with you slugging about," Jacques snapped. He reached to reclaim Alessandra.

At that moment Alessandra would have gone willingly to him, the known being far preferable to the daunting person who examined her as if she were a tasty morsel.

The woman, of uncertain descent and clothed like a man, sidestepped Jacques's attempt to take her prize from her. "Surely you're not having second thoughts?" she asked as her eyes raked Alessandra from head to toe.

"This one will certainly free you of your debts ... or nearly so."

The sly reminder stilled Jacques. She was right. He could not afford to change character at a time like this. He withdrew, turning so he would not have to face Alessandra.

"How much?" he asked over his shoulder.

The woman gripped Alessandra's chin and forced it up. "A bit red, wouldn't you say?" she reflected, her hooded gaze sweeping the mass of curling tresses.

Jacques swung back around. "Do not play games with me!" he barked, the delicate threads of his patience stretched taut. "What think you can get for the wench?"

She shrugged. "Soon we will know, but I promise you will do well."

Jaw clenched, Jacques took a step toward the door. "Today," he said.

"You would do better to wait. Word will spread and you will get a higher price in a few days."

He shook his head. "No, it must be today." Today, or else he might change his mind. And then where would he be?

The woman heaved a foul-smelling sigh. "Very well ... today."

He nodded. "And, Edith ..."

"*Oui*, Jacques?"

"The necklace." He indicated the silver collar around Alessandra's neck with a thrust of his chin. "It goes with her."

The woman's greedy eyes flitted over it, a sneer of disappointment making her face even less lovely than before. "As you like," she said.

Alessandra had forgotten about it, and her immediate thought was to tear it from her neck and fling it at Jacques's feet. And she would have, had the woman not been holding her arms.

Jacques snatched one last look at her, then turned away.

"Jacques!" she called after him, struggling in spite of the woman's greater strength.

He paused in the doorway, his shoulders bunching beneath the fine material covering them. *"Pardon, chérie,"* he muttered, and was gone.

A rage greater than any Alessandra had ever known overcame her. Uncaring that the vile woman could easily snap her neck, she began to fight.

As if she were but a nuisance, the woman encircled her throat with one rough, pudgy hand and squeezed until the lack of air sprayed color against the backs of Alessandra's eyelids. She did not stop there, content only when her captive sank into unconsciousness.

Had she not been such precious merchandise, Alessandra reflected with great bitterness, she would certainly have ended up much the same as the young girl she shared a cell with.

Clutching the accursed necklace still fastened about her throat, she peered at the girl's bruised and swollen face, which sleep had somehow managed to soften. A shudder rippled through her. It could as easily be her had Jacques not ordered that she be auctioned this day.

An hour past she had awakened in this cell, one of many, but separate from the others. From her tearful companion, a dark-skinned girl of fifteen who spoke halting Arabic, Alessandra had discovered the reason for the segregation. With the exception of the children, they alone were chaste. The other captives, a teeming mass of bodies pressed into cells filled to capacity, were men and women of varying races and languages. Though some were vocal in regard to their captivity, most seemed resigned to it.

What had it been like for Lucien? Alessandra wondered. He, a man of greater strength and will than any of those before her. Hell, she decided. The same—nay, worse—than that she found herself in.

Her imagination conjured visions of his giant's wrath. The ominous threats that must have battered those who had dared to make him their slave. The roar of curses that had seared his throat. His restless pacing in a cell he had likely shared with none. His large hands gripping the bars and straining their ability to hold him. His fists bludgeoning anyone who ventured too near.

And now he was free, likely on a ship set sail for his precious, chilly England. Would she ever be free?

"Aye," she whispered. Even if she died trying. She gripped the necklace tighter until its edges cut into her palm. As it was the only thing of value she possessed— the worth of the cosmetics negligible—she had grudgingly quelled the childish desire to be rid of Jacques's conscience-easing gift. Bereft of jewels, it was not terribly valuable, but it might aid in her escape.

A commotion at the far end of the warehouse gave way to a procession of men clad in various dress. They followed the man whom Alessandra's companion had earlier pointed out as being the auctioneer.

A sense of doom cast itself over Alessandra as she followed their advance into the bowels of this market of human flesh. They gathered before each cell, the auctioneer enthusiastically commented on the occupants, then they moved on.

Those with him were buyers, Alessandra quickly realized—a select few given the privilege of preview before the auction commenced. But that was not all.

In mounting horror, she watched as several women, and even some girls, were taken from their cells and given over to prospective buyers. Against a wall, before God and all those present, the men eagerly sampled the fruits the unfortunate slaves were forced to yield.

Their bestial rutting sickened and terrified Alessandra, who had never before witnessed copulation. It appeared nothing at all like what she had shared with Lucien.

She snapped her eyes closed on the image of him that rose before her. Always it came back to Lucien. Every notable twist and turn in her life was a result of the unforgettable man she had spurned in her bid for freedom. If only he had caught her in that alleyway . . .

No cloak to cover her, Alessandra shortly suffered the humiliation of the leering appraisals of the auctioneer and the buyers, who pressed close to the bars to better see her figure through her light garments.

Though fear filled her to overflowing, she did not cower. Instead, she sat erect on the pile of dank straw she had earlier gathered into her corner, and stared back.

Nothing to worry about—at least not yet, she thought in an attempt to calm the heart that beat fiercely in her chest. The price of her virtue was far too high to permit any to sample her as they had done the others.

Devastating blue eyes and a wicked smile caught Alessandra's attention and held it. The rake, a man of good height and carriage, smiled wider as his gaze lapped at her curves.

Alessandra's teetering temper flared. Why this particular man would give rise to it, she didn't understand. All she knew was a churning animosity for his brazen regard. It was as if he knew a secret—a secret that taunted her and turned her anger inside out.

Jumping to her feet, she rushed the bars and, to the surprise of those who stood without, hurled herself against them. "Damn you," she cursed, thrusting hooked hands between the iron rods. "Damn you all!"

Her nails drew only musty air, the blood of her intended victims maddeningly out of reach.

For a brief space of time a pall of silence fell over all, but was broken by the laughter that burst from the rake's throat.

"Sweet mother of mercy," he said in crisp English, his eyes dancing with delight. Fluid as the warm waters of the Mediterranean, he stepped forward and caught her wrist before she could pull it back to her mockery of a refuge. "Imagine this one in your beds!" he bantered, switching to lingua franca.

A tirade of profanity spewed from Alessandra's lips as she strained backward in an attempt to pull her arm free. However, her strength was easily surpassed by the man's. His audience captive, he leisurely reeled her in until her side was pressed hard against the bars.

"Release me, lecherous vermin," she spat, her fingers splayed but finding nothing to pierce with their nails.

Ignoring the scowl of the auctioneer, asking no man's permission, Alessandra's tormentor slid his fingers up her arm, brushing aside the sleeve of her chemise as he went.

The others drew near again, their faces alight with interest as the rake advanced on the breast nearest the bars.

Alessandra tried to twist away, to evade his loathsome touch, but was powerless to do so. "English swine!" she yelled, paying no heed to the bruises her continued struggle was inflicting upon her.

His smile turned stricken—mockingly so—then beamed wider. However, he did not violate her further. His fingers coming to rest on the firm flesh of her upper arm, he leaned in and whispered, "You will be in my bed by nightfall, hellion mine."

Alessandra stilled and turned her face to him. Through the wild tumble of her hair, she glared at him with all her anger. "With a knife," she snarled.

His eyebrows jerked upward. "Promise?" The word rolled off his tongue like a rapier-honed caress.

Startled by his response, Alessandra could only stare, her retort stoppered in her throat. This man was dangerous, as much, if not more so, than Lucien. Were all Englishmen the same? she wondered. If so, then what must her father be like?

She had been straining so hard against the rake that when he suddenly released her, she flew backward. She toppled unceremoniously into her corner, her hoarded straw flying in all directions and startling the young girl into wakefulness.

"Make ready, my lady," the Englishman tossed over his shoulder as he stepped away. "The day will be very long ... the night even longer."

A trembling in her belly, Alessandra watched him and the others go, their parting glances filled with lecherous imaginings. She wanted to cry, to scream, to pound her fists against her prison walls—everything and all at once—but she wouldn't allow herself. Instead, she drew up her knees, pressed her aching forehead against them, and turned to the only one who could save her now.

"Dear God," she whispered, low and miserable, "send me an angel. . . ."

CHAPTER 16

Alessandra would never forget the sea of eager, ravenous faces, or the fear of desperation flaying her insides as she looked out across it. She would not forget the three hundred and seventeen steps she had counted from her cell to the platform, or the merciless hands that had guided her there. She would forget nothing, she vowed, carrying it in her all the days of her life. And her remembrance of one man would be the anchor to which all was bound—Lucien de Gautier.

Surprising even to her, she did not blame him. Indeed, the blame was hers alone. Had she not run from him, even now she might be on a ship bound for England. Lucien had simply been providing a service, granting her mother's deepest wish—even if his motive had changed upon discovering it was his enemy's daughter he had agreed to assist. Nevertheless, it had all begun with him. If only it could also end with him . . .

A great emptiness lodged itself in Alessandra's chest. Though she vowed to fight and escape the man who would this day pay well to possess her body, gone forever was the one she would have given her soul to had the barriers they'd erected between them not become so insurmountable. If only—

The auctioneer's bellow startled Alessandra out of her memories and back to the reality of her world gone mad. Succinctly, the man began to tick off her qualities, some-

how managing to make the word *virgin* sound foul each
time he spoke it.

With a strength she had never known she possessed,
Alessandra stood proud and waited to be divested of her
clothing, as the woman before her had been. Although
she longed to resist such humiliation, she knew it would
be futile, and that it would only serve to excite the
wolves flanking her—a lesson she had learned only hours
before when the Englishman had taunted her.

Was he out there? she wondered, breaking her fixed
stare to search him out.

As if reading her thoughts, the rake moved into her
line of sight and smiled that secretive smile. Then, answering the auctioneer's summons to bid, he yelled out a
staggering sum that no doubt made many others rethink
their desire to have her.

Amazed to find herself still clothed, Alessandra sent
heartfelt thanks heavenward, then tentatively broached
the subject of an angel again.

A rotund Turk dressed in gilt-edged garments stepped
forward and topped the Englishman's price. No angel he.

A moment later an Arab raised it even higher—the farthest thing from an angel, with devilish eyes that raped
her where she stood.

Unperturbed, the Englishman countered. He certainly
was not an angel, but most likely one of the devil's own
henchmen.

At that moment, no hope in sight, Alessandra feared
she was going to lose the bile in her otherwise empty
stomach. Then, on second thought, she prayed she
would. If that did not curb their lust, nothing would.

The bidding continued, alternately creeping and jumping higher with each enthusiastic shout, until Alessandra's nerve endings jangled. In an attempt to retain
control, she squeezed her eyes closed and forced deep
breaths upon her constricted lungs.

It was then that something raw and warm touched her,
enveloping her from head to foot. Unearthly, she thought.
She opened her eyes wide to dispel the sensation, and her
gaze clashed with familiar violet.

Her breath knocked from her, she could only mouth his name. "Lucien . . ."

His gaze unwavering, his mouth set in a thin, hard line, the man who should have been long gone stared back at her from the shadowed folds of his headcloth. Still clothed in Arab dress, he would have melded with the others had not his manifest proportions set him so far above and apart from them. But even if he had been on a level with those around him, Alessandra would have known of his presence.

Momentarily forgetting that she stood at auction, she offered him a tentative smile—a blend of apology, regret, and gratitude.

As if sculpted from stone, his face remained impassive, giving no evidence of the emotions that must surely be there.

Aye, he would still be angry with her for running from him, that much was certain. But he would not forsake her. For what other reason would he have come if not to free her?

Even as she refused to look away for fear he would disappear and show himself to be only a figment of her imagination, the ashes of Alessandra's soul began to smolder with hope. As the bidding continued they turned to glowing embers, then leaped to flame.

She had never imagined angels capable of assuming the flesh of man, but in Lucien, one had found a way. As he had obviously come to rescue her, she wondered when he would bid her away from the others.

Her heart much lightened, she waited for him to step forward and offer a sizable portion of that which her mother had given him. She had seen the great amount of coin, as well as the several pouches of Sabine's precious jewelry. Though Alessandra had never had any dealings with money, there being no need for it, Lucien looked to have been given a king's ransom. Surely more than enough to assume the role of savior.

So why did he simply stand there and say nothing? she worried as time passed without his entrance into the fierce bidding. Why did his blank expression offer no reassurance? Was he looking at her or through her?

"To Captain Giraud!" the auctioneer pronounced with great satisfaction.

The warmth flooding Alessandra turned tide, chilling her as the man's words sank into her consciousness.

Captain Giraud? Shaking her head in disbelief, she tore her gaze from Lucien to look upon the other man—the rake who had vowed to make her his. Was it possible she now belonged to him? Belonged to this man whose mocking eyes held promise of the night to come?

Nay! What of Lucien? He had yet to offer for her. Even in his hate for the Bayards he would not desert her. Desperate for confirmation of a belief that was quickly losing its footing, Alessandra looked back to where he stood, but found that large space horribly vacant.

"Lucien," she gasped, searching the crowd for a glimpse of the giant. That was all she caught of him before he completely disappeared from sight.

"Lucien!" she cried, and lunged forward. She must follow him. Must—

Hands closed roughly around her arms and pulled her back from the edge of the platform. As she craned her neck for another glimpse of her would-be savior, she struggled to break free of the man who sought to keep her from him.

Raising her fists, she blindly pummeled the man, her knuckles contacting soft flesh, then bone that bruised and vibrated pain up her arm. A stinging slap jerked her head back, but she continued to fight, even when her mind warned of the futility of it. Nay! another part of her screamed as she was unceremoniously flipped over a shoulder and carried down the steps. She could not accept that Lucien would be so cold and unfeeling. That he would have stood there and made no effort to deliver her from rape when it was well within his means to do so.

But he had . . . and then he had turned his back on her without so much as a shrug of regret. Accept it she must, for he was gone. Was it revenge against her father that had hardened him to her plight? Had he only come to see her off to the hell she had made for herself?

Not wanting to believe, but having nothing left to believe in, she felt hot tears scald the backs of her eyes. To have been so close, only to discover how far she had really been, shook the adult foundation she'd laid over that of a child. Vowing she would not succumb to its crumbling, she set her jaw and fought back the evidence of her misery.

Dropped to her feet, Alessandra caught sight of the rake's—Captain Giraud's—approach. He wore that same damnable smile that had first fired her anger.

Soon, she told herself. Soon he would discover the poor bargain he had made. She would make him regret every gold piece he had paid for her.

Placing himself before her, his hands on his hips, Captain Giraud swept his gaze over her twice before returning his attention to her face. Triumphant, he leaned close.

" 'Tis as I said, hmm?" he provoked, a gleam in his blue eyes.

Alessandra needed no reminder of his threat to bed her. Soon, she promised herself. Nay, now! She launched herself at him, falling against him. He staggered backward, but did not topple as she'd hoped. Regaining his footing, he tried to extricate himself from her fierce grasp, then suddenly lurched forward as she landed a nasty blow.

Too late, the man who had carried Alessandra from the platform interceded. Though he tried to keep emotion from his hard-set features, there was no mistaking the quivering of his lips as he held tight to Alessandra and stared at the Englishman.

Curses clipped the air as Captain Giraud groped the pained part of his anatomy between his legs.

A small, bitter smile transformed Alessandra's face. "It is also as I said," she hissed.

Slowly, the hateful man drew himself erect. His jaw clenched, he growled, "Once you are on my ship, you will learn the folly of your actions, wench."

His threat bounced off Alessandra, leaving only its imprint on her closeted fears. "As will you," she tossed back.

Jacques LeBrec stood dockside and watched the small boat grow yet smaller as it was rowed toward an impressive merchant ship bearing the name *Jezebel*.

As he continued to watch he saw Alessandra rise up in the boat and hurl herself to the side. Expecting her to plunge into the waters of the Mediterranean, he held his breath, but released it a moment later.

The unmistakable figure of the English captain caught her around the waist and dragged her back down and onto his lap.

Though they were too far away for him to make out the exchange that followed, Jacques was certain Alessandra spewed curses as she struggled to free herself. The boat rocked, but continued on as if nothing untoward were occurring.

In spite of the ache in him, Jacques could not help but smile. Though Alessandra would no doubt find herself the mistress of *Jezebel*'s captain, she would be fine, he consoled himself. Indeed, she was bound for England, where her mother had said she belonged.

Pretending his conscience was eased, he turned and stepped into the waiting carriage.

CHAPTER 17

Footsteps. They had to be his.

Hefting the plank she had pried loose from the floor of the cabin, Alessandra flattened herself against the wall and spread her legs for balance. Just in time, too, for the ship suddenly pitched to the side and would have left her upended had she not.

Perhaps they were leaving port. She entertained the thought for a moment before thrusting it aside. She knew nothing of the captain's plans, for he had spoken not a single word to her all the way to the harbor. In his anger he had been silent, which had suited Alessandra just fine, for her mind had been awhirl with impossible plans and devices by which she might thwart his efforts to take what she would have given to only one man—one treacherous, vengeful man.

Silence fell as her unwelcome visitor paused before the cabin door, then came the metallic ring of keys being sorted. A moment later the chosen one rasped into the lock and turned. The mechanism released with a soft click.

Alessandra readied herself, calculating for the hundredth time where the blow must fall to assure the man was incapacitated long enough for her to flee him and the cabin he had made her prison.

Light, shadowed by the man who pushed the door inward, stole into the darkened cabin.

Refusing to falter in her resolve to escape, Alessandra

left the consequences of failure at the wall. Surging forward, she swung her weapon as the man stepped within.

The plank struck him hard, the force of the blow causing her to lose her grip on the splintery board. Humming, it sailed past her head and hit the opposite wall.

Alessandra had only a split second to anticipate the thud of the captain's body to the floor before the arm that had wielded her weapon was snatched and jerked forward. A gasp of surprise burst from her lungs.

"I am eternally grateful for my height," Lucien muttered, then began kneading the shoulder that had taken the brunt of her attack.

Speechless, Alessandra raised her eyes to pick out his gleaming bronze hair and the wonderfully familiar jags and angles of his face. Was she dreaming? Or had her mind twisted on her and conjured the impossible? She shook her head. Even the scar of the Islamic religion stood out in the dim light. Fingers itching to touch it, to know for certain if he was flesh or apparition, she reached up and traced the crescent.

Dare to believe, she told herself. Believe the warmth beneath your fingertips is real. Believe he did not abandon you. Believe there is some place in this angry giant that yearns for you as you yearn for him. Believe...

With a cry, she launched herself against Lucien's chest and shamelessly wrapped her arms around him. Grabbing handfuls of his tunic, she held tight for fear he might vanish again. Angels had a way of doing that.

The tears began to flow. For time immeasurable, she clung to Lucien, reveling in hesitant hands that quickly turned comforting.

He had not left her behind. Had not allowed his hate for the Bayards to rule his feelings for her. Admit it or not, he cared for her—Lord willing, the same as she cared for him.

She tilted her head back and met eyes she had thought never to see again. "Lucien," she breathed.

"Alessandra."

She smiled. "You did not forsake me."

His hands stilled. "Nay, though God knows I should have."

He had withdrawn, pulled back from his feelings, but it did not matter. Those feelings existed, and he could not keep them hidden forever.

"Forgive me," she said, then raised herself on tiptoe and pressed her wavering smile to his mouth. She breathed the scent of his wonderfully solid body, her nostrils filling with his masculinity and the salt of the sea issuing from his skin. His reined anger also rose to her senses—anger for who she was and what she had done.

In spite of his lack of response, nothing had ever seemed so marvelous, nor so worthy of savoring. Vowing she would make Lucien see her as a woman, and not the daughter of his enemy, Alessandra deepened the kiss.

Lucien pulled back, all emotion masked. "You were expecting the good captain, eh, my lady?"

The captain . . . Captain Giraud! How could she forget? Desperate, she grabbed his arm. "Lucien, the captain," she exclaimed, her eyes wide with alarm. "We must hurry, else he will discover us. He is an evil man and will—"

"Is that right?" Amusement replaced the irritation in his voice.

She blinked. Why was he so calm? Shouldn't he be using the time to spirit her away from the ship? Perhaps he had overwhelmed Giraud. But what, then, of the crew?

"You don't understand," she began.

"But I do." He turned away. "You have naught to fear, Alessandra. All is as it should be."

Confused, she watched him cross to the lantern she had earlier put out. His large hands, which should have been graceless, easily lit it.

He was dressed most peculiarly, she noticed. His Arab costume had been discarded in favor of tunic and hose that showed him to be more of a man than any caftan or robe could. Gone was the turban, his hair pulled back from his face and secured at his nape with a leather thong.

It was the European mode of dress, Alessandra knew. Jacques LeBrec had dressed similarly, though his clothes had been far finer and more embellished.

Lucien moved to the chest Alessandra had done her

best to pry open hours past. She had failed to discover its contents, but only for lack of the key, which he produced and inserted into the lock. Throwing back the lid, he probed within and removed a gown of dark green and an undergown of purplish red. He shook both out, then crossed back to her.

"You will need to change," he said, lifting her lax arm and turning the garments over it. "Then we will go above deck."

Immediately, a thousand questions rushed at Alessandra, followed by a host of suspicions. "I don't understand."

He turned away. "You will."

Nay, she needed to understand now. "Lucien, why did you bring me all the way to Tangier? Oran was less than half the distance." She spoke of the coastal city they had skirted halfway into their journey. Lucien had insisted on continuing to Tangier for reasons known only to him. At the time Alessandra had thought he chose to go farther west in order to throw off Rashid's pursuit. It had suited her fine, giving her that much more time to devise her escape. Now she wasn't so sure she had guessed right.

His hand on the door, Lucien looked back at her. "I will explain later," he said.

Still not good enough. "It's Captain Giraud, isn't it?" she said, voicing her strongest suspicion. "You know him, don't you? He's the reason you insisted on coming to Tangier."

It seemed Lucien was going to deny it, or at least put her off again, but then his wide shoulders rolled with a careless shrug. "Nicholas is my cousin."

Giraud was his cousin? Shock gave way to welling anger—anger that supplanted the relief Alessandra had felt when she'd discovered he had not forsaken her. "Bastard!" she cursed. Wadding the gowns, she pitched them across the room. They struck Lucien's chest before falling to the floor.

His jaw shifting side to side, he closed the door and leaned back against it. "It was necessary, Alessandra."

"Necessary?" She felt heat ripple over her neck and into her face. "You allowed me to be sold as if I were nothing but a piece of horseflesh. That—that man you call cousin taunted me. He—"

"Enough!" Eyebrows lowered, Lucien reached down and scooped up the gowns, then walked back to her. Seizing her arms, he raised them and shoved them full of the clothing.

"For all we knew," he said, "Rashid or one of his men might have been among the crowd. Though it proved otherwise when none opposed you being awarded to Nicholas. It was too great a risk, for had Rashid made Tangier ere the auction, death would surely have been upon my heels had he seen my face. And you, Alessandra, would have been returned to Algiers with none to carry out your mother's wishes."

Her rejoinder sputtered on her lips and died. He was right, of course. Had he bid for her, he would have drawn attention to himself. He would have risked his guise and shown himself to be an Englishman. She could not fault him for that.

Yet he had allowed her to believe the worst even when she'd been whisked away from the auction, and his ruthless cousin had not deigned to enlighten her. These past hours locked in his cabin had been horrid with wild imaginings.

As she calmed, Lucien felt a smattering of regret. There was something so appealing about Alessandra when she was angry. All that womanly fire excited him and reminded him of long legs wrapped around him, peaked breasts, and the keening cry of pleasure his hand had captured. Instantly, his body reacted to the memories. He scowled over his lack of control.

"Your cousin," she said. "Know you the words he spoke to me and the lascivious looks he cast upon my person?"

Lucien's scowl reversed into a grin. "I can well imagine."

"Well you needn't, for I'll tell you what he said. He said he would have me in his bed—"

"That is his bed." Lucien nodded to the cot suspended between wooden supports. "And that is where you will be sleeping. He did not lie."

"But it is what he meant when he spoke the words. He insinuated that he . . ." Alessandra blushed. "He purposely set out to frighten me."

Lucien's shoulders rose and fell again in a lazy shrug. "Likely, he took it upon himself to teach you a lesson."

"A lesson! What right—"

"We should have sailed two days ago, Alessandra." He planted his feet a stride apart. "Your escapade has cost him much in time and profit. Now his cargo will not reach England before the other ships bound for its ports."

It was the least he deserved for the terrible fright he had given her, Alessandra reasoned. However, guilt followed on the heels of that thought. Swallowing her retort, she cast her eyes down. "I'm sorry," she said. Sorry, but this was not the end of it.

"As you should be," Lucien said.

She clenched her teeth to keep her jaw from trembling. How was it that no matter how hard she tried to cast off the child in her, the little one refused to be shed? Could she do nothing right?

Lucien stared hard at the top of her head, mustering all the anger and frustration he had felt these last few days. In the end, though, he could not deny the jumble of warm feelings he had for this beautiful, freckled waif.

He tilted her chin up and looked into her miserable eyes. "It is done now," he said. "Soon you will be in England as your mother wished."

The mention of Sabine caused a lump to form in Alessandra's throat. "Yes," she choked. "As she wished."

Lucien lightly brushed his lips over hers. "Dress now," he said, drawing back. "The sun and sky promise a spectacular setting."

Her lips tingling from the brief contact, Alessandra drew a deep breath and lifted the garments. She was surprised to find they were as her mother had described, almost exact replicas of the small sketches of English costume Sabine had made.

The gown, with its low V-shaped neckline, high waist, flared sleeves, and dagged hem, could have been the same as her mother had worn as James Bayard's young bride. It did not remotely resemble the shapeless caftans

Alessandra was accustomed to wearing, and it was a far cry from the gossamer vest and trousers of the harem. Yet, beautiful as the gown was, it looked uncomfortable.

"Something is wrong?" Lucien asked.

She raised her eyes to his. "I—I have never worn such clothing."

His eyebrows shot straight up, then settled again. "Of course." His lips curved. "Will you need assistance?"

Though he clearly did not expect her to accept any, she nodded. "Will you show me?"

If the plank she had swung at him had struck him in the head as she'd intended, he could not have looked more surprised. It was short-lived, though, for he masked it with a shrug. "Very well."

As he moved toward her the flickering lantern put a gleam in his eye—or was it there of its own accord? His intent gaze locked with hers as he reached for the garments.

Dare she? Alessandra asked herself. Dare she allow him such familiarity? The reckless part of her that no amount of scolding had ever managed to curb, goaded her onward.

She wanted to feel again his hands on her bare limbs, to transport them back in time to the night he had made her body his. Sucking in a breath, she relinquished the gowns.

"You are sure?" he asked softly.

She nodded, turned, and began disrobing. Trembling fingers unfastened the vest and dropped it onto the cot. She hesitated, then hooked her thumbs into the waistband of the trousers. As she slid them down, exposing her legs beneath the hem of her chemise, her heart took up a staccato beat she was certain Lucien could hear. Braving it, she smoothed her hands down the remaining garment.

She had begun to lift it off when Lucien's warm hands covered hers and stayed their nervous quivering. She felt his breath near her ear, the cradle of his thighs settling against her buttocks, his hands gliding up beneath her sleeves.

"A siren," he said, his stubbled jaw grazing her smooth

cheekbone. "That is what you are, Alessandra Bayard. A flame-headed siren who would lure me to destruction. Is that your intent?"

He still did not trust her, she thought. And why should he, considering all she had put him through these past weeks? Repentant, she turned in his arms and lifted a hand to cup his jaw. "Lure you?" She searched his probing gaze, then nodded. "Aye, though not to destruction."

"What, then?"

"I want to give you what you gave me." Silently, she cursed that she could not speak so without a flush of color rising to her cheeks. So like a child.

Pressing one hand to the small of her back, Lucien reached with the other for the necklace she wore. "Le-Brec?" he asked.

Her hands flew to the forgotten reminder of the Frenchman. Realizing she had no further need of it, she began to search for the clasp. The accursed thing must go.

Lucien caught her wrists together. "LeBrec?" he growled.

Dare she hope it was jealousy responsible for darkening his eyes and curling his lip? "Yes," she answered.

"And what I gave you, did he also give you?"

How did he know of the man? Alessandra wondered. She did not think Jacques had been at the auction. Certainly, she had not seen him there. She tried to draw back to see Lucien better, but he would not allow it.

"Tell me," he demanded, tensing in anticipation of her answer.

She blinked. "How is it you know of him?"

"Tell me, Alessandra!"

It seemed she would have to answer first. "I am still a virgin," she said.

"That is not what I mean," he snapped. "You were also a virgin after lying with me. Did he touch you as I did?"

She shook her head. "No, Lucien. He was a gentleman."

His lids dropped over his eyes. When they lifted again, he smiled thinly. "Unlike myself," he said. Releasing her, he took a step back.

The necklace forgotten, Alessandra searched his face for a clue to his feelings. "It matters to you?"

He hesitated, his face remaining unreadable. "It matters," he said at last.

At least it was a start. "How do you know of Jacques?" she asked.

His mouth tightened. "Tale of the redheaded wench caught stealing the stores of a tavern spread quickly, though too late for me to intervene. LeBrec had already ensconced you in his home by the time I discovered what had happened."

"Why did you not come for me then?"

He shook his head. "His walls are high, Alessandra, his guards many. And not knowing what LeBrec intended, you would have fought me had I come for you. I had to content myself with what news the servant girl, Bea, brought."

Bea. The shy Circassian girl who had tended Alessandra's bath and grooming. In spite of her timidity, Bea's doe eyes had been ever watchful throughout Alessandra's stay. Now she understood why.

"As LeBrec has a reputation for leaving virgins intact," Lucien continued, "it seemed safer to take you at auction when next there was one."

She lowered her head and stared at his chest. "I won't fight you anymore, Lucien."

"I know."

So he did. "And I will go to England with you as my mother wished."

"It is already done."

She looked up at him. "Done?"

Humor shone from his eyes. "Aye. We have set sail. There is no turning back."

So final. England drew near while Algiers receded. Gone was the life she had known and embraced, while before her was a great, yawning hole she feared might swallow her completely. And at the center of that hole was Lucien. What were his plans for her? He had threatened to use her against her father. Was it still so?

"Lucien, what of me?" she asked. "Do you still intend to harm me that you might have revenge on my father?"

His silence was tangible, growing thick and tense as he considered her question. "Nay, Alessandra," he finally answered. "I will give you over to old man Bayard as soon as we reach Corburry."

But what of his earlier threats? she wondered. Dare she hope? "Then I am not to be the instrument of your revenge?"

His laughter warmed her brow. "It seems fitting enough revenge to give you to him. Let him deal with what I have had to these past weeks."

Alessandra's hope faltered and died. He had spoken no words of love. He simply wished to be rid of her as soon as possible. To hide her misery, she reached again for the hem of her chemise.

Lucien's words stayed her hands. "Leave it," he said. Raising the undergown over her head, he waited for her to lift her arms into it.

But the chemise would spoil the neckline, Alessandra thought. "The bodice—" she began.

"You are one woman among many men," he said sharply. "A bit of modesty would be in order."

Of course. It was not a harem she would be wandering about in, but a ship full of men from a world far removed from hers. Lucien was right.

Raising her arms, she stood unmoving while he lowered the garment over her head. Next came the gown—wonderfully roomy until he began buttoning the bodice. Its tightening diminished her breath, and the intimacy of his fingers brushing her breasts stole it completely.

"It fits well," he said as he looped the last button.

She dipped her head and stared at his hands. "It does?" Though the skirt was voluminous, the bodice was not at all proportionate. If she breathed deeply, surely the buttons would strain and burst free.

"I have no freedom in it," she murmured, feeling well and truly trussed.

Without comment, he belted the high waist.

She squirmed. "And even less now."

He arched a brow. "In English society, there is no place for a woman to wear caftans and trousers."

"None?" She looked longingly over her shoulder to the familiar garments she had shed.

He shook his head.

"What of a veil? I cannot go before men without one."

"Ladies of gentle birth dress as you are now," he said. "Some wear headdresses, but veils are of Muslim women only."

It was as her mother had told her, yet it still seemed such a foreign idea. Nervous, she knit her fingers together. "And I am of gentle birth?"

Lucien eyed her a long moment, then smiled. "By parentage only, I'm sure," he teased.

Alessandra rejoiced in the lessening of his anger. Accepting the risk of baring her soul to him yet again, she stepped close and stared up into his eyes.

"Lucien, do you not remember when you made love to me?" she asked.

His humor died a quick death. "I am not likely to forget," he answered, the tightening of his mouth causing the scar along his cheekbone to pucker slightly.

As he would not forget who her father was, his eyes told her. She sighed. "Nor am I," she said. Consoling herself with the thought that it would be many weeks before they reached England—time in which to change his mind about her—she swept past him.

Although her destination had been the door, she fell short of it by several feet—literally. Having trod on the hem of the undergown, she tripped and plummeted to the floor. Her outflung arms broke her fall, but were of little benefit to her dignity.

She had only a moment to contemplate the cleanliness of the floor before Lucien scooped her back onto her feet and began brushing her down. "You must either raise your skirts or shorten your stride when you walk," he said, speaking to her as if she were a child. "Preferably both."

She plucked at the skirt. "It is too long," she explained. "The hem will have to be raised."

He straightened. "The hem is where it should be for a proper English lady. *You* will have to adjust."

She wanted to argue otherwise, to tell him she was neither proper, nor an English lady, but decided it best to say nothing further on the subject. A needle and thread would solve her problem more readily than changing her behavior. In the meantime, she would hold the skirt up off the ground.

"I am ready," she said.

CHAPTER 18

"I owe you an apology." Pointedly, Alessandra lowered her gaze to the man's crotch.

Nicholas Giraud, a man more handsome than his cousin, though less in stature and presence, regarded her a long moment, then nodded. "That you do, my lady."

Remembering to lift the bothersome skirt out of her way, Alessandra stepped from Lucien's side, paused to catch her balance as the ship listed right, then placed herself before the captain. "Given," she said.

Frowning at her peculiar form of apology, he looked past her to Lucien, his left eyebrow quirked inquiringly.

His cousin shrugged.

Nicholas duplicated the gesture, then settled his gaze on the woman responsible for delaying his departure. "Accepted," he said.

She dipped her head, then met his gaze once again. "There is something else I owe you."

"Aye?"

Without warning, she swung her arm and landed her palm against his cheek. "You are no gentleman," she said evenly.

Nicholas resisted the urge to clap a hand to the fiery imprint of her palm. The little fool ought to turn tail and run, he thought. Captain Nicholas Giraud, former corsair and most recently Christian-turned-renegade, was not a man to allow such offenses to go unpunished—especially with his crew as witnesses.

But the woman did not move away. She made no attempt to gain the shelter of Lucien's great frame. Her lower lip thrust forward, her eyes blazing, she stood with hands on hips and waited to discover the consequences of her attack.

Too damn sure of herself was what she was. If not for Lucien and the twitching of his lips, Nicholas thought he might just turn her over his knee and repay her insult with a smack to her delectable bottom.

A vision of doing just that was his undoing. Laughter at himself and her rumbled up from his chest and caught on the same wind that filled his ship's sails. It grew louder at her openmouthed astonishment.

He glanced at Lucien, shared a moment of mirth with him, then threw his hands into the air. "Better you than me, cousin," he said. Too late, he wished he could pull back the words, for Lucien's face turned hard and serious.

Ah well, no matter, Nicholas thought.

Chuckling, he pivoted and stared across the bow of his ship, already forgetting his unexpected guests. Ahead, his treacherous mistress, the Atlantic, opened her arms and beckoned. Like the whore she proved herself to be each time he came to her, she lured him, seduced him, spread her legs, then betrayed him. And he savored every moment of it.

Aye, Lucien could have his redheaded paramour. As for him, he would make do with the occasional wench, always returning to the one who possessed his soul.

Alessandra stared at the arrogant captain who had laughed at her then wordlessly dismissed her, until Lucien's shadow fell over her. He would be angry, she knew. To ward off the chill creeping up the ridiculously flared sleeves of her gown, she crossed her arms over her chest. Then, with a toss of her head, she met his eyes.

"I don't know why I didn't anticipate that," he said, reaching to take her elbow.

Disconcerted by his calm, she sputtered for words. "He—he deserved it!"

Lucien guided her from the aftercastle. "It seems I've much to teach you ere we reach England."

"Teach me? And what would that be?"

"If you wish to continue being called a lady, then you must behave as one."

On the last step down from the aftercastle, Alessandra halted. "And I do not?" she asked, disbelievingly.

"Behave as an English noblewoman? Nay, you do not."

"But I am not an English—"

"You will be."

She closed her mouth. What he said was true. Before too long she would be in England, her name Bayard, and her standing that of lady. The thought overwhelmed her, making her wish she had paid closer attention to her mother's teachings on the conduct of ladies.

"Are ladies in England so very different from ladies of the Maghrib?" she asked.

"Aye, Alessandra, as you will soon see." He tried to urge her forward again, but she pulled back. His irritation showed. "Come to the rail and I will explain," he compromised.

Lucien did not want to miss his first sunset of true freedom, Alessandra realized, which was her first sunset of ominous change. Nodding, she followed at his side.

Though he appeared oblivious to the curious stares of the crew tending the sails, Alessandra was uncomfortably aware. When Nicholas Giraud had dragged her kicking and cursing onto the ship hours earlier, the men had enjoyed great laughter and jokes at her expense. Now, dressed as she was in European finery, they looked at her anew, though with little more respect than before. She longed for the security of a veil behind which she could hide all worry and unease.

Lucien settled his forearms on the railing and let the wind do with his hair as it pleased. And it pleased mightily, teasing it, lifting it, pulling at it, and finally freeing a number of the bronze strands from the leather thong.

It was not so kind with Alessandra's hair, tossing and dragging its unbound length into a mass of tangles she could hardly see past. Scowling, she gathered her hair, twisted it down to the ends, and tucked it into the neck of her chemise.

"How different?" she asked, returning to the question he had yet to answer.

He stared straight ahead, his eyes narrowed on the place where the ocean was busy swallowing the sun. "Very," he answered.

Alessandra scooted nearer. "So . . . tell me."

Though numerous examples came to mind, Lucien chose the one that stood out most in his memory. "The donkey game you played," he said, suppressing the smile tugging at his lips. "A proper English lady would never attempt such foolishness."

"And if she did?"

Lucien glanced at her from out of the corner of his eye. "Likely her papa would bundle her off to a convent."

"For riding a donkey backward?"

"For riding a donkey at all."

Alessandra's shoulders slumped. "How boring it must be," she muttered.

Giving up the sun, Lucien turned toward her. "Not at all," he said. "There are many diversions."

She tilted her head back and stared up at him. "Such as?"

"Hunting, hawking, dancing—"

"Dancing?" She pounced on the word.

"Aye, to dance well is an essential accomplishment of the nobility. You must learn if—"

"But I already know how to dance."

He shook his head. "I speak of dances unlike those you are accustomed to—very different, indeed."

Her face fell. "Stuffy, then."

Compared with the erotic dance he had watched her perform? Perhaps. However, European dance had something her dance had not—the interaction of male and female, man and woman, lovers. . . . "Not so," he said.

"Then?"

Lucien had the sudden urge to show rather than tell. Would she flow, her body following his? he wondered. Or would she be stiff and awkward, resistant to his lead?

He swept his gaze over her figure. Untried, perhaps, but awkward? Never.

His eyes moved from the curve of her neck to the hollow at the base of her throat, halting when he saw the damned necklace. She still wore it. Jealousy robbed him of the serenity that had been his for too short a time. Fiercely conscious of his actions, he reached out and grasped the offensive object. Ignoring Alessandra's start of surprise, he rotated it and disengaged the clasp.

"Do with it as you will," he said, pressing it into her hand, "but never again wear it in my presence."

Staring at the necklace, Alessandra realized she had no need of it. It was naught but a painful reminder of deception and the horror of slavery. She would do well to be rid of it forever.

Drawing her arm back, she hurled the necklace to the ocean. It glittered in the last of the sun's light, writhing madly before falling to the hungry waves.

"Gone," she said. "Monsieur LeBrec is no more."

Lucien's brow cleared. "Give me your hand, Alessandra."

"What?"

"Your hand."

Suspicious, she placed it in his. "Yes?"

He nodded, then reeled her to him and glided his other hand around her waist. Settling it at the small of her back, he urged her forward until they were chest to chest.

Was he going to kiss her? Alessandra wondered, her breasts tingling where they brushed the swell of his muscled chest. In front of the crew? Apprehensive and hopeful at the same time, she glanced past his shoulder to numerous eyes glazed with curiosity. They also wanted to know.

Looking up, she caught a glimpse of Lucien's smile. "Here?" she asked. "It is permissible?"

He nodded. "It is not usually done in private. More often in public."

Alessandra was shocked. Her mother had never made mention of such a thing. "Truly?"

"Aye, truly."

He was right, she thought. There were many things he had to teach her before they reached England, and though it would be awkward before an audience, she wanted that kiss. Tilting her head back, she offered her mouth to him.

There was no kiss, though. Instead, Lucien let go of her waist, put her away from him, and still holding to her left hand, led her forward.

" 'Tis known as the estampie," he said, "the noblest of all dances."

Dance? Was that what they were doing? "But I thought you were going to . . ." Her voice trailed off. She was too embarrassed to admit she had been expecting something far different.

The red sky reflected in Lucien's eyes. "I know," he said, "but first the dance."

And then the kiss? Alessandra didn't ask it, though she hoped it would be so.

The dance *was* noble, but dull, Alessandra realized a short time later as, side by side, she and Lucien worked through the slow, grave steps that had her yearning for more movement. For that reason—anticipation of lively movement—she caused her feet to trip over themselves time and again.

"Relax," Lucien told her. "You are making it more difficult than it is."

"If only it were more difficult," she muttered. Only the fact that she held to Lucien made the dance pleasurable at all. Wishing for his arm about her waist again and her breasts pressed to his chest, she followed obediently as he led her forward and backward across the deck.

"Can we not dance closer?" she asked after more time had dragged past them.

He looked at her. "Closer?"

"Aye, your arms about me. It would be more enjoyable than this."

He laughed. " 'Tis not the way English nobles dance, Alessandra. Such things are not permissible, except, perhaps, among the peasants."

"But we are not yet in England," she said, "and what is the harm in affecting that we are peasants?"

He smiled. "You will like the farandole better. Though a group dance, it has more movement." To demonstrate, he whirled her around, turned her again, and swept her across the deck to the music playing in his head.

"Lucien!" she gasped as he passed her under his arm.

Effortlessly, he coiled her into a spiral, then unwound her. "Is this better?" he asked.

"Much." She laughed. Giving herself over to his cadence, she found her feet again and attempted to match his movements. Simple, she realized a short time later. She had but to memorize a half-dozen steps and it always came back to the first. This dance of England was wholly predictable, and more enjoyable than the first, though still lacking in the excitement of the harem dance.

"Can we not dance the peasants' dance?" she asked when next Lucien came near her.

"Closer, then?"

"Aye. Surely the crew would not object."

There was a gleam in his eyes when he finally took her into his arms. "Just this one time," he said, "and never again, most especially once we are in England."

Alessandra nodded, then closed her eyes and felt. Lucien's body glided over hers, pressed, withdrew, then pressed again. His fingers clasped hers, the hand at her back slipping lower to the crest of her buttocks, reminding her of that first night. Almost, they were making love again.

"Another," she demanded when he came to the end of his silent music.

One eyebrow quirked expressively, a broad smile stretching his mouth, Lucien led her into deepening shadows where none could see, and eased her back against the mast. "In a moment," he said.

Alessandra leaned her head against the rough wood and met eyes shadowed by the fringe of lashes. "Are you going to kiss me now?" she asked, breathless with anticipation.

In answer, he lowered his head and covered her mouth with his. Easing his tongue between her lips, he drank from the well of passion no other man had ever drawn from.

Alessandra groaned and shoved her fingers deep into

his hair, clenching them against his scalp as his body enveloped her.

"Mine," he growled as he nipped her lower lip.

His? Had she heard right? Unfortunately, he did not give her the chance to ask, abruptly ending the kiss and pulling her into another dance.

Later, Alessandra decided, the wonderful rhythm beginning to move her. Later she would ask him what he had meant.

Lucien loved the feel of her, the uninhibited way she floated in his arms. She was the one he had been waiting for all these years, though he had never dreamed of actually finding her.

As night descended he vowed to no longer think of her as a spawn of James Bayard. Aye, from this point forward, she would simply be Alessandra—not that there was anything simple about her. And perhaps, the absurd thought crept into his consciousness, perhaps she was the key to finally settling the dispute between the Bayards and the De Gautiers. . . .

Danced out, weary, and her belly full of strange foodstuffs that only politeness had prevented her from refusing, Alessandra stepped into the dimly lit cabin and drew to an abrupt halt.

"Something is wrong?" Lucien asked from behind her.

"There are two cots now," she said, "where before there was only one."

He closed the door. "Aye, the second is mine," he said as if he saw nothing unusual about it.

She turned and looked up at him. "I did not know you intended to share the cabin with me."

"Do you object, then?"

Foolish question. More than anything, she wanted him near her. She shook her head. "Nay, it just seems odd, improper, considering all you have told me about the English."

He shrugged. "As space is limited, and there is no other whom I trust to keep you safe from the crew, 'tis for the best."

"But what will they think?"

"You need not worry what crusty men of the sea think, Alessandra," he reassured her. "Once we reach England, you will never see them again. 'Tis only the English nobles you must impress."

Turning away, Alessandra smiled the smile she had worked hard to keep from her face upon learning he was to share the cabin with her. Then, feeling much lightened, she moved forward and patted the cot that would be hers.

"I don't know that I will be able to sleep in such a contraption," she mused. "It looks uncomfortable."

"Looks, but is not," Lucien said as he came up behind her. "Shall I show you how to get into it?"

Wondering how that might be accomplished—if by words or deed—she peered over her shoulder at him. "Would you?"

"Aye, but first you must remove your gown." He tugged its skirt. " 'Twill be a mass of wrinkles if you sleep in it."

Blushing, she put her head down so he would not see her childish reaction to his words. How was she to seduce him if she continued behaving as one who was unworldly? she chastised herself. She must prove to him the woman she was.

Turning to him, she began unbuttoning her gown. However, Lucien walked past her and pretended interest in his own cot.

Wondering if he had spurned her, or if he was playing the gentleman—the same as he had played before Nicholas that evening during their meal—Alessandra freed the last of the bothersome loops and shrugged out of the gown. Gathering it together, she folded it and placed it atop the trunk.

"The undergown, too?" she asked.

He turned back around. "Nay, 'tis not necessary," he said, then beckoned her back to her cot. "One hand here," he said, taking it and placing it on the far side rail, "and the other here." He closed her other hand over the side rail she stood alongside. "Then a knee up and you roll your body into it. Quite simple, really."

"Or very humiliating," Alessandra said as she pulled back her skirts to lift her leg over the side of the cot.

Laughing, Lucien put one hand to the back of her knee, the other to her hip, and boosted her onto the cot.

Facedown in the soft mattress, Alessandra held tight, certain the swinging cot would land her on the cabin floor if she moved so much as a finger. It didn't happen, though, the cot steadying a minute later.

"Now turn over," Lucien directed.

She hesitated before releasing her handholds, then slowly made her way onto her back to find Lucien's grinning face above her.

"As I said, quite simple," he repeated.

She grimaced. "I don't think I'll ever become accustomed to it."

"Aye, you will." He reached for the folded blanket near her feet. " 'Tis a long voyage ahead of us, and sleep is better spent on a cot than the floor, which is of no comfort when the ship lists heavily." Shaking out the blanket, he dropped it over her.

"I take your leave now," he said, stepping back.

"What?" she exclaimed. "You are going to leave me?" Making no attempt to hide her dismay, she sat straight up, swallowed hard at the unsettled feeling of the swaying cot, then captured his gaze. "But I thought you were to share the cabin with me."

"I am," he said, steadying the cot with one hand, "but now I must speak with Nicholas."

"But you spoke with him this eve. Why again?"

His gaze turned serious. "There are some things, Alessandra, which are not discussed in front of ladies. Remember that."

What things? she wondered, but decided it best not to ask. "Cannot my being a lady wait until we reach England?" she suggested. "It seems such a dreary undertaking."

"Nay. You cannot simply act the lady, you must feel the lady."

He was right, of course. Sighing, she settled back upon the mattress. "Very well," she grumbled.

His stern countenance slipping, Lucien leaned over and

pulled the blanket to her chin. "I won't be gone long," he said. Then, to her surprise, he lowered his head and touched his lips to hers. "Slowly, Alessandra," he whispered against her mouth. " 'Tis how it must be."

Damn him for knowing what was in her heart, she silently cursed, and for denying them both.

"Dream well," he said as he drew back. Then he turned and left the cabin.

An insistent ache in that part of her that would never be English, Alessandra turned onto her side and squeezed her thighs together. Dream well, he had said—as if she would even sleep this night.

Though he knew that this early into the voyage it was safe to leave Alessandra alone in the cabin, Lucien took the added precaution of locking her inside. He wanted no seaman stumbling onto her and trying to take what was Lucien's. Another death on his conscience.

He located Nicholas aft, where he was busy overseeing the setting of a sail.

"Marvelous, isn't she?" Nicholas said as Lucien approached. "So calm, so placid."

Lucien knew better than to think his cousin referred to a woman. It was the ocean he spoke of with such adoration.

"She is pouting, you know," Nicholas added.

Coming to stand before him, Lucien spread his legs to counter the ship's gentle swaying. "Pouting?"

Nicholas grinned. "Aye, she only puffs at my sails, and all because I dared place my hull upon another's waters."

"The Mediterranean," Lucien supplied.

He nodded. "As if this ocean was only true to me." Sudden laughter burst from him as his white teeth flashed. "Imagine that, a tramp with a jealous streak."

"Perhaps you ought find another mistress," Lucien suggested, earning himself a scowl.

"Like that Alessandra, who will bleed your heart from you until you are less than even a woman, and then flit from your arms and into another's? Vincent's, perhaps?"

What little humor Lucien held to slipped away, and only just did he restrain himself from hitting Nicholas.

Vincent, his brother, whose handsome looks and win-

ning smile drew women to him like swarms of bees. It
had never bothered Lucien until those looks, and Vincent's shameless flirting, had twice ended Lucien's betrothal. To wed a woman who openly yearned for another
was a humiliation he had refused to submit to, most especially when the other man was his own brother.

Lucien breathed deeply through flared nostrils. "For all
your obsession with this accursed ocean, you are more
wise than I," he said.

Nicholas clapped a hand to his shoulder. "For a moment there, cousin, I was certain you meant to do me
harm."

"I did," Lucien muttered.

"Then I am fortunate, indeed, that you rethought it."

Deciding it was well past time for a change of topic,
Lucien turned to his reason for seeking his cousin out.
Since meeting up with him in Tangier, he'd not had the
time to address the concerns that now badgered him, his
worry for Alessandra having consumed him completely.

"I would know what you know of Falstaff," he said, referring to his home. "What changes have been wrought
since last I was there?"

Nicholas pushed a hand through his hair, kneaded the
muscles at the back of his neck, then shrugged. "I have
been no farther than London for more than a year now,
Lucien. I hardly dare venture too far from my ship lest
the Church clap me into irons for turning renegade."

"A fool thing to do."

Nicholas looked not the least bit remorseful. "At the
time it served its purpose."

"I am not even going to ask what that was."

Nicholas's eyes danced with merriment. "Wise," he
said, then returned to the subject at hand. "When last I
was at Falstaff, all was as it should be—with the exception that you were thought to be dead, Lucien." His voice
turned serious. "Your father was heartbroken to have let
you go to France with his angry words ringing in your
ears. It was his greatest sorrow that he would never be
able to make it right between the two of you."

Lucien nodded. For weeks he and his father had argued over Lucien going to France to fight a war his father

regarded as futile and witless. Harsh words had been spoken on both sides, with Lucien finally riding away from Falstaff angry and resentful. In the end, though, his father had been proven right, and Lucien intended to bend his knee to him and admit it once he stood before him again.

"All will be right when I return," he said, almost to himself. "I will make it right."

"The feud between the Bayards and your family was still being seeded and occasionally yielding bitter harvest," Nicholas continued. "Vincent was gambling away whatever he could lay his hands to, and Jervais ... You would not recognize your youngest brother, Lucien. He has become a worthy knight. His shoulders are broad, his muscles well developed, and when he speaks, one does turn an ear to him."

"And my mother?"

"Well."

"Giselle?" he asked of his little sister.

Nicholas smiled. "What can I say? The mite has a mouth on her which I would venture rivals that of Alessandra. Though your mother tries to discipline her, Giselle is more often out of control. Very strong of mind for a girl child."

Lucien did not say it, but it was Giselle he looked most forward to seeing again. "Any more?" he asked.

"That is really all I know."

"Though a year can change even that."

"Aye, that it can. A drink?"

Nicholas offered his wineskin, and Lucien took a draft of it.

"Change is not always bad, Lucien," Nicholas said after taking a swallow himself. "After all, it has brought you back from the dead."

What he was saying without saying it, Lucien thought, was that if things were different when Lucien arrived at Falstaff, he should be accepting of those changes—openminded.

Bidding Nicholas good eve, Lucien headed back across the deck.

Solemn, Nicholas went to the rail and looked across the

water to the moon's reflection on its sweet, sweet curves. He groaned at the analogy, well aware he sometimes took this thing about the ocean being a woman too far. If he was not careful—

He chuckled, then worked through the conversation he'd had with Lucien. Coming to the end of it, he heaved a sigh. There was only one thing he had neglected to mention—perhaps an important thing, but better overlooked for the time being.

Had he told Lucien of his father's illness, it would be a much longer voyage than it needed to be, for Nicholas knew the guilt that would be Lucien's. Also, there was always the possibility the old man had recovered. A very good possibility considering the stuff the De Gautiers were made of.

CHAPTER 19

Alessandra crinkled her nose. "It is an interesting game," she said, studying the ivory cubes Lucien and she had been tossing for the past half hour, "but not much fun."

Chuckling, he swept the cubes into his palm. " 'Tis called dice," he said, "a game quite popular in England. In fact, my brother Vincent has but to hold a pair in his hand and he loses all but the clothes upon his back."

Alessandra drew her knees up and rested her chin on them. "I prefer chess," she said, staring at the distant coast of Portugal.

"And your donkey game," he reminded her.

She hid her smile against her knees. "It makes me laugh. Were you not so English, you might see the fun of it."

"And were you not so Arab, you might see how ridiculous a game it is."

She pinned him with her gaze. "You surprise me," she said.

"How is that?"

She threw her hands into the air. "These past days you have been ceaseless in reminding me that I am English, instructing me in all manners of that culture, and now you call me Arab?"

Lucien frowned. "I said that?"

"Aye."

"Hmm, a mistake for certain," he said. "It must be your determination to cling to pagan ways that confuses me."

"Have I not been a willing pupil?" she asked huffily. "I

lift my skirts and measure my steps when I walk. I curtsy and use polite address even though there is not one seaman on board deserving of such respect. I eat that most terrible fare with a smile on my face. I have learned your dances and suffered the wearing of these gowns. I—"

"All that, and yet you refuse to wear head cover to preserve your fair skin." Leaning forward, he tapped a finger to each of the freckles the sun had warmed to a darker pigment.

Alessandra's lashes fluttered down—not to hide embarrassment, but to mask the emotion his touch aroused. Since they had left Tangier, he had played the gentleman well. Too well. All she'd had of him were kisses stolen amid laughter, frustration, and uncomfortable silence. As she had from the beginning, she wanted more of him, but he continued to distance himself.

"I like the sun," she said, excusing the overabundance of freckles. Tossing her head, she stood, propped her elbows on the railing, and cupped her chin in her palms.

Dropping the dice into a pouch, Lucien also rose. "You will not see much of it once we reach England," he said. "Especially now that summer is almost past."

"Mother said it could be a chill place."

" 'Tis the reason so many babes are born during high summer."

"How is that?"

Laughter in his eyes, Lucien turned her to face him. "When the clouds are weeping their rain and the air is so cold it bites, the best place to be is abed. With a lover."

Forcing herself to hold his teasing gaze, Alessandra swallowed hard. "Is—is that what you do?"

He raised his eyebrows, but left her question unanswered.

Alessandra felt a fool and, being a fool, decided some time alone in her cabin might be in order. "I suppose you do," she said, her attempt at flippancy sounding false to her ears. Smiling tightly, she stepped around him and descended the steps.

Though he followed her all the way to the cabin, she pretended ignorance, going so far as to close the door in his face.

His foot prevented it from seating itself. "You are angry with me?" he asked as he entered the cabin and closed the door behind him.

"Angry?" She shook her head. "Nay. I am tired, that is all." She busied herself with straightening her few possessions.

"What do you want from me, Alessandra?"

The unexpected question stunned her to stillness. He knew. He had to know. Had she not confessed it to him before? Very well, she would say it again if it meant she might reach him.

Squaring her shoulders, she walked over to him. "I want you, Lucien," she said, wishing her voice would not quake so. "I want to know what you have denied me—what you have denied yourself."

He stared at her, his eyes searching for something she wished she understood.

The air had grown heavy with his silence, and she tried to lighten it with wit. "And if you tell me that is not how an English noblewoman speaks, I shall scream."

Lucien frowned, his jaw clenching as he fought something Alessandra could only wonder at. Then his grievous sigh filled the cabin. "I make no lie of it," he said. "I desire you."

"Then why—"

"The time must be right when it happens, Alessandra, if it is to happen at all."

Cupping her face, he leaned down and touched his lips to hers. And that was all.

Tears brightening her eyes, Alessandra looked up at him. "I will not ask you again, Lucien," she vowed.

"You are coming along nicely," he replied, and was gone a moment later.

She tried to contain it. Tried her damnedest. But her frustration escaped. Yanking off a shoe, she threw it at the door.

Though Alessandra wanted to remain in the cabin and forgo the nooning meal, the woman in her scolded her for such immature thoughts.

"Very well," she said aloud. "I will come to you, Lucien."

She found both him and Nicholas in the small galley. They looked up when she entered, but did not pause in their consumption of the salted meat and fish laid out before them. Only when Alessandra came around the table to seat herself on the long bench next to Lucien did he speak.

"Sit next to Nicholas," he instructed her.

Was he so angry with her that he did not want her near him? she wondered.

"A lesson," he clarified upon seeing the distress cross her face.

Almost as bad as him being angry with her, Alessandra thought. Sighing, she took the bench alongside Nicholas, though she set herself several feet from him.

Truly, it could not be said there was any relationship between her and Lucien's cousin, but whatever little there was had remained strained—of both their doing.

Without looking up from the meat he was pulling a strip from, Lucien said, "Closer."

"Why?"

"Closer," he repeated.

Drawing a deep breath, she edged nearer, though not significantly so.

"More," Lucien said.

Entertaining the idea of abandoning the meal altogether, Alessandra looked to Nicholas. Though his attention was directed to the goblet he held, a smile quirked his lips.

He was laughing at her childishness, she realized, expecting her to jump up and run away. Determined to wipe the humor from his face, she lifted her bottom from the bench and seated herself so near him, their thighs touched. Immediately, his smile dropped, his startled gaze swinging to her.

It was Alessandra's turn to smile. "This close?" she asked, turning innocent eyes upon Lucien.

The meat no longer held his attention. "Nay," he growled. "No respectable English lady would sit so near a man—not even her own husband."

"I will remember that," she said, though she made no move to distance herself from Nicholas. Thus, it was he who moved away from her.

An uncomfortable silence fell among them until the wiry old cook came out from behind the screen in the corner. Bearing two great trenchers, he set one before Lucien, the other between Alessandra and Nicholas.

Wrinkling her nose at the smell wafting toward her, Alessandra leaned forward and looked into the rock-stale, scooped-out loaf of bread that served as a trencher. Within was a thick concoction in which pieces of meat, fish, lentils, and other unnameables floated. She swallowed hard, unable to imagine putting any of it down her throat.

Sitting back, she met Lucien's gaze. "I . . . am suddenly not very hungry," she said.

His left eyebrow arched. "Still, you will eat."

"Must I?"

"There is no lesson otherwise. Now try the stew."

Steeling herself, Alessandra picked up the spoon and reached to pull the trencher directly before her. However, Nicholas's hand shot out and prevented her from doing so.

Indignant, she stared at him. "Now what?" she asked.

" 'Tis also Nicholas's trencher," Lucien informed her. "In England, sharing food between two is common."

It was difficult enough becoming used to dining among men, but to share food as well? Alessandra shook her head.

"Did your mother never tell you of such things?" Lucien asked.

Vaguely, she remembered Sabine speaking of it, but it had been only talk. How primitive the reality. It seemed there were more things better left Arab than English. "Aye, she did," Alessandra admitted.

"Then I need not explain further."

Stamping down a retort, she dipped her spoon into the stew and carried it to her mouth. The broth crossed her lips with difficulty, but once it made her tongue, the going was much easier, as it proved more palatable than any meal she had had thus far aboard ship.

Hungry again, she dipped a second time, but her spoon clashed with Nicholas's.

"You must await your turn," Lucien said.

Withdrawing, Alessandra watched with growing irritation as Nicholas took his time fishing about the trencher for a morsel worthy of him. Finally, his spoon curved around a large piece of meat, dipped to take it up, but in the next moment abandoned it.

Vexed, Alessandra looked up and found him watching her. "Mayhap you would like to choose one for me, my lady," he said.

"I would not!"

"This is not a lesson in the code of love, Nicholas," Lucien said sharply.

Nicholas sighed. "Nay, I suppose not." Grinning, he took a spoonful of the stew and lifted it to his mouth, where it hovered a long moment. "Though it could be," he mused. "You must take care not to neglect that part of Alessandra's education."

" 'Tis none of your concern, cousin."

Alessandra reveled in Lucien's jealousy, for it could be nothing but that. Was this, then, what it would take to make him pay her more notice? Reckless, she scooted near Nicholas again and laid her hand to his arm.

"Tell me of this code of love," she invited him.

He looked momentarily taken aback. His brow furrowed, lips thinned, he glanced down to where her skirts brushed his chausses, then back up to her imploring gaze.

Knowing light entered his eyes—knowledge of what she intended. His gaze shifted to Lucien, but when he looked at her again, a smile twitched at his lips.

"Love," he said. "Let me think." He took another bite of the stew, chewed thoughtfully, then nodded. "Ah, yes, 'tis a fine thing."

Avoiding the bore of Lucien's eyes, Alessandra ate more of the stew while she awaited Nicholas's explanation.

"A lover must submit to his lady the same as a knight would his lord. He swears loyalty and enduring service to her. . . ." Trailing off, he licked from his fingers the juice that had run down them.

"And?" Alessandra prompted.

Lucien felt on the verge of eruption, the jealousy Alessandra sought tearing gaping holes in him. Fisting his hands to keep from giving over to the raw emotion, he stared at the two.

"The lady then offers him some favor," Nicholas continued. "Of course, you must not submit too soon, Alessandra, for your lover must suffer at least a little. And once you do accept him as your lover—"

"When you say lover, do you mean—"

"Enough!" Lucien shot straight up, and would have upended his bench had it not been secured to the floor. Rounding the table, he took Alessandra by the arm and pulled her off her bench and toward the door. "We will talk later of this, you and I," he warned Nicholas, then pushed Alessandra up the steps and into the sunlight.

From below, Nicholas's hearty laughter followed them.

Lifting her skirts, Alessandra matched Lucien's pace as he led her toward their cabin. Suddenly, though, he changed direction and steered her instead to the shadow thrown by the mainmast.

The way he felt, Lucien knew it would be a mistake to be alone with her, for his anger was likely to manifest itself in the sexual frustration that grew with each look, touch, and word from Alessandra. Here it was safer—for both of them.

Releasing her, he spread his legs and thrust his hands to his hips. "Have you learned naught from all I have taught you?" he demanded in a low, strained voice so none could overhear.

Alessandra also braced her feet apart to accommodate the roll of the ship. "I have learned plenty," she answered, "and found little of it enjoyable—except, of course, the dance and Nicholas's talk of love."

"Which he knows little enough of," Lucien retorted. "He who loves none but the ocean."

"And you know more?" she challenged.

Her arrow hit the mark. Shuttering his face and narrowing his eyes to fine slits, Lucien said, "I know what a lady does and does not discuss with a man who is not her husband. That the only lover a true lady takes is the one she is wed to."

He watched as regret—and something else—doused the spark of recklessness in Alessandra's eyes. Lowering her head, she stared at his booted feet. "Is that why you will not become my lover, Lucien? Why you give me no more than kisses when what I want—"

Belatedly, she remembered her promise not to be the one to mention lovemaking again. Lucien was silent for a minute, then he stepped forward and lifted her chin.

"I have told you, Alessandra. When the time is right—"

"But you have also said that a lady beds only her husband. Will you, then, marry me, Lucien?" Immediately, she regretted the words, but they had been said, and there was naught she could do to pull them back.

His jaw clenched, a flurry of emotions reflecting in his eyes, then a strange calm settled upon his face. He swept a strand of hair out of her eyes and tucked it behind her ear. "Twice I have been betrothed, Alessandra, and twice broken the betrothal. Marriage does not bode well for me."

Her breath caught. At last he had opened himself to her—given her a small piece of who he really was. "Why did you break them?" she asked.

As if it did not pain him, he shrugged. "Neither woman was faithful to me."

"You were cuckolded?"

He shook his head. "But I would have been."

She laid her hands to his arms. "How do you know this?"

Though he looked at her face, his eyes grew distant, as if he was staring through her. "The way they looked at my brother Vincent," he said. "Once they laid eyes upon his handsome face, 'twas obvious it was he they wanted."

Alessandra could not imagine why. True, Lucien was not the most handsome of men, but she still thought him quite generous of looks and character. "And you think I would do the same?" she asked softly.

" 'Twould seem likely."

"Then you do not know me," she said, sorrow making her turn from him.

He hesitated, then pulled her back against him, wrapping his arms around her. "But I *do* know you, Alessandra," he said into her hair. "I know you set out to make me jealous of Nicholas, and that you did it because you believe it is me you want. But you have too little experience with men to know for certain."

Sinking further into his body and thrilling at the feel of him against her backside, she dropped her head to his shoulder and peered up at him. "I have never been more certain of anything," she said.

His gaze stroked the curve of her face, then lower, the rise and fall of her chest. "You are not acting the lady," he murmured.

She felt the tremor go through him, his desire evidenced by the frank hardness of his manhood. "I do not need to pretend with you, Lucien," she whispered.

His eyes returned to hers, searched deeply, then he tilted her face higher. "Nay, you do not," he said, and he covered her mouth with his.

Alessandra did not feel the strain in her neck as he tenderly savored her lips. Instead, she felt his desire seep into her skin and coil about every part of her that was woman.

"Yes," she breathed into his mouth.

His answer was the tongue he touched to hers. And then he withdrew. When her eyes opened, he asked, "Truce?"

She smiled. "Aye, Lucien."

Stepping back, he slid his hand down her arm and twined his fingers with hers. "My trencher is still nearly full," he said. "Would you share it with me?"

More enthused than she had been when forced to share with Nicholas, Alessandra nodded.

CHAPTER 20

"Storm a-comin'!" cried the seaman as he monkeyed down the mast. "Storm a-comin'!"

Hands clasped behind his back, Nicholas slowly turned and stared at the horizon that had been open and clear when last he had looked. Now, however, swiftly advancing storm clouds blurred the line between ocean and sky.

He had thought it might come to this, that here in the Bay of Biscay his dark mistress would make him pay for his betrayal with the Mediterranean. He nearly laughed at himself, but sobered as the seriousness of the situation settled upon his shoulders.

For two days they had navigated the bay off the French coast. It was difficult and dangerous enough due to the prevailing northwest winds and a strong current, but now it might prove disastrous.

Knowing he could not chance hugging so near the coast and the rocks upon which his ship might be crushed, Nicholas called down to the helmsman, "Take her out!"

It would require vast open water for *Jezebel* to weather the storm if it proved to be a severe one—and there was little doubt of that.

Nicholas drew a deep breath of the heavy air, savored it, then began ordering his men. Like the well-trained and experienced sailors they were, each came alive and rushed to do his bidding. The sails were adjusted, the ropes corrected, and all with a deep awareness of peril—

and an excitement that only a man of the sea could appreciate.

"It looks serious," Lucien said as he mounted the steps to where Nicholas stood.

A slight smile betraying his grave expression, Nicholas nodded. "Aye, a tempest. Every hand will be needed to beat it back. Think you are up to it, cousin?"

"I am," Lucien said, staring at the gathering clouds and remembering other storms he had braved. On the galley he had slaved on, wind and rain and ocean water had beat upon him as he and the numerous other slaves had fought to save themselves and their masters from the wrath of a vicious sea. In fact, had he not been chained to his oar for a recently committed offense, one of those storms would have given him the same watery burial as several of the oarsmen who had rowed in front of and in back of him.

"Good," Nicholas said, then frowned. "Where is Alessandra?"

Lucien struggled out of the grip of bitter memories and back to the present. "She is in the cabin practicing her writing," he answered.

Though her Arabic lettering was quite beautiful, he'd discovered her English penmanship was appalling. As usual, she had argued with him over the necessity of the exercise, but had given in after extracting a promise from him that on the morrow she would have a day free of lessons.

"She is to remain there," Nicholas said.

Lucien nodded. "I will go tell her now, and return shortly to assist in securing the ship."

Nicholas watched him go, then looked again to the sky. It would not be so terrible if the storm had come upon them in daylight, but there was perhaps only an hour left before night descended.

He called for the sails to be brought about, then gazed far across the agitated water. "Whore," he muttered. "And what will be my reward if I win this one?"

Might he reach England before the other ships that had set sail before him? Might his cargo recover the value it had been reduced by when rescuing Alessandra had delayed his departure from Tangier? Though it was a slim possibility, he gave over to the challenge and smiled.

"That is quite a feat," Lucien commented with obvious pun.

The ink-dipped quill slipped from between Alessandra's toes and fell to the floor.

"Oh!" she exclaimed, sitting up in her cot and drawing her legs back onto the mattress. She had not heard him enter. "I did not expect you back so soon."

"Obviously." Striding forward, he bent and retrieved the quill. "Is this, then, how you earn your day free of lessons?"

She scrambled for the parchments she'd been practicing on. "My hand grew cramped," she explained, "so while I waited it out, I thought I would see if it was possible to hold the quill between my toes as I do my fingers." One by one, she raised each of the three examples of writing for him to see.

He grimaced. "Surely you can do better than that."

She turned one back around and studied it. "What do you mean? 'Tis much improved—by far."

Lucien shook his head, then shifted to the reason he had come below. "A storm is headed our way. You will remain here until I tell you 'tis safe to come out. Understood?"

"Oh, but I would see it!" she protested, swinging her legs over the cot to hop down from it.

Lucien stayed her with a hand to her shoulder. "You need only feel it, Alessandra," he said, his patience thinning. "Which you most definitely will here in the cabin."

"But—"

"If need be, I will lock you in."

Knowing he would do just that, Alessandra groaned her disappointment. "Very well, I will stay put. But you will come to me and tell me what is happening from time to time, won't you?"

"If I am able to."

Which, she knew, meant it was unlikely.

"Remain in the cot," he directed her. "It will take much of the turbulence." As if on cue, the ship lurched to the side, back to midpoint, then to the side again. "It has started," Lucien said.

Resignedly, Alessandra turned onto her side, pillowed her head on an outstretched arm, and peeked up at him. "You will take care, won't you, Lucien?" she asked, suddenly fearful for his safety.

His face softened. Leaning down, he stroked a finger along the curve of her jaw and laid it to her lips. "All will be well," he said.

Alessandra searched his eyes and, glimpsing his inner strength, gained courage from it.

At the door, he turned and looked at her. Their gazes locked, broken only when he turned to blow out the lantern. "Keep it unlit," he said. " 'Twill be safer."

Feeling rather melancholy, she stared at the door he closed behind him. "Lord, protect him . . . and the crew . . . and Nicholas," she prayed. Though she and the enigmatic captain would never be boon companions, she had discovered a liking for him, and it seemed only right she name him as well.

Alessandra tried to doze, to speed the storm on its way, but found no relief from mounting misgivings as the squall built, nor an easing of her troubled stomach.

Staring into the dark, she gripped the ropes of the cot as it pitched hard right, her ears straining to hear Nicholas's shouted orders.

"Down the mainsail!" she heard.

"Down the mainsail!" Another repeated the order to those who could not hear the captain above the wind's angry howl.

Shortly, there followed a terrible screeching sound, then a thunderous clapping as the sailcloth dropped from on high.

Immediately, the ship righted from its precipitous incline, then there was calm, almost as if the storm had come to an abrupt end.

Fooled, Alessandra loosed her hold on the ropes. In the next instant she was thrown from the cot as the ship slammed to the left. Reflexively, she threw her arms out, giving them the brunt of the fall, and slid across the floor on her belly. The cradle where floor met wall was where she came to rest, but only for a moment. Then she began to backslide.

"Dear God," she gasped, searching for something to hold on to. "Save us." She hooked an arm around the leg of the bolted-down table she came up against and listened for sounds above. All she heard was the pounding of the ocean against the creaking hull.

Had they all been swept overboard? she wondered, her mind a frenzy. Lucien? Fervently, she began to pray, her lips moving steadily, sobs paining her throat, and her mind groping for promises to God if He delivered them from the hands of death.

Then, mercifully, she heard shouted voices. Her relief was short-lived, though, for clearly she heard, "Man overboard!"

Lucien. Dear God, was it he? Lifting her head, she looked across the dark cabin to the door. Could she make it before the next swell knocked her aside? She had to try. Had to know.

Letting go of her life hold, she used the roll of the ship to hurry her to the door, then managed to make it to her feet. Twice she stumbled and fell, but on the third attempt, she wrenched the door open.

Staggering down the narrow passageway, hands to the walls on both sides of her, she wet her feet up to the ankles in water that had leaked through the hatch. The steps suddenly before her, she went down on hands and knees and crawled her way up them.

A sharp listing effortlessly tossed her against the wall, but she regained her footing. After what seemed an interminable time, she threw back the hatch to a night turned hellish.

Stinging spray lashed at her face and hands, the frigid wind seized her hair and whipped it into her eyes, and before her, men who were only shadows ran to unknown places in their bid to beat the storm.

"Lucien!" she called. The wind snatched her voice away and tossed it overboard with the hapless man who had gone before. Holding to the hatch with one hand to keep her balance, she cupped the other alongside her mouth and called again, but with the same result.

Fleetingly, she thought of the vow she had made Lucien to stay below, but just as quickly abandoned it. Dragging her skirts out of the way, she stepped onto the deck and seized the nearest handhold—a half-dozen casks that had been lashed together. Holding with both hands to the wet rope wound around them, she suffered the punishment of the storm and looked frantically about for a sign of Lucien.

"Please God," she mumbled, "let him show himself to me." In the near darkness, one shadow looked much like another, none differentiating itself by great height or width.

With the coming of another great swell, Alessandra's feet slipped out from beneath her, and though she continued to hold to her lifeline, she fell hard upon her knees. It was then she heard something—her name being called?

She had barely made her feet when the wave struck her and broke her hands free from the rope. Water all around her, in her mouth and nose, she was swept back toward the railing and the certain death of an unmerciful ocean. Desperately, she flailed for something to catch hold of. Nothing . . . nothing . . .

Something caught hold of her and slammed her to the deck.

The wave passed over the rail, but before she had time to drag a breath of air, another hit and beat upon the man stretched over her. When it also went the way of the other, the man surged to his feet and brought her with him.

"Lucien?" she said with the first breath she drew.

He didn't answer. Throwing her over his broad shoulder, he ran for the hatch, intent upon reaching it before the ocean. He did, but only just.

It had to be Lucien, Alessandra told herself. The feel of him was too familiar to be any other. Praying she was not mistaken, that it was not wishful thinking, she clung to him as he carried her down the steps. Behind them, the water pounded at the hatch that he had closed, but it could no more than trickle its way through the cracks.

In the cabin again, Alessandra was dropped to her feet. "You gave me your word and then broke it," Lucien growled into the darkness. "You were not to move from this cabin."

Wet and cold, but barely feeling either, Alessandra flung herself back into his arms. "You're alive," she cried, her desperate hands feeling up his back to know for certain it was he she clung to.

Lucien disengaged her hands and set her away from him. However, in the next instant, he pulled her back to him to keep her from tumbling with the ship's lurching roll.

"Aye, I'm alive," he said, "but only by the grace of God are you."

"And you," she reminded him.

His silence spoke anger at her more loudly than his words. "I'm sorry, Lucien," she apologized, pressing her face against his warm, wet chest. "I heard it called that a man had gone overboard and feared it might have been you."

"An unfortunate soul," Lucien muttered, then set her back from him. " 'Twas foolish of you, Alessandra. Even had it been me gone overboard, there was naught you could have done." His voice was gruff, but not as gruff as she deserved.

"You are right," she admitted. "But I had to know."

"Why?" he asked, wondering what answer he hoped for.

The violent heaving of the ship denied him any answer. Steadying her, Lucien waited out the worst of it, then lifted Alessandra and felt his way to her cot. With its swaying, it was no mean feat depositing her on it, but he managed it without mishap.

She reached for him. "Lucien, I—"

" 'Twill keep until later," he said. Though he started to turn away, the brush of her hand along his arm made him pause. Giving in to the weakness only she was capable of arousing, he captured her hand, held it a long moment between his, then laid it upon her breast. "I am needed on deck," he said, and swung away.

Alone again, Alessandra heard the unmistakable scrape

of metal on metal as Lucien locked her in the cabin. He had made good his threat, but for how long? she wondered. How long before she saw him again?

Shivering more from fear that she would not see him again than from the cold of her wet, beaten body, she dragged the blanket over her and curled up with prayers tumbling from her lips.

He came to her again, pressing his forehead to hers, touching her mouth, nose, and eyes with soft kisses, and feathering fingers down her neck—though she wasn't sure whether or not it was a dream until the cot swung and his wet body stretched out beside her.

As her cot became wonderfully cramped with his large frame, Alessandra opened her eyes and gazed at the man who lay facing her. Though he looked fatigued, his eyes shot with red and darkly ringed from his battle with Nicholas's mistress, he had a smile for her.

She returned the smile, though hers was born more of relief—relief that it was done with. There had been times when she had thought the storm would never end, and though the long night had continually grown longer, it had finally given way to a rough dawn. However, only when she'd heard Lucien's shouted voice had she surrendered to her exhaustion. Mumbling thanks, she had drifted off to the sway of an ocean finally calmed.

"Lucien," she murmured, reaching a hand to touch his unshaven jaw.

He kissed her palm. " 'Tis over," he said.

"I know." She curled her fingers around the kiss. "You are still angry with me?"

His weary smile curved larger. "Nay, though I ought to be."

Encouraged, she edged nearer. "There were no more lost to the ocean, were there?"

Regret stiffened his body and drew his smile tight. "Nay, only the one, though that is one too many."

Impulsively, she reached up to smooth his furrowed brow. "I'm sorry," she said.

He nodded, then closed his eyes.

They lay silent a long time, though neither slept. Finally, Alessandra gathered the courage to ask the question she so wanted to know the answer to. "Why have you come to lie with me?"

Opening his eyes, he stared into hers. "To hold you," he said. Lifting the blanket from her, he smoothed a hand down her hip. " 'Tis what I promised myself once the storm was out—what kept me going."

Though his words blossomed hope within her, she could not help but wonder at them. To hold her, he'd said. Naught else? "Will you kiss me, Lucien?" she ventured, her color rising with the words. "Like you did that first time?"

Truly, all Lucien had wanted was to hold her in the curve of his body and breathe the scent of her, but her words stirred his battered body to life.

Though he knew he should not, he levered up onto an elbow and stared at her. "And how did I kiss you that first time?" he asked.

She blinked surprise. "You do not remember?"

"Well I remember, but I wish to hear it from you."

Her cheeks flamed. "I . . . you . . ." She sighed. "I do not know the words to tell you. 'Twas perfect, that is all I know."

"And my other kisses have not been perfect?"

"Nearly," she breathed, "but not as that first."

"Then let us see if we can re-create it." Lowering his head, Lucien claimed her lips with the hunger of a man who had been too long without such caresses.

Fortunately or not, it took no prompting for Alessandra to open to him, her own hunger demanding as he demanded. Taking his tongue in her mouth, she tasted the salt on it and marveled at the breath he filled her with. Wanting more of him, she slid her hands up his back to tangle in his hair, then arched to the masculine strength of him and let go of the small, desperate sounds of need mounting within her.

Deepening the kiss, Lucien glided his hand from her hip to her waist, then higher to her breast. His thumb and forefinger finding her seeking nipple, he stroked it rigid.

Alessandra pressed her restless body closer to his, wanting so badly she thought she might cry out. His mouth still possessing hers, Lucien turned her onto her back and settled his body over hers. She felt his need— the need he had thus far denied them both. Would he again? Praying that he would not, she lifted her hips into his and felt his need grow stronger.

Lucien muttered something as he tugged her damp skirts up, then his fingers found the inside of her thigh. Rough and callused, their stroking caused her to jerk with remembered response, then they moved higher. Lightly, he touched that place she so longed him to know better, but then he slid his hand back to her thigh.

His harsh sigh rippled the air. "You know what I feel for you, don't you?" he asked, lifting his head and seeking her gaze.

Surely he loved her as she loved him, Alessandra thought hopefully. Surely that was what he felt for her. "What do you feel for me, Lucien?" she asked, breathless as she awaited the answer she most desired.

Regret in his eyes, he pushed her skirts down and lay back. " 'Tis enough that I feel," he said, his eyes fixed overhead, "which is why this can go no further."

Hardly able to believe he meant to put an end to it, Alessandra sat up. "Are you toying with me, Lucien?" she asked, suddenly fearful this could be his revenge against the Bayards.

"Nay, I am not. I did not intend that this would happen."

Defeated, she looked away. He still would not say he loved her . . . and she would not ask him to. If it was love he felt for her, the words must come from him.

"Though you may not wish it," he said, "you are still a lady, Alessandra, and 'tis how I will give you over to old man Bayard—not with my whelp growing in your belly." Certainly not until they had lain together as man and wife.

That last thought shook Lucien, but he used the lame excuse of being tired so he would not have to ponder it. It was far too disturbing a notion for a man twice betrothed and twice of broken betrothal.

Pulling Alessandra's unresisting body down beside him, he nestled her against him as he'd originally intended. "Let us sleep now," he said. " 'Twill do us both good."

pillati i.aappti nie in ban. braune bbuirscrlatter, oncauni-

※❀✿❀※

CHAPTER 21

"I see it," Alessandra exclaimed.

Proud and austere, the distant keep of Falstaff rose from a still fog, almost as if floating atop a cloud. Of the walls surrounding it, only intermittent crenellations were visible, and only if one peered closely. Even the village Lucien had spoken of was nowhere to be seen, cloaked in the same curious morning haze.

Since arriving in England, Alessandra had marveled at this new land. Granted, it was rather chill and damp compared with Algiers, but its newness satisfied a hunger in her she had long known.

The London of lore, where the ship had laid anchor, had been thoroughly intriguing, beckoning her to explore its crowded streets and shops. And she would have, had Lucien not been in such a hurry. To her disappointment, shortly after securing horses and provisions, he had announced it time to ride north. Nicholas had accompanied them to the outskirts of the city. Far more genial since discovering he'd been granted the wind to reach London ahead of the ships that had left Tangier before him, he had kissed Alessandra's hand, then waved her and Lucien on their way.

Verdant countryside and wooded forests had passed by in a blur. Inns with their coarse English-speaking people had provided a place to bed down for the night. Strange food and drink, which Alessandra had been given only a brief introduction to during the weeks aboard ship, was palatable, though more often than not unsettled her stomach.

It was an adventure, but one that would soon end once Lucien fulfilled the bargain he had struck with her mother and delivered her to James Bayard.

She swallowed hard to dislodge the anxiety in her throat. If only she could delay the inevitable a bit longer. If only Lucien would give in and take her with him to Falstaff.

Looking at him, she caught a glimpse of longing in his eyes as he stared at his home. Then, becoming aware of her regard, he blinked the emotion away and twisted in his saddle to meet her imploring gaze.

"Lucien, I do not think I am ready for Corburry," she said.

He smiled. "More likely Corburry is not ready for you."

He'd said it before, and always with humor, but this time Alessandra found the comment less than amusing. "Perhaps," she said, averting her gaze.

A lengthy quiet ensued, then Lucien sidled his mount alongside hers. "We have discussed this many times," he reminded her.

She tilted her head back. "Aye, but still I would prefer to travel to Falstaff first. What can it hurt?"

There was no hesitation in his response. "Nay. What awaits me there, I cannot say, but I will not have you witness it."

She knew it impetuous to throw into his face, but his obstinacy and her fear of what awaited her at Corburry forced the foolish words from her mouth. "What is it you're frightened of?"

His face darkened. "Frightened? Such emotions are for children, Alessandra, and that I no longer am."

The relationship that had evolved between them during the long voyage was strained. It was not a relationship born of friendship, nor one of lovers, but a curious mix of the two. And now it appeared to be crumbling.

Attempting to salvage what her words had wreaked havoc on, Alessandra mustered a brave face. "I'm sorry," she said. "I understand your reasons."

Lucien crooked a finger beneath her chin. "Nay, you do not, but you will see it is for the best."

Though she did not believe him, she nodded, then pressed her heels into the sides of her mare.

Bracing himself for what awaited him at Corburry, Lucien overtook her and set the pace that would see them at their destination by midday.

The castle of Corburry was a fortress, erected of ponderous blocks of stone, silent testimony to the perpetual feud that had been waged between the Bayards and the De Gautiers for nearly one hundred and fifty years. Its imposing gatehouse and curtain walls bore evidence of that conflict, various sections having been repaired with stone of differing shades. From the center of the inner ward rose a nondescript cylindrical keep. According to Lucien, therein resided her family.

Misgiving upon misgiving weighted Alessandra's shoulders as she stared at the destiny her mother had forced upon her. Though dear, sweet Catherine Bayard had been certain this was where her daughter belonged, Alessandra was doubtful. The adventure now come to an end, what awaited her?

"Something is wrong." Lucien's voice broke into her thoughts. His mouth set in a grim line, his gaze riveted upon the castle, he touched the hilt of his dagger, then his sword.

Alessandra looked at him. "Wrong? What do you mean?"

He did not glance her way. "I can count on one hand the number of soldiers that walk the walls."

She looked back at the castle, quickly tallying the four figures there. "How many hands does it usually take?"

Her innocent query brought his head around, his grim mouth softening. "Many, Alessandra. James Bayard is not a man to take chances."

"Unlike you," she said, quick to remind him of the many chances he had taken to bring her out of Algiers.

His eyebrows dropped low, then settled back into place. "Aye, unlike me," he agreed.

Disconcerted by the intensity of his stare, she looked away. "Think you it a ruse, then?"

"Likely."

More than the scarcity of soldiers at the walls, Lucien wondered why none had appeared to halt their progress. Only by stealth had he and his kin advanced so near without meeting resistance.

"Perchance the castle folk are in worship," Alessandra suggested. " 'Tis Sunday, after all." Purposely, she melded *it* and *is* into one, a nuance of the English language she had been working at mastering these past weeks. However, she had no intention of masking the accent that marked her as a foreigner.

"You still have much to learn," Lucien muttered.

It did not get past her. "Then teach me," she challenged.

He urged his horse forward and down the rise. "Nay, I leave that to your father," he tossed over his shoulder.

Alessandra trailing, they approached the castle in clear view, finally stirring those atop the walls from their listlessness.

"Cover your hair," Lucien instructed.

Alessandra tugged at a curl falling past her shoulder. "Why?" she asked. Though it had been difficult for her to become accustomed to going about with face and hair uncovered, she was beginning to like the freedom. In fact, all would be agreeable if not for the awkward clothing that still hindered her movements.

"Do as I ask!" Lucien snapped.

Her indignation flared, but she resisted argument. Lifting the hood of her mantle, she adjusted it atop her head and tucked her hair out of sight. "Better?" she asked.

Without confirming that she had done as ordered, for his eyes were trained straight ahead, he nodded.

Alessandra sighed. She much preferred the Lucien she had come to know on board ship to this one. Once again he had turned warrior—alert, calculating, predatory—his guise of gentleman conspicuously absent.

His suspicions mounting steadily, Lucien proceeded toward the castle with even greater caution than before. When would the attack come, and from where? he wondered, following each move of those visible to him while searching for those who must lie in wait.

It made no sense. Though the portcullis was in place, effectively barring entrance to the castle, the drawbridge remained lowered—and no attempt was being made to raise this all-important bastion of defense. Why? Peace? He scoffed at the thought, refusing to believe two years' absence had brought about such inconceivable change. But what else might it be?

He reined his horse in before the drawbridge, ignoring Alessandra when she drew alongside him.

In no hurry, a bearded man appeared at the portcullis. "Who calls?" he demanded.

Peering closely, Lucien dredged up recognition of the man he had encountered in a skirmish when he had been all of ten and four summers old.

"Do you not recognize the one responsible for your hobble, Sully?" he called.

Pregnant silence.

Lucien smiled a hard smile. He had come close to killing the bastard that wet, miserable morn. In spite of his upbringing, however, he had been unprepared to take his first life. Within the year, that had changed forever.

"Lucien de Gautier," the man said hoarsely, awkwardly crossing himself.

"Aye, 'tis I who comes to call on your heathen lord. Summon him."

Sully grasped the bars and pressed his long face between them. "By the fury of hell, be ye a ghost, man?"

So it was as Nicholas had said. Everyone thought he had died. "I am of flesh, the same as that which your dagger once cleaved," he shouted. "Now rouse old man Bayard and tell him I have come."

Sully did not look convinced, his gaze skittering to the cloaked figure alongside Lucien. "And who be that with ye?" he asked, obviously trying to see past the shadows the hood threw over Alessandra's face.

"Tell your lord 'tis long-lost kin I have brought him," Lucien answered.

"Long-lost kin," Sully repeated, glancing down at the

bit of Alessandra's gown, that peeked from beneath the hem of her mantle. "Do she have a name?"

" 'Twill be revealed for your lord," Lucien growled, his patience on the verge of disintegrating. "Now waste no more time and bring him hither."

Mumbling crude words, Sully turned and limped out of sight.

"You did not tell him," Alessandra said.

Lucien looked at her. "He will know soon enough."

She held his gaze a long moment, then looked at the castle again. There was no turning back now, she knew. Nothing left to argue.

Sully returned within minutes. "Lady Bayard requests you proceed to the keep," he said.

Lady Bayard? Alessandra thought. And who might that be? Foolish, she chastised herself. It had never occurred to her that her father might have remarried. Feeling a twinge of misplaced hurt, she quickly pushed it aside.

Lucien considered Sully and his invitation. Only once, as a youth, had he been within these walls, and then it had been as a captive. Did the Bayards think him foolish enough to go willingly into their viper's nest a second time? And why would they risk it? Even Lady Bayard would know better.

"What of Lord James?" Lucien asked.

"Ah . . ." Sully shuffled his feet in the damp earth. "The lord'll be along shortly."

Meaning he was elsewhere. Perhaps burning off his midday meal with his favorite pastime of pillaging and plundering De Gautier villages.

Lucien shook his head. "We will await him here—"

An ear-piercing squeal heralded the ascent of the iron portcullis, startling Alessandra's mount. Skittering back a step, the mare threw her head and would have bolted had Lucien not caught hold of the reins and brought the animal under control.

Alessandra opened her mouth to thank him, but he quieted her with a shake of his head. Returning the reins to her, he drew his sword and watched as Sully ducked beneath the gate and traversed the drawbridge.

Wide of shoulders and chest, but painfully short of stature, the man positioned himself a good ten feet from Lucien. Stroking the dagger at his waist, he eyed the sword raised against him, then lifted his gaze to Lucien's scarred face.

"Come back from the dead, did ye?" he said, the rounding of his cheeks the only evidence of his bearded smile. "Imagine that."

When Lucien's silence threatened to be without end, Sully shrugged. "Ye never were quite handsome, lad, and even less so now."

Alessandra was surprised at Lucien's control. Though his grip on the sword drained color from his hand, and his anger heated the cool air, he did not waver.

"'Tis fortunate for you and me," he said, "that how deeply a man buries his sword is not dependent on his countenance."

Sully laughed. "Is that what you proved in France?"

The leather of Lucien's saddle creaked with the tensing of his frame, but still he did not retaliate.

Alessandra glanced at Sully and was surprised by the disappointment reflected in his face. Did he strive to antagonize Lucien into a contest of weapons?

Thunder behind them brought all heads around. At first Alessandra saw only the empty meadow, but then a large party of riders crested the hill beyond it.

"See now, my lord Bayard has returned from a-hawking," Sully announced.

Lucien wheeled his steed around to face their coming.

Stamping down her anxiety, Alessandra did likewise, though with far less grace and ease.

Which one was her father? she wondered, scanning the approaching riders. Guessing he would be among those at the fore, she concentrated on the half dozen who rode there. It was a futile exercise, though, for they were still too distant for her to match one with the description her mother had occasionally given her.

"There," Lucien said, as if reading her thoughts. "Off center, left. He wears the green."

As he neared, the man Lucien had indicated became a

tall, stately figure whose russet-colored hair had not yet gone gray.

Lucien surprised Alessandra by reaching across and giving her hand a quick, reassuring squeeze. "Say nothing," he instructed, then straightened.

She nodded.

On the final approach, all but one of the riders slowed—James Bayard. Extricating himself from the pack, he galloped his horse forward.

If he was surprised to see it was Lucien who awaited him, he did not show it. Instead, he guided his horse to a place before his visitors, leaned forward, and wordlessly peered at the De Gautier come back from the grave.

Faced with the man who had sown her in her mother's womb, but had no knowledge his seed had born fruit, Alessandra began to tremble—not from fear, but an unexpected emotion. This handsome man was her father, the man who had loved her mother. Kind, Catherine had insisted, but driven by past generations to hate his neighbor.

In spite of his forty or more years, he appeared to be in good form, the wrinkles at the corners of his eyes and mouth surely created by laughter, not anger.

Until that moment Alessandra had wanted naught to do with him, but now she had a peculiar yearning to know him. After all, he was all she had—providing he accepted her.

James Bayard glanced at the cloaked woman beside De Gautier, attempted to see beyond her hood, then returned his gaze to Lucien. Behind him, his men assembled, muttering in surprise as they recognized the man they had all thought dead.

Sensing tension, the hooded falcon perched upon James's wrist bristled, its glossy feathers standing on end. Without breaking eye contact with Lucien, James calmed it with a caressing hand. "I knew it," he said, an ambivalent smile on his lips. "If a Bayard could not bring you down, neither could a Frenchman."

" 'Tis encouraging not all believed me dead," Lucien returned.

James shifted his gaze to Lucien's sword. "You come armed. I take it you demand satisfaction?"

"Two years' absence cannot have changed things so much that you should expect otherwise."

"But they have changed, haven't they?"

Lucien did not respond.

With a sweep of his arm, James indicated those behind him. "Only you would stand alone against so many."

"I've done it before."

"Aye, and nearly died for it."

"Nearly."

Regretful, James shook his head. "Ironic, isn't it? At last we are at peace with the De Gautiers and you return."

Lucien's sword wavered. "At peace?" he echoed.

Surprise flashed through James. "You've not been to Falstaff yet?"

"Nay, I came here first."

"Why?"

Sully pushed his way between Lucien and Alessandra's horses. "Kin, milord," he said, nodding to the cloaked figure. "He says this one be of Bayard stock."

His eyebrows drawing together in question, James looked again at the stranger. "Bayard, hmm? Let me see you."

Her moment at hand, her heart beating a wild tattoo, Alessandra raised her arm to push back the hood. However, Lucien stayed the unveiling. "Nay," he said to James. "In a moment, perhaps, but first I will hear more of this peace."

James looked ready to argue, but then shrugged. "Come out of this damned cold and we will talk," he said, and spurred his horse forward with a tap of his heels.

At Lucien's hesitation, he added, "As Bayards are welcome at Falstaff, De Gautiers are welcome at Corburry. Lay your suspicions aside and come share a warm fire with me."

Alessandra could see no harm in it, but felt Lucien's misgivings straight through. In the end, though, he acquiesced and turned his mount toward the drawbridge.

"And Lucien ..." James twisted in his saddle to address him.

"Aye?"

"There is no need for arms."

Another hesitation, then Lucien sheathed his weapon.

Riding silent beside a tense, suspicious Lucien, Alessandra marveled at the goings-on of the bailey they entered. Though it was fairly quiet this Sabbath day, it was a world unto itself with its towering granary, thatched barn and stables, odorous piggery, and sprawling smithy. It appealed to every curious bone in her body. She could not wait to explore it all.

Prior to reaching the inner bailey, the procession of men and horses split and disassembled. Only a handful continued on to the keep with their lord.

Passing over a smaller drawbridge, Alessandra began a search for the marbled walks, splashing fountains, and lush gardens with their fruit-bearing trees and multitude of flowers. They were nowhere in sight, only the austere keep and lesser buildings. It was a world far removed from the elegance of Jabbar's home, she realized with disappointment.

Pray, let it be handsome within, she thought. It seemed ages since last she'd been surrounded by beauty—beauty she'd always taken for granted.

Swinging out of the saddle, James tossed his reins to an attending squire and waited patiently at the base of the keep's steps for Lucien to join him.

Lucien dismounted, untied three of the four packs from his saddle, then came around his horse to assist Alessandra.

"Remember, say nothing." He spoke low as he gently set her to her feet.

"He does not seem so bad," Alessandra whispered, earning herself a malevolent glare.

"You do not know him as I do," Lucien growled.

True, but her mother had known James best and said he was kind. Thus far, Alessandra saw nothing to dissuade her from adopting the same opinion. However, accepting this was neither the time nor place to argue the matter, she closed her mouth and preceded Lucien up the steps.

Disappointment filled her as the man soon to learn he was her father stepped aside to allow her a view of Corburry's immense hall.

Though it appeared clean and orderly, the room's only claim to beauty were its colorful wall hangings. All else was stark and unappealing, including the castle folk with their drab clothing and air of indifference.

A bittersweet longing for the harem and its tumult of spirited personalities swept Alessandra. What dull lives these people must lead, she thought. Had no one ever told them of color and form? And where was the lively chatter and laughter that warmed a room as no fire ever could?

Aboard the ship, and later in the inns she and Lucien had stayed at, there had seemed no lack of gaiety and enthusiasm, though it had been of a different sort from that she was accustomed to. So why was Corburry cheerless?

Knowing it selfish of her, she prayed for a reasonable explanation. Perhaps someone had died . . . ?

As the massive door they had passed through groaned closed, a spot of color made its entrance via the stairs at the far end of the hall. A woman, Alessandra realized. Lady Bayard, perhaps?

James seemed not to notice her. Stepping to a raised dais, he lifted the falcon from his wrist, settled it on the back of an immense chair, then eased himself into the chair's embrace.

Halting twenty feet before the dais, Lucien caught Alessandra's arm and steered her from his right side to his left. She understood that he wanted no interference with his sword arm if it became necessary to wield his weapon.

Those of James's men who had accompanied him within scattered, though they did not go far. As if anticipating trouble, they positioned themselves about the hall.

"Come sit with me," James invited.

"Nay, I will stand," Lucien said, his gaze following the

brightly garbed woman as she took her position alongside James's chair.

"Lady Bayard," James introduced her.

Lucien inclined his head, prompting Alessandra to do the same.

Standing tall and proud, the woman lifted her chin and acknowledged the visitors with a lift of her plucked eyebrows. In spite of her haughty demeanor, Alessandra thought Lady Bayard looked flustered, even upset.

"It seems the De Gautier has come back from the dead, dear wife," James informed her with a half smile.

Obviously, she did not share his humor, her mouth tightening until her lips pinched gray-white.

"What of this peace you spoke of?" Lucien asked, blatantly ignoring propriety.

James motioned a hesitant serving woman forward and accepted the tankard of ale she brought him. "Some for you, friend?" he asked.

Alessandra watched the hollows beneath Lucien's cheekbones deepen, and the veins in his neck swell. "The peace," he reminded his host.

Shrugging, James lifted the tankard to his lips and took a long, deep swallow.

Doubting she saw right, Alessandra blinked and peered closer. Nay, she was not mistaken. The bottom of James's tankard *was* fit with glass, allowing him to keep his eyes on Lucien while he quaffed his ale. It could have no other purpose, could it?

James set the tankard on the arm of his chair, reclined, and clasped his hands across his middle. "We have been at peace with your family for nearly a year now," he said. "There is no more fighting. No more needless bloodshed. Your family—"

"How did it come to be?" Lucien interrupted.

"Your family and mine now come and go as they please without threat of injury," James continued, unabashed. "The villagers and their crops thrive. Children play in the meadows where once they feared to go. Peace has finally come to our lands, Lucien."

At that moment Alessandra thought Lucien looked capable of murder. Anxiously, she watched his hand go to his sword hilt and curl around it.

James's men must have also seen it, for they stepped from the shadows in readiness.

"At what price, peace?" Lucien ground out between clenched jaws.

James reclined farther, thrusting both legs out and crossing them at the ankles. "Do you intend to undo what has taken so long to be done?"

"That depends."

"On?"

"Your answer."

A sound, half groan, half sigh, escaped James's lips. "That which our families have fought over for more than a hundred years is now resolved," he said. "All rights and claims to Dewmoor Pass have been given to the Bayards."

Lucien's hand tightened on his weapon. "Never would my father agree to it."

"True ... he did not." James righted himself in the chair, his pretense at nonchalance at an end. "Neither could he. You see, young Lucien, Sebastian de Gautier is dead."

Stillness momentarily fell over Lucien, then a terrible, inhuman roar broke from his throat. Dropping the packs and thrusting Alessandra aside, he wrenched his sword from its scabbard and rushed at James Bayard.

It all happened much too fast for Alessandra to react, the commotion following Lucien's charge appearing to her like a warped dream.

A high-pitched scream—Lady Bayard's?—and the ring of iron resounded throughout the hall. Bodies flew past Alessandra, one knocking her to the floor. Like an angry swarm of bees, James's men fell upon Lucien a moment before he would have impaled the man where he sat.

"Bastard!" Lucien shouted, throwing his arm back and cracking his fist into the jaw of one of the men attempting to hold him. The man fell off him, but was immediately replaced by two others who met with the same fate. In the end, it took four brawny men to keep him from rising again. Small victory it was, though, for they were unable to wrest the sword from his clenched fist.

Appearing only slightly ruffled, James rose from his chair, dirk in hand, and came forward.

Her eyes lighting upon the weapon her father carried, Alessandra struggled to her feet, unaware that the hood of her mantle had fallen to her shoulders. Dear God, did he intend to slay Lucien? She could not allow it.

"Do not harm him!" she cried as she lunged forward, fear causing her to lapse into Arabic. Beneath the mantle, the accursed skirts wrapped around her legs and caught beneath her feet. Though they hindered her advance, they blessedly failed to topple her.

If not for her father halting midstep, Alessandra would not have reached Lucien first. Amazed that she had, she tossed her head back and stared into James's shaken countenance. Only then did she realize she'd come unveiled, her molten hair tumbling past her shoulders.

The dirk slipped from James's fingers and clattered to the floor. "God . . . Catherine," he murmured, "is it you?"

The angry words Alessandra had been about to throw at him slipped her mind. Speechless, she looked into eyes the same shape and color as hers, and saw hope and disbelief battle in their depths.

An awed silence blanketed the hall as all turned their attention to her, including Lady Bayard. Eyes like saucers, her mouth agape, the woman stared.

Though still pinned to the floor, Lucien was the first to break the spell. " 'Tis your daughter, you murdering bastard," he said.

Immediately, Lady Bayard emerged from her stupor and rushed to James's side. "You lie!" she exclaimed, looking from Alessandra to Lucien. " 'Tis a hoax you work on my beloved husband."

"No lie. No hoax," Lucien said. "Alessandra is the child James and Lady Catherine made nearly a full-score years ago."

James blinked. "Alessandra?" he whispered, his gaze moving from feature to feature before settling on her hair. "My daughter?"

His wife grabbed his arm. "James, they lie!" she cried. "Catherine carried no babe when she disappeared."

Unmindful of her station, James shook her off. Then, as if fearful Alessandra might shatter before his eyes, he reached out and lightly ran his hand down the curve of her face. "You've my eyes," he said.

"Aye."

He swallowed. "Is it true, then?"

Without thinking, guided only by strange emotions, Alessandra turned her mouth into his palm and laid her lips against it. She wanted to become a part of this man—to belong to him, and him to her, as had once been with her mother. "It is true," she said.

His brow wrinkled. "But how? Catherine was not pregnant when she vanished."

"But she was," Alessandra said, acutely aware of her accent, "though she did not know it."

"I tell you she lies," Lady Bayard screeched. "She may be Catherine's bastard child, but she is certainly not yours."

Outraged that this woman would label her so, Alessandra spun around to face her. "I am no bastard." She angrily enunciated each word. "And neither is my mother a—"

"Agnes, do you open your mouth once more," James interrupted, "I vow to cast you out of the hall myself!"

Agnes? While the woman sputtered indignation Alessandra gaped at her. Could this be her mother's cousin who was now wedded to James? she wondered, recalling Sabine's warnings about the woman. It would certainly make sense considering Agnes had desired marriage to him.

Gaining his wife's grudging acquiescence, James turned back to Alessandra. "I must know all," he said.

Alessandra looked to where Lucien lay beneath his captors, his eyes ablaze with malevolent fire. "Release him," she said.

James considered the angry young man. "And give him another chance to slit my throat?"

" 'Twas not what I had in mind," Lucien taunted.

"Disembowelment, then?" James said, his offhandedness startling Alessandra.

"For a start."

James sighed. Looking to have added ten years to his life these past minutes, he raked a hand through his hair, then plunged his fingers into his trim beard. "The Bayards are not responsible for your father's death, Lucien. I assure you, Sebastian died of natural causes."

"Natural for whom?" Lucien demanded. "You?"

"I hear tale 'twas his heart—that it gave out."

"And I am to believe you?"

As if he could not bear being too long without a glimpse of Alessandra, James stole a look at her before returning to Lucien's accusing stare.

"Nay, I suppose that would be asking too much," he said. "But when you return to Falstaff, your family will serve as witness that I had naught to do with his death."

"And what remains of them?"

James muttered a curse beneath his breath—at least Alessandra assumed that was what it was, for she had never before encountered the word.

"Have you not heard anything I have said?" he snapped. "We are at peace. Your family is well."

"Not till I see it will I believe it."

James threw his hands into the air. "Release him," he commanded his men.

Grumbling disappointment at having their prey taken from them, the men warily rose, backing away from Lucien but assuming a stance of preparedness.

Obviously, not all were content with the peace the Bayards and De Gautiers had made, Alessandra realized, and the knowledge chilled her.

With one fluid movement, Lucien regained his feet. Though he did not raise his sword to James, he held it ready.

"What now, Lucien?" James asked.

Lucien glanced at Alessandra, then back at his enemy. "Who of the De Gautiers made peace with you?" he asked.

"He who was thought to be Sebastian's heir—your brother Vincent."

Of course, Lucien thought. Reckless Vincent, who hadn't a responsible bone in his body. Vincent, who must have been the one to refuse his ransoming.

There was more to this peace than James Bayard was letting on, Lucien was certain. And if the man would not enlighten him, he would have his answer this eve when he showed himself at Falstaff. "And what were the terms?" he asked.

James looked reluctant to speak further, but he answered. "Our daughter, Melissant," he said. " 'Twas planned that she and Vincent seal the peace with marriage next spring."

"A De Gautier wed a Bayard?" Lucien said, incredulous.

"Aye, 'twas agreeable to Vincent. Now, though, as you are Sebastian's true heir, it would fall to you to wed her."

Nearly, Alessandra protested. However, Lucien made it unnecessary.

"There will be no wedding," he said, his nostrils flared, his giant's body bunching.

Alessandra held her breath as she awaited her father's reaction.

"Your hate threatens all the good we have achieved," James said.

Lucien spread his legs. "I see no benefit in lying with one of your offspring."

Remembering when last they had lain together following the storm aboard ship, Alessandra could not help but be hurt by his callous words.

"The benefit is peace," James said.

Lucien's laughter crackled on the air. " 'Tis too high a price," he said. "Methinks better the war than a Bayard wife."

"You are refusing, then?"

"Aye."

James was silent a minute. "Vincent, then," he said at last. " 'Twill still bind our families together."

Agnes's face flushed red. "My daughter will not marry a landless noble," she exclaimed. "Melissant marries the heir or none at all."

"It will be none, Lady Bayard," Lucien said. "As I

would not allow Vincent to wed your daughter, neither would I consider such an unsavory union."

"You arrogant—"

"Agnes!" James rebuked.

She swung around to face him. "How dare you allow him to speak to me in such a manner!"

James pointed to the stairs. "Out!" he commanded.

Her jaw worked as she searched for a retort, but no further word passed her lips. With an indignant huff, she stamped toward the stairs.

Seeing the last of her disappear from sight, James turned his attention back to Lucien. "Very well," he said. "No marriage, but will you honor the peace?"

Lucien did not answer immediately. "Perhaps," he said, offering a thread of hope. "But I make no promises until I reach Falstaff."

Although James's face mirrored detachment, Alessandra felt his uneasiness. "Then go," he said.

Silently, Alessandra implored Lucien to look at her, to give her hope that this was not the end of them, but he did not.

He slid his sword into its scabbard, then went to the packs and picked them up. Opening one, he pulled out a folded letter. "From Lady Catherine to her aunt and uncle," he said, holding it for James to see. "It explains Alessandra."

Another letter? Alessandra thought. And he had not told her of it? As her own letter from her mother had been left behind at Jacques Le Brec's home, she fought the impulse to run forward and snatch it from him.

James's eyes turned hungry. "And Catherine?" he asked. "Where is she?"

Lucien stepped forward, laid the packs at James's feet, and handed him the letter. "She is now dead."

"Dead," James choked. He had obviously hoped she lived.

Alessandra's heart went out to him. For certain, he had loved her mother and suffered greatly over her loss.

James unfolded the letter. "What form of writing is this?" he asked.

"Arabic," Lucien answered. "Alessandra can translate it for you."

"Arabic?"

"Aye, Catherine was sold into slavery after she disappeared from Corburry, and was all those years in Algiers."

Of a sudden, James's face flushed red, his nostrils flaring and lips drawing back. "Then the De Gautiers have known all along where she was—were responsible for thieving her away!"

Lucien laid his fingers to his sword hilt. "Nay, we were wrongly accused," he maintained. "Only by chance did I meet up with Catherine."

James stared hard at him.

"He speaks true," Alessandra said as she moved to stand alongside her father, hoping to avert disaster. She looked into Lucien's eyes. "Never did my mother say it was the De Gautiers who abducted her."

"Then who?" James asked.

"She did not know."

"And that absolves the De Gautiers of the crime?"

"They were not responsible." She spoke with conviction.

James looked unconvinced, but, miraculously, let the matter drop. "You are off to Falstaff?" he asked Lucien.

"Aye, though be assured this is not over with, Bayard."

"What more is there to discuss?"

"Dewmoor Pass."

James shook his head. "The matter is settled, Lucien. It belongs to the Bayards."

"Perhaps."

James's lips thinned. With contained anger, he nudged the packs with his boot. "What are these?"

"Alessandra's dowry."

Surprised that Lucien had no intention of keeping any of her mother's possessions for himself, Alessandra sought his gaze. "What of your share?" she asked.

"I have my reward." His cool eyes swept her face. "I am home again."

Knowing he was about to depart and leave her with strangers, she stepped forward and gripped his arms.

"Pray, Lucien, do not forget me." She whispered her plea so no others might hear.

Softening. She was certain she saw it in the depths of his eyes. "How could I?" he murmured, then set her away and pivoted on his heel.

Lucien was at the door when James called to him. He looked over his shoulder.

"You will find much changed at Falstaff," James said. "Accept it and let us go on in peace."

Lucien stood poised on the threshold, as if trying to unravel the mystery of James's words, then he was gone.

Alessandra felt as if her heart were cracking. Reminding herself of her vow to behave as a woman and not a child, she quelled the impulse to go after Lucien. She would see him again, she consoled herself. Even if it was she who must go to him.

One of the knights came forward and placed himself before James. "My lord," he said, "when he discovers Falstaff is but a shadow of its former self, he will be back."

James nodded. "I am counting on it."

Puzzled and concerned by the exchange, Alessandra touched her father's arm. "What does your man speak of?"

He turned to her. Then, as if she had not spoken, he enfolded her in arms that might have been comforting had he not avoided answering her. "Welcome, daughter," he said. "Welcome to Corburry."

❦❧

CHAPTER 22

Whether apparition or flesh and blood, the Lion of Falstaff had come home. He spoke not a word to the villagers he passed as he spurred his mount toward the castle, but his bearing roared anger and kept all from venturing too near.

None opposed Lucien when he rode into their midst—not the guard at the gatehouse, not the men-at-arms within the walled fortress, nor the few knights straggling about the hall. Awed, all stood back and let him pass unhindered.

Intent on one man who had yet to notice his coming, Lucien ignored the gasps of surprise and whispers of disbelief as he strode to the high table.

Vincent did not look up, his attention centered on the woman perched upon his knee.

Quelling the desire to upend the table, Lucien slammed his palms to its top and leaned forward.

Vincent started violently, then shot up from his chair, tumbling the wench to the floor. "My God, you're alive!" he exclaimed.

"Disappointed, brother?" Lucien snarled.

Like a cornered animal, Vincent backed away, his eyes darting left, right, then left again. He would get no aid from his knights, he realized. Lucien's coming had robbed him of his rule over them. They now belonged to another.

"Nay, of course not, Lucien. I am—I am surprised, that is all."

"I daresay."

"Lucien!" a woman cried.

Lucien turned and sought out the lone figure across the hall. Frozen with disbelief, his mother stared at him, the glow upon her face evidencing that she had just come from the kitchens.

"My prayers have been answered," she said, then fell to her knees and lifted her hands in praise of God.

Shooting a warning look at Vincent, Lucien strode across the hall and raised Lady Dorothea to her feet. "Mother," he said.

Tears in her eyes, Dorothea stared up at her eldest son. "You have come home," she said.

Lucien nodded. " 'Twas a promise not to be broken."

She smiled and, in the next instant, was in his arms. Holding to him as if fearful he might disappear, she sobbed into his tunic.

Lucien soothed a hand over her head and held her close.

"Your father," she mumbled. "He is dead."

"I know. How?"

"His heart, it grew old." She clung tighter, her weeping turning to moans of grief.

It was a beautiful child of perhaps six who brought an end to her crying. "Mama." The curly-headed girl tugged insistently on Dorothea's skirt.

Wiping a hand across her eyes, Dorothea pulled back and looked down at her daughter. "Ah, Giselle," she said, "have you come to give welcome to your brother?"

The little girl shifted her blue-eyed gaze to Lucien's face, examined it, then scowled. "He is not my brother," she declared.

Dorothea disengaged herself from Lucien and bent to Giselle's level. "Aye, 'tis Lucien come home from France, little one," she said, caressing an apple-red cheek. "Give him a kiss, hmm?"

Willfully, Giselle crossed her arms over her chest and shook her head. "He is not Lucien," she said, narrowing her gaze on the crescent-shaped scar. "Lucien had a nice face."

Dorothea looked over her shoulder at Lucien and, as if noticing the scar for the first time, frowned. Quickly, though, she recovered. "Giselle, 'tis Lucien indeed. He is a warrior."

Giselle's pert mouth puckered.

"Sometimes when warriors go into battle, they are injured. 'Tis certainly what happened to your brother. Now be a good girl and give him a proper welcome."

She stamped her slipperless foot. "No!"

Yielding, Dorothea straightened and offered Lucien an apologetic smile. "Give her time," she said.

What Lucien wanted was to sweep his little sister into his arms and whirl her around. Before he'd left for France, she had been forever chasing after him and getting underfoot. He had pretended annoyance, but had loved every minute of it.

During long nights aboard the galley, he had calmed his tortured soul with memories of her guileless giggles and screams of delight, her innocent questions and boundless curiosity. She had been a beacon, this miracle child who should never have been conceived, much less survived the arduous birthing by a woman well past childbearing age. But Giselle had, and she'd been born to parents who, until then, had only been blessed with boy children—five in all, of which three had survived to adulthood.

Lucien bent low and put himself level with Giselle. "When you wish to ride on my shoulders again, you will let me know, won't you?" he asked.

Her eyes grew wide and round, her mouth slackening as her memory stirred. "Oh," she murmured. Then, not ready to give in, she gave a disdainful toss of her head. "Only my *brothers* get to be my horse," she stated.

Lucien drew back. "Ah, then you will have to pretend I am your brother if you are ever to see what is up here."

Though it was obvious curiosity urged her to ask what that might be, Giselle pressed her lips together and stood unmoving.

Sighing, Dorothea gave her daughter a push toward the stairs. "Summon Jervais," she said.

Giselle moved to comply, but turned back around. "My *brother*," she informed Lucien, then flounced off.

"She will be in your lap by nightfall," Dorothea said, then looped an arm through her son's and urged him to where Vincent and the others waited.

Seating his mother at his side, Lucien dropped into the chair recently vacated by Vincent. "Leave us now," he ordered the knights and servants.

Reluctantly, they withdrew, leaving a gaping silence Dorothea tried to fill. "Tell us, Lucien—"

"Nay, Mother, when Jervais is here," he said.

Puzzled by Lucien's mood that should have been joyous, rather than churlish, Dorothea turned her gaze upon Vincent. "Sit with us," she invited.

He fidgeted a moment, then assumed a seat conspicuously out of Lucien's reach.

With the mounting tension, it seemed ages before Jervais appeared, but finally he did. Pausing at the foot of the stairs, the youngest De Gautier brother stared at Lucien.

"I did not believe Giselle," he said, "but 'tis true." As if a great burden had been lifted from his shoulders, he smiled and practically ran across the hall.

Lucien rose to accept his embrace, surprised at the bulk and power Jervais's once slender body had attained during his absence. Nicholas had not exaggerated.

" 'Tis good you are home," Jervais said as Lucien drew back. "Very good." He made the table his seat.

"Much has changed," Lucien said, remaining standing. He marked Vincent with his stare. "And I would know all of it, but first there is one question that must be answered."

Vincent surged to his feet. "I know your question, Lucien," he said, his handsome face distraught and pale.

To contain his rage was one of the most difficult things Lucien had ever had to do. But he knew he must, if only for his mother's sake. "I thought you would, but do they?" he asked.

Vincent looked to his mother and younger brother, then reluctantly back to Lucien. "Nay, they thought you dead."

"We all thought you dead," Dorothea interjected, her brow puckered with puzzlement. "When you did not return from France, and there came no word, there was no other conclusion to be drawn."

"But word did come, didn't it, Vincent?"

In a quandary over the strange current passing between her two eldest sons, Dorothea stood. "Make sense, Lucien," she implored. "What speak you of?"

It was probably the bravest thing Vincent had ever done, but he bridged the gap separating him and Lucien.

"He *is* making sense, Mother," he said, meeting the fury in his brother's eyes. "A message did come that he lived."

"What!" Dorothea clapped a hand to her heart.

"Aye, and with it a ransom demand from one of those pagan Muslims."

It was too much for her. Staggering, she dropped into her chair. "You never spoke of it," she whispered.

Vincent turned pleading eyes on his mother. "How could I? The coffers were near empty. There wasn't enough to bring him home."

"What do you mean there wasn't enough?" Lucien growled.

Vincent cast his eyes down. "After Father died, and when there was still no word from you, I thought I was heir. I thought it all mine."

"All yours," Lucien repeated, forcing his fists to his hips to prevent him from attacking. "And what did you do with it?"

Jervais was the one to give the bitter answer. "He gambled it away. Near every last bloody coin."

"I tried to get it back," Vincent said. "To make your ransom."

"Which is why we are now reduced to near poverty," Jervais announced.

It was as Bayard had warned, Lucien thought. Much had changed at Falstaff, the loss of Dewmoor Pass the least of its troubles. His gut twisting, Lucien looked to Jervais. "Explain," he ordered.

Jervais crossed his arms over his chest and began swinging a leg back and forth. "Tell him, Vincent," he urged. "Tell the heir of Falstaff who now holds the greater of the De Gautier lands."

At that moment Vincent could not have been said to be handsome. Indeed, the beauty that had forever eclipsed his brothers was reduced to a caricature, a vague shadow of manliness.

"Each time I thought I had him, the bastard took another piece," he said, dragging a hand down his face. "I should have stopped, but I thought the next time my luck would turn and all would be restored."

Now Lucien understood the scarcity of knights when he had come into the hall. No longer did the vassals answer to the De Gautiers, but to another. Though he knew, he demanded, "Who holds the lands, Vincent?"

His brother heaved a sigh. "Bayard."

Bayard. Lucien's muscles bunched so tightly, his arms began to shake from the effort to keep them at his sides. *Accept it and let us go on in peace*, the bastard had said, knowing full well what awaited Lucien when he returned home.

Unable to contain himself, Lucien threw himself on Vincent, making the floor their battleground. Vaguely, he heard his mother's cry of distress, which restored just enough sanity to prevent him from drawing his dirk instead of his fists.

Vincent's was a lost cause, for even had he attempted to defend himself, he was no match for Lucien. Accepting it as his brother's due, he opened himself to wrathful blows that broke his nose, bruised both eyes, and battered his torso. Yet for all the pain, he was silent.

Eventually, Lucien became conscious of the one-sidedness of the fight. Why didn't Vincent defend himself? he wondered. At least throw up an arm to protect that beautiful face of his? Abruptly, he ended his attack.

Breathing raggedly, his knuckles raw and stained with both his and Vincent's blood, Lucien pushed back onto his knees and looked down at his irresponsible brother.

"Do it!" Vincent beseeched, peering up at him through

lids that were swelling already. "End it all. 'Tis no more than I deserve."

" 'Twould be far better than you deserve," Lucien muttered. Rising abruptly, he wrenched his tunic off over his head.

Dorothea and Jervais gasped at the mutilation of his scarred back.

"This"—Lucien traced the scar upon his face—"and this"—he turned to show Vincent his back—"is no more than you deserve."

Vincent groaned his horror and shame. "God, Lucien. I did not know."

"Did not know!" Lucien swung back around.

"I—I tried not to think about it."

"It happened, Vincent, and 'tis a burden you will shoulder the rest of your days."

Wiping the back of his hand across his bloody mouth, Vincent raised his head. "You would let me live after all I have done?"

"Though you haven't the backbone to be a De Gautier," Lucien said, "you are still my mother's son."

Vincent flinched. "I am also our father's son—and your brother."

"That you will have to prove."

Vincent pulled his battered body into a sitting position. "How?" he asked.

Lucien left the question unanswered. "What did Bayard promise you for marriage to his daughter?"

"How do you know of that?"

"What did he promise you, Vincent? Falstaff?"

"Nay, Lucien! Falstaff and its immediate environs I—you—still hold. 'Twas lasting peace he offered."

"Naught else? No dowry? No return of the property he stole?"

Vincent stumbled to his feet. " 'Twas agreed that with the birth of a child made of Melissant and myself, he would gift all De Gautier properties back to me."

"And Dewmoor Pass?"

"Dear God, Lucien!" Vincent exclaimed. "Isn't it enough that Bayard would restore the lands? Haven't both our families shed enough of the other's blood over that useless pass?"

"It is ours!" Lucien stormed. He swung away, knowing that if he did not, he would attack again, mayhap even give Vincent what he had pleaded for.

"I will have the lands and the pass back," he said, looking from his mother's distressed countenance to Jervais's expectant face. "By blood or by guile, I will have them back."

"You speak the same nonsense our father spoke," Vincent spat. "You'd rather spill blood than accept peace through marriage to a Bayard."

Lucien turned back around. "Aye, 'tis the way of warriors, Vincent. But you wouldn't know that, would you?"

Vincent looked away, but then forced his gaze back to his older brother's. "I know what it is to be at peace," he said. "Do you?"

Much to their father's disappointment, Vincent had always been better with words than weapons, and his words now struck Lucien hard. So hard, in fact, he felt gutted. Having no response, he turned away.

"What do you intend?" Jervais asked.

Lucien asked himself the same question. In the past, making war on the Bayards had been the only means of retribution. Now, however, the loss of vassals and household knights hindered such a solution. Or did it?

He raked a hand through his tangled mane. God. If only he had brought Alessandra to Falstaff first as she'd pleaded. Judging by James's reaction to her return, she might have played a powerful role in restoring De Gautier lands. She could have been a pawn, the same as Sabine—Catherine Bayard—had made him. Too late . . .

"I must think on it," he said, suddenly weary.

Jervais laid a hand to his shoulder. "I stand with you, Lucien," he said. "Together we will restore the name of De Gautier."

Lucien looked at where Vincent stood forlorn. "Have you the stomach for it, Vincent?" he asked.

Vincent's hesitation earned him a scowl from both brothers.

"Nay, I thought not," Lucien muttered.

Eyes averted, his jaw clenched on whatever it was he was tempted to respond with, Vincent strode from the hall and out into the last of day.

Lucien turned to his mother. "I've need of a long, hot bath."

"I will have water delivered to the solar," she said, standing.

"The solar," Lucien repeated. That place where his mother and father had slept and made their children. Where Dorothea had birthed her babes. Where, when young, he and his brothers had gathered around their father to hear tales of the cowardly Bayards and the fearless De Gautiers. It seemed so long ago.

"'Tis yours now," Dorothea said.

Hastened from his memories, Lucien struggled to put meaning to her words. A moment later he realized it was the solar she spoke of. Aye, his, and would he one day share it with a wife as his father and generations before him had done?

Unbidden, visions of Alessandra rose before his eyes. Alessandra in the great bed, her red hair spread upon a pillow, her arms beckoning. Alessandra in the chair before the fire, a babe in her arms. Alessandra—

Lord, but he was tired. He dragged a hand across his stubbled jaw. "I must needs shave," he said.

"I shall do it," Dorothea said. Smiling as if steeped in memories of her own, she turned and hurried across the hall.

Watching her go, Lucien pondered whether or not a bed would hold him in better stead than a shave. His shoulders were weighted, his eyelids heavy, and the ache in his chest grew sharper each time his thoughts turned to Alessandra. A short sleep seemed definitely in order. But the blade first, and then—

"What *is* up there?" a petulant voice asked.

Lucien had not seen Giselle come back into the hall, and was thus surprised to find her staring up at him.

Momentarily forgetting his fatigue, he smiled. "Magic," he said.

"Magic?"

He nodded. "Up here"—his hand stirred the air above his head—"one can fly—or very nearly."

Thoughtful, she tapped her pursed mouth. "But only birds can fly, Lucien."

With her naming of him, the ache in his heart eased. "And little girls who have big brothers with broad shoulders," he said.

She scowled. "I have not said you are my brother."

"True, but mayhap you are ready to pretend I am."

For a moment she looked as if she might denounce him again, but then she raised her arms for him to lift her up. "I think that would be all right."

Trying not to smile too wide for fear she might pridefully change her mind, he plucked her from the ground, told her to hold back her skirts, then settled her upon his shoulders.

"Ooh," she crooned after taking a thorough look about her. " 'Tis magic just as you said."

"Think you can fly up there?" Lucien asked.

Her whole body shrugged. "If I knew how."

"Put your arms out to the sides."

"But I might fall."

"Nay, you will not. I will hold you steady." He clasped her legs more tightly to reassure her.

"Very well, but if I fall, 'twill prove you are not my brother," she warned.

"I am prepared to accept the consequences."

With a laugh, she let go of him and put her arms out. "I am ready, Lucien."

His troubles and fatigue forgotten for the time being, Lucien dashed about the hall amid the giggles and gleeful cries of the small treasure upon his shoulders. And though Jervais looked at him as if he had lost his mind, he gave all of himself to his little sister.

CHAPTER 23

As Jabbar had wept upon Sabine's deathbed, so did James when Alessandra finished translating her mother's poignant letter—or nearly so. He was far too English to allow any to witness his tears, though the back he turned to her quaked with his silent sobs.

The letter had been addressed to Catherine's aunt and uncle but its message was clearly meant for James. It explained all—her abduction from Corburry, her first months in the harem, the birth of Alessandra, the intervening years, the sickness thieving her body, and finally, Lucien's role in delivering Alessandra to Corburry.

Only one detail was missing, Alessandra realized when she came to the last, beseeching line of the letter. Not once had her mother mentioned her great love for Jabbar. She had been wise not to, for there was no doubt James had loved her deeply. No good could possibly come of telling him.

For hours, Alessandra and James had sat alone in the great hall, even now forgoing the evening meal as they attempted to bridge the gap created by nearly twenty years of separation.

Though there were some facets to James's personality that might take years to know, Alessandra was soon certain of one thing. As her mother had said, he was kind, his one failing the same as Lucien's—the legacy of hate between their families.

Still, James spoke often of the new peace, reveled in the

word each time he uttered it, and expressed concern over
whether it would last now that Lucien had returned.

Tentatively, Alessandra asked the question uppermost
in her mind—what would Lucien find upon arriving at
Falstaff?

Though James attempted to turn her attention to other
topics, in the end, he gave over to her willfulness and
told her the truth.

"You won the lands from his brother?" she repeated.

"Aye, but fairly I assure you—and with good intention."

She lifted a questioning eyebrow. "What was that?"

He smiled. "Surely you can guess."

"Peace?"

"Exactly. Had it been Lucien, I never would have attempted such a thing, but with Vincent it was simple. The
idea was to gain what the De Gautiers treasured most
and offer it back to them at a price."

"Being peace?"

"Aye, and a grandchild that would forever bind our
families and put an end to our feud."

"And Vincent was agreeable?"

"As agreeable as a De Gautier can be," James quipped.

Alessandra looked past him to a tapestry that depicted
men engaged in battle. "Lucien will return," she said,
"but I do not think it will be in peace."

James also looked at the tapestry. "The battle at Crest-
ing Ridge in the year 1342," he said with bitterness. "The
De Gautiers lost six men, the Bayards five—Bayard victory by the death of a lad too young to heft the sword he
carried."

A shiver stole up Alessandra'a spine for what the tapestry represented—death and a repulsive gloating over it.

James sighed. "I fear you may be right, Alessandra.
Still, I pray Lucien will put aside his pride and reconsider
marriage to Melissant."

Alessandra's silence was her undoing.

Her father gave her a searching stare. "What happened
between you and De Gautier?" he asked.

She blinked, then blushed. Obviously, he referred to
any intimacy they might have shared. "I—" she began,

clenching her hands in the blanket James had earlier sent for when she'd begun shivering. "Lucien was kind to me."

Her father chuckled. "Not likely. Tolerant, perhaps, but never kind."

She averted her gaze to her hands. "You are wrong about him."

His face grew serious, his eyes distant. "I pray I am." A moment later he shrugged himself free of his melancholy. "But you have not answered my question, have you?"

"I . . ." Though this man was her father, it was not easy what he asked. "I am chaste," she said.

James considered her a moment, then covered her hands with one of his. " 'Tis as I had hoped," he said, "but what of your feelings for him?"

Should she tell her father of her love for his enemy? she wondered. How would he react?

The appearance of James's wife saved Alessandra from responding. Stepping from the stairs, the woman crossed the hall with a young woman and boy on her heels.

James stood, his brow set with irritation. "I had thought you would await my summons."

Agnes held her tongue until she stood before him. "And I would have thought you would have summoned me sooner," she retorted. Her sharp gaze flickered over Alessandra, dismissed her, and returned to her husband. "With darkness upon us and no meal laid, it has fallen to me to interrupt your conversation."

James's jaw worked side to side. "Which you've succeeded in doing very well."

The young woman stepped forward, easing the tension with her sweet smile. "Is it true, Father, that she"—she swept a hand toward Alessandra—"is also your daughter?"

James cupped a hand beneath Alessandra's elbow and urged her to stand.

With great reluctance, Alessandra gave up the warmth of the blanket, feeling anew the draft of cool air that crept in through every crack and window in the hall. She could not remember ever being so cold. Even on the deck of the ship, the night wind blowing through her clothes, she had been warmer. But then, Lucien had been at her back, his arms encircling her. Would they ever again?

She sighed. If only her father would instruct a servant to set a fire in the hearth. She looked longingly at that gaping hole and wished a roaring fire there.

"Aye, Melissant," James said, forcing Alessandra back to the present. "She is my daughter—your half sister."

"Is she also mine, Father?" the boy piped in.

With pride, James looked upon the lad who had all of eleven years to his credit. "Aye, Ethan, that she is."

Alessandra was tempted to embrace this brother and sister as she'd done her father. However, uncertain as to how she might be received, she fought the impulse and linked her hands before her.

A serious frown aged Ethan's young face as he focused on Alessandra's mouth. "Mother says she speaks strange," he said. "That she has the sound of the infidel."

A look passed between Agnes and James, his eyes shining with the promise of reprimand, hers assuring him she was up to the challenge.

Forgetting her mother's warnings about her cousin, Alessandra silently sympathized with Agnes. It could not have been easy for her to live in the shadow of one James had loved so deeply—most especially her childhood rival.

James laid a hand upon Ethan's shoulder. "Aye, 'tis true Alessandra speaks different—with a song in her voice. But she is Christian, the same as you and I."

"Let me hear," Ethan said.

Surprised by his request, Alessandra studied him for a moment, then obliged him. "It is most pleasurable to meet you, young Ethan," she said, then looked to the one she might call sister. "And you, Melissant."

To her discomfort, neither responded. They simply stared.

Agnes interrupted the silence. "What of our daughter's betrothal, James?" she asked.

With a sigh of regret, James took Melissant's hands in his. "I am sorry," he said. "Lucien de Gautier's return has spoiled all plans."

"Then I am not to wed Vincent?"

"Nay, you are not."

Alessandra did not think the girl looked the least disappointed. In fact, her eyes brightened.

"But perhaps Lucien," Agnes said.

Annoyance flared in James's face. "Have you forgotten he refused?"

"He may reconsider once he learns there is more than peace to be gained in wedding Melissant."

The land, Alessandra thought. "You are wrong," she spoke up. "Lucien will take back his lands by force before he will bend a knee to a Bayard."

Slowly, Agnes turned from her husband to the woman she obviously considered a trespasser. "You do not know that," she said in a voice chill with dislike.

"But I do. I—"

"Because you have lain with a man," Agnes snapped, "does not mean you know his mind."

And she had sympathized with this woman only minutes earlier? Alessandra would have responded most vehemently to her accusation if James had not growled, "Stand down, Agnes."

"'Tis true," the woman continued. "Look at her. Do you think a man like De Gautier would not take what she so blatantly offers?"

Pressing her lips tightly together, Alessandra glanced down at her attire, then back up to compare it with that of Agnes and Melissant. It seemed little different from what they wore. In fact, hers was more modest of cut.

What then? Her hair hanging unbound past her shoulders? Both Agnes's and Melissant's hair was braided, Agnes's mostly concealed by a jeweled cap, and Melissant's plaits pinned on each side of her head over the ears. It must be this.

While Alessandra had been preoccupied with discovering what it was that made her so different from the other women, James had moved to stand before his wife.

"You are acting the shrew, Agnes," he said, his anger apparent in the stiffness of his posture. "Alessandra is my daughter, and—"

"As is Melissant," she was quick to remind him. "And do not forget your son."

He ignored her outburst. "Henceforth you will keep your nasty thoughts inside your head or suffer my displeasure."

The standoff lasted several minutes, abandoned only when Agnes resentfully conceded. "Very well," she said, "but do not forget to whom your first duty is."

"To the Bayard name," James said. "As it has always been."

Her plucked eyebrows soared up her forehead. "You know 'tis your children of whom I speak."

"Of which Alessandra is the firstborn," James reminded her.

"If what she says is true, which—"

"It is true, Agnes. And 'twould be to your benefit to accept it."

Though Agnes wisely decided against further argument, the way she crossed her arms over her chest said she was not finished with the matter, and had no intention of embracing this intruder who had come into their midst.

James turned back to his children and found all three staring expectantly at him with eyes that were identical to his.

He smiled. "Methinks a tourney would best introduce Alessandra to the gentry," he said. "What think you of that?"

"Oh, yes, Father," Ethan exclaimed.

"Alessandra?" James asked.

"A tourney," she mused. She had heard tales of such celebrations, but knew very little of them. "It sounds . . . interesting."

"Then 'tis done," James decreed, quelling Agnes's incipient objection with a withering look. "A month hence, Corburry will have its first tournament in nearly a decade."

CHAPTER 24

"Where is the sun?" Alessandra moaned, regretting its absence as she had every day for the past fortnight. Nearly a month at Corburry now and she had yet to see a blue sky or feel the sun's heat upon skin that was too often covered with prickly bumps.

At first it had been an interesting change from the Maghrib, but too soon it had turned monotonous. Though the green of England was beyond compare, she thought the price it paid for such beauty far too high.

"I thought never to tire of rainbows," she muttered, "but now I am quite sick of them."

"Come away from the window," Melissant urged.

Lifting her chin from her hands, Alessandra looked over her shoulder at her sister.

Dressed in a gown of lustrous velvet, its buttons loosened in defense of the overheated room, Melissant sat upon the bed as far from the fire as possible. Propped in her lap, and receiving considerable attention, was an illuminated tome, its warped and discolored pages attesting to its respectable age.

Alessandra's mouth curled into a contented smile as she reflected on her friendship with Melissant.

In spite of Agnes's ardent attempts to keep James's daughters apart, the girl was proving herself to be a rebel. At every opportunity, she sought Alessandra out, begging for tales of Algiers and life in the harem in exchange for demonstrations of the English way of things.

Having a sister filled a void in Alessandra's life that she had not known was there. However, the void left by Lucien's absence grew more terrible with each passing day.

His silence was unbearable. Though James's men kept an eye out for his vengeful coming, their efforts were for naught. All appeared quiet at Falstaff.

If only Lucien would send word—

"Come," Melissant beckoned a second time, her head remaining bent. "I want to show you something."

Sighing, Alessandra straightened from the window. However, she had only gone a few steps when she turned to the fireplace, whose fire had not been allowed to extinguish since she had been given this chamber.

Poker in hand, she bent and stoked the fire, then reached for another log to feed its hungry flames.

"Oh, must you?" Melissant groaned, sweeping a hand across her damp brow. "I am near to burning up."

Alessandra dropped her arms back to her sides. "I've not been warm since leaving the Maghrib," she explained for probably the hundredth time.

Melissant lowered the book and stared at her. " 'Twill be a miserable winter for you if you do not adapt soon."

"I cannot believe it could get any colder than this," Alessandra grumbled. "Why, never before have I seen my breath upon the air, and now when I awaken in the morn, it is there when I come out from beneath the covers."

Melissant giggled. "And yet you sleep fully clothed, right down to your slippers."

"Did I not, I would be like the frost upon the window," Alessandra retorted. "And likely, you would find me dead come morn."

"You need a man to warm you," Melissant said boldly. At the widening of Alessandra's eyes, she quickly explained, " 'Tis what Hellie says when I complain of cold."

Hellie. The robust cook who had groused about modifying the foods Alessandra ate, but had finally complied when Alessandra had become sick right in front of her.

Alessandra sighed. Aye, the woman was right. Were Lucien to share her bed, there would be no need for covers or fire.

"Shall I guess who 'tis occupies your mind?" Melissant said, blundering into the vision Alessandra had conjured.

Caught, Alessandra straightened abruptly and looked at her sister. "None occupies my mind," she said.

"None but Lucien de Gautier." With a knowing smile, Melissant drew her knees up and settled her chin on them.

"How—how do you know that?"

She shrugged. "A guess, but a good one, aye?"

Frowning, Alessandra crossed to the bed. Though she had told Melissant of the escape from Algiers and the events straight up to Lucien rescuing her from slavery, she had been careful to downplay their relationship. What had given her away?

Lowering herself to the bed, she pulled the coverlet over her legs and turned to the girl. " 'Tis wrong of me, I know—improper, you English would say—but I cannot stop thinking of him."

"Then you love him?"

Alessandra nodded, forgetting what Melissant had told her earlier about playing coy with men.

"And he you?"

"Nay. Perhaps if I had remained Alessandra, daughter of Jabbar, he might have come to care for me. But I am Alessandra Bayard now, daughter of his enemy. That he cannot forget."

Melissant looked down to study the bitten nails of her right hand. " 'Twould seem our father should offer you in marriage to keep the peace, rather than me."

Alessandra shook her head. "Nay, methinks Lucien would refuse me as readily as he did you."

"One does not know until one asks."

"I know," Alessandra said. Wishing she had thrown another log on the fire, she dragged the coverlet around her shoulders and burrowed her cold nose in it.

Melissant sighed. "I suppose you know him better than most."

Alessandra peeked at her. "Only what he allowed me to know."

A knock preceded Ethan's appearance. Cheeks flushed, he thrust his head around the door. Catching sight of his sisters—one of whom he was still uncertain about—he beamed. "A messenger has come," he said. "From Falstaff."

Forgetting her chill, Alessandra sprang from the bed and rushed forward to pull the door open wider. "He brings word of Lucien?" she asked in an excited rush.

Ethan wrinkled his nose. "What did you say?" he asked, unable to grasp her flood of words amid her accent.

"She asked if the messenger brings word of Falstaff's lord, Lucien de Gautier," Melissant interpreted.

Ethan rolled his eyes. "Nay, the message is simply that the De Gautiers will be attending the tourney."

Alessandra gripped the edge of the door. She had not known James had issued them an invitation. What did Lucien's acceptance mean? That he would embrace the peace and overlook the loss of his lands? It did not seem possible, but what other explanation was there?

"Does Mother know?" Melissant asked.

"Not yet. She is with the physician and won't allow any in her chamber until he is finished."

Melissant grimaced. "I suppose she is being bled again?"

Ethan nodded. "Again."

Alessandra shuddered at the mention of that repugnant thing English noblewomen did to attain a pale complexion. Melissant had described the procedure in great detail, admitting she had once undergone it herself—and been sick for days thereafter. Now she opted for painting and powdering her face to achieve a similar look.

Alessandra thought both methods unsavory and had refused Melissant's well-intentioned offer to instruct her in applying paint and powder. She had always preferred her skin honey-colored, and now without sun, it was more pale than she cared. Even Agnes's taunts and Ethan's teasing about her freckles were not enough to make her give in to the bleaching Melissant suggested.

Kohl for her eyes and rouge for her lips would have suited her far better, but she hesitated to use either, as she had not seen them worn by her stepmother or Melissant.

Ethan touched Alessandra's arm. "It's not something

you've eaten again, is it?" he asked, grudging concern upon his face.

"What? Oh, nay, Ethan. 'Tis nothing."

Realizing it was the best he would get from her, he turned and ran down the corridor and out of sight.

Feeling herself watched, Alessandra looked back at Melissant's grinning face.

"Father says things meant to be are, and not meant to be aren't," the young woman said. "Methinks you and Lucien de Gautier are meant to be."

Alessandra wished she could believe it, too, but felt strangely dejected. Had the messenger carried a note from Lucien to her, then she might believe. But Lucien appeared to have forgotten her completely.

She shook her head. "Nay, Melissant. Though you may fancy it possible, it is clear Lucien has no thought of me other than as a Bayard."

Still grinning, Melissant swept from the room and tossed over her shoulder, "Do you not put another log on that fire, 'twill surely die."

Arriving in the hall before the evening meal, Alessandra was surprised to find Agnes and Melissant poring over the books that, until that moment, had seemed the constant companions of the steward.

Pale, and looking more than a little weakened by her recent bloodletting, Agnes flipped through the pages, muttered something beneath her breath, then pushed the book in front of Melissant.

How curious, Alessandra thought. Her mother had told her it was not uncommon for women in England to be versed in the household accounting, but she hadn't given it much thought. She stood back and watched as mother and daughter discussed the numbers.

"Now figure these two." Agnes jabbed her finger to the numbers at top and bottom of a page.

How Alessandra itched to know what the two numbers were that she might figure them herself. It was something she'd always had a flair for, adding and subtracting in her head without the need for quill and parchment.

Quill in hand, bottom lip clamped between her teeth,

Melissant set the figures down and, a few minutes later, provided her mother with the answer. "Two hundred seventeen," she said.

Agnes shook her head. "Nay, Melissant, two hundred twenty-seven," she corrected, her annoyance dragging small spots of color to each cheek. "Where is your head today, child?"

Melissant groaned. "Elsewhere. Why must I know the books, Mother? Is this not the job of the steward?"

Agnes heaved an unladylike harrumph. "As you will someday run your husband's household, so, too, must you know the numbers your steward puts before you."

"But why?"

"I have told you before—so that you will not be cheated. 'Tis your duty to your husband to keep an eye on all that is his. Did I not do it for your father, much would be lost to the thieving hands of others."

"Is it not duty enough to bear my husband's children?" Melissant complained. "Surely he can do this as well as I. I detest numbers."

Agnes looked ready to vent her anger, but then the spots of color drained clean away and left her chalky white. She lowered her head, bracing it in her hands. "If I have to explain it to you one more time," she mumbled, "I think I will scream."

A hand to her mother's shoulder, concern etched in her young face, Melissant leaned near her. "You let him take too much," she said. "Why not just use powder and paint?"

Agnes tried to lift her head, but quickly laid it back down. "I must needs look my very best for your father," she said, "else those memories he carries everywhere with him, and which now grow stronger with the coming of Catherine's daughter, will supplant me completely." As if pained, she rolled her head side to side. "What am I to do about Alessandra? What?"

Guilt washed over Alessandra—guilt that James's memories could hurt so much and that they had grown with her arrival at Corburry, and guilt that she had not revealed herself to Agnes and Melissant. It was a private moment, one that did not, and never would, include her.

Thinking to retreat without showing herself and embarrassing Agnes, Alessandra turned. However, her foot caught the leg of the small table she had stood alongside, and set it to rocking.

"Alessandra," Melissant called to her. "I did not see you there."

Feeling terrible, Alessandra turned back around, her gaze going first to Agnes.

Though Agnes did not look up, her heartfelt groan revealed her chagrin.

"I was just . . . I . . ." Alessandra turned her hands palm up into the air. "I did not mean to intrude."

Melissant nodded understanding. "Come," she beckoned. "I will need help in conducting Mother to her chamber. She is not well."

As Alessandra stepped forward, Agnes's head came straight up, her body following a moment later. "I do not need any assistance," she snapped, though she swayed as she stood. "Think you I am an old lady who must be cosseted and carried about?" Her voice rising, she stared haughtily at Alessandra. "Well, I am not, and you ought not forget it."

Looking as if she might collapse at any moment, Agnes came around the table on shaky legs and, chin thrust high, walked past Alessandra.

Neither Alessandra nor Melissant spoke until enough time had passed that they were certain Agnes wouldn't overhear them.

"I'm sorry," Alessandra said.

Melissant shrugged. " 'Tis not your fault." After closing the books and stacking them neatly, she walked around the table to stand before Alessandra. "The only one to blame is whoever stole your mother away. One day he will no doubt be found out."

"You think so?"

Melissant nodded, then changed the subject. "Mother has given me the tedious task of overseeing the supper preparations this eve. Would you like to help?"

Another lesson in being an English noblewoman, Alessandra mused. At least it sounded more interesting than spinning wool or embroidery. Nodding, she followed Melissant to the kitchens.

Within seconds of stepping into that cavernous room, Alessandra knew it was a place she belonged. It was not the wonderful smells wafting from bubbling pots. It was not the joyous clatter of cooking utensils. Nor was it the laughter and excited chatter of the cooks and kitchen maids. Though all these things certainly made her feel welcome, it was the wonderful heat that appealed to every cold bump on her body. It was so intense, it raised a sweat on every brow and caused clothes to stick in places they ought to—just like in Algiers when she had gone onto the rooftop at midday.

"Wonderful," Alessandra breathed. Having never before entered a kitchen, for it had been considered beneath harem women to frequent that place, she found herself deeply curious.

Wandering from Melissant's side, she leaned over a cook's shoulder to peek into the pot he stirred. "What is it?" she asked.

He stepped aside to give her a closer look. "Spiced wine custard, milady. One of yer father's favorites."

And soon to be hers, Alessandra thought as she inhaled a deep breath of it. "How is it made?" she asked.

He smiled widely. "Ye really wish to know?"

"Of course."

His chest puffing with self-importance, he handed the spoon to her. "Taste it, and then I'll tell ye."

Uncertain, Alessandra looked around to see where Melissant had taken herself to. Across the room, she stood with elbows propped on a huge block table at which two women were kneading dough. With a wink, she nodded for Alessandra to try the custard.

Grinning, Alessandra dipped up a spoonful, blew on it, and tasted. "Delicious," she stated, wishing for a whole bowl of it. Knowing it would likely be improper to request more, she handed the spoon back to the cook. "Now tell me, how is it you make it?"

He looked like a proud father. "Ye warm good wine," he began, "cast yolks of eggs in it, and stir awhile—but let it not boil, milady—and when 'tis thick, ye throw in sugar, saffron, salt, mace. . . ." Finger to his forehead, he searched for the remainder of the ingredients. "Ah, yes. Some galingale, and then flower of Canelle."

Impressed with the knowledge that had come straight off the top of his head, Alessandra thanked him and went to where Melissant now stood at a spit lined with roasting hares.

"More sauce," Melissant instructed the man who tended the meat. " 'Twould not do for them to be dry."

Nodding, he reached for the bowl of honey-colored sauce and did as she instructed.

"What do you think?" Melissant asked Alessandra.

"I like it. Had I known 'twas such an interesting place, I would have ventured here sooner."

Taking Alessandra's arm, Melissant drew her away from the spit. "What were the kitchens like in Algiers? Quite different, I would imagine."

"I don't know. I was never allowed within."

Melissant halted. "Truly? Why?"

Alessandra shrugged. "Food preparation was the duty of slaves, often overseen by the chief eunuch, but never the master's wives or daughters."

"Ah, heavenly," Melissant said. "How I detest this hot, smelly place." She sighed. "But Mother says a wife must assure her husband's food is good and plentiful."

Though she did not say it, Alessandra thought the kitchen one of the best things about England thus far, and also the household accounting. To test the steward's numbers would be far more enjoyable than what she had thus far learned about being an English lady. Of course, those things paled next to Lucien. More than anything else, he made England appealing. Without him . . .

Shaking her head to clear it of wayward thoughts, Alessandra turned her attention back to the busy kitchen.

CHAPTER 25

At last he had come. All the others having arrived hours before, Alessandra had nearly given up hope that Lucien would attend the tournament.

Her first sight of him was from the window of her chamber, where she stood naked and dripping wet. Though he was far too distant for her to make out his features, she knew because he sat head and shoulders above the others.

In spite of his loss of property, his was an impressive entourage, numbering twenty or more and outfitted in gold splashed on red. Banners of the same colors fluttered in the stir created by the speed at which they approached Corburry's walls.

Would he come to the keep this eve to dine with the others? Alessandra wondered. Or would he stay in the encampment outside the walls?

"Lady, come back to your bath," Alessandra's new maid, Bernadette, called.

"I will not catch chill," Alessandra said, her eyes following Lucien's advance.

The twelve-year-old girl snickered. "Aye, for certain not in this room," she said, fanning herself with the washrag she held.

Alessandra smiled. The temperature suited her just fine, even with the draft coming from the window. It was heavenly to be without garments and feel none of the English cold. In fact, had she not been averse to losing sight of Lucien, she would have closed her eyes and conjured up the lovely heat of Jabbar's bathhouse.

"Come, milady, I must needs rinse the soap from your hair," Bernadette beseeched.

Not until the walls stole Lucien from sight did Alessandra respond. Leaning against the window ledge, she looked over her shoulder to the wooden tub.

"Hurry," the girl insisted, motioning her forward. "There is much to do ere the banquet."

Alessandra dropped her gaze to the murky gray water she had hastily emerged from minutes ago. Nay, she had absolutely no intention of going back into that!

The English way of bathing was something she did not think she would ever grow accustomed to. Rather than sitting upon stools and allowing their filth to be washed from them, they preferred to soak, bathe, and rinse in the same fouled water. Unfortunately for Alessandra, she found herself with no other choice but to do the same. No doubt she would never again be as clean as she'd been before England.

Though she was forced to use a tub, there was one thing she refused to compromise on—the frequency of her baths. Worse than their mode of bathing, the English infrequently bothered to do it, using heavy perfumes to mask the scent of their foul, unwashed bodies.

Several days earlier Agnes had taken up a vehement protest when Alessandra had called for heated water, and had refused to allow the servant to bring it to her. Determined to have her bath, Alessandra had fetched the water up the stairs herself and, if not for James's intervention, might still be doing so. Regrettably, his intervention had only added fuel to Agnes's fire.

"Ah, milady, have you no modesty?" Bernadette scolded as she draped a robe around Alessandra's shoulders.

Alessandra straightened. "There is only you in this room with me."

"Aye, but 'tis improper that you wander about with nary a stitch of clothing on."

Fitting her arms into the sleeves of the robe, Alessandra humored herself by casting Bernadette in the role of serving girl in a bathhouse. It would certainly terrorize the poor thing to see so many naked women in one place.

"Come, come," Bernadette said, "I must rinse your hair."

Much to the maid's chagrin, Alessandra shunned further immersion in the water. Instead, she knelt beside the tub, leaned forward, and instructed Bernadette to pour what remained of the fresh water over her hair.

It was done, but not without much grumbling.

With an adeptness that surprised Alessandra, Bernadette made quick work of pressing the moisture from her lady's hair and arranging it in thick braids that she then wound around Alessandra's head like a coronet. It was a compromise, really, for Alessandra had refused the weighty headdress Agnes had sent her to wear. She was not ashamed of her hair's color, and had no intention of hiding it beneath the contraption.

An hour later Alessandra had but to don her gown before going belowstairs to the banquet held in her honor. Though she would likely have to find a way into the garments by herself, for Agnes had called Bernadette away, she was grateful for a few minutes alone.

Nervous, she paced her chamber and fingered the jeweled necklace that had been her mother's, finding consolation in the wearing of it. Though she had been tempted to put on belled bracelets and anklets as well, she had decided against it. Agnes's unmerciful chastisement of days earlier when she had worn but a single bracelet precluded that.

Alessandra pressed her palms together, trying not to be daunted by the great number of people she was soon to face. Of course, meeting all of them was nothing compared with the possibility of seeing Lucien again.

Melissant had promised to send word if he appeared. Thus far, none had come to announce it.

Glimpsing her reflection in her mirror, Alessandra drew to a halt. Lord, but she was pale. Moving to stand directly before the mirror, she peered at her powdered face.

No paint, she had insisted, but had given in to a light dusting of powder so Bernadette could cover her freckles.

It had been a mistake. What little warmth of color remained in her face was concealed beneath pasty white.

"God's rood!" She muttered James's favorite curse. Grabbing a cloth, she dipped it in the stagnant water of the washbasin and began scrubbing her face.

Relieved to see the smattering of freckles resurface, she smiled. "Much better." She would have been content with the transformation had not the small wooden box sitting on her dressing table caught her eye.

She lifted the lid and considered the kohl and rouge there. Such simple enhancements compared with the painting and powdering, she thought.

Nipping at her bottom lip, she looked at her reflection again and found it wanting. Perhaps just a little . . .

Alessandra was well pleased with her image when the knock sounded a short time later. Knowing it would be her father come to escort her belowstairs, she hurried to the door and flung it open.

To her great discomfort, James's smile faltered at the sight of her. However, he quickly recovered and offered her his arm.

"Something is wrong?" she asked. "The kohl?" Though she had applied it much more lightly than when she had lived in the harem, it might still be a shock to those unaccustomed to the look.

James shook his head. "Nay, everything is right," he said. "Perfect, in fact. You are beyond lovely, Catherine's daughter."

Unconvinced, Alessandra peered down the front of her gown to the raised hemline. "I know I should not have," she said, putting a foot forward to show him the space between gown and floor, "but I feared if I did not shorten it, I might trip and embarrass you."

Stepping back, James eyed the curve of stockinged ankle she had exposed. "I have always wondered why women wear gowns so long," he said, a corner of his mouth twitching. " 'Tis not very practical, is it?"

Alessandra's mouth relaxed into a smile. "Not at all," she said. "Were it permissible, I would choose a nice caftan and trousers instead."

James's smile came through. "Pray, give me fair warning ere you think to wear such garments in Agnes's presence."

Alessandra laughed, then looped her arm through his and walked beside him down the corridor.

"Father," she said tentatively, "will the house of Falstaff be represented at the banquet?"

"Methinks you are asking if Lucien has arrived," he said as they began their descent of the three flights of stairs.

The excited buzz of hundreds of guests in the hall floated up to them, but went unnoticed by Alessandra. "Why—why would you think that?" she asked.

He looked sideways at her. "On the way to your chamber, I intercepted Melissant's messenger."

Inwardly, Alessandra groaned. "And what was the message?"

James inclined his head. "He is here."

Alessandra's being sparked with a mix of apprehension and excitement. "Has he come in peace, Father?"

"As far as I can tell. Still, I have set men to watch him and those he brought with him."

"Then you and Lucien have not spoken?"

"Exchanged only glances, I'm afraid."

Alessandra sighed.

"You think he has come to make war?" James asked, halting a half-dozen steps from the entry into the hall.

She looked up at him. "War?" After some thought, she shrugged. "All I know for certain is he has come to reclaim what was taken from him."

"Aye, that he has."

Alessandra was surprised at her father's concurrence. "Then what will you do?"

He patted her hand and led her down the last steps. "It has always been my intention that De Gautier lands be returned," he said, "but it must be with marriage to a Bayard."

"To keep the peace."

"Aye."

"It's important to you, isn't it?"

He nodded. "The feud will end with me. 'Twas the promise I made Catherine before she disappeared.

Though many times since I have broken that promise, as when I thought the De Gautiers were responsible for her taking, I am determined to see this peace through."

Alessandra wanted to know more, but suddenly found herself before an audience whose conversation quickly rippled to silence.

"Smile, Alessa," James said, using the pet name he had adopted for her shortly after she had arrived at Corburry. "Let them see that Catherine lives on in you."

Forcing a smile, Alessandra stiffened her spine and lifted her chin. Everywhere, nobility flanked nobility, men and women alike turning their attention upon her. Stares dropped from her lined eyes to the hem of her gown, the women looking positively scandalized, the men appreciative.

Oh, why hadn't her father ordered her to pull out the stitches in her hem and remove the kohl? Alessandra wondered as she shifted from one foot to the other.

Only once before had she ever been faced with so many intent on her—at the slave auction in Tangier. But Lucien had been there, her savior in disguise. He was here now, wasn't he?

"Allow me to introduce my daughter," James said in a booming voice that carried across the hall. "Alessandra Bayard."

Forcing the uncertain child in her aside, Alessandra raised her chin even higher and smiled wide.

A murmur of acknowledgment rose, along with whispers behind hands and judgmental mutterings. Though a few stepped forward to present themselves, the rest held back.

"Worry not," James whispered into Alessandra's ear. "Once I have taken you around that all might know your charm, they will be clamoring to stand alongside you."

Agnes's sudden appearance boded no good. However, instead of disapproval, her eyes shone with satisfaction as they swept Alessandra. "Your daughter is most becoming," she told James. "Most becoming, indeed."

Alessandra's suspicions echoed those her father voiced. "What?" he said in a low voice. "You are laying down your sword, wife?"

"Wrongly you have judged me," Agnes said, softly rebuking him. "Never did I take it up."

"Is that so?"

Her smile gay, Agnes slipped her arm through the one Alessandra held to and wedged a place for herself. "Come," she said, tugging James free. "The steward wishes to have a word with you ere the banquet commences."

"Whatever for?"

" 'Twould seem several knives are missing."

James's eyebrows drew together, his concern evident.

Knives and spoons—precious articles, Alessandra had learned during her first meal at Corburry. They represented a good portion of the portable wealth of a castle, and it fell to the steward to hand the utensils out prior to each meal, and to collect and count them carefully afterward. Though Alessandra found it humorous, at Corburry it was taken quite seriously.

Motioning Melissant forward, James passed Alessandra into her care. "I should not be long," he assured Alessandra. "In the meantime, Melissant can introduce you about. In fact . . ." He tapped his chin. " 'Twould probably be better if she did." Agnes on his arm, he turned and disappeared among the throng.

When he was gone, Alessandra pushed her shoulders back and convinced herself to stand proud. None, she vowed, would know of her discomfort.

"Clever," Melissant said, eyeing the hem of her sister's gown. "Though I would never be brave enough to do it myself."

"Bravery had naught to do with it," Alessandra said. "It was purely functional."

Melissant shrugged. "You needn't explain to me. But come, I've scores of people to introduce you to ere the call to feast."

Alessandra leaned near her. "And Lucien?"

Melissant smiled a secretive smile. "As was my message, he has come."

"But where is he?"

"I don't know, but be assured he is somewhere among this melee."

"You are certain?"

Melissant nodded. "Though I've yet to see him myself, I am told he has created quite a stir." At Alessandra's questioning frown, she added, "Turning up alive when all thought him long dead."

Having to content herself with that, Alessandra allowed herself to be led into a whirlwind of introductions. To further her discomfort, however, she was followed and watched closely by a man in the lavish robes of one who held high office with the Church.

"Who is that?" she asked Melissant after they had extricated themselves from a group of giggling young women.

Melissant followed her line of sight. "Bishop Armis," she said.

"There is only one of him?"

"Aye, thank the heavens," she whispered. "Why do you ask?"

"He seems everywhere at once."

"Ah." A faint smile curved Melissant's lips. " 'Tis the way of things. The good bishop wants to be certain you are of the Holy Church's beliefs and not those of pagan Islam."

What must he think of her clothed and made up as she was? "And if I were of that faith?"

Melissant's smile was wiped clean away. "Alessandra, do not even think such thoughts!" she said into her ear. " 'Tis heresy for sure. Did your mother never tell you the Church is tolerant of only one religion—theirs?"

Alessandra was surprised by her vehemence. True, Sabine had told her of the Church's staunch position, but she'd never detailed the consequences of holding conflicting religious beliefs.

"I don't understand," she said.

Melissant linked her hand with Alessandra's and steered her away from the bishop. "Later, I will explain," she said.

A man who looked to be a male rendering of Agnes, though some years older and sporting a good-natured demeanor, suddenly appeared before them. "I would not have believed it had I not seen it with my own eyes," he said, his stare engulfing Alessandra.

In spite of his advanced years, he was handsome. Liberally peppered hair cut short to control it sprang from his scalp and waved back from a face that had captured the elements of masculinity without sacrificing beauty. The trim beard tracing his jaw was silver gray, his mustache lifting with his smile.

"Uncle Keith," Melissant greeted him. Stepping forward, she went up on tiptoe and pressed a kiss to his cheek.

Tearing his gaze from Alessandra, he looked at his niece. "You have grown since last I was at Corburry," he said, and ruffled her hair as if she were a pet he held in high affection.

"Did you visit more often, you would not even notice."

"True," he agreed, "but then I would have to endure your mother's incessant matchmaking."

Melissant giggled at some remembered event. "Aye, but 'twould be good for a laugh, wouldn't it?"

"At my expense," Keith grumbled.

Another giggle. "How are Grandmother and Grandfather?"

He shrugged. "Well, I would guess. They have been in London for over a month now."

"At court?"

"Aye."

Melissant wrinkled her nose. "Stuffy," she said, then asked, "Does Mother know you're here?"

"I have just come from her."

"And no doubt she was as surprised to see you as I. Everyone knows how much you dislike these events."

"Is that right?"

Sharing a secretive smile with her uncle, Melissant turned back to Alessandra. "As you have already guessed," she said, "this is my half sister, Alessandra Bayard."

Without hesitation, Keith bridged the distance separating them. "Catherine's daughter," he said, catching Alessandra's hand. "I did not think it possible, but you are more lovely than your mother." He brushed his lips across the backs of her fingers.

"You knew her, then?" she asked.

A reminiscent smile appearing, Keith released her hand. "Of course. Did she never speak of me?"

Alessandra searched her memory for mention of Agnes's brother, but came up empty. "I . . . don't believe so," she said with apology.

He shrugged. "Ah well, as I was several years older than she, and not often around due to my training for knighthood, 'tis not surprising she would have forgotten me."

"I—"

"Pray, excuse me, ladies," he said, looking past them. "There is an old friend I must needs speak with." Smiling, he strode away and was quickly swallowed by the mass of bodies.

"Too bad 'tis not a lady friend he seeks," Melissant said on a sigh.

"He is not wed?" Alessandra asked.

"Nay, he is not, and has never been."

"Why? He seems most eligible."

Melissant pursed her lips. "Mother says he loved once and lost to another, and that he foolishly waits to find such love again."

Alessandra was struck with sadness—not only for Keith, but for herself. Would she also wander the rest of her days in search of the love Lucien denied her? Would she grow old never knowing the happiness of a love returned?

"Do not cry for him," Melissant said, noticing the huge tears welling in Alessandra's eyes. "Uncle Keith is quite content with his lot."

Alessandra blinked the moisture away, then summoned a smile.

"You can do better than that," Melissant said. She poked a tickling finger in Alessandra's ribs.

Humor restored, Alessandra rolled her eyes and allowed herself to be pulled along after her sister. A moment later, though, she bumped into her when Melissant came to an abrupt halt.

A gurgle of laughter parted Alessandra's lips, but died when she looked up to find Lucien standing two strides in front of them.

Or was it he? Such fine clothes he wore, and so well groomed was he that he did not seem the man who had brought her out of Algiers. But it was he, and the same brilliant eyes that had once shone with desire were as flat and condemning as they had been following her revelation about her parentage.

As they stared at each other he scrutinized her more thoroughly than any of the others—except, perhaps, Bishop Armis—making her realize her entrance into the great hall had been far less of an ordeal than she had thought.

On the ship, he had warned her about the use of kohl and forbidden her to stitch up her hem when she had commented in passing on how much easier it would be to wear the gowns shorter. He had told her it was not English, and now she knew him to be right.

Though her heart constricted, she made herself smile. Then, pulling her hand free of Melissant's, she stepped forward to greet him. Before she could speak, though, the call to feast came.

The press of men and women eager to take their places at the well-laid tables forced Alessandra back. Again, she collided with Melissant, who steadied her and saved her from plunging to her knees.

Lucien disappeared.

" 'Twas him, wasn't it?" Melissant asked with awe.

Alessandra looked over her shoulder. "Aye, but where did he go?"

Melissant frowned. "Probably to his table," she said, then added, "which is what we should be doing."

Seated at the high table beside the bishop, Alessandra knew even greater discomfort. When the man stood and said grace over the meal, she knew without raising her bowed head that he watched her. When she answered the question put to her by the knight at her other side, she was certain he listened. By presence alone, Bishop Armis made himself all-seeing and all-hearing. It was an uncomfortable situation, made even less comfortable by Lucien's presence and his slighting of her.

A lady on either side of him, he sat at one of the side tables—a respectable distance from the high table, considering the past feud between the two families. Likely it was the first time a De Gautier had ever dined with a Bayard.

As the meal commenced Alessandra marveled for the hundredth time at the experience of dining among men. Most were without manners of any sort, which, unfortunately, included her father. They overstuffed their mouths, spoke before swallowing, wiped their dribbled chins on their sleeves, and often belched.

Now she better understood why Muslim ladies dined separate from men. It was a most unsightly experience, though she had to admit that she herself preferred it. After all, it created an interesting diversion during a meal made far too long.

Feeling isolated, Alessandra broached a conversation with the knight—one Sir Rexalt—who sat beside her. Fortunately, he turned out to be of a talkative nature and inclined to bouts of laughter, which helped to take her mind off Lucien. Conversely, he touched her hand and arm often, though he made it seem quite innocent.

Only when James rose between courses to toast Lucien's return to the living did Alessandra glance Lucien's way again—and met eyes brimming with reproach. Was he angry with her for conversing with the knight? she wondered.

"I welcome home to England he who has given my daughter back to me—Lucien de Gautier," James bellowed that all might take notice. Having gained their attention, he raised his goblet. "To everlasting peace," he said, "and the union of our families."

Lucien remained seated while the other men in the hall quickly rose to their feet—all except two seated near Lucien.

Relations? Alessandra wondered. The younger definitely looked to be a brother. Though smaller in stature, his features were too similar to Lucien's not to be. And the handsome one had to be the middle brother, Vincent.

Melissant had told her what a beautiful man he was, and none other fit the description so well. Alessandra wondered why Melissant had so readily accepted the breaking of her betrothal to him.

She looked back at Lucien. Although a half smile turned his mouth, she felt the anger seething beneath his schooled facade. What did he intend? she anxiously wondered.

In unison, goblets were carried to a hundred pair of lips. However, few found their mark as Lucien suddenly surged upright.

"To the return of my lands," he said, his goblet raised higher than the rest, "and then peace." Eyes fixed on James, he drained the last of his wine, then slammed the vessel to the table.

A stunned silence enveloped the hall, the tension Lucien had brought to it increasing tenfold before James finally lightened it with forced laughter.

"Do you hope to escape marriage, young Lucien, 'twill cost you much in coin."

Coin that all knew the De Gautiers were sorely lacking due to Vincent's penchant for gambling.

Lucien's smile widened. "Better coin than a Bayard," he said.

Gasps of disbelief sounded around the room—mostly from women who cast pitying looks on Melissant.

Alessandra also looked at Melissant, who appeared more like a girl than the young woman she had earlier. Coloring prettily, she sat erect beside her gaping brother, her mouth trembling, her moist eyes on the giant of a man who had just paid insult to her.

Alessandra could not help herself, anger at Lucien's callousness forcing her to her feet. "A shared sentiment," she railed, uncaring what any thought of her outburst.

Lucien shifted his cold gaze to her. "Is it?" he asked. "Then what of you, Lady Alessandra? Would you also find such a match objectionable?"

"Indeed." Though the word did not echo what was in her heart, she easily threw it at this arrogant man who had completely forgotten her in the weeks gone by.

His jaw hardened. His eyes snapped with rancor.

If the speculation about their relationship had been spoken aloud, it could have been no more tangible. Melissant forgotten, the guests waited to see what would follow.

James ended the waiting. "We will settle this in the lists tomorrow, Lucien." He spoke between clenched teeth.

Lucien released Alessandra from his scrutiny and looked to his host. "Think you are up to it, old man?"

James's nostrils flared and the corners of his mouth tightened until they were pinched white. However, he did not let go of his control. "I will be there, Lucien. Will you?"

Lucien inclined his head. " 'Tis my reason for attending the tourney."

Lifting his glass-bottomed tankard, James quaffed his drink and sat.

The others followed suit, though it was more to wet throats that had gone dry from unease than to participate in the toast gone awry.

It took quantities more wine and ale before the life of the banquet returned. Regardless, throughout the festivities that followed—the music of the jongleurs, the songs of the minstrels, and dancing—a pall hung over Alessandra that forbade her to enjoy her celebration.

What would the morrow bring? she wondered, watching from the shadows as an actor performed a mime. Peace or bloodshed?

Her searching eyes found Lucien, flanked by his brothers, across the hall. Lounging against a wall, he watched the mime's performance with no more interest than she. And then, as if aware of her regard, he looked her way.

Unnerved, Alessandra stepped deeper into the shadows. Who would be victor on the morrow? she wondered. A father she was growing to love, or the man who possessed her heart?

CHAPTER 26

"I do not see Lucien's," Alessandra whispered to Melissant.

Frowning, Melissant popped up on tiptoe to peer over the ladies crowded before the table that displayed the contenders' banners and crested helms. "There," she said, pointing to the far end of the canopied table where the De Gautier red and gold fluttered in the morning breeze.

Alessandra nodded. "I see it, but why is his last?"

"You would ask that after what happened yestereve?"

So, this was the penalty James had levied against Lucien. "I see," Alessandra muttered.

"Oh, look!" Melissant exclaimed. "Sir Simeon's helm is being taken down."

An excited stir rippled through the ranks of women as they attempted to guess what had warranted the removal of the intricately embossed helm.

"I don't understand," Alessandra said.

"It means a lady has accused him of doing wrong," Melissant explained. "Thus he is banished from the lists."

"He will not be allowed to compete?"

"Nay. To watch, and that is all. Likely, though, his disgrace will keep him from the tournament altogether."

For a moment Alessandra considered this a means by which she might prevent Lucien and James from publicly carrying out their private battle.

She sighed. Nay, that would only fuel Lucien's revenge. If he did not do battle with the blunt and dull-edged weapons of tournament, he would likely do battle with those that let blood.

Pushing her way between two older ladies, Melissant gained for herself and Alessandra a place before the helms. "Aren't they marvelous?" she exclaimed with childish glee.

While Melissant chattered over the decorated helms Alessandra craned her neck to better see the one Lucien would don a short time from now. Directly beneath his banner, several helms rested on the table, red and gold plumes projecting over their crowns.

As the ladies began to drift away, their destination the pavilions to watch the opening ceremony of the tournament, Alessandra took the opportunity to get closer. Hitching up skirts that skimmed the ground—after her reception yestereve, she had decided it best to leave their hems be and her cosmetics in their pots—she walked to the magnificent panoply that was the De Gautiers'.

Thinking herself alone and unseen, she reached a hand to the helm she guessed to be Lucien's and found the metal warm beneath her fingertips. Sun, she realized, amazed she had not noticed before. Peering over her shoulder, she saw the clouds were beginning to disperse and give way to the golden orb. She beamed. At last, evidence of England's earthliness.

"He will defeat your father, you know."

Alessandra swiveled her head back around, her gaze clashing with heavily lashed blue eyes. Vincent de Gautier.

"You are speaking to me?" she asked, thankful he stood on the opposite side of the table.

"Aye."

"Why?"

He smiled beautifully—exactly as Melissant had described to her. "Curiosity," he said.

She raised questioning eyebrows.

Vincent's lower lip dropped, enlarging his white smile. "My brother is much changed from when he left for France," he explained. "Now I am beginning to understand why."

Was he implying she was responsible for that change—

whatever it might be? Farfetched. If she had touched Lucien's life in any way, it had only been briefly, with no lasting effect, as proven these past weeks by his silence, and last night by his contempt.

"Methinks you ought to look elsewhere for answers," she said. "Namely, the war he fought on French soil and the slavery he was pressed into thereafter. Therein lies your answer, Sir Vincent."

His smile slipped. " 'Twas not what I was referring to," he said. "That side of him I understand."

"Obviously not," she returned.

Melissant chose that moment to come join Alessandra. "Ah, 'tis you," she said to Vincent. Had she slapped him, her scorn could not have been more apparent.

"Lady Melissant," he said, inclining his head.

Her mouth compressed into a lipless line.

Vincent must have found something humorous about her behavior, for his smile returned. "Ladies, I take your leave," he said, and pivoted away.

"Knave," Melissant muttered, her narrowed eyes following him out of sight.

"You do not like him, do you?" Alessandra asked.

Melissant looked at her. "You put it mildly. That I do not have to wed with that whoremonger is evidence enough of a God."

"Now who speaks heresy?" Alessandra teased.

Melissant's nose crinkled. "But 'tis true," she said. "He would have made a most unsatisfactory husband."

Though Melissant had never expounded on the matter, it had remained an item of curiosity for Alessandra, especially considering Melissant's inclination toward handsome men. "Surely you find him attractive?" she prompted.

Shrugging, Melissant pulled the golden plume atop Lucien's helm through her hand. "Who would not? But Vincent is neither responsible, nor faithful, his only gift a face women make themselves fools over. God willing, I will wed a man who wisely guards his money and shares only my bed."

Aye, God willing. Though to Alessandra the Christian law of one man to one woman seemed a wonderful institution, unlike Algiers where a man could take several wives, she had learned it was not uncommon for Englishmen to bed with other women. And yet they condemned the practice of polygamy. Hypocrites.

"You would do poorly in a harem," she said, remembering Melissant's enthusiasm for stories of that exotic place.

"You think?"

"Most assuredly."

Melissant exaggerated a sigh. "Then in England I must remain."

"Let the jousters make ready!" an unseen herald called loudly as he wound his way through the avenues of tents, rousing the knights within.

Linking an arm through Alessandra's, Melissant turned them toward the pavilions.

"A moment," Alessandra said. Pulling free, she turned back to Lucien's helm. Considering the words they had exchanged the night before, it was foolish what she did, but she had to. Her body shielding her, she quickly traced the sign of the cross above the eye slit of the visor. "The Lord protect," she whispered, then swung back to Melissant.

"What did you do?" Melissant asked.

Alessandra took her arm. "Naught. To the pavilions?"

Melissant grimaced. "You are an odd one."

"Verily."

Grudgingly accepting Alessandra's evasion, Melissant jutted her chin toward the pavilions that were nearly filled to capacity. "We are late," she said. "Mother will not be pleased."

Though Alessandra did not say it, she was disappointed to discover they were not to join the other ladies. Instead, they were seated in the center pavilion reserved for the family of Bayard and visiting dignitaries.

Unfortunately, that included Bishop Armis, whose seat provided him full view of Alessandra. Beside him sat Agnes, her smile false, her eyes hawking Alessandra's every move.

The mass sung, the parade commenced shortly thereafter.

The display was like nothing Alessandra had ever seen. As giver of the tournament, her father came first. Resplendent in Bayard blue, he led four camp marshals—senior knights chosen to oversee the contests—into the lists. They were followed by heralds who cried encouragement to the combatants.

The knights, riding two by two, outfitted in burnished armor and long spurs, and each preceded by a banner bearer, sat atop warhorses. Though the destriers of the lesser knights were modestly arrayed, several wore complete head-and-neck armor, elaborately worked muzzles and stirrups, double reins, and richly decorated coverings Melissant called trappers.

As the first of the knights completed the circuit of the tilt—a wooden barrier erected to separate jousters and to prevent their horses from colliding—and passed by the pavilions, he began to sing. Soon the rousing melody was taken up by the other knights and ladies in the pavilions, causing the lists to quake with their joyously raised voices.

Alessandra was just recovering from the unexpected singing when a most peculiar thing happened. Married and unmarried ladies alike began removing items of clothing with great enthusiasm—stockings, hair ribbons, gloves, girdles, and even sleeves that they tore from their gowns. Alessandra looked to Melissant for an explanation, but found her bent over in the process of removing a stocking. Nay, both stockings!

Turning back to the knights, Alessandra saw that as they pranced their mounts before the pavilions, unabashed ladies leaned forward and tied their castoffs to the tips of proffered lances. Even terribly dignified and proper Agnes joined in.

What did it all mean, this strange ritual? she wondered, feeling more out of place than ever. And where was Lucien? She stretched her neck to see past the contestants waiting to enter the lists, but could not pick him out among the numerous armored knights.

"Be mindful where you place your favor," Melissant warned, "lest you find yourself pursued by one you would rather not."

Alessandra looked around in time to observe the enthusiasm with which Melissant's uncle Keith received an array of favors. "Is that what the ladies are doing?" she asked. "Showing favor?"

"Aye, and so shall I." Proudly, Melissant held up her stockings.

"To whom will you give them?"

Melissant played coy for a moment, her lashes fluttering, her lips pinched into a puckered smile. "Hmm." She touched the tip of a finger to her lips. "Methinks the youngest De Gautier quite fair, don't you?"

Jervais? "He is also competing?"

"Of course."

"And Vincent?"

Melissant shrugged. "Likely he is too busy consorting with the joy women to prove himself a man."

"Joy women?"

"Ah, Alessandra, you have much to learn. See yon woman with her skirts hiked high?" She pointed across the lists to where the tents of the competing knights were pitched, then put her lips to Alessandra's ear. "For but a coin," she whispered, "she will service a man and give him what a lady would never allow."

Alessandra started. "Truly?"

"Would I play you false?" She sat back in her chair and smiled impishly. "Now tell me which knight you intend to favor. Perhaps Lucien de Gautier?"

"Never," Alessandra blurted.

"Father says 'tis a word one should never use."

Alessandra folded her hands in her lap and turned her attention back to the colorful knights. "Methinks Lucien would rather dangle the stocking of a joy woman from his lance than that of a Bayard," she muttered.

Melissant sighed. "You must choose someone. I would suggest Sir Simeon, but he has been banned from competing." She cogitated a moment, then her eyes lit. "Sir Rexalt," she said. "He would be perfect."

Alessandra recalled the good-natured knight who had sat beside her during the banquet yestereve. Though he had been a bit on the short side—barely topping her—he had been amiable and pleasing to the eye. "Aye, Sir Rexalt it is," she agreed.

"The ribbon in your hair would do nicely," Melissant suggested.

Alessandra fingered it. "Not my sleeve?"

Melissant giggled. "Only if you wish to ruin your gown. And then the poor knight will think you are most serious about him."

Which was the furthest thing from Alessandra's mind. "Very well," she said, beginning to unbraid her hair through which she had woven the red ribbon.

Suddenly Melissant jumped to her feet and waved her stockings. "Sir John!" she called to an approaching knight. "Come hither."

Grinning, the knight led his horse in a caper as he neared the pavilion.

"What of Sir Jervais?" Alessandra asked.

Melissant looked over her shoulder. "I've two stockings, haven't I?"

Amused, Alessandra watched as her sister tied a stocking to the lance Sir John leveled at her.

"Much honored, Lady," the knight said, reverence in his voice. Inclining his head, he urged his horse onward.

A pretty blush on her cheeks, Melissant sank into her chair again.

When next Alessandra looked up, she glimpsed the end of the procession, which surely numbered in excess of sixty knights. There, waiting to enter the lists, sat Lucien atop an enormous destrier draped with an emblazoned trapper. Unlike its rider, however, the spirited animal wore no armor.

Visor raised, Lucien stared across the lists to the pavilions, blatantly ignoring the center pavilion where Alessandra sat.

Her ire flared. He would not so much as acknowledge her, easily forgetting all they had shared in favor of his godforsaken revenge. Gladly, she told herself, she would tie her ribbon to the lance of Sir Rexalt, who was only now entering the lists himself.

"I do not believe it." Melissant's voice broke into her thoughts.

"What?" Alessandra asked.

"Just look." She pointed toward Lucien. "Sir Vincent also competes."

True. Alessandra had been too intent on Lucien to notice his brothers making up the rear of the procession. Side by side, Vincent and Jervais waited patiently for their turn at the lists. "Perhaps you have judged Vincent too harshly," she said.

Melissant harrumphed. "I do not think so."

Not for the first time Alessandra wondered if she had also judged wrongly. Lucien was entitled to his anger. After all, he had left England the heir to wealthy lands and returned to an estate far diminished by the actions of his brother and James Bayard. If only he would not direct his anger at her . . .

His banner bearer going before him, Lucien angled his lance upright and spurred his horse forward. Vincent and Jervais followed.

Though it was by no means an esteemed position to be the last to parade the lists, the ladies grew more enthusiastic with the coming of the De Gautiers. Or perhaps, Alessandra thought, it was just her imagination.

Nay, it was not. The excitement was real, the shrieks unimagined.

"I am told they fight fierce," Melissant said. "Lucien and Jervais, that is. Ere he left for France, Lucien was a favorite among the ladies."

Jealousy warmed Alessandra. "You have never witnessed it yourself?"

"Nay. 'Tis rare Bayards and De Gautiers come together anywhere other than on a battlefield."

Until now. Of course, Lucien might well turn the lists into his own private battlefield.

So caught up was Alessandra in watching Lucien that if not for Melissant elbowing her, Sir Rexalt would have passed by unnoticed.

Gripping the ribbon, she stood and beckoned to him. His smile, seemingly perpetual, grew wider.

"Lady Alessandra," he said, lowering his lance. "I am most grateful for your regard."

Head bent to the task of securing the ribbon between

the sleeve and girdle of two other ladies, Alessandra became aware of Lucien's eyes boring into her. She jerked the bow tight. What did he care whom she bestowed favor upon? He did not want it.

Sir Rexalt hoisted his lance and waved it jubilantly, then urged his destrier forward again.

Still standing, Alessandra raised her chin and looked across to Lucien, who had only just completed his parade at the tilt. Their eyes met. Was the anger in his gaze simply that, or was there some jealousy to it?

Riding to the far pavilion, Lucien lowered his lance for the favors the women clamored to bestow upon him. Like brightly colored streamers, more than a half-dozen articles adorned it when he came away.

Next, he advanced to the center pavilion and positioned his destrier before Alessandra. However, he did not lower his lance—even when the lady seated beside Agnes waved him to her.

The roar of the pavilions lapsed into speculative murmurs as all turned their attention upon the two.

Not realizing she was onstage, Alessandra continued to stare at Lucien. In spite of the distinct scar tracing his cheekbone, the hard planes of his face, and a mouth that offered no hint of a smile, he suddenly seemed a most handsome man.

Thinking that if he would only give her some encouragement she would gladly tear both sleeves from her gown, Alessandra offered him a tentative smile. But the eyes he swept her with gave no encouragement.

As she sank back into her chair Lucien moved on and gained several more favors before exiting the lists.

Jervais and Vincent also paused before the center pavilion. Completely ignoring Vincent, Melissant tied her second stocking to Jervais's lance.

Though Vincent certainly had no more need of favors, he ill disguised his disappointment at being snubbed.

"Did you see Mother?" Melissant whispered as the lists cleared. "I thought she was going to snatch my stocking right off Jervais's lance."

Alessandra frowned. "She does not like him?"

"She does not know him."

"Then?"

"He is not the heir, and only an heir will satisfy her."

And Lucien was the De Gautier heir. Yet he had made it abundantly clear that not even for the return of his lands would he wed a Bayard.

A herald crying the commencement of the contests started the clamor anew. "Come joust he who wishes to do battle!" he called.

Trumpets blared, and favors that had escaped being bestowed upon knights were scattered to the sanded ground of the lists.

With the appearance of the two champions chosen to be the first to joust, a collective gasp wended through the pavilions.

Alessandra looked up to see Lucien and James being led upon their destriers by their respective squires to opposite ends of the lists. For a moment it seemed as if her heart stopped beating, then she gulped air and felt it race with fear. No doubt it was a fitting opening to the tournament to face these two adversaries off after the events of yestereve, but it boded no good as far as she was concerned.

Facing each other from opposite sides of the tilt, Lucien and James lowered their visors and made ready for the confrontation.

Moving away, the squires nodded to the chief marshal, who called loudly, "In the name of God and King Henry, do battle!"

As one body, all in the pavilions rose and began to shout as the knights and their destriers came to life. They raced down the lists toward each other, the ground trembling, sand spraying, and all Alessandra could do was join her hands in prayer.

Unable to move out of her chair, she tensed as Lucien and James simultaneously bent low over their saddles, brought their shields up, and dropped their lances before them.

The sound of their meeting was deafening, the splintering of wood like the crack of thunder. Clapping her hands over her ears, Alessandra watched in disbelief as the destriers struggled to regain their balance, both riders brandished broken lances and scraped shields, and the spectators shouted their excitement.

Though Melissant had described to Alessandra the contest of the joust, never had she imagined such a horrific display. It seemed so primitive.

Lucien and James turned their destriers and cantered back to position, where they were met by their squires wielding new lances. Once again they rushed at each other and met the same fate as before, both sustaining broken lances and battered shields. And again—with the same result. Finally, each having broken three lances, it should have been called a draw and ended there. Instead, the contestants took up fresh lances and rode a fourth time.

The moment before they met, James swerved slightly, enough to cause him to miss his mark and to take the full impact of Lucien's lance across his shield. Propelled out of the saddle, he fell to the ground and narrowly escaped being trampled by his destrier.

Melissant's shriek was muted by shouts of enthusiasm all around.

Dear God, let it be over that I might wander the garden instead, Alessandra prayed. That I might put my nose into a most boring book. Anything but watch grown men behave as animals.

Melissant turned to her. "Now Father must pay De Gautier a ransom for his horse and armor," she said.

"Whatever for?"

" 'Tis the price of the victor."

A commotion in the lists brought Alessandra's and Melissant's attention back to it. On his feet, his armor dulled by the dust and scratch of sand, James thrust his sword toward Lucien. An unspoken challenge.

Alessandra leaped to her feet to stand alongside Melissant. "Is it not done with?" she asked, panic-stricken.

" 'Twould appear otherwise," Melissant answered around the thumbnail she was steadily chewing.

Lucien slid his visor back. "The ransom, first," he said.

A hushed silence descended as all awaited James's response. "Name it." His angry voice rang from the depths of his helm.

"De Gautier lands."

James shoved his visor back. "You know the price, Lucien. 'Tis not coin that will buy them back."

Lucien glanced to where Alessandra and her half sister stood. "Nor Bayard wife," he said. Damn her for the sun in her hair that reminded him of gentler moments and emotions he had never thought to feel, that called to his baser needs and warmed his loins with urgency, that stirred jealousy at the remembrance of her giving favor to Rexalt.

" 'Tis your last insult," James shouted, his sword gleaming in the sun. "Come down from your horse, De Gautier bastard."

Dancing his destrier sideways, Lucien bided his time in a waiting silence that was so tangible, he felt it on his indrawn breath. "For a price," he said at last.

James issued a burst of harsh laughter. "The lands are mine," he reiterated. "Only under my terms will they be restored to you."

"And only under my terms will I enter swordplay with you, old man," Lucien retorted, then set forth what those terms would be. "Should I be victor, you agree to sell the De Gautier lands to me for the price you paid. Should I lose"—he glanced to the pavilions, then back—"I will agree to your peace through marriage."

How the words burned his throat. But they were only words, he assured himself. Words that would never be acted upon. He'd spent these past weeks in merciless training for this confrontation, and if his sword arm remained as true as he had honed it, he need not worry about the humiliation of being forced to wed in order to regain his lands. Aye, he would better James Bayard— and however many others it took to raise the money.

Though it was clear to all that James burned to test his skill against Lucien's, he lowered his sword. "Naught, then."

Lucien smiled. "You need not fear my sword, Lord Bayard," he taunted, pulling the weapon from its sheath. "As you can see, 'tis dull-edged for the tourney and would draw little blood. Too, I would be gentle with you."

James's sword swept the air again. "I fear no man's sword," he shouted. The portion of his face that was visible colored at the insult.

Drawing his quarry in, Lucien resheathed his sword. "You fear mine, else you would trust yours to keep the lands. Perhaps your sword arm has grown infirm with age?"

James's struggle lasted less than a half minute before he hurled his sword to the sand and shouted to his squire, "Bring me a blade worthy of piercing this bastard!"

Lucien's blood surged, his heart pumping fiercely with anticipation. "My terms, Bayard?" he asked.

"Aye, but also your blood," James snarled.

Triumphant, Lucien called for a cutting sword as well. Then, accompanied by the shouts of a goading crowd, he dismounted and slapped a hand to the destrier's rump. The animal swung about and trotted across the lists.

Her throat dry, fear squeezing the breath from her, Alessandra turned disbelieving eyes to Melissant. "True weapons are not permitted at tourneys," she said, repeating what she had been told earlier.

Her face mirroring Alessandra's concern, Melissant nodded. "Aye, 'tis not looked kindly upon by the Church."

Both turned to Bishop Armis.

His attention on the scene unfolding before him, the man appeared not the least disconcerted by the challenge that was being taken up. In fact, he seemed most eager for it, leaning forward in his chair, his gaze intent with the interest a worldly man might show a comely wench.

Even more obvious was Agnes, her eager smile, sparkling eyes, and shifting carriage evidence that she was not averse to a contest that might see one or both men wounded, perhaps even dead.

It appalled Alessandra, this blood lust echoed by ladies and men alike.

"What say you we dispense with the armor?" James yelled. "Excepting the breastplate."

Honed sword in hand, Lucien motioned for his squire to remain. Then, unhurriedly, he held the weapon before him and looked down one edge, twisted his wrist, and looked down the other. "We may dispense with it altogether if you prefer," he finally answered.

James refused the bait. "For the love of the ladies, the breastplate remains."

Lucien shrugged. "As you will."

Immediately, the squires began the painstaking process of removing the armor piece by piece.

Desperate, Alessandra glanced at the bishop again, but found him as unmoving as before, though a poorly suppressed smile tightened the corners of his mouth. Thinking to appeal to him, she made to step around Melissant. However, Melissant caught her arm and pulled her back.

"What think you you are doing?" she asked.

"I would speak with the bishop. Surely he cannot allow this to go forward."

Melissant shook her head. "He more than any enjoys such sport, Alessandra. You will only anger him by interfering."

"But if I do not, who will?" Alessandra demanded.

"None. 'Tis a part of England, these contests. You cannot change that."

Catching her bottom lip between her teeth, Alessandra looked back to the lists. The squires and varlets were carrying away the armor. All that remained were the breastplates and arming doublets they were attached to.

"Fools," she muttered.

The chief marshal called for the contestants to take position, then cried, "Make worthy of your ancestry. Do battle!"

For Alessandra, what followed was a blur, the coming together of Lucien and James and the clash of their swords a terrible thing to witness. Hugging her arms about her, she forced herself to watch the confrontation, unconsciously tensing with each blow of steel on steel.

Though Lucien had the advantage of height, James appeared a good match, his greater experience making up for the ten inches he lacked in stature. Still, Lucien was the first to land his sword, piercing James's mailed sleeve and causing the links to color bright red.

Amid the roar of the crowd, James cursed vehemently, retreated, then raised his shield and lunged forward again. "Get your fill, De Gautier," he yelled, "for 'tis all you will have of a Bayard."

But it was not all.

Lucien landed another blow, denting James's breast-plate, but for all his effort, left himself open and vulnerable. Taking advantage of the moment, James swung his sword and slashed through Lucien's unprotected thigh.

Blood discolored Lucien's chausses, but he showed no reaction, guarding his pain well. Without pause, he continued to hack and slice forward, his sword point slashing his opponent's jaw, then cutting downward and catching the edge of James's shield and sending it flying.

Without his shield, James's fate was questionable. But he did not appear to question it. Roaring wrath, he pressed ahead and was granted a swipe at Lucien's arm. More blood flowed, alternately Lucien's and James's.

The crowd grew more frenzied with each blow, their cheers and excited voices closing in on Alessandra until she could hardly breathe. With her teeth clenched so hard it was painful, her mind reeled with every prayer she had ever memorized. Unbeknownst to her, hot tears slipped to her lashes, clung a moment, then slid down her cheeks to wet the neck of her gown.

When the continually shifting battleground moved to a place directly before the center pavilion, she took a faltering step back, but not before her father's blood sprayed the air and flecked her and the others in the front row.

Alessandra stared disbelievingly at the erratic pattern of red across her bodice, then cried, "No more!"

Pushing past a stunned Melissant, who was also horrified to find herself marked by the battle, she placed herself before the bishop.

"You must stop this!" she entreated, uncaring that she drew attention to herself. "It cannot continue."

Annoyed by her outburst, the bishop waved a fluttery hand at her. "You block my view, child," he said.

"Your view?" she repeated, hardly able to believe she

had heard right. Enraged, she set herself more fully before him and completely obliterated his view of the lists.

"Is it not the edict of the Church that only weapons of peace be used at tournaments?" she demanded.

The bishop's nostrils flared, all pretense of tolerance gone. "Remove yourself from my presence," he ordered.

Though Alessandra intended to stand firm, Agnes pulled her off balance and out of the way. " 'Tis the way of men, Alessandra," she hissed. "Now take your seat or I will have you returned to the keep."

"I will not!" Alessandra said. "It is wrong. A tournament—"

Agnes shook her. " 'Tis no longer a tournament. A vendetta is what it is, and one that ought to have been settled long ago."

Alessandra broke free of her hold and stumbled back a step. "Not this way," she said. "Not with blood."

"Aye, with blood," the woman shot back. "As much blood as it takes to bring the De Gautier dog to heel."

Disbelief rendered Alessandra speechless. Such hate. Such venomous loathing. Dear God, though her mother had said England was where she belonged, it seemed no better than Algiers. Nay, worse. This woman was James's wife, yet it mattered not that he was injured, or doing injury to another—to the De Gautier dog as she had called Lucien.

Alessandra straightened to her full height. "You are a pitiful excuse for a Christian," she said, knowing her voice carried, but making no attempt to lower it. She turned to the bishop and met his imperious gaze. "As are you."

She heard the crack of stricken flesh before she felt the heated sting. Shock knelling through her, Alessandra touched her cheek where Agnes had slapped her, then looked to the woman's disdainful face.

Odd, but Agnes's expression reminded her of another. Another who had shown little emotion in the face of death, Sabine's death, whose eyes had challenged Alessandra to prove her wrongdoing. Who would have been equally content, perhaps more so, had it been Alessandra who had taken the poison.

Alessandra blinked to dispel the face of the woman more familiar than Agnes, but it came before her again, and again, drawing her back to a past she had nearly convinced herself was closed.

As disquiet gave rise to anger Alessandra found it impossible to hold back from what she knew could not possibly be. Lunging forward, she fell upon the one who wore Leila's face.

Though Agnes's husky grunt of surprise distinguished her from Leila, all Alessandra could think was that this woman was responsible for her mother's murder. And this time she would pay.

A chair collapsing beneath the thrust of their combined weight carried them to the floor of the pavilion. Blocking out the commotion around her, Alessandra clenched her hands around Leila's neck. Against her fingers she felt straining muscles; her palms, the vibrations of a rasping scream; and her thumbs, the swift flow of blood that would soon flow no more. But it was not Leila's face that stared in horror up at her. It was Agnes's come back to the present.

Alessandra faltered, her hands slackening, and in the next instant was gripped beneath the arms and lifted.

Feeling as if she'd been startled awake from a dream, she looked over her shoulder and into Lucien's beautiful eyes. How had he come to be there? What of the contest with her father? She turned to him, trying to make sense of the last few minutes. "I thought ... Leila ..." She shook her head, then pressed her face against the warm metal of his armor.

Lucien's arms coming around her was the most wonderful thing she had felt in weeks.

From her haven, she heard her father's voice, Agnes's enraged shrieks, the bishop's condemning words, and the chatter of the crowd, but she refused to give up Lucien. Quelling the urge to cover her ears, she held to him and tried not to think of the rejection that might come at any moment.

"Quiet, woman!" she heard James order.

Agnes finished her accusation, claiming Alessandra had attacked her without just cause, then she fell silent.

The bishop's self-important voice filled the air then. He asserted that the "infidel"—being herself, Alessandra assumed—had insulted both Agnes and himself, and been corrected with a slap that in no way made recompense for what she had said.

"Lord Bishop, I assure you Alessandra is a Christian." James's own voice was carefully schooled to reflect veneration and humility. "Her mother raised her by our faith without taint of the infidel. 'Tis simply a matter of England and its ways being foreign to Alessandra, but in time she will learn. I implore you to accept my apologies for her conduct."

Alessandra started to protest her father's apology, but Lucien pressed a hand to the back of her head and held her still. "Be silent," he hissed.

"I am not so sure she is without taint, as you say," the bishop argued. "Methinks she ought to be questioned to determine the truth of the matter."

Alessandra felt Lucien stiffen.

"I attest to her purity of heart, Lord Bishop," James said. "Each morning she attends mass and offers prayers to our Lord. She knows the Bible well and quotes scripture quite capably. She—"

"Yet she shows her body like a common trollop, lines her eyes with the black of the devil, speaks out of turn, shows no respect for the clergy or her elders, and has just now attacked your good wife."

"Lord Bishop," James said, "do you speak of the gown she wore yestereve, 'twas a simple mistake that it was hemmed improperly. It was too late to correct the problem by the time it was discovered. As for the cosmetics, she has been told it is improper and does not wear any today. The rest . . . the rest she will learn."

An expectant silence followed, grew, then was burst by the bishop. "You excuse all her sin as trivial, yet even now she clings to a man who is not her husband."

"She is frightened, Lord Bishop. This is her first tourney, and no doubt a shock to her."

"Methinks you do not understand the gravity of the situation, Bayard," the bishop reproved. "Your daughter could be tried as a heretic. She—"

"No doubt," Lucien smoothly interrupted, "you are also shocked to see blood shed in a manner condemned by the Church. 'Tis verily the reason you did not protest, is it not?"

It was clearly a threat, and one that the bishop was wise not to dismiss. A tense silence followed, then he began to sputter. "But she ... I ..."

"No harm has been done," Lucien concluded. "Though methinks 'twould be best if Lady Alessandra attends no more contests."

"Aye," James agreed. "For the best."

"Very well," the bishop grudgingly conceded. "This matter is concluded, then."

"But what of the attack upon my person!" Agnes protested. "Look at my throat. Surely I will be bruised come noon. I demand punishment where punishment is due."

Whatever James rasped into her ear, none but she knew. However, it silenced her.

Lucien turned a willing Alessandra toward the steps that led down from the pavilion and headed for the castle walls. However, James stepped into their path.

"I will take her," he said.

Lifting her head, Alessandra looked at her father's battered figure, then his face. He did not look the enraged warrior any longer. Indeed, he looked weary and more than a little gaunt.

Wordlessly, Lucien stepped around him and led her away from the lists. He wanted her as far from them as possible before he set his plan fully into motion. Though he believed she still cared for him, he did not wish her to see the animal he must become these next days to have what he sought.

"Did you not hear me, De Gautier?"

Lucien halted and turned to face James. "I hear well enough, Bayard," he said, then nodded over his shoulder. "Do you?"

From the lists came the booming voice of the chief marshal as he announced the points given to each of the contestants. Twice he named Lucien the victor—once in the joust, once in foot combat.

Dazed, Alessandra was slow to make sense of the

words, but as they unraveled she could not help but feel dirtied by them. Aye, Lucien had won, gaining the ability to purchase his lands from her father, but it seemed such an unholy price to pay.

"The ransom for your horse and armor will be high," Lucien said, then continued across the drawbridge.

James followed. "As I would expect, but 'twill not be near enough to buy back your lands."

Lucien's smile was bitter, the arm around Alessandra's waist tensing. "A start only," he said, "but be assured that by the end of this tourney, I will have amassed enough to have it all back—and then some."

"Not even you have the endurance to challenge enough comers to raise it," James retorted.

The same might have been said for the amount of soul he had given to survive the ordeal of slaving a galley, Lucien thought. But he had survived, his scarred body testimony to that. The question was, had he enough soul left to survive the quest to retrieve his lands? Aye, he told himself, but whether he would come out of this entirely soulless would be told at the end of three days.

The remainder of the way to Alessandra's chamber was walked in silence.

Once there, Alessandra reluctantly released her hold on Lucien. Sinking down upon the mattress, she drew her knees to her chest and stared at the two men facing her.

It was not just her father who was battered, she realized, but Lucien as well. His breastplate was dented, the mail of his arming doublet in disrepair, and the stain of his blood abundant. She shivered.

Immediately, James was at her side. Dragging the coverlet from the bed, he pulled it around her. "You are ill?" he asked.

"Not ill," Lucien answered for her. "Just in shock."

James touched her cheek. "Is that true?"

"I'm fine," Alessandra mumbled, hating herself for feeling the child again.

"Keep her away from the tournament," Lucien ordered, then turned to go.

"Lucien," James called after him.

Lucien stopped at the door. "Aye?"

"I have not thanked you for intervening with the bishop. Know that I am most grateful."

"I did it for her, not you."

" 'Tis obvious," James said, a knowing smile slanting his mouth.

Anxious to return to the lists where the future of the De Gautier lands lay, Lucien pulled the door open. "I take your leave now."

"Why don't you make it easy on yourself?" James said. "Wed my daughter and there will be no need for any of this."

Lucien glanced at Alessandra. "You are offering Alessandra?" he asked.

She felt as if struck by a bolt of the blue lightning that often preceded the rain in England. Would Lucien truly consider a match with her?

James nodded. "Though I do not wish to relinquish her just yet, if it would bring peace, I would."

"Nay, Bayard," Lucien said, emotionless. "I would rather spill blood than wed a Bayard to gain back De Gautier lands." Stepping through the portal, he disappeared down the corridor.

Alessandra stared at the empty doorway and knew Melissant's humiliation of yestereve, and an incredible desire to go after Lucien and repay him with every vile word—Arabic and English—she could think of. Instead, she hugged the coverlet tighter and cursed him silently.

"You love him, don't you?" James asked.

She raised startled eyes to him. How had he guessed? Did it show so clearly on her face? If so, then did Lucien also know? Her humiliation increased twentyfold.

"Why do you fear the bishop?" she asked, changing the topic.

Unmindful of soiling the bedclothes, James settled himself on the edge of the bed. "A secret, hmm?" he said. "Very well, keep it, but do not think you fool me, Catherine's daughter." Affectionately, he patted her hands.

"What of the bishop?"

His smile turned wry. "If the bishop determines you are a ..."

"What? Tell me."

"A heretic, of the Islamic belief—"

Alessandra threw off the coverlet and surged to her feet. "But you know that is not so. I am a Christian. In fact, more than he!"

"It does not matter. Many Christians whose only crime was in being different have been made to suffer terrible persecution, even put to death, Alessandra. You must suppress those things Arabic in you if you are to assuage his suspicions."

" 'Tis not fair."

"Aye, not fair, but neither is Bishop Armis. He is a powerful man in the Church and easily inflamed."

Alessandra felt her stubborn streak surface, but decided it best she keep it hidden from her father. Pretending submission, she lowered her eyes and sighed. "I will try," she said, "but it will not be easy."

CHAPTER 27

That evening in the great hall, the talk was all of Lucien's triumphs at the lists. Though he was conspicuously absent from the banquet, his deeds filled the mouths of men and women alike. Even those who had challenged him and lost spoke of the jousting and foot combat, of the blows they had successfully landed on him, the ransom they had paid for horse and armor, and their eagerness to try again.

Sitting erect and alert beside Agnes's brother, Keith, Alessandra tried not to think of Lucien and the injuries he had sustained. Over and over she told herself she didn't care what became of him, that he was undeserving of her worry, but she knew it to be false.

Rhythmically, she swung her foot beneath skirts that were overly long, but for which she'd finally found a use. The soft peal of the bells fastened about her ankle eased her anxiety. Though she pretended ignorance each time someone glanced her way, a questioning frown upon his face as he caught the sound, she continued to swing her foot.

It was rebellious of her, she knew—potentially dangerous if the bishop discovered whence the sound came—but the satisfaction she experienced in resisting some things English was worth it. Though her blood was English, in many ways she would always be of the Arabs.

"You will be found out," Keith whispered near her ear.

Feigning puzzlement, she met his eyes. "Whatever are you talking about?"

He grinned. "Perhaps I am mistaken," he said, "but methinks I hear the sound of bells coming from 'neath your skirts."

"Aye, Sir Knight, you are mistaken," she agreed, then swung her foot more vigorously.

Keith's grin melted to a charming smile. "Forgive me. It just seemed something your mother might have done."

Charged with sudden need, Alessandra stilled. "Tell me about when she was young."

"Ah, now 'tis silent," Keith said, cocking an ear to the air. "Methinks the wearer of the bells has departed the hall."

Alessandra gave her foot a shake, then checked the movement. "Nay, she is still near—just curious."

"About Catherine, I presume?"

She nodded. "As am I."

Keith's telling of Catherine as a child was animated. His food forgotten, he spoke fondly of her, grew solemn when he talked of her sadness upon first coming to live with his family, laughed when he related her antics, exaggerated grimaces when he spoke of the rivalry between Catherine and Agnes, and even became teary-eyed when he spoke of the last time he had seen her—a few months following her marriage to James.

"Though she was a cousin, I thought of her as a sister," he concluded. "In fact, it seemed I was closer to her than to Agnes."

Alessandra smiled. "Thank you for telling me," she said. "It is easier knowing my mother had you for a friend."

"Though she never spoke of me," he said, a flash of hurt entering his eyes. He blinked and it was gone.

Alessandra felt sorry for him. "I am sure Mother thought of you often," she said. "It is just that when she spoke of England, it was usually as my father's wife. She did not often mention her childhood."

Keith leaned back in his chair. "Now you must tell me of the Catherine who mothered you."

Alessandra was about to launch into an account of life in Algiers when the end of the meal was called.

"Perhaps later," Keith said as he rose.

Alessandra also stood. "I am indebted, Sir Keith," she said. "You have been very kind."

He snapped a gallant bow, then strode to the hearth where the senior knights had gathered.

Left on her own, Alessandra turned to search out Melissant and came face-to-face with a red-faced Agnes. "You will remove those pagan bells at once!" she commanded.

Determined not to be bested by a woman who thrived on throwing obstacles in her path, Alessandra crossed her arms over her chest and tipped her chin high. "I know not what you speak of," she said.

"No?" Without warning, Agnes grabbed Alessandra's skirts, clearly intending to wrench them high and expose the anklet to those whose curiosity had gotten the better of them—including Bishop Armis.

Alessandra's youthful reflexes saved her. Catching Agnes's wrist, she averted disaster. "You would reveal my limbs when the good bishop has directed they remain covered?" she asked with mock disbelief.

"I would show what it is you've hidden beneath your skirts," Agnes spat, jerking her hand free.

"I've my ankles, my knees, and my thighs," Alessandra listed, "none of which would be appropriate to bare in the hall." Her movements causing the bells to tinkle, she stepped around a scandalized Agnes and walked to where Melissant stood before a group of minstrels who were tuning their instruments.

Having watched the encounter, Melissant moaned when Alessandra reached her. "No doubt, Mother will forbid me your company yet again," she said.

And again, Alessandra thought, Melissant would appeal to their father, who would overrule Agnes.

"I wish she did not hate me so," she said. "I have done naught to earn her enmity, yet she behaves as if I have wounded her badly."

"But you have," Melissant said. "You remind our father of your mother, whom he has never made a secret of hav-

ing loved above all others. Ere you came to Corburry, my
mother was lady of the castle and had Father's affection.
Now she finds herself eclipsed by Lady Catherine once
again."

She spoke true, reminding Alessandra of the day she
had come upon mother and daughter while they studied
the household accounts. The older woman's pain at being
second in James's life had been clear then, though
Alessandra had overlooked it as she became enmeshed in
Agnes's animosity. A mistake. "It was never my intention," she said. "I will apologize."

She started to move away, but Melissant pulled her
back. "Later," she said, looking past Alessandra to her
mother. "Just now I do not think she would be very re-
ceptive."

One glance confirmed that to Alessandra. The bishop
her companion, Agnes looked anything but approacha-
ble. "Yes, later," she agreed.

Music burst upon the air as the minstrels began a
rousing tune that instantly brought the young people together.

Alessandra and Melissant stepped back to give them
the floor and watched from the sidelines as the dancing
turned vigorous.

"It surprises me," said Alessandra.

"The dance?"

"Yes. I did not know the English could dance so. Those
which Lucien taught me were slower and more con-
trolled. This reminds me—"

"Lucien taught you to dance? When?"

Inwardly, Alessandra groaned. She had not meant to
reveal so much. "On the ship," she admitted. "He
schooled me in things English, dance being one of them."

A smile lit Melissant's face. "Interesting," she murmured. "Only the slow dances, hmm? Those where he
held your hand and turned you about?"

Remembering Lucien's warning, Alessandra did not
mention that he had also showed her a more intimate
dance. Her toes curled in her slippers as she remembered
the feel of his body brushing hers, pressing, then with-

drawing. "What is this dance called?" she asked, desperate to turn the conversation.

Melissant laughed, but obliged. "The tourdion," she said.

"It looks great fun."

Melissant leaned near. "It is. Would you like to try?"

A more ridiculous question had never been asked Alessandra. Under the watchful gaze of Agnes and the bishop, she was reluctant. "Nay, I am content to watch."

"Liar," Melissant accused.

Alessandra smiled. "That I am."

Giggling, Melissant quit Alessandra's side and crossed to where a group of young noblemen stood watching. A moment later, her chosen partner in tow, she joined the others on the dance floor.

As Alessandra watched the couples move faster, their actions almost violent, she felt that familiar stirring—a yearning for her feet to move and her body to sway to the music creeping beneath her skin.

With effort, she suppressed the desire to know the music better. However, it rose again and filled her with a need impossible to deny.

She closed her eyes and learned the music, felt it wash over her and infuse her limbs. In her mind, she saw the women dancers of the harem, their filmy clothing billowing around them as they danced a dance far older than any knew.

Suddenly Alessandra was there again, joining them with a recklessness that would undoubtedly earn her Jabbar's reproach. Now, as then, she didn't care. All that mattered was the dance.

She gave herself to it, throwing her head back, lifting her arms, circling her hips, allowing her feet the rhythm to bring it all together. Marvelous! her body sang. More! the bells around her ankle cried.

The music was in her head now, pulling her deeper into its seductive embrace. It beckoned. She went to it. It wrapped itself around her. She held to it.

Still, something was missing, denying her complete immersion. Where was the caress of light garments, the

brush and tickle of unbound hair catching in her eyes and
mouth?

Without interrupting the dance, she drew her hands up
over her confining garments, wondered at their heavi-
ness, then pushed her fingers into her hair. The clothes
she could do nothing about, but her hair . . .

Finding the pins that secured the braids to her head,
she pulled them free, then unraveled the plaits. She
laughed softly as her tresses tumbled past her shoulders
and joined her in the sway of the dance.

Raising her arms again to tease the air with her fingertips, she smiled. Free. She was free.

Something came into her path, reaching for her, but she
whirled away to empty space that had not yet known the
dance.

The obstruction came again, and this time hands
caught her arms and squelched her resistance.

An angry protest on her lips, Alessandra opened her
eyes and stared at the one person she had not expected to
see that evening—Lucien. But a Lucien without the turban and robes of a eunuch. A Lucien whose stern countenance returned her to England and Corburry with a
disheartening thud.

Breathless, Alessandra looked past him to dozens of
shocked faces, including Agnes's and the bishop's. Even
the musicians, their instruments now silent, stared at her
with the same disbelief. The couples who had been dancing, including Melissant and her young man, stood on
the outskirts of the dance floor, leaving Alessandra and
Lucien alone at its center.

"Give me your hand," Lucien said.

Horrified at what she had done, she looked at him
again. "I don't know. . . ." She shook her head.

"Your hand," he repeated.

When she still did not respond, he took it himself and
lifted it within his. Then, with a nod to the minstrels, who
scrambled to accommodate the giant, he led Alessandra
into the first of the dances he had taught her, the noble
estampie.

"Smile," he said, "and do not forget your feet."

In silence, Alessandra did as told, turning her head to

focus on Lucien's face so she would not have to look upon the others who would condemn her for the rash, improper thing she had done.

Though he was not entirely pleasant to look at, the numerous cuts and bruises he had suffered that day standing out in sharp relief and making his crescent-shaped scar pale to insignificance, she could not imagine anyone she would rather rest her eyes upon. But whence had he come?

"Lucien," she began.

"Not yet," he quieted her.

Not until well into the dance did the other couples step onto the dance floor, and only then with reluctance. However, the dance that followed—a lively number—lessened the rapt attention with which Alessandra and Lucien were regarded, luring young and old alike.

"Now?" Alessandra asked.

"Later," Lucien replied.

Telling herself she must be content with being so near him, Alessandra pushed aside her questions and concentrated on the steps he guided her through. It still amazed her that one so large could move so smoothly, without hitch or strain. As it had been on the ship, he made her feel as one with him, the meeting of their hands the point at which they flowed together.

With the start of the next dance, Lucien ushered her from the dance floor and into a shadowy alcove. Turning her to him, he whispered harshly, "Did your father not warn you of the punishment of heretics?"

Another lecture, Alessandra thought, though it was probably well deserved considering the predicament she had put herself in a short time ago. "I am not a heretic," she said evenly, squinting to pick out his features.

"You learned naught from what happened today, did you? You don the bells and flaunt the dance of an infidel without thought to the consequences."

Alessandra swallowed the lump in her throat. Though the bells she had purposely donned, the dance had been beyond her control. "What do you care, anyway?" she tossed back at him. "I hear nothing from you for weeks, and when you finally appear, you cast me aside as if we had never shared a kiss."

Lucien caught her chin and lifted it. "We shared more than a kiss, Alessandra," he reminded her.

"Aye," she admitted, grateful the shadows hid her embarrassed flush, "and yet it appears to have meant naught to you."

"If I did not care, I would have left you to your dance and the bishop's denunciation."

She searched the glint of his eyes, but could read nothing in their darkened depths. "If that is true, why do you suffer abuse when all you seek could be attained through marriage?"

"I am not a coward, Alessandra," he growled.

"Nay, you are an animal," she snapped. "An animal who prefers bloodshed to peace. Who cares only for himself and the name of De Gautier."

His hand on her shoulder clenched painfully. "You do not understand," he said.

She wrenched free of him and stumbled back a step. The bells pealed softly. "But I do," she declared. "I understand you don't love me as I love you." Though she spoke aloud her heart's innermost secret, she was too angered to regret its disclosure. "And even if you did, you would not allow yourself to feel it past your loathing of the Bayards."

Whatever emotion might have shown on Lucien's face was concealed by the unlit alcove. After a time he said, "There is one rule of war you would benefit from knowing, Alessandra. Never let your enemy know the emotions which drive you, for most assuredly he will turn them against you."

War. Enemy. Emotions. The words he had chosen were like a fist to Alessandra's belly. "It is good to know you and I are at war, Lucien de Gautier," she said past the constriction in her throat. "Until now I had not realized you considered me your enemy."

Not in the broader sense of the word, Lucien thought, but as the enemy of his heart. However, if it would keep her from the lists and mock carnage, he would not disabuse her of the notion that she was his enemy. Later, once he regained his lands, there would be time for explanation. Later.

"All Bayards are my enemy," he said. Words only—hurtful words to send her away until the time was right. They served him well.

Alessandra turned and hurried from the alcove.

Brave shoulders, Lucien thought as he watched her go. They did not slump or sag, but remained squared as if she went into battle. But something was missing.

He frowned, a moment later recalling the bells. Her leaving had not been accompanied by their music. Pulling his gaze from her, he scanned the floor and caught the glint of gold where she had stood.

He scooped up the belled anklet and found it still warm from Alessandra's flesh. He smiled. Damned bells. They were the very reason he had come from his tent in the first place. Having left the banquet early, Vincent had mentioned in passing the speculation caused by the sound coming from beneath Alessandra's skirts.

Though he ached from head to foot, his spent body demanding rest, Lucien had once again appointed himself savior and arrived in the hall to discover her the center of attention. Like the others, he had stared in disbelief at the exotic dance she performed. Unlike the others, he had momentarily slipped into memories of the first time he had laid eyes upon her.

His loins uncomfortably taut, he had forced himself to action and brought Alessandra back to the present. He had not intended to dance with her, but rather, drag her from the dance floor. However, dancing with her had seemed the natural thing to do.

Stepping into the light, Lucien opened his palm and stared at the miniature bells. Alessandra would not know it, but he would carry them into the tournament on the morrow. A favor ill-gotten, but nonetheless his.

Closing the door of her chamber, Alessandra leaned back against it and gasped the sob she'd had so much trouble keeping down. Though she hated herself for the self-pity that choked her, she could not prevent the bitter tears that spilled over and streaked down her cheeks.

"Why?" she asked the darkness. "What more must I do to gain his love?" He cared for her, she knew that much, but obviously not as she did for him.

Wiping the back of her hand across her eyes, she started to move away from the door. However, laughter without stilled her. Straining to hear who it was that passed her chamber, she recognized Agnes's voice. She spoke husky words to whomever she was with, then laughed again, in a way that spoke of intimacy.

Did Agnes intend to cuckold James? Alessandra wondered. Did she seek to lessen the pain of his love for Catherine in another's arms?

Knowing she should not, but unable to ignore her worries, Alessandra eased her door open once the couple had passed by, and looked down the corridor.

Through her misery, she managed a smile.

It was James to whom Agnes spoke words of love, his arm that curved around her waist and guided them toward their chamber, he that paused and briefly covered her mouth with his, his voice that said, "I love you, Agnes."

Tipping her head back, Agnes met his gaze. "Even though I am not Catherine?" she asked.

Exasperated, as if this was not the first time she had asked the question, he shook his head. "Foolish woman. How you anger me, how you test every whit of my patience, how you make me want to shake you till your teeth clack together." Vented, he sighed. "Of course I love you," he said, "but do not ask me again to prove it. I have done enough."

Lifting onto her toes, Agnes pressed her lips to his, then accepted his lead and walked beside him the last steps to their chamber.

Gently, Alessandra pushed her door closed, her heart much lightened by the unexpected sight she had just witnessed. It was a side to both Agnes and James she would never have thought possible. Well they played the warring lord and lady of Corburry, but there was tenderness, too—as there had been between her mother and Jabbar.

The difference was that did Agnes and James remain faithful to each other, there would be no other to share their affections with. On the other hand, though Jabbar had loved Sabine, his other wives and concubines had time and again come between them.

Sinking down upon her bed, Alessandra dragged the covers up over her and snuggled deep. "I see, Mother," she said, better understanding why Sabine had insisted she was unsuited to life and marriage in the Muslim world. One man, one woman. Lucien and Alessandra. But dare she continue to hope?

CHAPTER 28

Alessandra had vowed to stay away—had not wanted to witness any more bloodshed—but the final day of the tournament had drawn her back to the lists. It was not that she wished to join in the revelry, but rather she thought it might be her last chance to see Lucien before he returned to Falstaff.

Lest her father send her away, she had dressed inconspicuously, hiding her hair beneath the hood of a cloak and keeping her head bent as she moved among the people. Eschewing the pavilions, she made herself a place at the sidelines where the lesser nobles and villeins watched.

The jousts that followed, and the occasional foot combats, were tame compared with the battle she had witnessed between Lucien and her father that first day. In fact, Alessandra found herself somewhat interested, though she still thought it a rather primitive contest whereby Englishmen proved their valor.

Vincent de Gautier's entrance into the lists sometime later caused a stir. Surprised, Alessandra listened as the chief marshal called out his victories. Of the four jousts he had taken part in, he had lost only one—to Melissant's uncle Keith.

In the evenings, Alessandra had heard only tales of Lucien's stream of victories, each bringing him closer to his goal of regaining his lands. Having heard naught of

Vincent's and Jervais's successes, she had assumed there
were none.

Now, curious as to how this De Gautier fought compared with his older brother, Alessandra watched with
avid interest as he readied himself at one end of the tilt.
The cry to "do battle" sounded, and Vincent and his opponent sent their horses charging at each other.

Crash!

Lances broken, Vincent and the other knight took up
position again, and again met midway down the tilt. This
time, however, Vincent unseated his opponent and sent
him tumbling to the ground amid a clamor of armor.

"Fairly downed!" the crowd shouted.

Triumphant, Vincent thrust his lance into the air and
waved it side to side.

A movement in the pavilions caught Alessandra's eye.
Melissant, standing beside her mother, shrieked applause
and clapped her hands with unquestionable enthusiasm.
Agnes, however, quickly squelched it.

So, Melissant was not immune to Vincent, after all,
Alessandra thought. Obviously, he had redeemed himself
with this show of mastery at the tilt.

Two jousts later, Jervais also proved himself capable,
gaining ransom from his opponent after only one run
down the lists.

How close were the De Gautiers to regaining their
land? Alessandra wondered, thinking the ransom of
horse and armor must be quite high.

The chief marshal interrupted her ponderings with the
announcement of a break in the tournament. He was
quick to whet the appetites of the crowd with the promise of two challenges Lucien had accepted, which would
be played out following the short respite.

Hungry for the savory meat pies and pastries of the
vendors, the crowd dispersed, leaving Alessandra staring
toward the tents pitched nearby. Among them would be
Lucien's.

Resisting the urge to go to him, she abruptly turned
and walked into a wall of flesh over muscle. A resonant
chuckle rose from the chest her chin bumped, and a moment later hands pushed the hood from her head.

"I thought 'twas you," Sir Keith said, grinning.

Frantic that no others see, Alessandra reached to cover herself again, but was stayed by his hands.

"So like Catherine," he said, smoothing back her unbound hair. "The looks, the spirit . . . She lives again in you."

"Please, Sir Keith," she beseeched, "if I am seen, my father will insist I return to the keep."

Sighing, he dropped his arms back to his sides. "And we would not want that, would we?"

She pulled the hood back over her hair, then peered up at him. "No," she said. "As it is the last day, I am determined to see the end of it."

"Then you will also see my joust," he said, smiling.

"I had thought you finished. Yestereve you said—"

"Aye, but I could not resist one more try," he interrupted. "But tell me, will you bestow a favor upon me, little cousin?"

His request was so unexpected, Alessandra stumbled back a step. "A favor? From me?"

He laughed. "You need not tell me I am too old for you, Lady Alessandra. That I am well aware of. 'Twould be in remembrance of Catherine only."

Alessandra did not pause to think at all before she asked, "Sir Keith, were you in love with my mother?"

He looked taken aback, but quickly recovered. "Nay, Alessandra. As I have said, Catherine was like a sister to me—well loved in that respect, but no other."

Alessandra blushed. "I am sorry. It was rude of me to ask." Dipping her head, she pulled off one of the embroidered red gloves Melissant had given her. "For my mother," she said, handing it to him. Instantly, she regretted the loss of its warmth, for though it had dawned another sunny day, the air was chilly.

He tucked the glove beneath his belt. "I will do it honor," he said, then grinned. "Now, though, I must needs seek out the brew ere 'tis all drunk and I am left dry."

Alessandra watched him go, then looked over her shoulder to the tents. Perhaps . . . She half turned, then hesitated.

If she did discover which of the tents was Lucien's,

would he receive her well? Though the answer was in the negative, she gave over to impulsiveness and headed for them.

Weaving through the crowd of others who had eschewed food in favor of wandering around the tournament tent and watching the preparations of the knights, Alessandra quickly found the De Gautier tents of red and gold stripes. Outside the center one, Lucien's squire was busy cleaning and polishing his armor. Was Lucien within?

Alessandra stood a long moment debating whether she should turn around or go forward. In the end, she went forward. Intent on his task, the squire did not look up, and she passed him unnoticed.

Hand to the flap, Alessandra listened for sounds from within. Silence. Perhaps Lucien had joined the others in feasting? She peeled a corner of the flap back and peeked inside.

His scarred back to her, his head bowed, Lucien sat on a stool while Jervais pressed pungent, herb-soaked cloths to his injuries.

Braving whatever Lucien might throw at her, Alessandra stepped within and met Jervais's startled gaze over Lucien's head. She hesitated, then pushed back her hood.

Jervais frowned, but did not react in any other way that might alert Lucien to her presence. Still staring at her, he dipped the cloth in the bowl of herbs and pressed it to a purpled swelling on his brother's shoulder.

Her footsteps muffled by thick carpets that patched the dirt floor, Alessandra walked to Lucien, then held out her ungloved hand.

Jervais regarded her with skepticism, but relinquished the cloth and moved away.

Her hands trembling, she dipped the cloth once again and put it to Lucien's shoulder. Holding it there, she craned her neck and saw that his eyes were closed. Did he sleep, or simply rest?

Quietly, she moved from behind to stand before him. Though she had known his injuries were likely many, she was unprepared for what she saw.

These past days of jousting had left ugly bruises and gashes all over his arms, chest, and abdomen. None looked life-threatening, but all looked painful. Yet he continued to accept challengers and subject himself to this punishment. All in the name of the De Gautier lands.

Damn him! Damn his precious lands! Damn the De Gautiers—and the Bayards!

Fairly seething, her skin grown uncomfortably warm, she swept her gaze up to his face and found him watching her.

Too angered to be surprised, she flung the medicinal cloth to the floor and slapped her hands to her hips. "All this to avoid wedding a Bayard," she said bitterly.

He rolled his shoulders, as if to loosen tight muscles. "I cannot think of a more worthy cause," he said. "Can you?" Retrieving his tunic, he pulled it on.

She stared at him, striving to hold back her tears. "Once I might have," she said, "but now? Nay." Drawing herself fully upright, she stalked past him, her destination anywhere away from this heartless man.

Lucin let her go. But then Jervais called his name, and Lucien turned to see his brother blocking Alessandra's exit.

Lucien turned to see his brother blocking Alessandra's exit. Later, he reminded himself as her stiffly erect figure pulled at his caged emotions. One more challenge and he would have enough coin to pay Bayard. Then he would explain it all to her. Damn, but he was weary.

"Stay, Alessandra," he heard himself say. "Stay and we will talk while Jervais armors me."

Her shoulders lifted with the deep breath she drew. She turned and glowered at him. " 'Tis abundantly clear where your heart is, Lucien de Gautier. And I want no part of it."

"You are sure? Not even a small piece?" He had not meant to taunt her, but the words came so easily to his fatigued mind. "What of the love you professed?"

"I do love you," she shot back, "though I am ashamed to have ever admitted it."

Lucien stood. "Leave us, Jervais."

Looking doubtful, Jervais withdrew.

Alone. How long had it been since she and Lucien had shared space with no others? Alessandra wondered. Too long. She clasped her hands before her and met his gaze.

He appeared stiff as he walked toward her, though his carefully schooled features gave no hint of how his body must ache.

He stopped an arm's length from her. "You are missing a glove," he said, looking pointedly at her hands.

It was unnecessary, but Alessandra glanced at the remaining red glove. "So I am," she said.

"Perhaps 'twas given as a favor?"

She shrugged. "Perhaps."

His eyebrows rose. "Sir Rexalt again?"

"Nay, another."

Lucien stepped nearer. "And what of my favor?" he asked, brushing the hair back from her face and tucking it behind her ear. "What will you give me to remember you by when next I battle?"

Reminding herself that she was angry with him, Alessandra fought the impulse to turn her mouth to his palm. "What would you have me give you?" she asked, pretending flippancy. "My girdle? A stocking? What say you to a glove that has sadly parted ways with its match?"

Lucien looked into her eyes a long moment, then turned his attention to the brooch fastening her cloak closed. He touched it, his fingers skimming her throat and starting an ache in Alessandra's lower regions. A moment later the cloak slipped to the floor.

"A memory is all I want," he said, his eyes burning into hers.

Alessandra knew she should spurn him as he had spurned her, but could not move—even when his fingers began to work their way down the buttons of her gown. Anger, she reminded herself. He trampled your pride, don't let him take this from you, too.

His rough, callused hand curved over a breast, making her shiver and jerk against him. Her anger receded. "You ... should not," she protested.

He brushed his thumb over the taut, straining nipple.

"Whom do you belong to, Alessandra?" he asked, lowering his head so his mouth was only a moment from hers.

Him. Only him. Never any other. "I . . ." Her breath came out in a rush. "Lucien, do not enter the lists again." She lifted her hands to cup his bruised face. "Take me to wife and the lands will be yours."

He brushed his lips over hers. "I cannot," he murmured, then repeated, "Who, Alessandra?"

Searching his determined face, she saw she had no choice. He would not be swayed from the course he had set himself. "You," she whispered. "I belong to you, Lucien de Gautier."

He smiled. "Good. And now the favor."

Crushing her to his bare chest, he parted her lips beneath his and sweetly ringed the soft, inner tissue of her mouth.

Alessandra forced her mind to push away the events of these past weeks as she moaned her surrender and wrapped her arms around his neck. This was what she wanted—the initiation to the greater possession he had once denied her. And this time perhaps she would know it.

One hand stroking her breast, the other ranging down her spine to the curve of her buttocks, Lucien plunged his tongue deeper. As if he knew well what havoc it would make of her senses, he tickled the ridge behind her front teeth, then lapped her sensitive palate before entwining his tongue with hers.

Alessandra thrilled at the sensations, felt triumph as his masculinity grew hard against her belly. His hand slid up her bare inner thigh, and she gasped and tossed her head back. And then he touched her. Softly.

"Please, Lucien," she begged in a voice so strained it could not possibly be hers. "Now."

His hand drifted up from that secret place to rest against her quivering hip. He groaned. "There is not time," he said. "I must armor for the joust."

It took a moment for his words to make sense, but once they did, Alessandra squeezed her eyes tightly closed in an attempt to obliterate them. However, they remained clear and true.

She opened her eyes. "I beg you, please don't. . . ."

The hard, unmoving look in his eyes, which had supplanted the passion, told her it was futile to argue. Dejected, she fell silent.

Lucien pushed her skirts back down, then lifted his hand from her breast and laid a finger to her swollen lips. "Are you certain 'tis love you feel for me?" he asked.

She nodded.

He looked unconvinced. "Look at me," he said, centering his face before hers. "I am no prize. Everywhere I am scarred. Even before this"—he touched the crescent scar—"I had not the beauty of Vincent—not even Jervais."

Boldly, she touched the scar, tracing its sweeping course to the corner of his eye. "Aye, 'tis true you are not handsome," she agreed, holding his gaze. "Not like Vincent . . . or Rashid. But here." She laid her palm to his breast where his heart beat heavily. "Here you are most beautiful, Lucien—or will be if you ever let yourself feel it. It is that which I love."

Was it possible she was different? Lucien wondered. Different from the two he had been betrothed to?

Since coming to Corburry, he'd watched closely, but had not seen her look at Vincent with the same cow-eyed longing as other women did. In fact, the first day of the tournament, when he'd glimpsed her viewing the banners and helms, she had seemed reluctant—even annoyed—when Vincent tried to talk with her. And when Vincent had gone, she had done something out of sight of all.

Later, and only by accident, did he discover what that was. When he'd taken his helm from his squire, the smudge of a cross where it broke the perfect polish had caught the light of the sun. Alessandra had blessed it.

The renewal of faith in womankind had spread tentatively through him. And then she had given her favor to Sir Rexalt. . . .

The bitterness had nearly choked him, but that memory, more than the need to regain his lands, was what had driven him to fight that day, and to fight again these last days. It had given him the strength to defeat each of his challengers and accept new ones, even when the weight of his armor threatened to bear him to the ground.

"We will talk later," he said, drawing back.

Alessandra had prayed he would speak words of love to her, that he would lay open his heart as she had done, but he refused to. Either he was too proud to confess his love, or it was only love of the flesh he felt for her.

A mix of anger, frustration, and fear that he might suffer serious hurt in his next joust was responsible for her words. "If you truly cared about me, you would not do this thing," she said. "You would lay down your arms and turn aside your challengers."

His eyes hardened. " 'Tis an ultimatum you give me?" he asked.

An ultimatum? She had not thought of it as such, but if there was the possibility of it keeping him from the lists, then why not call it that? "Aye, an ultimatum," she said.

Fists clenched, Lucien stepped back. "Then you lose."

To keep him from seeing the tears that sprang to her eyes, she turned and scooped up her cloak. Head bent, she settled it on her shoulders and began to fumble with the brooch.

The tent flap parted.

"Pardon," Jervais said, his gaze sweeping from Lucien to Alessandra, "but methinks the good bishop comes this way."

Alessandra turned stricken eyes to Lucien. It seemed a replay of the night she had gone to the eunuchs' quarters. Though she knew the punishment in Algiers for being alone with a man who was not her husband, what was the price here in England?

"Someone shadows you," Lucien said wryly, then turned to his brother. "Delay him if you can."

Eyes rolling, Jervais disappeared.

Quickly, Lucien refastened the brooch, then took Alessandra's arm and pulled her across the tent.

Did he intend to hide her here, in his tent? she wondered. There was no other opening but the one she had come through. She had her answer a moment later when he drew his dagger.

Punching it through the heavy canvas of the tent, he sliced an opening waist-high to the ground. Then, assuring none were without, he drew Alessandra to it. "Go," he ordered. "We will not be caught again."

She bent to slip through the opening, but something made her turn around. That something was the look in his eyes, tenderness and longing that he quickly masked. "Lucien—"

"Alessandra, the punishment will not be mine this time," he growled, giving her a push. "Now go!"

It was true. He would not be beaten like an animal. Rather, the bishop would put all the blame on her, which she certainly was more deserving of than Lucien.

"Just tell me this," she said. "Do you love me?"

His jaw working, Lucien looked across the tent to where voices sounded just outside. "Love is an emotion reserved for children," he scoffed, then looked back at her. "We are not children, Alessandra."

Did something die in her eyes? he wondered, thinking himself the most despicable cur. Later, he assured himself. Now was not the time to work out the hash of emotions he had battled with ever since he'd first laid eyes on her. Always later . . .

"Farewell, Lucien," she said, her jaw quivering, then she ducked and disappeared through the opening.

Lucien wasted no time. Pulling a stool over to block the opening, he lowered himself onto it just as Bishop Armis entered.

"You are alone," the man said, sounding surprised.

"You expected otherwise?"

"I thought, perhaps, you would be enjoying the company of a woman." His darting gaze searched out the corners of the tent as he leisurely walked around it, confirming Lucien's suspicions that Alessandra had been followed.

"I speak of a joy woman, of course," the bishop added, brushing his fingers across the dusty top of the trunk that contained Lucien's belongings.

"Then you have mistaken me."

"Aye, 'twould seem so." Coming to stand before Lucien, Bishop Armis grimaced at the sight of his battered body. "You will provide us a good show this afternoon, hmm?"

Lucien resisted the urge to personally demonstrate his prowess, unclenching his hands and laying them open on his knees. "A performance worthy of you, Bishop Armis," he said.

"I look forward to it." His mouth a tight pucker, the bishop turned and swept from the tent in a flurry of silken robes.

Something was unfolding, Lucien knew. Something that would do Alessandra harm if she did not tread more carefully. Pondering what that might be, and who the players were, he stood and went to the small box he'd earlier thrown onto the cot. Lifting the lid, he picked out the belled anklet to which he'd added a length of chain. He clasped it around his neck, then pressed a palm to it and smiled.

Since the night Alessandra had unknowingly left it behind, he had worn it beneath his armor, the noise of the crowd and the clank of metal masking its soft peal. It had brought him incredible fortune, and within the hour it would deliver his lands back to him.

"You belong to me, Alessandra," he said aloud, then crossed the tent and called to his squire to bring on the armor.

He was sick of it all, Lucien realized as he wheeled his horse around to discover the fate of his fallen opponent.

The man lay motionless upon the sand, his left pauldron—that piece of articulated shoulder armor which Lucien's lance had broken free—thrown to the opposite end of the lists.

Lucien pushed his visor back and waited with the crowd as the squire of the downed man came running. Dropping to his knees, the young man threw back his master's visor and peered inside.

A long silence followed that boded ill.

Had the knight broken his neck in the fall? Lucien wondered, guilt and disgust overwhelming him. Though it would be said to have been a fair joust, and many would see it as confirmation of his mastery of the game,

Lucien wanted to yell to the heavens at the injustice of it all.

Searching the crowd, he located Alessandra's hooded figure. In spite of the shadows that hid her face, he knew her eyes were on him, and imagined the accusation that must be there—the contempt and loathing.

She had been right. No matter his reasons, he was an animal and, like an animal, had carelessly taken the life of another—just as he had done time and again in the name of his king. If it was hate, not love, that now shone from her eyes, he deserved no better.

No more, he vowed, tossing the remains of his lance to the ground. He had reestablished himself and his family's name, and he and his brothers had taken enough ransom to pay off Bayard. There was naught more to be gained.

A loud groan broke the silence, followed by the crowd's collective sigh of relief.

Releasing a breath he had not realized he held, Lucien looked back at his opponent and saw him move, then begin to flounder as his senses returned.

Three varlets were summoned, and a short time later the knight, his vehement curses amusing the onlookers, was carried away on an elongated shield.

Immediately, Lucien's final opponent entered the lists.

A red glove fluttering from the shoulder strap of his armor, Sir Keith Crennan took position as the chief marshal called out his challenge.

Lucien tensed with what he knew had to be called jealousy. What had possessed Alessandra to give the glove to her cousin? he wondered. Not only was the man too old for her, but they were related within the degrees prohibited by the Church.

A token favor only, he told himself, her declaration of love forever imprinted on his mind and blazoned across his heart.

"Take position, Sir Lucien," the chief marshal ordered.

Lucien looked over his shoulder at the man. "Nay, I am finished." Snapping the reins, he cantered his destrier to the center pavilion where James sat.

"Lord Bayard," he said, "as we agreed, the De Gautier

lands for gold. This eve, if you will have the papers drawn and ready, I shall deliver the entire sum to you."

James rose. "My offer stands, Lucien. Do you take a Bayard to wife, the lands I will give you, and that which you have gained these past days will keep you in good stead for a lifetime."

"You are mistaken to believe a Bayard bride is all it would take to keep peace between our families."

James's nostrils flared. "Dewmoor Pass?" he guessed.

Laughter, unexpected and coarse, rumbled from Lucien's chest. Not since arriving at Falstaff had he thought of the pass, which had been the cause of so much bloodshed. Thinking of it now, he realized it was beyond ludicrous that so many battles had been fought in the name of a piece of land that comprised fewer than fifty hectares.

"Keep it, Bayard," he said, then turned and galloped from the lists.

Stunned, the people looked to where Sir Keith rigidly sat his destrier before the tilt. A questioning murmur arose, but was put to rest when he doffed his helm. "It seems the Lion of Falstaff has forfeited the tourney to me," he said. His smile askew, he drew his sword and triumphantly trotted the lists.

The people tittered. Though Sir Keith was among the most competent of jousters, his chances against De Gautier had been little better than they had been for all the others who had challenged before him and been defeated.

As Sir Keith left the lists, the revelries that always followed a tournament commenced.

He was fine. He assured himself of that over and over as he led his destrier to the stables, but still the anger brewed in him until everything he laid eyes upon was splotched red.

He barely even noticed the appearance of his squire. "I will take him, Sir Keith," the young man said, reaching for the destrier's reins.

The terrible desire to strike the squire surged through Keith, but he managed to keep his fists at his side. "Nay,

I will tend him myself," he said. "Go and enjoy the festivities."

"But—"

Keith drew to an abrupt halt. "Leave me!" he thundered in a voice that was not his own.

The squire jumped back. "Aye, my lord," he said, then turned and quickly retreated.

Sparing only a moment to regret his outburst, Keith resumed his walk to the stables. "All is well," he muttered. "Quite well." To prove it, he smiled and lifted a hand to an approaching knight.

Nodding, the man passed by on his way to the tournament grounds.

Feeling as if his smile might shatter at any moment and leave a gaping hole that would howl his emotions to all— that would expose him—Keith let the smile drop.

"I'm not angry," he tried again to convince himself. "I'm ... disappointed. Aye, that is all." With more self-talk he might have convinced himself of it had Agnes not appeared to rub his nose in the humiliation Lucien de Gautier had subjected him to.

"A bastard," she said, linking her arm through his. "Who does he think he is?"

Again, Keith experienced a nearly overwhelming urge to strike out, to shove his sister and upend her in the dirt. He fought it down. Agnes must never know of the demons in him that, though their appearances were rare, had wreaked havoc on his and others' lives, that haunted him with memories that he could not bear to examine.

" 'Tis De Gautier you speak of?" he asked, turning his mind back to the present.

"Of course. Who else would I call 'bastard'?"

"Your husband, perhaps?"

She laughed. "Only when he disagrees with me."

Entering the stables, Keith led his destrier to the far stall. He lifted Agnes's arm from his and began tending the animal's needs. "He gave forfeit, did he not? What better victory than that, Agnes?"

"What better victory?" she echoed. "Why, knocking him from his destrier, of course. Bringing him to his knees."

He eyed her a moment, then unbuckled the saddle. "I am content," he lied, wishing she would leave so he could be alone with his demons.

"He humiliated you, Keith," Agnes exclaimed, "and yet you say you are content?"

"I am."

Her face reddened. "Do you know what they will say about you?" When he did not respond, she continued, "They will say De Gautier forfeited the joust not because he feared your lance, but because he thought you too unworthy an adversary."

Keith moved around the horse so Agnes would not see the seething anger her words aroused. "Nay, methinks he did it for Alessandra," he said.

"Alessandra! Aye, 'twas bad enough Lucien's homecoming, but her arrival has taken away any hope of Melissant ever wedding the De Gautier heir."

"And what has Alessandra to do with that? 'Tis Lucien's decision to wed, not hers."

"You are wrong. Lucien and Alessandra are enamored of one another. Do you know where she went after she spoke with you this morn during the break in the tourney?"

Keith had not known he'd had an audience when he had unhooded Alessandra and requested a favor of her. It made him uncomfortable—intensely so. "Nay, I do not know where she went," he said.

"She went to *him*—to his tent. If he weds a Bayard, 'twill be that one, not my poor Melissant." Shaking her head, Agnes looked to the stable floor. "Oh, what am I to do, Keith?" she moaned.

Alessandra had given him her favor, then gone to another. . . . Shaking off the demons again, Keith walked around his horse and laid a comforting arm across Agnes's shoulders. "There will be one more worthy of Melissant than Lucien de Gautier," he said, giving her a reassuring squeeze. " 'Tis truly for the best that he does not wed her."

Agnes pulled away from him. "Do you think that is what I wish to hear?" she snapped. "You who would have fallen at the feet of a De Gautier had he not deemed you unfit to raise his lance against?" Swinging away, she crossed to the stall portal, but stopped herself with a hand to the frame.

She stood there a minute, then turned back around. "Ah, God, I am sorry, Keith," she apologized, her eyes glistening tears. "Alessandra's coming has been difficult for me."

"I can well imagine," he said, the words strangled past the constriction in his throat.

Agnes nodded. "She has brought with her Catherine's ghost, and I know not how to do battle with it . . . but I will." Gaining strength from her own words, she smiled another apology at Keith, then left him to his own private battle.

He held them back until he was certain his sister was out of earshot, then he let the demons out.

His eyes painting everything red, he tore the saddle from his destrier's back, threw it against the wall, and howled rage. While the horse cried its distress and sidled away, Keith kicked at the walls and hurled buckets, brushes, reins, a whip . . . anything he could get his hands on. When there was nothing left to throw, he threw himself—to the ground, where he pounded his fists.

At last the fit passed, leaving him drained and moist with the heat of his anger.

"Something must be done," he said as he picked himself up off the straw-covered floor. His demons must be laid to rest.

CHAPTER 29

"It could all be yours, and the land," Vincent said as he sifted through a pile of coins, "if you married the red."

Lucien did not comment until his squire, struggling under the load of armor, exited the tent. "The red, hmm?" he said with a weary smile.

"Aye, the red," Jervais said, agreeing with Vincent.

Lucien dragged his arming doublet off over his head. "Her name is Alessandra," he said, tossing the mailed garment to the cot, "and I am going to marry her once order is restored to Falstaff."

"What?" Vincent exclaimed. "If you were going to marry her, then . . ." Confused, he shook his head.

"Then why not accept Bayard's offer?" Lucien supplied.

"Aye."

Lucien picked a coin from the pile and turned it front to back. "For one thing, De Gautier pride," he said.

"Which you have little enough of," Jervais was quick to point out to Vincent.

His face contorting, Vincent shot to his feet and lunged for his younger brother.

Having anticipated the confrontation, Lucien stepped between them. "Enough," he growled.

Flushed scarlet, Vincent tore his gaze from Jervais. "I do not need him"—he jabbed a finger past Lucien—"reminding me of my mistakes. I am paying for them, and will no doubt continue to pay the remainder of my life."

Lucien knew that among other things, Vincent referred to the jousting, a contest abhorrent to him. Prior to coming to Corburry, he had voluntarily submitted himself to weeks of grueling practice alongside his more capable brothers. Yet for all the humiliation and pain he had borne, he had not once uttered a protest.

Though Lucien was certain it would be a long time before he could completely forgive his brother his trespass, he had been proud of the man Vincent had become.

"We will speak no more of this," he said. "Come dawn . . ." His voice trailed off as a skittering sound caught his ear. Looking over his shoulder to the partially concealed opening he had slashed for Alessandra's escape, he saw a shadow move over the red and gold stripes.

Coming alert to Lucien's discovery, his brothers started across the tent. Lucien stopped them and motioned for them to continue speaking.

Too late. The shadow dissolved, and by the time Lucien thrust his head through the opening, only the trampled scrub attested to an eavesdropper having been there.

"Who was it?" Vincent asked.

"The bishop?" Jervais said.

Lucien shook his head. "Possibly."

That evening, following the repast, the return of the De Gautier lands took place behind closed doors. A long hour after entering the lord's solar, the parties emerged.

Lucien, carrying a sheaf of papers, a brother on either side of him, traversed the great hall without pause, though his eyes flickered once over Alessandra. Then he was gone, passing through the doors with nary a word to those who watched.

Alessandra slumped where she sat before a blazing fire. On the morrow, before first light, Corburry's guests would depart en masse. Would Lucien go without further word to her, believing the angry words she had last spoken to him?

"You look unhappy," Sir Keith said, his voice reminding her that they had been conversing before Lucien's appearance. "Is it something I said?"

Alessandra tore her gaze from the doorway and met his kind eyes. "Nay, I—"

" 'Tis what was not said," Melissant interrupted.

Alessandra turned to find her sister hanging over her shoulder. "What are you talking about?" she asked.

"You cannot hide it from me," Melissant teased, winking at her uncle. "You had hoped to have words with Lucien de Gautier, am I right?"

Embarrassment colored Alessandra's cheeks. How could Melissant speak so boldly of matters of the heart before Sir Keith? "You are mistaken," she said.

"Nay, I am not," Melissant replied in a singsong voice.

Grinning, Sir Keith caught Alessandra's eye. "So 'tis Lucien de Gautier who occupies your mind," he said. "I should have guessed."

As both Melissant and Keith appeared firm in their beliefs, Alessandra decided it would be useless to protest any further.

She sighed. "We are friends," she said. "He was good to me when he brought me out of Algiers."

Melissant plopped down beside her. "Good to you? Is that all?"

"Melissant!" Alessandra exclaimed, for once thinking the fire far too warm for her taste.

"You have your mother's foolhardiness if you think you can tame that one," Sir Keith said.

"Perhaps she does not wish to tame him," Melissant slyly suggested.

With an affectionate chuckle, Keith mussed his niece's hair. "And what of you, Melissant? Would you want him tame?"

"I do not want him at all!" she said.

"But 'twas you who was to have wed the De Gautier heir," he reminded her.

"Aye, Vincent," she spat. "And good riddance to him."

"But now Lucien is heir," Keith pointed out.

"And a far better choice, that."

Grateful the conversation had shifted from her involvement with Lucien, Alessandra glanced around the hall and found it emptying as the guests went to bed down for the night. Which, she told herself, she should also do if she was to rise early enough to seek out Lucien before he departed.

Out of the corner of her eye, she glimpsed Agnes and Bishop Armis. Side by side, they stood at the far end of the hall, their intent gaze making her feel like their prey.

Gritting her teeth, she rose and turned to bid good eve to Melissant and Keith, but discovered Melissant absent. Looking around, she saw her sister had gone to one of the side tables to pick at the platters of cold meats and cheeses.

She looked back at Sir Keith; his eyes were closed in rest. Lightly, she touched his shoulder. "Good eve," she said.

His lids flickered open. "Caught me," he teased. "Good eve, Alessandra."

She turned to go, but was detained by the appearance of a serving girl.

"I've a missive for you, milady," the girl whispered. Taking Alessandra's hand, she pressed a folded square of paper into it, then scampered off.

It was from Lucien, Alessandra knew, her heart fluttering with anticipation. It had to be.

Still, she grimaced. Though the girl had tried to be secretive about her mission, she clearly had not succeeded. Alessandra knew it without scanning the hall again, the feeling of being watched stronger than ever.

Curling her fingers around the paper, she glanced at Sir Keith's questioning face, then smiled. "Good eve," she said again.

Once out of sight of the hall, Alessandra threw her skirts over her arm and took the stairs two at a time. Not until she was firmly ensconced in her chamber did she nervously open the message.

It was from Lucien, his boldly scrawled initials overlapping the final sentence. Standing before the fire, she read the note through, then clasped it to her breast.

He asked her to come to his tent, and urged her to hasten so she might slip out of the keep unnoticed, mingling

with those heading for their camps outside the castle
walls.

Hope surging through her, Alessandra quickly changed
into inconspicuous clothes, donning again the cloak and
hood that had allowed her to attend the tournament unnoticed. Of course, it had not fooled Sir Keith. . . .

Keeping him in mind, she descended to the hall. Standing in the shadow of the stairs, she searched for him, but
he was nowhere to be seen.

Counting herself blessed, she waited for the right moment and, when it came, hurried from the stairs to the
kitchens. Though some of the servants looked up from
their toil, they allowed her to pass without question.

The crisp air of night greeted her when she stepped
outside. She shivered, her body stiffening with the abrupt
appearance of goose bumps over every square inch of her
skin.

Grumbling beneath her breath about the damnable English cold, she briskly rubbed her hand over her arms as
she traversed the inner and outer bailey. At the portcullis,
it proved beyond easy to merge with a group of de-
parting nobles, and moments later she impatiently skirted
them and ran the rest of the way to the pitched tents.

She paused as she neared the red-and-gold-striped De
Gautier tents, briefly worried that the note might have
been a ruse. But light shone from within Lucien's tent. He
was there. Breathing a sigh of relief, she hitched up her
skirts and hurried forward again, but in the next instant
lost her footing.

Her first thought was that she had not raised her skirts
high enough and had tripped on them. However, instead
of falling forward, she found herself being dragged backward.

Her cry of surprise was caught by the hand that
clapped over her mouth, and she knew sudden fear. But
the fear immediately yielded to the instinct for survival.

Her arms free, she twisted from side to side and thrust
her elbows into the chest of the person behind her.
Though he grunted discomfort, instead of lessening his
hold, he gripped her more tightly about the waist and
continued pulling her backward.

Alessandra fought harder. Kicking a leg back, she connected with a vulnerable shin, then the other. When that failed to result in her release, she sank her teeth into the fleshy palm, that bruised her mouth. All to no avail. Her captor held tight as he maneuvered her from the camp toward the border woods.

Still flailing, all manner of horrible thoughts lit Alessandra's imagination. Did this person intend to violate her? Perhaps even murder her? Who was he? Had he followed her from the keep, or been among the nobles she had trailed out of the bailey?

Lucien? Though she knew from the height and build of her attacker that it was not he, perhaps he had arranged it. . . . Nay. Not even at his angriest would he do such a thing.

The crunch of leaves and the ghostly shadow of trees alerted her to their entrance into the woods. Her heart beating so heavily she thought it might burst from her chest, she reached over her shoulder and raked her nails down the man's face.

He retaliated by shifting his hand so that it also covered her nose.

The air stolen from her, Alessandra's panic soared. Whimpering, she tossed her head in an attempt to dislodge the hand, but it only bit more deeply into her face. She opened her mouth and screamed against it, but the sound was loud only in her head. As unconsciousness dragged at her and her impotent struggles weakened, one lucid thought came to her. Embracing it, she grew still, then became a deadweight in her captor's arms.

As she hung there she sensed his hesitation, his uncertainty. Then there was air again. Greed entreated her to gulp the precious stuff, but she forced herself to draw silent, shallow breaths. Her hazy senses were slow to clear, and not until she felt the cold, moist undergrowth beneath her did she realize she had been lowered to the ground.

Fearful the night was not dark enough for her to open her eyes unseen, she lay still and waited to discover what the man intended. She did not have long to wait.

He whistled softly, and a moment later she heard the

sound of approaching horses. Chancing being caught, she lifted her lashes just enough to see the dark silhouettes of three horses and two riders picking their way to where she lay. Her captor, his back to her, motioned them forward.

Alessandra had to fight hard to keep her breathing even. Her heart was pounding so furiously, she feared she might in fact lose consciousness.

Think, she commanded herself. Think. She had to devise a plan before the man's accomplices reached them. Her futile search ended with only one possibility of escape—run and scream, and perhaps draw the attention of the camp.

Acting immediately, she rolled to her stomach, pushed to her feet, grabbed handfuls of her skirts, and lunged toward the flickering lights.

Behind her a man shouted angrily, then she heard the sounds of her captor giving chase.

Her hair flying out behind her snagged something—a branch, perhaps? Or the grasping fingers of the one who pursued her? She ran faster, felt the roots of her hair pull free, and knew it must have been the man.

Was it blood pounding in her ears, or the beating hooves of riders bearing down upon her? Sending up a prayer that just this one time she would not trip over her damnably long skirts, she stretched her legs as far as they would reach and filled her lungs with the air needed to scream.

The first scream sounded pitiful to her ears, wheezing from her mouth and cut short by the need to draw further breath to fuel her flight. She tried again, but with little more success. Abandoning the idea, she put her remaining energy into legs that had always known how to run.

As her feet touched meadow her heart soared. Nearly free, she encouraged herself. But then something slammed into her back and knocked the breath from her. An arm, she realized as it wrapped around her waist, lifted her from the ground, and held her like a rag doll against a galloping horse.

Alessandra threw her head back as the horse wheeled,

and saw the woods rise up before her again—a refuge for those who meant to steal her from Corburry. Gasping, she vainly lashed out at her captor, but knew herself defeated.

Bruised and shaken to the core, she was finally released and fell to the ground in a heap.

Dazed, she heard voices, all sounding familiar, yet strangely distorted. A dream? she wondered. Was that all this was? She rolled onto her back and stared up through her tangled hair at those above her.

"I want her gone from here now!" ordered the man who had thwarted her escape.

Who was it? Alessandra wondered. She knew the voice, but could not place it.

She heard an answering murmur, then the man who had first captured her dropped to his knees beside her and thrust his face near hers.

It was a face Alessandra knew well, but it made absolutely no sense. Accepting that it was only a dream she found herself in, she closed her heavy lids. "I always could outrun you," she murmured, then gave over to unconsciousness.

"She did not come?"

Lucien dragged his gaze from Corburry's darkened keep and mounted his horse. Taking up the reins, he looked over his shoulder to where Jervais awaited an answer.

"Nay," he said. "She stayed true to her word."

Jervais urged his horse near his brother's. "She will change her mind," he said. "Methinks within a sennight you will have word from her."

Lucien tapped his heels to his horse's sides and maneuvered to the head of the De Gautier procession. As it had been nearly impossible for him to sleep through the night, they would be the first to leave Corburry. It suited him fine, leaving ahead of the dawn and ensuring their arrival at Falstaff well before the noon hour.

"Even so," Lucien said when Jervais sidled alongside, " 'tis probably best Alessandra remain a Bayard."

"Best for whom?"

"Both of us."

"But—"

"She has made her decision, Jervais. Now leave it be!" Seeing his outburst had brought him unwanted attention, Lucien jabbed his heels into his mount's sides and left his brother and the others behind.

Falstaff, he told himself as the invigorating cool air sifted through his hair. All his former holdings now restored to him, it was there he would find peace.

In time, Alessandra would fade from memory. All that would remain of her would be the occasional encounter that was bound to happen so long as there was peace between the De Gautiers and the Bayards.

However long that might be . . .

drawing. "What is this dance called?" she asked, deeper...

※◦∩☥∩◦※

CHAPTER 30

"She is awake, my friend."

The heavily accented voice drifted into Alessandra's consciousness, then started to drift out. Blinking against the light of a sun muted by cloud cover, she played the words over again and wondered who the person was speaking of. Her?

She turned her head and attempted to focus on the man who rose from beside a campfire, the warmth of which barely reached her chilled limbs. However, not until he knelt beside her and pushed the hair out of her eyes did she see who it was.

The same dream, she thought, and closed her eyes in hopes of awakening later to the warmth of her chamber at Corburry. But the man would not allow it.

"Alessandra," he said, giving her a shake.

Funny, but it even sounded like him, she thought.

"Do you hear me?" His warm breath caressed her face.

She opened her eyes again and met those familiar black orbs. "Go away," she muttered. "You do not belong in England." Rubbing her hands up and down her arms, she curled into a ball in a vain attempt to warm herself.

"Neither do you belong in England," he snapped, then shook her more vigorously.

Was it possible this was not a dream after all? she mused. Frowning, she looked again at the man and found his features undeniably distinct. His black brows drawn together with irritation, his mouth a tight line, he looked more real than any dream she had ever had. And the four lines that scored his right cheek . . .

"Rashid?" she breathed.

The line of his mouth softened. "Yes, Rashid," he said.

She sat up so abruptly, she bumped his chin. "It cannot be," she said, switching to her native language with an awkwardness that surprised her. Though she had continued to think in Arabic, she realized now she spoke the English language without conscious effort.

Rashid caught her hand. "It is me," he said, placing her palm alongside his jaw.

She shook her head. "What are you doing in England?"

"I came for you," he said, hurt flickering in his eyes. "I came to take you home."

The events of the night before rushed at her. It was Rashid who had abducted her from the camp, she realized. He who had stolen the breath from her when she'd fought him and scratched his face. But what of the other two? She had known one of them—or thought she had—but could not think who it was now.

"Why did you come for me?" she asked.

His nostrils flared with a hint of the anger she had glimpsed the night he had beat Lucien. "Algiers is where you belong," he said. "As my bride."

As his bride—not Lucien's. Lucien. Realizing that he had likely left Corburry by now, she closed her eyes and let regret wash over her. He would have gone believing she had spurned him.

"Alessandra!" Rashid jogged her.

"What? Oh . . ." She blinked.

"We are returning to Algiers," he said.

That was what she had thought she wanted when Lucien had forced her to Tangier, but now she knew differently. She absolutely could not return to Algiers and the life she would have as Rashid's wife. She needed freedom, not to be cosseted and locked away without thought of her own feelings.

Even though in England women were regarded as a man's chattel, their lives were much fuller, what with the running of the household, accounting, outings where they were not required to hide their faces, and all other manner of independence she would never be allowed in Algiers. For all its cold weather, strange food, and primitive means of men proving their valor, she belonged here—with Lucien, providing he would have her.

"I cannot," she said, pulling her hand from Rashid's. "I no longer belong in Algiers, Rashid."

Jumping to his feet, he stood looking down at her, his body tensed and seeming ready to burst with the fury she saw clearly on his face. "And you think you belong in this godforsaken country of little sun and damning cold?" he demanded.

Though she feared it, Alessandra knew she deserved his anger. After all, he had come across an ocean to take her back to Algiers.

Pulling her to her feet, he gripped her upper arms. "Are you still mine, Alessandra?" he asked.

"Yours?" Had she ever really been? Regardless, she no longer was. It was Lucien she belonged to now. "I'm sorry, Rashid," she began, wishing there was an easier way to tell him, "but England is my home now."

"I have asked if you are still mine."

She shook her head. "I am not yours, Rashid."

"Then it is true you lust after the De Gautier bastard," he growled. "Have even lain with him."

The truth would hurt him, she knew, but she could not lie to him. "I am still chaste," she said, "but 'tis true I love him."

Though she had not anticipated his striking her, only her quick reflexes saved her from the hand he raised against her. Holding his wrist, she stared into his fierce eyes and tried not to tremble with the fear rushing through her.

"Do not strike me." She spoke as evenly as she could manage.

He wavered, then thrust her backward, so that she fell onto the blanket she'd been lying on. "You are a witch and a whore," he accused. "Just as my mother tried to tell me." He slammed a fist against his forehead. "I would not listen."

"No, Rashid," Alessandra said, rising to stand again. "You know that is not true."

"I know you have betrayed me," he said. "And for that, Allah would not blink once if I took your life."

She put a tentative hand to his shoulder. "You could not do that to me," she said, her mouth gone terribly dry. "We are friends, and will always be."

"Friends!" Shrugging off her hand, he lurched away.

For the first time Alessandra saw who it was that had accompanied Rashid to England. Perched on a rock, one knee drawn up, his arm draped over it, Jacques LeBrec offered her a slow, cool smile.

She stumbled back. Could it be? Nay! It was only a dream, after all—a strange, crazy dream that had brought two men together who could not possibly have ever crossed paths outside her dreams. Could they?

"*Chérie,*" Jacques said as he gracefully stood. As if Rashid's curses did not abrade the air, he walked over to her and caught up her limp hands. He brushed his lips over the backs of her fingers, then released her just as Rashid spun around to face them.

"You are surprised, no?" he said, his smile broad and offensive even for a dream.

"This is not possible," Alessandra whispered. Thinking to dispel the illusion altogether, she shook her head, but both Rashid and Jacques remained.

"But I *am* here, Alessandra." Jacques laughed. "And so is your betrothed."

She glanced at Rashid, felt the anger still emanating from him, then looked back at the very real person of Jacques LeBrec. "You sold me into slavery!" she yelled at him. "You lied to me!"

He shrugged apology. "*Pardon,*" he said, then attempted to coax understanding from her with the same smile he had used to gain her trust in Tangier. "But now I am redeemed, hmm? Soon you will be back in Algiers, as was your wish."

"Redeemed?" she shrieked. Drenched in memories of the slave auction, and the terrible humiliation and fear she had suffered, she flew at him.

Her fury made it nearly impossible for Jacques to catch hold of her, but finally he succeeded in grabbing her upper arms and reducing the havoc she wreaked upon him to her kicking legs. Rashid grabbed her from behind and forced her to the ground. Straddling her, he held her down until, at last, she tired.

"I demand your obedience, woman," he ordered.

Defiant, Alessandra used her last reserve of strength to buck and twist, but it was a futile struggle. "You demand?" she gasped, her breathing strained. "I am not your wife, Rashid, nor am I of the Muslim faith that I must obey your every word."

"You are not my wife," he agreed, "but you will be."

"I am not leaving England."

His chin dimpled with anger. "Yes, you are," he said, then swooped down and covered her mouth with his.

Not having expected ravishment, Alessandra lay stunned, unmoving, while his lips bruised hers. However, when his tongue invaded her mouth, she tossed her head to the side. "No, Rashid."

He met her gaze. "You wanted it once," he said.

She remembered—when she had kissed him on the rooftop in an attempt to prove to herself she was not attracted to Seif—Lucien. She swallowed the lump in her throat. "Not like this," she said. "Not this way."

"How?" he demanded. "Tell me how De Gautier pleasured you and perhaps I can accommodate better." He waited for her to speak, but when she didn't, he dropped his head and dipped his tongue into her ear.

Alessandra would have protested, but the appearance of Jacques, dropping down on his haunches beside them, silenced her.

"Rashid, my friend," he interrupted, speaking lingua franca. "This is neither the time, nor the place, to tame her."

Although Alessandra expected Rashid to rain his fury on Jacques, she was surprised when his face softened into familiar planes. He blinked, looked from her to Jacques, and in the next moment was on his feet.

"Allah," he said, rubbing a hand down his face. Suddenly he fell to his knees and lifted his arms in supplication. "Allah, Allah," he moaned.

"Heathen," Jacques muttered as he helped Alessandra

to a sitting position. Then he put his arm around her as if to offer solace.

She immediately pulled back and distanced herself from the hateful Frenchman.

He took her withdrawal in stride. "I do not blame you, *chérie*," he said, standing. "But eventually, you will have to forgive me."

She shook her head. "Never."

"Truly?" He tsked. "Ah, but never is a very long time."

"It is forever," she shot back.

Sighing, Jacques walked to the fire and picked a piece of dried meat from the battered platter beside it. "And here I thought I was making amends by leading your betrothed to you." Pulling the meat apart, he thrust his hand forward, silently offering a piece to her.

She shook her head. "How is it you come to be with Rashid?"

He chewed the tough meat, swallowed, then smiled apologetically. "You must know that I suffered terrible guilt selling you at auction," he said.

"I know nothing of the sort," she retorted.

His expression was sorrowful. "I did, *chérie*. But when I saw that the English captain had bought you, I knew you would be fine. You had family in England, and would no doubt escape him once you reached its shores."

"And Rashid?" she prompted.

"Two days after you set sail, he came to me—angry!" Jacques threw his hands into the air, glanced at Rashid's bent, praying form, then continued. "Talk was still fresh of the redheaded woman sold at auction. Thus he had learned it was I who had offered you."

As if recalling an unpleasantness, he rubbed a hand over his throat. "There was a moment, *chérie*, when I was certain my life was over—and then, Blessed Virgin, I remembered something very important."

"What?"

He walked to where a large pack sat beside the rock he had earlier perched upon.

It did not take him long to find what he was looking for. Brandishing a crumpled, folded letter, he walked back to her and dropped it in her lap.

Alessandra knew without opening it that it was the letter her mother had written her—a precious letter she had been forced to leave behind when Jacques had sold her into slavery, and for which she'd shed many tears.

"Read it," he invited.

"I know what it says," she snapped.

"Then you also know that it is how Rashid and I came to discover your whereabouts. It was—"

Rashid's long-suffering wail rent the air.

Jacques rolled his eyes. "It was not very difficult."

"But the letter said I was to be taken to my aunt and uncle," she said. "So how is it you found me at Corburry?"

He sank to his haunches and took another chew of meat before answering. "I am not at liberty to say."

"What do you mean, 'not at liberty'?"

"Alessandra, you are an intelligent woman. Surely you can figure it out for yourself."

"I would prefer you save me the trouble."

He shook his head. "I cannot."

Frustrated, Alessandra dragged the blanket around her shoulders to ward off the cutting cold of morning.

Glasbrook, she thought. Her mother had instructed Lucien to take her there first, where Sabine's aunt and uncle—Agnes and Keith's parents—lived. So, since they had Sabine's letter, Rashid and Jacques would have gone there. But who would have sent two strangers on to Corburry? The aunt and uncle? Sir Keith?

Nay, foolish thought. Sir Keith was too wise to be duped by two of obvious foreign descent. It must have been his unsuspecting parents. Still, it made no sense.

A memory niggled at the back of Alessandra's mind. She pulled at it, tried to free it of the muddle, but lost hold of it.

"I cannot think now," she said.

"It will come to you," Jacques assured her.

Determined to wring the truth from him, she opened her mouth to question him further. However, Rashid's return silenced her.

"Get up," he said.

Taking the blanket with her, Alessandra rose, and was surprised to find his eyes filled with tears.

"Forgive me," he implored. "It has been difficult these last months." Putting his arms around her, he pressed her face to his shoulder.

Hope soared through her. Then he would let her go—allow her to return to Corbury. However, his next words told her otherwise.

"Everything I ever knew has either changed or been done away with completely," he said, his voice muffled. "I cannot lose you, Alessandra. You're all I have left of what was good in my life. I need you."

His loss and sorrow tugged at her heartstrings, made her wish she could love him as he did her so he would suffer no more hurt, but there would always be Lucien—only Lucien.

Pulling back, Rashid looked into her eyes. "We will be wed as soon as we reach Algiers, then you will be my wife as it was always meant to be."

Pretending acquiescence, she nodded. If Rashid was set on taking her back to Algiers, it would be unwise to alert him to her continued defiance. Let him think she would go willingly, then she might catch him off guard and escape when an opportunity presented itself. Over Rashid's shoulder, she met Jacques's bewildered gaze.

"We must go," Rashid said, setting her away from him. "There is a ship that leaves in four days for the Mediterranean. We will be on it."

Alessandra summoned a smile that she hoped showed nothing of her true feelings.

Placated, his boyish handsomeness returned, Rashid looked around at Jacques. "Clear the camp and I will bring the horses," he said.

Less than a half hour later they rode east.

CHAPTER 31

"My lord, the Bayards come."

Frowning, Lucien pushed away the ledger he'd been examining and sat forward. "In peace?" he asked.

His brow puckered, the captain of the guard shook his head. "Armored, my lord, with knights abounding."

Lucien surged to his feet. "Damnation," he cursed. After old man Bayard had made such a pretense of wanting peace, he'd fully intended to continue their feud even as he'd signed over the De Gautier holdings but two days ago.

Still, Lucien would have thought James would have given it some time before taking up the dispute again—and for what reason did he do it? The bastard now possessed Dewmoor Pass, and without contest.

"Secure the castle," Lucien ordered.

" 'Tis being done now," his man assured him.

Throwing off his fur-lined robe, Lucien called for his squire.

The young man came running. "You would have me arm you, my lord?" he asked, breathless.

"For now, I require only my mail tunic, boots, and sword."

The squire disappeared, returning minutes later with the items. In the center of the great hall, knights and family members abounding, Lucien took the mail tunic and donned it himself, then shoved his feet into the leather boots and secured his sword.

"I thought 'twas finally over with," Dorothea said, placing a hand on Lucien's arm.

Lucien shifted his jaw to ease the tension there. "You are not the only one who was duped, Mother," he said.

She looked down and whispered, "It will never end."

Making no comment, Lucien tilted her face up, pressed a kiss to her pale cheek, then called for his knights to follow him outside.

On the roof of the gatehouse, Lucien and his brothers stared out at the assembled Bayard knights. No question about it, they had not come in peace.

"Are the cannons ready?" he asked the captain of the guard.

"They are being loaded now."

Lucien turned back to contemplate what move Bayard would make next.

"I cannot believe it," Vincent murmured. "It must be a misunderstanding."

"No misunderstanding," Jervais said. " 'Tis typical Bayard trickery."

James Bayard, a knight on either side of him, broke formation and urged his horse forward. "Lucien de Gautier," he called. "Where are you, man?"

Without regard for his safety, Lucien leaped to the embrasure of the crenellation. "I am here," he shouted.

James pushed back his visor and stared up at him. "I want her back," he demanded.

Lucien was sure he hadn't heard right. "What speak you of?"

A long silence, then James growled, "Very well, I will play your game, Lucien, but know that you will die on your knees."

Was it possible there was more to this than met the eye? Lucien wondered. "I play no children's games," he replied. " 'Tis you who plays them—you who professed to want peace and yet now ride against me without provocation."

"Without provocation! You De Gautiers would steal my daughter as you did my wife and then dare say I am unjustified in murdering every last one of you?"

Alessandra ... Something terrible gripped Lucien at the very core of him. "Alessandra is missing?"

"Missing?" James spat. " 'Twas you who took her, you whoreson, just as your father took Catherine."

Ignoring the insult, which years ago he would have made the man pay dearly for, Lucien shook his head. "You are wrong," he said. "I am coming down." Turning, he dropped back to the rooftop.

"Nay, Lucien," Jervais said, "do not trust him. 'Tis a trap, I am certain."

With one hand, Lucien touched his dagger, with the other, the hilt of his sword. "If it be such, you need not worry whose blood will spill."

Grudgingly, Jervais nodded. "I will watch your back, brother," he said.

Turning on his heel, Lucien descended to the bailey and motioned for the portcullis to be raised. Less than a minute later he had traversed the drawbridge and stood before James Bayard, who, up close, looked half-mad.

"Tell me all of it," Lucien said, fighting the urgency to know every detail that moment.

Sword in hand, James leaned forward in his saddle. "What are you up to?" he demanded. "Where is my daughter?"

Though the desire was great to draw his own sword lest James challenge him, Lucien merely settled his legs wide apart and clenched his fist around an imaginary hilt. "I did not take her," he said.

"Then you deny having sent her a message ere you left Corburry?"

"I deny no such thing. The message was sent, but that is all."

"That is all," James sarcastically echoed. "You are saying she did not come to you that night?"

"Aye, that is what I am saying."

James slashed the air with his sword, its point coming within inches of Lucien's chest.

Though he stood stock-still, Lucien knew the flight of his dagger—a split second away—would likely do more harm than the sword he was threatened with.

"You lie!" James shouted. " 'Twas you who took her,

and no doubt have sold her into slavery as your father did her mother." He waved his sword again.

A moment's calculation was all it took, then Lucien was dragging an unsuspecting James Bayard from his horse. Ignoring the Bayard knights who swiftly drew their swords, he gripped James's wrist to arrest the flailing of his sword, then pressed his dagger to the man's throat.

Shooting warning looks at the two knights who'd accompanied James from the ranks, one of whom was James's brother-in-law, Sir Keith, Lucien said in a raspy voice, "Hear me well, James. As my father was not responsible for your wife's disappearance, neither am I responsible for Alessandra's."

"You expect me to believe you?"

"Do you so soon forget that 'twas I who brought her to you?"

James's eyes bulged. "No doubt so you could do me injury by then taking her away."

Patience, Lucien reminded himself. "You are wrong," he said. "Though 'twas originally my intent to use Alessandra against you, in the end I could not do it."

James looked about to challenge him, then a spark of sanity returned to his eyes. "Why?" he demanded. "Why would you, a De Gautier, leave her untouched and then hand her over to your enemy—without demand of ransom?"

The question momentarily disconcerted Lucien, then the answer struck him, and he found he could no longer deny his feelings. "I love her," he said. Those three simple words echoing in his head, he released James and sheathed his dagger.

Stumbling back a step, James touched his throat where the blade had scored a thin line. "If that is true," he said, still suspicious, "then why did you not accept marriage to her?"

"For De Gautier lands?" Lucien shook his head. "Two reasons, pride being one of them."

"And the other?"

He dragged his fingers through his hair. "Would you have taken a woman that you loved to wife and have her always believe you did so only for gain?"

James stared at him a long moment, then nodded understanding. "I see."

"Do you? Then you no longer believe I stole her?"

Though he looked reluctant to abandon the belief that had brought him to Falstaff, James inclined his head. "It seems I have no other choice," he said.

"Good. Leave your men without and we will go to the keep and talk while my men make ready to join your search. I want to know everything." Turning, Lucien headed back across the drawbridge.

Still too wary to trust a De Gautier completely, James brought Sir Keith with him.

"When did Alessandra disappear?" Lucien asked once they were seated at the high table.

"Melissant discovered her missing the morning after the tournament," James said.

"Then yesterday."

"Aye."

"She should not have ventured out at night," Sir Keith said. "It is the same as when her mother was taken."

Lucien frowned. "You believe she disappeared the night before?"

Keith shrugged. " 'Twould follow, wouldn't it? You send her a message and she is gone the next day. Likely she was caught out in the open on her way to see you."

"And how did you determine the message was from me?" Lucien asked.

Keith smiled. "The look on her face when she received it. Did you know she loves you?"

Lucien did not answer. Instead, he turned back to James.

"My men spent all day yesterday scouring the surrounding countryside," James said, picking up where he'd left off, "but without result."

"You did not set out the dogs to track her?"

James shook his head. "I would have, but there is malady among them. Too, once I was convinced 'twas you responsible for her disappearance, it seemed an unnecessary exercise."

Lucien heaved a disgusted sigh. "And now it may be too late to find her scent."

"Aye, but if her fate be the same as her mother's," James said, "then it follows that whoever has taken her is headed for London—the nearest port."

Lucien rose. "Then London is where we must go."

"Too obvious," Sir Keith disagreed. "More likely Southampton."

Lucien considered the older man's wisdom, then nodded. "You are probably right, but I would still send on to London to be certain."

"Two parties, then?"

"Two parties," Lucien agreed. "My men and I will take Southampton. James?"

"Nay, I go with you," he said.

Keith stood. "I will take my men and go to London," he volunteered.

Sensing Lucien's uncertainty, Vincent also stood. "And I will accompany him," he said.

Keith frowned. "With your dice?"

Vincent colored. "Nay, with my sword, Crennan," he snapped.

"You might have better luck with dice."

Vincent clenched his fists. "Like it or not, you will suffer my company."

Lucien was pleased Vincent had not backed down, his determination to redeem himself growing stronger with each passing day.

"Let us delay no longer," Lucien said. "We will have to ride hard to cover ground this day."

CHAPTER 32

"It will be good to be back in Algiers," Rashid said, his chest pressed to Alessandra's back. "This damn English cold is unfit for humans."

Funny, Alessandra thought as she stared into the fire, but she was growing accustomed to it. And even if she never fully adapted, the cold of her body would be far preferable to the cold of her heart.

Looking past the fire, she focused on Jacques where he lay on his side beneath a single blanket. Not surprisingly, he watched her, as he'd done throughout the day.

He was her hope, she realized. In spite of what he had done to her in Tangier, his concern for her welfare seemed genuine. He had truly believed he was making amends by leading Rashid to her, but he now knew different. How, though, could she enlist his help in escaping?

She offered him a tentative smile. His face showed surprise, then he returned the gesture.

"Are you awake, Alessandra?" Rashid asked, interrupting the silent exchange.

Should she pretend to be asleep? Perhaps then he might loosen his hold on her. . . . "I am awake," she admitted.

"And what are you thinking?"

"How nice it would have been had we stayed at the inn we passed earlier," she lied. "As you say, it is quite cold."

Raising himself onto his elbow, Rashid rolled her to her

back and looked down at her. "Do I not keep you warm enough?" he asked.

"It is not you, Rashid. It is the weather."

He smoothed the hair back from her face. "There are other ways to be warm," he said, then feathered a finger down her throat to the neckline of her gown. "We need not wait until we are wed."

Grasping his meaning, she said quickly, "We are not alone."

His gaze flicked to the Frenchman. "But we could be."

"Nay, Rashid, I ... I want to be pure on our wedding day. It is the Islamic way."

"But you are not of that belief."

She floundered a moment, then responded, "It is also the Christian belief."

His eyebrows shot straight up. "So it is," he said.

"Then we should wait—yes?"

"If that is what you desire," he conceded, then lowered his head and kissed her.

Fortunately, Alessandra did not have to pretend a response she didn't feel, for Rashid drew back immediately.

"You love me, don't you, Alessandra?" he asked. "Like your mother loved my father?"

Nay. Only as her childhood friend. Never as a woman should a man. Never as she loved Lucien. "I have always loved you," she half lied.

He smiled, closed his eyes as if to hold her words a bit longer, then opened them again. "Our parents' love was great," he said. "Even now my father mourns Sabine's death."

His words hurt terribly, reminding Alessandra of a loss too recent to have healed. However, they opened the door to the question she had been grappling with ever since that morn. "And your mother, Rashid, what was her punishment?"

In the light of the fire, his pain showed. Gone was the carnal desire Alessandra feared. "Leila is dead," he said.

Alessandra knew she should not, yet she couldn't help but feel relief that the murdering woman could injure no others. All were free from any further wickedness she might devise—and she, Alessandra, need never worry about her retribution.

"How?" she asked, though she wasn't certain she really wished to know.

Rashid's dark eyes became distant. "It should not have happened," he said, his voice choking. "For my sake, Father agreed to return her to her family for what she had done—to be done with her forever—but she wouldn't let well enough be."

"What do you mean?"

Rashid drew a deep breath. "Mother asked for a farewell embrace, and when Father complied, she tried to stab him. He wrested the dirk from her, then, in anger, turned it on her. She died laughing, Alessandra. It was the most awful thing."

"Laughing?"

"Yes. Laughing and cursing Father ... Sabine ... you ... even me. I will never forget it."

Feeling Rashid's pain, Alessandra tenderly cupped his jaw. "I am sorry," she said. "I know how it hurts to lose one's mother."

His bitter smile turned sweet as he looked into her eyes. "Of course you do." He kissed her again, but with more intensity than before.

Alessandra held herself still and tried to feel something for him, but found herself as empty as before. "And Khalid?" She spoke past his searching lips. "How does he now that my mother is gone?"

Rashid pulled back, then shook his head as if to clear it. "Khalid," he repeated, a short, deprecating laugh following. "He would be dead now had he not vanished."

"He vanished—left Algiers?"

"That surprises you?"

She frowned. "Yes. Algiers was his home. But why do you say he would be dead?"

"You do not know it was he who assisted De Gautier in your escape?"

Aye, she knew, but feared confirming Rashid's belief should Khalid ever resurface. "No," she said, "and I do not believe it."

"Believe it, Alessandra, for it is the truth. It was he who

purchased a eunuch who was not a eunuch, he who did not give punishment where punishment was due—"

"How do you know that?" she interrupted.

"That he did not bastinado De Gautier as I ordered?" Again, she found herself looking at a man she did not recognize. "Aye, how do you know?"

"Had Khalid obeyed me, the Englishman could not have escaped, Alessandra, much less taken you with him. He would have been crippled—or nearly so."

"Was that what you wanted?" she whispered, horrified at the ease with which he spoke.

"Do not look at me like that," he snapped. "What I wanted was him dead—and he would have been had I not feared what you might think of me."

At the risk of further inciting him, she asked, "Why do you want me, Rashid?"

He stared at her a long time, then lay back down. "You have been mine since the beginning," he said. "From the moment your mother turned back the blanket and let me see the girl child within."

She turned her head to look at him and saw his face had softened again. "You cannot have been more than two," she pointed out.

"About that, but I remember it well. My mother had been sent away because of Sabine."

Alessandra nearly told him the reason Jabbar had banished Leila—for trying to poison her mother—but there was nothing to be gained in paining him with the truth.

"To stop my crying," he continued, "Father promised me that one day you would be mine. Perhaps it would have appeased me, but your mother would not even let me hold you. She said I was too young. I could look, but not touch."

"And then Leila came back."

"Yes, and she would not even let me look. She tried to keep me from you, Alessandra, but I was determined to claim you . . . and finally I did."

"As you are claiming me now," she murmured.

"There is nothing dishonorable in it," he said. "It is as Allah wills a woman to be."

"And if I do not wish to be claimed?"

His eyebrows descended. "You will be happy with me," he assured her. "As first wife, the harem will be yours to govern, and do you give me a son, you will be mother of my heir."

What Alessandra had once accepted with wide-eyed innocence was no longer enough. Yes, she wanted a husband and children, but it was Lucien she loved, and the children they would make together. No longer did Rashid figure into her world. She had left him far behind the day Lucien had come into the harem and their eyes had met. The boy in Rashid might have understood that, but not the man.

She closed her eyes and turned her head to the side. "I am tired," she said. "It has been a long day."

She felt his strange silence, then his arm curved around her again. Trapped, she lifted her lids a fraction and met Jacques's eyes, just visible above the blanket he had pulled up over his nose.

You are going to help me out of this, she told him silently.

Implying he understood, he nodded.

Something didn't fit. There was a piece out of place—and conspicuously so. For perhaps the hundredth time Lucien measured the length of the camp while the others slept. Reaching the outer margin, he turned and started back.

Something . . . Halting abruptly, his booted feet kicked up dust. He slapped a reproving hand to his head, then searched out James.

James was wide-awake when Lucien knelt beside him. "Surely your father taught you stealth in murdering a man in his sleep," James said, his attempt at humor falling flat beneath the burden of worry he shouldered.

"Tell me, James." Lucien spoke with urgency. "Did you ever discover the means by which Catherine was stolen from Corburry?"

James frowned. "Nay. I returned early morning from a two-day trip and discovered her missing myself. Sometime between eve and dawn she was taken."

"You do not know if she received a message that would have summoned her out of the castle during the night?"

"How would I know that? 'Twas assumed a De Gautier had taken her directly from our bed."

Lucien issued a litany of curses. "You assumed wrong," he said. "Just as we assumed wrong in thinking Alessandra's captor would take her to Southampton."

"What do you mean?"

Lucien wasted no more breath. Surging to his feet, he roused the camp with a loud bellow. Less than half an hour later all were mounted and headed for London in the dark of middle night.

CHAPTER 33

"Mon dieu," Jacques grunted as he swept his disbelieving gaze over the room the rotund woman had led them to.

Peeking out from beneath the overhang of her hood, Alessandra agreed with his assessment, but kept her head bent as Rashid had instructed her.

"You want," the woman said, "I could send a girl up to sweep out the place."

"No," Rashid said, pushing Alessandra ahead of him. "It will do fine."

The woman eyed him with suspicion, trying to see beyond the shadows of his hood, then she shrugged. She turned her regard back to the Frenchman, who had charmed her so completely, she had forgotten the not-so-distant defeat suffered by the English at the hands of the French.

"If there's anything you be needing," she said, giving him a gray-toothed smile, "you'll let Anna know, won't you?"

Jacques smiled in return. "Of course, mademoiselle. I will come to you myself."

A ruddy blush staining her face, the woman flounced back down the murky corridor.

"Done," Rashid said. Closing the door behind him, he tossed off the hood to reveal his distinctly Arabic countenance. "Now we wait."

For the ship that, on the morrow, would deliver Rashid to his homeland, Alessandra thought. Though he did not know it, she would not be with him, not if the hastily conceived plan she had worked out with Jacques succeeded. It had to, since her scheme of delaying their journey had failed.

Knowing the time constraints they were under to reach the ship before it departed, she had done her all to slow their progress these past days. However, not feigned malaise, poor weather, a saddle that had mysteriously come uncinched, nor the disappearance of their provisions had hindered Rashid's determination. Now they were in London, and tomorrow would tell what was to be her fate.

"It is only for one night," Rashid assured her, misinterpreting her silence.

She pushed her hood back and looked past him to where Jacques stood at the window. "Only one night," she echoed.

Missing their exchange, Rashid went to the lopsided bed, gingerly patted the lumpy mattress, then threw back the blanket to reveal the frantic scattering of insects. Disgusted, he stepped back from the bed. "This you prefer to sleeping out-of-doors?" he asked.

Alessandra hurried forward and began brushing the nasty little insects aside. "At least it will be warmer," she said, "and there is food to be had belowstairs."

"The English are a nasty lot," Rashid grumbled. "It will be bliss to be back in Algiers."

"Yes, it will," she absently agreed.

He smiled at her. "Perhaps it will not be so bad," he said, lowering himself to the bed. "At least it is soft between the lumps."

Abruptly, Jacques crossed to the door. "I will see what food is to be had," he said. "You are hungry, yes?"

"Very," Alessandra answered.

"Rashid?"

He looked uncertain, then nodded. "Not for English fare," he qualified, "but I suppose it will have to suffice."

Slowly, Alessandra released her held breath. For a moment she had feared Rashid would not allow Jacques to leave alone.

"Sorry, my friend," Jacques said. "You will have to wait until we reach the Maghrib before you can satisfy your yearning." He slipped Alessandra a cryptic look, then was gone.

The silence following his departure was of the waiting kind, Rashid's eyes appreciative of Alessandra, hers wary. It was their first time alone—truly alone—since he had taken her from Corburry. Though all had gone as Alessandra had planned, it was not the ideal situation.

She removed her cloak and wandered to the window to look down at the filthy street below. It was only a moment before she saw Jacques emerge from the inn and take off at a run. Settling her cloak over the back of a rickety chair, she dragged her fingers through her hair and followed his passage until he disappeared from sight.

Hurry, she silently urged him, then she turned her attention to the bits of gray water visible between the tumble of buildings that separated the inn from the harbor. Somewhere, beyond her vision, the ship that would return Rashid to his home was anchored. Only the morn would tell whether or not she would be returning with him.

She heard the bed creak, then Rashid's footsteps over the gritty floor. At her back, he hesitated, then he put his arms around her.

Alessandra tensed. Surely he wouldn't try to take her with Jacques's return imminent? She looked down at where his hands linked over her abdomen.

They were nice hands, she nervously acknowledged. Though smaller than Lucien's, Rashid's were so smooth and unblemished, she imagined they would glide over her like silk. Odd thing was, she longed for the rasp of Lucien's worn hands, their strength and familiarity. Between silk and coarse wool, she would choose the latter.

"You will soon forget him, and then you will be mine again," Rashid said, as if reading her thoughts. "Trust me."

She jerked with surprise. How had he known? And what of the ruse she had played these past days, affecting an attitude of acceptance and favor toward him? Had it been for naught?

"What speak you of?" she asked, continuing the deception.

He brushed her hair aside and placed his lips near her ear. "Though you say you love me, I know it is not true, Alessandra. Still, I am certain in time you will love as your mother loved my father, and all that fire in you will belong to me."

"But . . . I do love you, Rashid."

He touched his mouth to her earlobe, then trailed it down her neck to her shoulder. "As a brother," he said, "but soon as your lover."

She tried to turn to him, but he wouldn't allow it. Gripping her firmly about the waist, he lifted a hand to the lower curve of her breast—but nothing more.

"You think the Englishman would make you happy," he said, nuzzling her nape, "but once I lie with you, you will know different."

How vain, Alessandra thought, then reminded herself of the culture she had been raised in, where a man was the supreme master. His wives, especially if there were many, magnified his ego in their eagerness to gain his sexual favors. Still, Rashid seemed in an amiable mood at the moment, perhaps enough to be reasoned with. She owed it to him to try one last time. . . .

"Rashid," she began, "your mother, my mother, even Jabbar said I would not make you a good wife. Do you remember?"

He let her hair fall back into place and turned her to face him. "I remember, but they were wrong."

"No, Rashid, they were not. These English you detest so much—I am one of them. I always have been, will always be, and need to be. This is where I belong."

Smiling indulgently, he shook his head. "With me is where you belong. You are mine—"

"I am not a possession," she interrupted. "I am Alessandra—your friend—and that is all."

"But it will be more when we are wed. Then you will feel for me what your mother felt for my father."

She wanted to shake sense into him, to knock this crazy ideal of love from his head. Instead, she squared her shoulders and stared into his eyes.

"Yes, Rashid, my mother did love Jabbar, but I am not she. Never will we have the great love our parents had.

Friends is all we will ever be—and perhaps not even that if you force me to return to Algiers with you."

Rashid pecked a kiss to her lips, then released her and walked back to the bed. Removing his cloak, he laid it over the mattress, then settled down upon it and eyed her through narrowed lids.

"Join me?" he invited.

Feeling disjointed, she shook her head. "What of our discussion?" she asked.

He clasped his hands behind his head. "It is over with."

"Over with? But we've only just begun."

"Over, Alessandra. Let us speak no more of it."

"But—"

"Enough said."

Fighting tears, she swung back to the window. He left her no choice. No choice at all . . .

CHAPTER 34

Dread in his soul, Lucien bent and turned Vincent faceup. Blood caked his face from where it had run in rivulets from the hideous gash on his forehead.

"God, Vincent," Lucien choked as he pulled his brother into his arms. "Let it not be."

James and Jervais's entrance into the tent went unnoticed until Jervais sank to his knees beside his wounded brother.

Eldest and youngest exchanged glances, then Lucien lowered his head. Putting his ear to Vincent's mouth, he looked for the rise and fall of his chest. Breath. Let there be breath, he silently pleaded.

Was it his imagination, or did life flutter through Vincent? He raised his head and looked into his brother's half-open eyes.

"I am sorry, Lucien," Vincent murmured. "I tried...."

All past grievances forgotten, Lucien clasped Vincent to him. "You are alive," he said. "Only that matters."

"No time." Vincent's muffled voice rose from Lucien's embrace. "You must reach her ere he does."

Lucien lowered Vincent to the ground. "Sir Keith," he said.

"Aye, 'twas he who did this to me."

Lucien looked to James, conveying what the man had refused to believe—until now. Sir Keith's undoing had been the words he had spoken in the great hall at Falstaff.

They had festered at the back of Lucien's mind, finally coming forward for closer examination.

She should not have ventured out at night, he had said of Alessandra. *It is the same as when her mother was taken.* Yet the man should not have known how Catherine had been stolen from Corburry. And then the bastard had thrown them off the trail with the cool logic that Alessandra's captor would flee England by way of Southampton.

"Why did Crennan do this to you?" Lucien asked.

Vincent raised a wavering arm and touched the open wound. He flinched. "I found the letter."

"Letter?"

"Aye. When I questioned him as to the leisure with which we rode on London, he became strangely defensive. We argued, and when he went to bathe in the stream tonight—it is still night, isn't it?" At Lucien's nod, he continued. "I came here to his tent and went through his things. That's when I found the letter. I—" He broke off, rolled onto his side, and violently retched the contents of his stomach.

When he was finished, Lucien hefted Vincent into his arms and carried him to the cot. He laid him down gently, then sent Jervais for a basin of water.

Shuddering, Vincent feebly hugged his arms about himself. "You ... waste ... time," he said through chattering teeth.

Lucien dragged blankets over Vincent and tucked them around him. "Tell me about the letter, Vincent," he urged.

Not until Jervais returned with the basin and a cloth did Vincent find the strength to comply. As Lucien mopped his brow, cleaning away the blood and perspiration, Vincent continued. "The letter you gave me ... to have delivered to Alessandra the night before our ... our departure. It was in his possession, Lucien."

Lucien looked over his shoulder at James. "Now are you convinced?" he asked.

James sank down upon the nearest object that would support his weight—a trunk. Covering his face with his hands, he shook his head. "How could I have known? We were always good friends. Surely Agnes must have known."

Lucien turned back to Vincent. "Then what happened?"

Vincent swallowed hard. "He returned before I expected him and discovered me here. I confronted him with the letter, and that's when he struck me."

"And left you for dead," Lucien said bitterly. Rising, he passed the job of comforting Vincent to Jervais. "Now that Sir Keith is found out," he said, "doubtless he has gone to London to make certain his plans for Alessandra do not go awry."

With much effort, Vincent raised himself up from the cot. "Before I lost consciousness, I heard him, Lucien. He muttered something about Marietta. A woman? A—"

"A ship," Lucien guessed. He touched James's shoulder. "Do you ride, or stay?"

His face hardened by determination and suppressed fury, James stood. "I ride. Crennan is mine."

Rather than argue who had first rights to the man, Lucien turned on his heel and strode from the tent. At the flap, he hesitated, then looked over his shoulder and into Jervais's anxious eyes.

"I trust no other with Vincent," he said. "There will be other times for us to do battle together, brother." Though he prayed this would be his last battle, that there would finally be peace, Lucien knew such a possibility was very real.

Outside, Sir Keith's men waited anxiously to discover what had transpired while they'd slept. Though the unexpected arrival of Lucien and James had sent them scrambling for their weapons before they realized who it was that had come upon their camp, they were still none the wiser as to the reason for their coming.

And Lucien had no intention of wasting any more time explaining it to them. Soon enough they would learn of the sins of their lord.

Calling for his men to hasten to their saddles, Lucien mounted his destrier and turned it toward London. It would be morning before they reached the city, but God willing, Crennan was not too far ahead.

Alessandra, he silently pleaded, be impetuous, be wild, be reckless, but do not go quietly. Though the thought struck him that she might that moment be on a ship sailing south, he tossed it aside. He had to believe she was still in London, waiting for him to come for her. Otherwise, he would surely shatter.

Regardless, he assured the image of her that came to mind, if needs be I will go back into Algiers and bring you out again.

The blow struck, then Rashid's hold on her loosened.

Instantly, remorse rushed through Alessandra. It should not have been this way, she thought as she turned to face Rashid. He lay upon the pillow as if he still slept. And in a way, he did.

Sitting up, she looked at a grinning Jacques, his weapon, a badly rotted board, propped against his shoulder.

"You hit him too hard," she protested.

He shrugged. "No more than he deserved. Besides, it will assure he does not come to before he ought."

Which would be disaster for certain. Scrambling off the bed, Alessandra went to the window. "Soon it will be light," she said, catching a glimpse of the day's first rays.

"Too soon," Jacques agreed. "There is no time to waste." Throwing the board onto the bed, he walked to the door, opened it a crack, and peered down the dim corridor. Assured all was clear, he crept out and returned shortly with a trunk burdening his shoulders.

Alessandra closed the door behind him, bolted it, then went to the table where quill and parchment awaited her. While Jacques struggled to fit Rashid's bound and gagged body into a trunk that would have better served had it been a bit larger, she lit a lamp and set herself to writing.

It was a letter to Rashid—one of apology, explanation, and poignant reminiscing of a childhood that belonged in the past. As she signed her name tears stung her eyes.

"Farewell, old friend," she whispered, then folded the letter and walked to the trunk. Placing it in Rashid's hand, she curled his fingers around it and stepped back.

"I am ready," she said.

Jacques closed the trunk lid and locked it.

"Will he be able to breathe?" she asked.

"I have punched holes here . . . and here." He pointed to them. "He will not want for air."

She nodded relief.

"Now I am forgiven, no?" he asked.

Forgiven? Alessandra frowned, then jolted herself back to the reality of her relationship with the Frenchman. No doubt he referred to having sold her into slavery after the promises he had made her, and for helping Rashid steal her from Corburry.

Though her first thought was that she would never forgive him, in all fairness she had to concede that he seemed truly repentant for what he had done, and that he was attempting to make amends by assisting her.

"I am trying to forgive you," she said honestly, "but it is not so easily done."

He pretended nonchalance. "Then you will let me know when I am forgiven, *chérie*?"

She summoned a smile. "Of course."

Straightening, Jacques walked to his pallet and took up his cloak. As he settled it about his shoulders he crossed to the door. "Dress quickly," he said, glancing from her chemise to her stockinged feet. "I will return shortly with the men."

He was gone perhaps all of ten minutes, but when he returned, Alessandra had donned her overgown, slippers, and cloak, and was ready.

The two men Jacques had hired the day before entered the room without caution. But then, caution was hardly needed for men of such size and countenance. Both stood nearly a foot taller than Jacques and were of such breadth, they'd had to turn sideways to pass through the door.

Caps pulled down over their ears to ward off the cold of the gusty English morning, they turned beastly faces to Alessandra, who immediately stepped back into the shadows.

Grateful she had covered her own head against the chill, she peered at them from beneath her hood and wondered where Jacques had unearthed such unsavory characters. Surely they were criminals.

"There." Jacques pointed to the trunk. "Carry it to the dock and you will have the reward I promised."

The older of the two men cocked his head to the side. "Who be the lady?" he asked in a deep voice that vibrated through the floorboards.

Jacques hurried to Alessandra's side and put an arm around her. "This is my wife, gentlemen. Madame Félice LeBrec."

Alessandra was not about to dispute his claim, her heart beating so heavily she was relieved to have his support.

A moment of tense silence followed, then the younger ruffian elbowed the older. "Let's go," he said. "Sooner done, the sooner we have the man's coin."

The older one grunted, then lumbered to the trunk and hefted one end of it. A moment later Rashid was borne from the room and began a hazardous journey down stairs that protested loudly beneath the weight.

Leaving their few possessions in the room—they would return before journeying back to Corburry—Jacques and Alessandra followed the hired men through and around the dirt and garbage of streets just awakening to the first light of morning.

The docks, in contrast, were practically teeming with life when they arrived. Here and there men darted as they readied for the departure of the ship that would return Rashid to his homeland.

Walking beside Jacques, Alessandra marveled at the beauty of the berthed vessel. Though Nicholas's ship had been splendid, it could hardly compare with this one. "*Marietta*," she murmured, reading the embellished, gold-lettered name.

"So it is," Jacques mused. "The same as my mother was called." Glancing into Alessandra's wide, questioning eyes, he shook his head before she could ask. "A coincidence only," he said, then led her to the railing along the edge of the dock.

"Wait here," he said, "and I will take care of the men."

Huddled in her cloak, the moist air cold upon her cheeks, she watched Jacques direct the men to the area where baggage was stacked, waiting to be hauled on board.

They dropped the trunk to the dock without any care, making her wince at the bruises Rashid would likely suffer from such handling.

Jacques paid them from a pouch he brought out from his tunic, then started to walk away. However, the men blocked his way and held out their hands for more. Haggling followed, angry words were exchanged, but in the end, Jacques pressed more coins into their palms and sent them on their way.

After speaking briefly with one of the crew, and handing that man a coin, Jacques returned to Alessandra's side. "Thieves," he muttered. "I had to pay those men more than twice what they agreed to yesterday."

"You expected better?"

His scowl ascended to a smile. "Foolish, no?"

She shrugged, then looked past him to the ship. "What now?"

"If I had my way, we would start for Corburry," he said, "but since you refuse to leave Rashid to his fate, we wait."

Of their hastily worked plan, it was the one thing Alessandra had refused to concede. Bound and gagged as he was, Rashid would not likely make his presence known—or survive the voyage in the trunk. She simply could not do that to him.

Instead, Jacques would accompany the trunk to the cabin Rashid had reserved and get him out of the trunk, but leave him bound and gagged. Alessandra was certain he'd be discovered, though not until long after the *Marietta* had sailed. Then she and Jacques would be on their way to Corburry.

It was a tense hour before the boarding began, and the docks swarmed with passengers eager to set sail.

Perhaps it was good that Jacques had struck Rashid so hard, after all, Alessandra thought. His awakening and subsequent commotion might otherwise have foiled their plan. Gripping the folds of her hood to keep it from being blown off her head, she watched as two sailors lifted the trunk and carried it up the sharply inclined ramp.

Jacques patted her hand. "All goes well, *chérie*," he reassured her, smiling. "I will return shortly." He confidently strode the dock, mounted the ramp, and disappeared from sight.

Alessandra turned and leaned her elbows on the railing. Cupping her chin in one hand, still holding her hood with the other, she looked down into the stir of murky water. Cold, she thought, and shivered.

Sometime later the call to board was bellowed across the docks. Nervously tapping a finger to her teeth, unmindful that her hood had fluttered down upon her shoulders, she watched as the queue of people advanced up the ramp.

Where was Jacques? she wondered. What was taking him so long? Had Rashid come to and overpowered him? Those thoughts and others worried her as she searched the deck for sight of the Frenchman.

Then she saw him. At the top of the ramp, his progress hindered by the upward surge of people, he waved his arms—frantically.

Peculiar, she thought, then excused his behavior as another of his idiosyncrasies. Shrugging, she waved back. In response, he waved more vigorously and shouted something she could not hear above the din of the docks.

A touch on her shoulder brought her around. Sir Keith stood behind her, a friendly smile lighting his handsome face.

"Good day, Alessandra," he said.

Stunned, she opened her mouth to answer, but could only gape. What was he doing there? Had he and her father tracked Rashid to London and come to rescue her? She glanced past him, but saw no other faces that looked familiar.

And then the pieces came together. *I want her gone from here now!* She heard again the words of the man who had lifted her onto his horse after she had run from Rashid at Corburry. She had known the voice then, but it had not registered. Now it did.

Too late, she understood the passionate flailing of Jacques's arms—a warning, not a greeting. Moreover, she understood why Keith had never mentioned Rashid and

Jacques coming to Glasbrook in search of her. It was not
that his parents had known and not told him, as she'd
imagined. Indeed, the nagging memory of what Keith
had said the night she had met him finally came back to
her.

When Melissant had inquired as to her grandparents,
he had said they'd been in London for more than a
month. Thus, they could not have been at Glasbrook
when Rashid and Jacques arrived. But Keith had to have
been there, and for reasons known only to himself, he
had assisted Rashid in abducting her, which meant he
had also . . .

Alessandra jumped away and attempted to lose herself
among the throng. It was not to be, though, for Keith reacted quickly, catching her cloak and jerking her back to
him.

With the cloak binding about her neck and threatening
her breath, she stumbled against him. His arms came
around her, holding her firmly to him.

"So you know," he said into her ear.

With desperate fingers, she dragged the cloak away
from her neck and looked for Jacques. He was frantically
but ineffectually struggling through the crowd to reach
her. He would be too late, she realized.

Pretending defeat, she went lax in Keith's arms. When
he turned her to face him, she strained back, clenched her
fist, and punched him between the eyes.

He released her instantly, staggering back. Spurring
herself to flight, Alessandra turned and jostled her way
through the melee. Thankfully, the crowd closed around
her, separating her from the man who would too soon be
close on her heels.

Where she was going, Alessandra had no idea, but it
was not toward the ship Keith had intended her to be on.
When she could, she ran. When she couldn't, she stepped
as quickly as her feet and the obstacles in her path allowed.

Breathing raggedly, and denying herself a look behind
lest she come face-to-face with Keith again, she left the
docks and turned onto a street that looked familiar. She

couldn't be certain, though, for it was now daylight, and
the people milling around had not been present earlier.

As she ran she was reminded of her flight from Lucien
in Tangier. The irony of it all was that she would likely
not be running now if she had never run from him then.
Too, there would have been no Jacques to lead Rashid to
her.

There would still be Sir Keith, though, she told herself.
Sir Keith who had abducted her mother nearly twenty
years ago and sold her into slavery. But why? Why?

The ramshackle inn she had spent a sleepless night in
peeked at her from between two larger buildings. Familiarity and the hope of a haven drew her to it.

Rushing past the large woman who had let the room to
Jacques the day before, Alessandra clambered up the
stairs and ran to the room at the end of the corridor. It
was locked. She looked over her shoulder to see if she
was followed. The corridor was empty save for herself,
and she grappled with the pouch fastened to her girdle.

Jacques had given her the key, hadn't he? Cool metal
brushed her fingers, and a moment later she was fitting
the key into the lock. She had just turned it when she
heard the pounding on the stairs. She looked back to see
Keith taking the last steps to the second floor.

Their eyes met briefly before Alessandra surged into
the room, slammed the door closed, and locked it. Shaking from head to foot, she backed away from the door as
Keith's footsteps neared.

Surprisingly, he advanced without hurry. When he
reached the door, his shadow crept beneath it and spread
to touch the toes of her shoes. She jumped back.

A light tap made her jump a second time. "Alessandra," he called, "open the door."

A weapon. Her gaze skittered around the room in
search of a makeshift weapon with which to defend herself, and fell upon the board Jacques had used to render
Rashid unconscious. Grabbing it, she held it behind her
in hopes of catching Keith unawares a second time.

He knocked again, though more loudly this time. "I
need to speak with you, Alessandra," he said in a voice
that sounded completely harmless.

Mutely, she shook her head.

"Please, Alessandra. There are so many things I need to explain."

Indeed there were, but she would not be the one to let him in.

He waited, giving her the opportunity to open the door, then put his weight against it. It strained and creaked warningly, but did not give. He tried again, this time using thrust to break the lock, but, blessedly, it held.

Though not for much longer, Alessandra realized. Tilting her face to heaven, she closed her eyes tightly. "Lord, I need another angel," she whispered. Preferably in the form of Lucien, she added.

The abrasive sound of splintering wood snapped her eyes open in time to see the door swing inward, strike the wall, and rebound.

Throwing up a hand to avert being struck by it, Keith pushed the door away from him and stepped inside. Quickly, he located Alessandra where she stood beside the window. Pausing in the middle of the room, he stared at her.

"You're afraid of me," he said, "but you shouldn't be. I would never hurt you."

Though slivers pierced her skin where she gripped the board behind her, she curled her hand more tightly around it. "Is that what you told my mother—that you would never hurt her? You don't think she was injured when you stole her from my father and sent her into slavery?"

A corner of his mouth pulled up into a half smile. "You are guessing, Alessandra," he said, almost as if speaking to a child.

She shook her head. "Nay, I know. I know it was you."

"And how do you know that?"

She put her free hand to her heart. "I feel it here," she said. "And that you would do the same to me—steal me from my father—proves it."

His gaze shifted to the floor as if he were considering her words, then he looked at her face again. "Give it to me," he said, holding out a hand.

She started. "What?" she asked.

"What you've behind your back."

Shadows. Shadows that the dim lamp threw had revealed her secret. Though she brought the board out from behind her, Alessandra did not relinquish it. Holding it before her, she warned, "Do not come any nearer."

As if settling in for a long stay, he spread his legs wide and crossed his arms over his chest. "Do you want to know why I did it?" he asked.

A nasty, impulsive rejoinder nearly denied Alessandra the right to know what had motivated him all those years ago, but she bit it back. "Yes," she said.

He contemplated her a long moment, then began. "You guessed it," he said. "I loved Catherine. When she chose James Bayard over me—"

"You were cousins!" Alessandra burst out.

He shrugged. "It didn't matter. All those years watching her grow up and waiting for her to come of age . . ." He drew a deep breath. "And then Bayard took her from me. Do you know she didn't even love him?"

"But she didn't love you either."

His nostrils flared. "She would have come to love me had she only given me the chance."

Alessandra locked her teeth to keep from responding. It would do more harm than good to argue with him, she knew—to throw in his face the great love her mother had had for Jabbar.

"When she wed James," he continued, "a part of me withered—nearly died. I promised myself I would not break, that I would turn my mind and heart elsewhere. And I thought I was succeeding, but then Catherine summoned me to Corburry."

He fell silent, and Alessandra had to prompt him out of the place he had drifted to. "Why?" she asked.

He came back with a start. "Why?" He shook his head. "My heart rejoicing, I hastened to Corburry believing she meant to tell me of the mistake she had made in wedding James. That she loved me—only me."

"But that wasn't the reason, was it?"

His bitterness staining the air, he pinned his gaze to her. "Nay. She thought I was teasing her when I went down on my knees and kissed her hands. She laughed at me—told me I must be serious if I was to assist her in obtaining a birthday present for James. James. The only reason she had summoned me."

Feeling that his anger was mounting, Alessandra took a step back.

"She was so damn oblivious to my feelings for her, always treating me like a brother when it was her husband I should have been." He pressed fingers to his forehead as if suffering pain there. "While I sat beside her in the gardens, her chattering about whether a new sword or a saddle would make a better gift, it occurred to me that if she couldn't be mine, then neither should James have her."

"So you sold her into slavery," Alessandra concluded, unable to keep condemnation from her voice.

"She should not have flaunted her happiness!" Keith exploded. "Some regret—just a little—that was all I asked."

Worrying he'd come at her, Alessandra raised her weapon higher. "You were her friend," she said. "How could you have betrayed her?"

"She betrayed first," he countered, his angry color alternately rising and waning.

"But she didn't know what you felt for her, did she? You never told her."

He blinked. "And be laughed at? Nay, she should have known. I could not have made it any clearer."

"Except with words."

Abruptly, he turned and walked to the table where the lamp burned dimly. Laying his palms on it, he leaned forward and hung his head between his outstretched arms.

The temptation of the open doorway beckoned to Alessandra, but she could not go yet. Not until she knew everything.

"How did you do it?" she asked. "How did you lure my mother from Corburry and into slavery?"

"She never told you what happened?"

Alessandra shook her head.

"Fortunately, James was out visiting one of his vassals when I came to Corburry. Otherwise, it would have been impossible to do what I did. Knowing I could not spirit

Catherine away without being seen, I sent her a message—from James. It asked her to meet him at the stream at dusk. A tryst, you see. And like a lamb, she came."

"And you abducted her."

He peered at her from beneath his arm. "Aye. I stole upon her and bound her up. Though I was careful so she would not know who 'twas, I always feared she might have guessed it was me, which is the reason I led Rashid and Jacques to you. If Catherine had known and told you, you would undoubtedly have revealed me."

"She never knew."

"Aye, I guessed as much when I met you." He pushed a hand through his hair, then stepped toward her.

Delay! Alessandra's mind screamed. "You're proud of what you did, aren't you?" she accused.

He halted, a distant look entering his eyes. "Never proud," he said. "Haunted, but never proud."

She frowned. "I don't understand."

He did not look at her, but through her. "For an entire day I fought the demons—after all, I loved Catherine— but once the idea entered my head, they would not let it go. Don't you see?" He pleaded for her understanding. "It wasn't me who did it, but them. I had no control. What I would have given to have Catherine back the day after I sent her into slavery!"

Though he spoke in riddles, Alessandra unraveled enough of what he said to understand it was not evil that drove him, but unrequited love and an unbalanced mind—a dangerous combination. "If that is true, then why have you done the same to me?" she asked.

He was looking at her again. "As with your mother, I fought it, but again I lost."

"But why harm me? I am not my mother."

"You looked at me the same way she did. You were her all over again, tearing at my heart and making me want something I could not have."

"You wanted me?" Alessandra asked with disbelief.

"I wanted Catherine," he corrected her. "But in you I could have had her, or nearly. You, however, wanted De Gautier—went to his tent after giving me your favor."

Understanding washed over Alessandra. "Then 'twas you who set the bishop upon me. You who sent him to Lucien's tent."

"The bishop?" He shook his head. "Nay, I did not. 'Twas likely Agnes who did that."

Agnes? Did he speak true? Insecure in James's love, had Agnes purposely set out to do her harm? Absurd question, Alessandra chastised herself. Of course she had.

"You betrayed me with De Gautier," Keith continued.

"I did not betray you," she said. "The favor I gave you was in remembrance of my mother only. You said so yourself."

Uncertainty came and went on his face. "Aye, but you led me to believe differently."

He was fooling himself. "I love Lucien," she said boldly.

He ignored her declaration. "Your betrayal still fresh and hurting, I knew I had to act quickly when I overheard a conversation Lucien had with his brothers."

"What conversation?"

He shrugged. "One he had in his tent."

"And what was said?"

"Enough to make me realize you must disappear as Catherine had."

"But I know it was Lucien who sent the message for me to come to him. It could not have been you."

Keith smiled. "A coincidence, but a timely one. I had planned to have a message delivered to you later that night, but then De Gautier unknowingly accommodated me. It was perfect, throwing suspicion on his family for the second time. And it would have worked if . . ." He shook his head.

"If what?" Alessandra prodded. Was her father this moment making war with Lucien for something he'd had no hand in?

Again he shrugged off her question. "I am not selfish, Alessandra. What I did to your mother and you was not only for myself."

"You are making no sense."

As if agreeing with her, he nodded. "Just like Catherine, you were taking from another woman for your own gain."

"What are you talking about?"

"When Catherine wed James, she not only wounded me, but Agnes."

Agnes who had wanted James for herself, Alessandra thought, recalling the story her mother had told her.

"Agnes loved James," Keith continued. "It was always assumed they would eventually wed. So, you see, what I did in sending Catherine away also helped my sister."

"But what have I to do with it?"

"Melissant," he hissed. "She was to wed the heir of Falstaff—and then you came and took it all from her."

"She didn't want to marry Vincent," Alessandra protested.

"Agnes wanted it, and if not Vincent, then Lucien would have done as well. 'Tis the same, can't you see? Catherine all over again."

Alessandra swallowed hard. "It is the same only because you make it so."

"Nay, not I." His eyes suddenly widened with mad fire. "You made it so, Alessandra, not I!" he shouted.

She wisely decided not to argue the matter further, turning instead to Agnes's role in her mother's abduction. "Did Agnes know what you had done?" she asked. "Did she help you?"

He did not answer for a long time, but when he did, the quick fire of his anger had lessened. "Not at the time, though I did tell her years later."

"And?"

His laughter was bitter. "She didn't believe me, didn't appreciate what I had done for her. Now, though, she will have to."

"Because of my disappearance."

"Aye. But enough of that. Tell me how you convinced the Frenchman to assist you in escaping the infidel."

"I can answer for myself," an unexpected voice said.

Both Alessandra and Keith jerked in surprise, looking to where Jacques stood in the doorway.

"You are all right, Alessandra?" he asked, his gaze sweeping over her, then lighting upon the board she held.

"I think so."

Keith turned to face Jacques, though he kept Alessandra within his peripheral vision. "Where is Rashid?" he demanded.

"Comfortably settled on the *Marietta*," Jacques replied, "and soon bound for the Maghrib."

"Not without Alessandra," Keith returned.

Jacques stepped into the room. "Yes, without her. Alessandra stays in England."

Keith drew his sword. "She goes."

"It is over, Crennan. Run, and you may escape the wrath of the Bayards and De Gautiers. Stay, and surely you will know death at their hands."

"I am no coward," Keith growled. "I've never run from anything before—"

"Except the truth," Jacques interrupted.

Keith tensed, then in the next moment charged toward Jacques, his sword aimed at the other man's heart.

It all happened too quickly for Alessandra to follow. A dagger flew and with uncanny precision caught Keith's sword arm. He bellowed in pain, but tenaciously held to his weapon. Jacques rushed to meet him, and they fell heavily to the floor.

Alessandra jumped out of the path of their struggling bodies as they rolled across the dirt-crusted floor. She had to help Jacques, but which was he? One moment he was atop, the next Keith. Their violent shifting made the chance of landing a blow on the right man nearly impossible.

"Run, Alessandra," she heard Jacques cry. She could not leave him, though.

The two men rolled farther across the floor and into the table, nearly upsetting it and the lamp upon it. Knowing the room might catch fire if the lamp overturned, Alessandra rushed forward to rescue it, but too late. One of Keith's legs kicked the table and the lamp crashed to the floor, bursting into flames that greedily licked the hem of her skirts.

Crying with surprise and fear, Alessandra dropped the board and jumped backward. The material had caught, though, and was quickly being consumed.

Lifting her skirts to keep them from burning her legs, she ran to the bed, grabbed the grubby blanket from it, and began slapping at the fire. Blessedly, the flames died, their smoldering causing an acrid scent to burn her nasal passages.

Looking back around, Alessandra saw the room had caught fire, and that Keith and Jacques's fight had not abated in spite of the danger. Running forward, she dropped onto her knees beside them.

"Stop!" she screamed, trying to pry them apart. "We must hurry. The room is afire."

Something struck her temple and sent her sprawling onto her back. Though dazed, she fought off the yearning to close her eyes, and instead struggled onto her knees and began crawling after Jacques and Keith. Fire leaped into her path, keeping her from them.

The smell of singed hair gagging her, she searched for a glimpse of the two men, but the smoke had grown too thick for her to see clearly.

"No!" she screamed, pounding her fists on the floor. "No!"

"Alessandra!"

Squinting, she tossed her head and looked over her shoulder to see Lucien running toward her. He had come. Her prayers had been answered.

She struggled to her feet and fell into the arms he wrapped around her. For only a moment did she indulge in the wonderful feel of them, then she pushed back. "Jacques," she gasped. "And Keith."

Lucien lifted her against his chest and ran for the door. "Jacques," she protested.

"I will come back for him," Lucien promised. Surefooted, he traversed the smoky corridor and the stairs without slowing.

The air outside struck Alessandra as wonderfully clean and fresh, though it had not seemed so earlier. Looking up, she saw that a crowd had gathered before the inn. Among them was her father.

"Your daughter," Lucien said as he set her to her feet. James put an arm around her. "You are well, Alessa?"

he asked, concern evident in the lines around his eyes and mouth.

Nodding, she looked past him to Lucien, but he had already plunged back into the burning inn. "Lucien," she cried.

James hugged her closer. "He will be fine."

Would he? she wondered as she watched the flames burst from the window of the room she had shared with Jacques and Rashid. It did not seem possible.

"Father, it was Keith." The words tumbled from her mouth. "He—"

"I know," he said. "It is as Lucien guessed. What I have yet to know is why, though soon I shall have my answer from the bastard."

Alessandra recognized the pain he was trying to hide, but knew he needed to know it all. "He was also responsible for my mother's abduction," she said.

"Aye." James nodded as if he already knew. "But tell me, Alessandra, do you know if Agnes had a hand in it?" His breathing checked, he awaited her answer, his eyes pleading that it not be so.

That Keith had told Agnes of what he had done all those years ago seemed no longer relevant. Too, he had said she had not believed him. Reasoning that there was no need to ruin any more lives, and that Agnes should not be made to suffer for her brother's sins, Alessandra shook her head.

"Nay, Father. Agnes did not know."

"You are sure?"

"Very."

Lucien emerged then, carrying a man over his shoulder—Jacques. Gently lowering him to the muddy street, he glanced at Alessandra and James. Though his face was smudged black and his hair hung singed about his shoulders, a more welcome sight Alessandra had never seen.

"Keith is dead," he said.

A hoarse moan rose from Jacques.

Breaking free of her father, Alessandra rushed forward. "Nay," Lucien snapped, "stay back." Though he stood to block her, she slipped past him and went down on her knees beside Jacques. A moment later Lucien also knelt.

Jacques was badly burned, his beautiful clothes charred and hanging in smoldering tatters, his face red and puckered where the fire had tasted him. His eyes were glazed, though he opened them wider to look at her.

"Forgive me?" he asked, trying for a charming smile, but sadly missing the mark.

She nodded. "Of course."

He raised a hand to her, but it fell limp to his abdomen.

Understanding, she entwined her fingers with his. "You are going to be fine," she said.

"No, *chérie*, I am not."

"Do not—"

"Did you know I have never lain with a woman?" he said. "Never."

Confused, Alessandra shook her head. "Why are you telling me this?"

"Because were I man enough, you would have been the one, Alessandra."

She glanced at Lucien and saw his displeasure, then looked to Jacques again.

"Just tell me," he begged. "Tell me you could have loved me." His plea was followed by a bout of coughing.

Beside her, Lucien remained silent.

"Lie if you must," Jacques entreated, "but tell me it is so."

Feeling his pain, she leaned forward. "I . . . I do love you, Jacques."

He smiled. "That is the best lie I have ever heard, though I might believe it a little if you kissed me."

"I . . ."

"Here." He touched the side of his face that was not burned.

Her heart crying for him, she pressed her lips to that place, then slowly drew back.

"You have made me very happy, you know," he said, the light in his eyes diminishing further. "Now I can rest." His smile slight, his lashes fluttered down.

It seemed a long time before either Alessandra or Lucien moved, but when they did, Jacques had passed beyond their world and into the next. Oblivious to his audience, to the clamor of men running for water to put out the fire, he lay unmoving—silent testimony to bravery gone awry.

Lucien helped Alessandra to her feet, then pulled her into his arms and laid his cheek against the crown of her head. "I am sorry, Alessandra," he said. "I wish he could have been saved."

Eyes burning with tears, she nodded. "He helped me," she said. "After all the deception, he helped me to escape Rashid."

Lucien raised his head and held her away from him. "It was Rashid, then," he said, better understanding Keith's scheme. "Was he in the room as well?"

"Nay. He is on the ship. Jacques bound him in his cabin and was returning to take me to Corburry when Sir Keith found me on the docks." She frowned. "How did you know where to find me, Lucien?"

"A long tale that would be better told elsewhere," he said.

"But how did you know I was at the inn?"

He rubbed a smudge of ash from her face. "We were on our way to the docks when we saw the smoke from the fire. Something told me it was here I would find you."

"My prayers," she whispered. "I prayed you would come."

"Then you still want me?" he asked.

He seemed so uncertain, it tugged at her heart. Always he had been confident and in control, but now she saw something of the boy Lucien must have been before the war between the Bayards and De Gautiers had consumed him. She cupped his face in her hands. "I have never stopped wanting you," she said.

"Even when I became an animal in the lists?"

"Even then."

Reaching into the neck of his tunic, he brought out her anklet of miniature bells. "I wore these that day," he said. "To keep you close."

She touched the bells. "I had thought I'd lost them, and you had them all along."

"What does it tell you, Alessandra?" he asked, his stare intent.

Dare she hope it meant more than desire? That he loved her as she did him? "That you love me," she ventured. "Do you?"

Lowering his head, he kissed her. "Aye," he said, against her mouth.

He did not say the words, but it was enough for now, Alessandra told herself.

" 'Tis hardly the place," he went on, "but I need to know. Will you marry me?"

She stared at him. "You want to marry me? But you said—"

"I know, but I could not have you believe I had wed you only for the land."

So it had been more than foolish pride. "Is that why you sent me the message?" she asked.

He nodded. "When you didn't come . . ." A distant look briefly clouded his eyes. "You are the only one who can control me, Alessandra. Will you marry me and tame the beast?"

Into the dark of death came the light of life—two people uniting in love. "Yes," she said. "Yes."

Though what Lucien really wanted was to take Alessandra from this place, to ride to Falstaff with her and carry her to his solar, he knew it was too soon. Not before her time.

back and looked down at her. "Do I not keep you warm

CHAPTER 35

She had put him off long enough. Peeking around the screen, Alessandra searched Lucien out and found him seated before the hearth on a stool. His back to her, he leaned forward and stared into the fire.

At last, she rejoiced, their wedding night had arrived. On this cold autumn night they would finally be joined in the flesh. It was not too soon, either, for Lucien had insisted on courting her these past two months. To prove himself worthy, he had said.

Suddenly nervous, she smoothed the embroidered chemise over her limbs and wondered how long it would be before it lay crumpled at her feet. Would he be gentle, or would he take her like the storm that raged outside Falstaff's keep?

Stepping lightly, she came out from behind the screen and walked to him. From the tilt of his head, she knew he heard her, but he did not look around.

Standing at his back, she laid her hands on his broad shoulders and bent forward. "Are you ready for me, my lord?"

"Perhaps I should ask that of you."

Smiling, she slid her hands down his chest and lifted his tunic. Her fingers had only brushed his hard abdominal muscles when he caught her wrists together, preventing her from drawing the tunic up.

"Come around," he said.

"Not yet," she breathed into his ear. "First I must make you ready."

"Which you can do standing before me." He started to pull her around, but she resisted.

"I know you do not want me to see your back, Lucien, but I am going to. It is a part of you, and as we are wed now, I want to know all of you."

"Not that," he growled.

" 'Tis not as if I have not seen it before," she reminded him.

"Not tonight, Alessandra."

"You are ashamed of it?"

He looked over his shoulder at her, displeasure, not passion, shining in his brilliant eyes. "It was not by cowardice I earned those stripes," he said, his voice evidencing the control he exercised, "but by mettle."

She nodded. "I know, but they stand between us. Won't you trust me?"

He looked ready to deny her, but then his eyes softened. "Very well." Releasing her wrists, he made to lift the tunic. However, Alessandra took the task from him and drew the garment over his head.

She stood silent a long time, her gaze tracing the worst scars, and then she touched them. Though she felt Lucien tense beneath her fingertips, she did not pause in her exploration.

Slowly, he began to ease, stiffening only when she knelt and began caressing his back with her lips.

"I love you, Lucien," she said, "every bit of you."

Turning, he captured her between his legs. "Then why do you waste time at my back?" he asked. Though he attempted humor, his eyes searched hers.

She smiled, then leaned forward and put her arms around his waist. "Because, husband, I once overheard a concubine say that to love a man is to love all of him— from the soles of his feet to the ends of his hair." Lowering her head, she planted a kiss on his navel.

Lucien groaned. "This is not going as I planned."

She peered up at him. "And how did you plan?"

Remaining seated, he raised her to her feet and began

picking at the buttons of her chemise. "Let me show you."

When she stood bare before him, her chemise pooled about her ankles, she felt no shame, only desire. "And now?" she asked after several minutes had passed and Lucien had made no further move, other than to caress her every hollow and curve with his gaze.

"Now, Alessandra Bayard de Gautier, we make love." Pulling her against him, he buried his face between her breasts, breathed in the scent of her, then shifted to take a taut nipple in his mouth.

"Ah, blessed," she moaned. Wrapping her arms around his shoulders, she clung to him.

As his hands glided over her backside Lucien teased the other breast until she gasped with pleasure. Then he ducked lower and put his mouth to the surprisingly sensitive flesh in the curve above her hip.

Alessandra surged against him. "Teach me, Lucien," she pleaded.

Laughter rumbled up from his throat. "I intend to," he said, then stood and swept her into his arms. Carrying her to the bed, he laid her on the mattress and stood looking at her.

She reached to him. "We have already waited too long. Come to me, Lucien."

Slowly, he stretched out his length beside her and propped his head on one hand. "What are we to do about these?" he asked, sweeping his other hand downward to indicate his chausses.

Smiling, Alessandra turned onto her side to face him and reached for his laces. Tugging them free, she slipped a hand inside and slid the material off his hip. Lucien raised himself, and the chausses fell away to reveal his manhood.

He was ready for her.

Suddenly uncertain, she looked up and saw that he watched her. "Touch me, Alessandra," he said. "Know me."

She hesitated. "I don't know how."

"Aye, you do. You just do not realize it." He took her

hand, curled it around his length, and held it there as if fearful she might pull back.

Alessandra had never anticipated he would feel as he did. Against her palm, he was feverish, hard, and alive with straining power. He was a man to her woman, and the realization that he would soon make her a woman in every sense of the word had her imagining he already had.

Burning to know him, she drew her hand up over him and was amazed at the sound that strangled from his throat.

"God, Alessandra," he groaned, "if you are going to do that, I will not last long. I will take you here and now."

"But that is what I want," she said innocently. "You would make me wait?"

"It will be better for you if we go slowly."

"I have waited long enough to know you, Lucien de Gautier," she teased. "Later we can go slowly."

He needed no more encouragement. Pushing her onto her back, he kicked off his chausses and straddled her. "It will hurt," he warned.

"Do you tell me that, it most certainly will," she exclaimed.

"I would not lie to you."

"But you would make me wait. . . ."

He smiled. "Patience is something you really must work at, my pagan bride."

She reached around him, cupped his buttocks, and urged him to her. "Later," she said. "Much later."

He resisted her pull. "A moment, Alessandra. There is something I must first say to you."

Through the hair that had fallen over her face, she stared up at him. "Now?"

He nodded. "It can't wait. You see, it's waited too long already."

He seemed so serious, she knew it was a matter of great import. Perhaps something was wrong. . . . "What is it?" she asked, worriedly compressing her lips.

Dipping his head, he eased her mouth with a gentle kiss and said, "I love you."

She gaped at him, her mind repeating the words again

and again. It was the first time he had spoken them, and
there was something so sweet in the memory of their
birth that she didn't want to let go of the moment.

"Tell me again," she beseeched.

He did, and at least a dozen times more before he
made her a woman in every sense of the word. He was
tender, waiting out her discomfort before venting months
of longing. And then came the storm.

Alessandra clung to him. Moved with him. Cried out at
the swells of sensation he aroused in her. And when his
final thrust culminated in their joint satiation, she knew
they had become one.

Lying spent beneath him, she drew her hands up his
back. "Ah, Lucien, you never told me it could be like
this."

He raised his head and kissed her. "Had I told you,
would you have believed me?"

She reflected on it a moment, then laughed. "Words
could never do it justice."

"And that was only the beginning."

"There is more?"

"Of course, as I will prove to you."

"Now?"

"Shortly."

She stroked a finger down his face. "I love you," she
said.

"I love you, Alessandra."

The letter arrived a month later. Lucien brought it to
Alessandra, his mouth set in a grim line as he handed it
to her.

"Something is wrong?" she asked.

"Vincent has just returned from Corburry," he said.
"He brought this with him."

Dear Vincent, whose most recent aspiration was to recapture Melissant's hand in marriage. Unfortunately, he
faced a serious obstacle—Agnes.

Though she knew it would be manipulative of her,
Alessandra was tempted to aid him in doing away with
that obstacle, as she had done away with her own upon
returning to Corburry from London.

No longer need she fear that Agnes would conspire with the bishop to name her a heretic. Nay, there was peace between them, Agnes eternally grateful that Alessandra would not tell James of her knowledge of Catherine's abduction. Both well understood that though Agnes had not believed her brother's claim, that would have little bearing on the anger and punishment James would dole out if he ever discovered the truth.

Perhaps next time Vincent went to Corburry, Alessandra mused, she would accompany him. She abandoned the idea, though, knowing it wrong of her. This was a battle Vincent must win alone.

Taking the letter from Lucien, she turned it over.

"It is from Algiers," he said.

"Yes, I see."

"Rashid?"

She bit her bottom lip, then nodded. "I would guess."

Lucien turned toward the door. "I will leave you alone, then."

"Nay, Lucien, stay."

His back to her, he stood rigid, but finally came and sat beside her.

Unfolding the letter, Alessandra read it, then smiled.

"What does it say?" Lucien asked.

She passed it to him so he could see the two lines of Arabic. "He asks my forgiveness," she translated, "and wishes us well."

Lucien frowned. "That is all?"

"As you can see," she said, tears filling her eyes.

"You are sad."

She shook her head. "Nay, all is well. I have never been more happy in all my life. And you, Lucien? Is it everything you hoped it to be?"

He pulled her into his arms and kissed her. "More," he murmured. "So much more."

ABOUT THE AUTHOR

TAMARA LEIGH has a Master's Degree in Speech and Language Pathology. She lives in the small town of Gardnerville located at the base of the Sierra Nevada Mountains with her husband David, who is a former "Cosmopolitan Bachelor of the Month." Tamara says her husband is incredibly romantic, and is the inspiration for her writing. They have one child. You may write to her at: P.O. Box 1088, Gardnerville, NV 89410.

England, 1068

"A thousand times I curse you!" the fallen knight shouted at the woman who cradled his head in her lap, her blue skirts turned purple by his blood.

Lifting an arm, he closed his fingers around the dagger protruding from his chest, dragged it from his body, and let it fall to the ground. Splaying his hand over the mortal wound, he turned his glazed eyes back to the woman.

"To eternity I curse you, Rhiannyn of Etcheverry," he said. "If you will not belong to a Pendery, you will belong to no man. Your days and nights will be yawning pits of deepest despair."

With fingers that trembled, Rhiannyn brushed the tawny hair back from his damp brow. "Forgive me, Thomas," she whispered. "Pray, forgive me."

"The Devil forgive you!" Jerking his head back, he lifted his bloodied hand to her throat and encircled it.

Though approaching death weakened him, his grip was cruel, strangling. Rhiannyn did not draw back, telling herself it would be no less than she deserved if he ended her life. For a fleeting moment, she even wished he would. Then the torment of these past years, which had seen so many dead, would also end.

Too late, she wished she could relive the past few hours. Given a second chance, Thomas would not be dying in her arms. If only she had not run from him . . . If only he had not come after her . . .

Her tears brimmed over and coursed a slow path down her dirt-smudged face. "I never wanted this," she said, a sob catching her voice.

"Curse you," Thomas choked, then dragged his hand down her bodice, leaving a scarlet trail. Letting his arm fall back to his side, he shifted his gaze to the gray sky above.

"Avenge me, brother," he cried to the heavens with his last breath. His body spasmed, and though his eyelids did not fall, death took him.

"Nay!" Rhiannyn wailed, staring into sightless eyes that would never again darken with annoyance at her defiance, nor smile at her.

Thrusting clenched fists into the air, she stared up at the God who had allowed this terrible thing to happen. "Why?" she cried. "It did not have to be!"

In answer, the bank of clouds rolled with the sound of an approaching storm.

"Now more will die," Rhiannyn screamed. "Is that your will?"

Chill droplets sputtered from the clouds, spotting her fair hair and mingling with her tears. A moment later, the rain was loosed in sheets that drenched her to the skin.

Rhiannyn did not turn at the sound of approaching horses, did not flee as she ought to. Instead, uncaring whether those who came were her kin or

Thomas's avenging men, she bent over the man who lay silent in her lap.

"I will belong to none," she whispered, the salt of tears bitter on her tongue. " 'Twill be a burden I will carry the rest of my days." No husband, no children, only the great emptiness Thomas had banished her to.

She heard voices. Raised in anger, they shouted foreign words—the French of the Norman conquerors.

First fear, then relief swept her. She would not be made to carry her burden of guilt for long. With the coming of the Pendery knights, she was assured her own death was not far off.

Though she thought herself prepared for the fury, Rhiannyn cried out when merciless hands wrenched her upright, causing Thomas's body to roll off her.

"Saxon bitch!" Sir Ancel snarled at her. "What have you done to our lord?"

Rain pelting her upturned face, she met the livid gaze of the man who had been Thomas's friend. "He is dead." She spoke in French so he might understand. "I—"

The back of his hand struck her hard, sending her to her knees amidst the sludge of the muddy road. She expected him to come at her again, but instead he turned to the prone figure of his liege, around which the others had gathered.

"Thomas," he groaned as he turned him faceup. "Thomas."

She could run, Rhiannyn knew, the bordering woods only a short sprint away. However, though the survivor in her urged her to do just that, she found herself curiously resigned to the fate awaiting her. Lifting her head, she looked past Thomas's men to the lone rider who had not dismounted.

His countenance mirroring disbelief, Thomas's fourteen-year-old brother stared at her a long moment before shifting his stricken gaze to the man Sir Ancel had pulled into his arms. The youth's name was Christophe, and he had always been kind to Rhiannyn. Lame from birth, he was a gentle soul destined to know books rather than weapons. And now he would certainly hate her, would cheer her demise when all was done, but he would not avenge his brother's death as Thomas had bid him to. He was incapable of such violence.

"Lady Rhiannyn, rise," Sir Ancel commanded.

Lady only because Thomas had named her one, Rhiannon mused. Intent on wedding her, though she had shamed him with her public refusal, Thomas had bestowed the title on her. After all, it would not have done for a favorite of the Norman king to take a Saxon commoner to wife.

Imagining her blood would soon soak the same ground as Thomas's did, Rhiannyn rose and faced those who would stand in judgment of her.

"Who did this?" Sir Ancel demanded, his face contorted with loathing, his short-cropped hair plastered to his head.

Rhiannyn lowered her eyes so the lie could be more easily told. "It was I who killed him."

Sir Ancel grabbed her shoulders, his grip punishing. "No more of your Saxon lies," he said, shaking her so hard she thought the end was surely upon her. "Tell me the truth!"

"I have told it," she gasped. "It was I who did it."

"Do you think me a fool?" he snapped. "It was your lover who put the sword to him, wasn't it?"

He spoke of Edwin, the second son of the Saxon thane who had ruled Etcheverry before the Normans came. Edwin, whose bitterness kept the enmity alive between the conquering Normans and the vanquished Saxons. Edwin, who had never been her lover, though he would have been her husband had the Normans not conquered a land they had no right to.

Though Rhiannyn would never admit it, it was Edwin who aided in her escape that morn, he who had fought Thomas such a short time ago and been wounded by his opponent's blade. But it was not Edwin who had landed the death blow.

Some other person, unseen and surely of Saxon blood, had done the deed. He had thrown his dagger from the concealing woods a bare moment after Thomas had sliced through Edwin's sword arm.

Bolstering her courage, Rhiannyn met Sir Ancel's gaze. "Nay," she answered him, "it was I who killed him."

He sneered at her, not believing her. "And where is your weapon?"

The dagger. What had become of it? Blinking, Rhiannyn lowered her head and searched for a glint of blade among the grass. It hid itself well, and only by going down on her hands and knees was she able to find it. Grasping its hilt, she stumbled back to her feet and raised it for Sir Ancel to see.

"This," she said. "This is what I used."

Still, disbelief showed on Sir Ancel's face and those behind him.

Was it that they did not believe her capable of such an atrocity? Rhiannyn wondered. Or that they did not believe she possessed the strength required to kill a man, especially one the size of Thomas?

Desperate, she stepped forward. "God is my witness," she lied, promising herself she would repent later. "It was I who killed your lord."

Rage replaced Sir Ancel's disbelief. Knocking her hand aside, he sent the dagger into the rain-beaten grass. "Lying whore," he spat. "It was the Saxon coward who did it—Edwin!"

Nursing her pained wrist and wondering if he had broken it, Rhiannyn shook her head. "You are wrong. I hated Thomas. I—"

"Non!" Christophe shouted. Dismounting, he hobbled to where she and Sir Ancel stood. "You do not speak true, Lady Rhiannyn. You did not hate my brother. Never could you have done this."

Finding it impossible to hold his gaze, which begged her to say otherwise, Rhiannyn looked away. "I am responsible," she said, which was true, whether it was she who had wielded the weapon or that other who had slipped away unseen.

Grabbing a handful of her wet hair, Sir Ancel forced her head back. "Fear not, young Christophe," he said. "Either way, justice will be done."

Rhiannyn quelled the impulse to struggle against the pain. After the death she had just witnessed, it shamed her to feel anything other than a twinge of discomfort.

"Do it now," she pleaded. "Be done with it."

Sir Ancel bared his teeth. "I am tempted," he said, "but it would be too good for the likes of you, too facile. Nay, when it is time, you will suffer as Thomas did. A slow and painful death."

For the first time, Rhiannyn felt the cold of wet clothes soaked through—or was it simply fear? Though she tried to suppress the answering shudder, it racked her body.

"I am resigned to my fate," she said through teeth that had begun to chatter. "Do with me as you will."

"Such brave words from a Saxon," Sir Ancel said. "We will see how well you fare in the dungeon." He thrust her from him.

Caught off balance, Rhiannyn stumbled and fell. Unmoving, she lay on the ground, arms splayed in the mud. Dear God, she prayed, be merciful.

It was Christophe who assisted her to her feet. "Lady Rhiannyn—"

"Do not call her that, boy!" Sir Ancel snapped. "She has never been, and will never be, a lady."

"She was to have been my brother's bride," Christophe reminded him.

"Aye, and Thomas was a fool to think he could trust her. Look at him." Sir Ancel jabbed a finger to where his lord's body was pitifully draped over the back of a horse. "He is dead, boy. Dead."

Stepping away, Christophe reached down and retrieved the dagger. Seeing his brother's blood upon it, he squeezed his eyes closed, his lower jaw trembling as he fought his emotions.

He must be strong—had to be strong. With Thomas gone, the estates would now fall to him, a boy who had never trained for knighthood, whose single aspiration had been to one day serve as his brother's steward. He wanted none of it, most especially the stuggle for power that would ensue, but what other course was there? Of the four sons born to Lydia Pendery, only two survived, himself and the eldest.

"Maxen," he murmured. Maxen, to whom all that was the Penderys' should have belonged had he not shunned it in favor of a different life.

Would he come out? Christophe wondered. And once out, would he stay?

His demons quieted, the tension finally drained from him, the lone figure rose from before the altar and lifted his tonsured head to stare at the array of holy relics, the only witnesses to the fervent prayers he had offered.

"Answer them, Lord," he said. He waited, as he did each time he prostrated himself in the chapel, and again he was denied deliverance from the memories that had brought him to this place.

Defeated by a God who was not yet ready to forgive him his atrocities, he turned and walked from the chapel. He would try again on the morrow, and the morrow after that. And one day there would be peace for his soul, a place for it other than perdition.

Paying no heed to the chill wind that cried the coming of winter, he left his head uncovered and crossed to the cloister, where his studies awaited him.

It was Brother Aelfred who stopped him. "There is a messenger come from Pendery to speak with you, Brother Maxen," he said, his voice muffled by his hood.

Maxen frowned. What ill had befallen the house of Pendery that Thomas would call upon him now? For the past two years there had been only silence, as he had directed upon entering the monastery. Why had Thomas broken his vow to leave him be?

"He awaits you in the outer house," Brother Aelfred continued.

Maxen nodded.

At the outer house, the messenger stood without, his back to Maxen. The wind sifting through his short black hair and tugging at his clothes, he stared at the walls surrounding the monastery. Then, as if sensing he was no longer alone, he slowly turned and met Maxen's questioning gaze.

Maxen drew to an abrupt halt, his heavy clerical gown eddying about his feet. "Guy," he said, recognizing the man who had fought beside him at Hastings.

Guy's lips whipped into a grin. "No other," he said. Stepping forward, he clapped a hand to Maxen's shoulder. "It is good to see you again."

His demons roused, his body grown tense, Maxen pulled back. "Why have you come? Is something wrong at Pendery?"

Clearly, Guy was taken aback by the chilly reception, but he quickly assumed an impassive face.

Tamara Leigh

"Very wrong, Maxen. Otherwise I would not have come."

"Thomas sent you?"

Guy shook his head. "Nay, it was Christophe."

Christophe, Maxen thought, who must be . . . fourteen summers old? It could only mean something had happened to Thomas. An unbearable constriction in his chest, Maxen asked, "What of Thomas?"

A silence ensued as Guy struggled with the words. In the end, though, he could find no way to soften them. "Thomas is dead."

Maxen stared at him. "Dead," he echoed. Another brother dead. The memories he had worked so diligently to put from his mind came surging back. As if there again, he saw the sloping meadow of Senlac that had been the battlefield. He saw the careless strew of ravaged bodies and heard the Norman battle cries of "Dex aie" and "God's help"; the English war cries of "Holy Cross" and "Out! Out!" He smelled the wasted blood and felt the heat of too many bodies pressing in around him. And he saw Nils . . .

Maxen forced himself back to the present. Nils was dead, and now, too, was Thomas. There was only Christophe and himself.

So Guy would not see his torment, he turned his back to him and clenched a hand over his face. "How?" he asked. "Saxons?"

"A Saxon woman. She whom he was going to wed."

Maxen swung back around. "A woman? His betrothed?"

"She claims to have been the one," Guy said.

"Why did she turn on him?"

"Rhiannyn—that is her name—is the daughter of a villein who died at Hastings. She blames the Normans for the death of her family—her father and two brothers at Hastings, her mother during a raid on their village shortly before the battle. Foolish Thomas." Guy shook his head sadly. "He thought he could make her forget what she had lost by bringing her into the castle and grooming her to become his wife."

His hands hidden in the long sleeves of his monk's robe, Maxen clenched them into fists in an attempt to control the emotions he had thought never again to experience. "It was Thomas who lost," he growled.

"Aye. Rhiannyn refused to wed him, and though he could have forced her to marriage, he was determined that she come to him willingly."

"And she did not?"

Guy issued a regretful sigh. "Over a sennight past she slipped free of the castle. When Thomas discovered her gone, he rode after her, would not wait for any to accompany him, though the forests are replete with Saxon rebels."

An old anger in his blood, Maxen inclined his head for Guy to continue.

"It was too late when we found them. Thomas was already dead."

"And the woman?"

"Rhiannyn was there. She claimed she had killed Thomas, but all knew it not likely. Though the murdering blood of the Saxons surely runs through her veins, she does not have the strength to do such a thing."

"Then she protects another."

"Aye, 'twould be Edwin Harwolfson, to whom she was betrothed ere William claimed England's throne."

"And who is this Edwin?"

"The second son of the thane who possessed those lands which King William awarded to Thomas. Edwin was a royal housecarle to King Edward before his death, and then later to the usurper, Harold. Now he makes havoc on Normans he catches out in the open, and those who dare pass through the forest of Andredeswald. A half dozen times now he has led attacks against Pendery Castle."

Maxen wondered if he had ever met this Edwin. By invitation of the now deceased King Edward, who had had a particular fondness for Normans, the Penderys had resided on English soil for nearly a quarter century. It was for this reason the first language of the Pendery offspring was Anglo-Saxon, though they were equally fluent in Norman French. However, following King Edward's death, the Penderys had not supported Harold Godwinson's claim to the throne, siding instead with their liege, Duke William of Normandy, in overthrowing the usurper. So much bloodshed . . .

Maxen shook his head in an attempt to dispel the haunting images. With what he'd heard these last minutes, those images had grown sharper and more detailed, almost as if only yesterday he had pierced the blood-soaked soil of Senlac with his sword and walked away from the abomination.

Damn Thomas for his obsession with the deceitful Saxon wench. Damn him for dying and leaving none but Christophe to deal with the responsibility of the Pendery estates. Damn—

"There is only you." Guy broke through his silent cursing.

Maxen met his intense gaze. "What speak you of?" he demanded, knowing but not wanting to.

Guy shook his head. "Christophe cannot do it, Maxen—nor does he want to. If that which is the Penderys is to remain theirs, you must come out of the monastery."

Leave the monastery, the refuge which, with prayer, might someday free him of his demons? "I cannot," Maxen said, grasping at a resolve that was fast slipping through his fingers. "My vows have been spoken. My life is here."

"A petition has been dispatched to King William. If he agrees, which he would be a fool not to, you will be freed of your vows—at a price, of course," Guy added.

Maxen stared at him, his insides madly churning emotions that would be better left buried. With their rekindling, he was viciously reminded of who he was and what he had done. Here were the reasons he had come to this place, never again to know the outside world that had made him bloodthirsty and merciless.

Incited, his monk's calm thrown to the four corners of the earth, he smote a fist into his palm. "Christophe sent the petition?" he growled.

Guy swallowed hard, then shook his head. "Nay, Maxen, it was I, though it was with Christophe's blessings that I did it."

Maxen stepped toward him. "You?"

Guy retreated. "Forgive me, but I had to."

Landing his hands on the smaller man's shoulders, Maxen shook him. "Why?" he snarled. "Who gave you the right to meddle in my life?"

Beneath the pressing weight, Guy squared his shoulders. "In the name of our friendship I did it. I could not bear to see all lost."

"But Christophe—"

"Nay, I have told you. Christophe is not fit to lord over Pendery, nor to lord over Brionne once your father passes on. If you do not come out, then it will be Sir Ancel Rogere who controls Pendery lands."

"Rogere?"

"Aye, Thomas's friend. Surely you remember him?"

Vaguely. Thomas had first become acquainted with the Norman prior to the battle at Hastings.

"Continue," Maxen ordered.

"It is he who sits at the high table in Christophe's stead. He who directs the household knights and to whom the steward answers. He whose intent it is to take your sister, Elan, to wife."

Guy's words sank in with finality. Loosing his grip on him, Maxen turned away. Lost. All was lost. Duty bound him to defend his family's holdings, even if it be at the cost of the very soul he'd worked so diligently to save these past two years. It seemed he had no choice in the matter.

"How long ere the king's reply?" he asked, feeling suddenly weary.

"I would think the abbot would receive it within the next few days, no more than a sennight," Guy answered.

Maxen knew William would not dally long over

the decision, nor did he have any delusions as to what that decision would be. After all, William had wanted to award the barony to Maxen, and had only grudgingly conferred it upon Thomas when Maxen refused and entered the monastery instead.

"I will ready myself," he said, and turned to go.

"Maxen?"

He looked over his shoulder. "Aye?"

Guy's regretful smile did not quite reach his eyes. "It is for the better," he said.

Maxen's laugh was bitter. "Better for the house of Pendery," he said scornfully. "But me? Nay, Guy, this is where I belong." And she who had forced him from his sanctuary would pay dearly for what she had done.

"The woman, Guy. Does she yet live?"

"Aye, my lord, but only by the grace of your brother. Sir Ancel would have had her put to death, but it was the one thing Christophe would not allow."

"Why?"

"Regretfully, it would seem he is as enamored of her as was Thomas."

Foolish boy. Directly or not, the woman was as responsible for Thomas's death as her lover was. "Then she still dwells in the castle."

"Not . . . exactly."

"Where, then?"

"The dungeons, my lord. Sir Ancel insisted."

Rightly so, Maxen thought, and realized the Maxen of old had edged out the Maxen he had struggled to shape these past two years. Suddenly, the vows he had taken seemed so hollow. They were never meant to be, and now they would be no more. And all because of a treacherous woman.

So be it, Maxen thought. If he must give up the monastery, then damn compassion, charity, and forgiveness. Damn them all, every last one of those kindnesses he had been taught. And God help the Saxon wench.

DON'T MISS THESE FABULOUS
BANTAM WOMEN'S FICTION TITLES